N.J. CROSSKEY

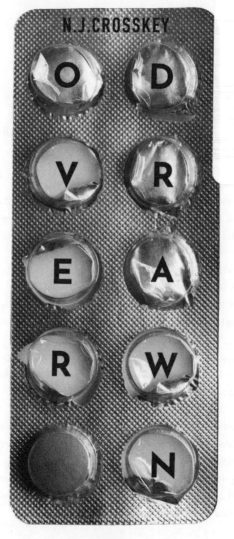

Legend Press Ltd, 107-111 Fleet Street, London, EC4A 2AB
info@legend-paperbooks.co.uk I www.legendpress.co.uk

Print ISBN 978-1-78955-022-1
Ebook ISBN 978-1-78955-021-4
Set in Times. Printing managed by Jellyfish Solutions Ltd.
Cover design by Kari Brownlie I www.karibrownlie.co.uk

N.J. Crosskey lives with her husband and two children in the seaside town of Worthing, West Sussex. She has worked in the care sector for almost twenty years, but has always yearned to be an author. In 2014 she finally found the courage to chase her dream, and began by writing short fiction which has since been published in various ezines and online literary magazines.

Her debut novel, *Poster Boy*, was published by Legend Press in 2019.

Visit N.J. at
www.njcrosskey.com
or follow her
@NJCrosskey

For my wonderful daughter Mya.
Thank you for teaching me what it is to be a mother.

PART 1

STEPHEN JENSEN IS
ONE HUNDRED AND TWO

"The importance of the Moving On initiative simply cannot be overstated. In many ways, it is the second revolution of our time; offering both an effective solution to our current economic crisis, and a personal solution to thousands who have, in the past, suffered needlessly and seemingly without end.

"Just as the advent of the contraceptive pill gave our great, great grandmothers autonomy over their own fertility for the first time, the Moving On Corporation now offers us an even greater freedom. The freedom to choose our own destiny. The power to decide our own fate."

Maria Drake, Spokesperson for the
Collective Council

1

Henry had never liked doctors. They were always harbingers of pain. Even when he was a boy, he'd never been wooed by their shiny red lollipops. No amount of shrink-wrapped sugar could distract him from their lies about what constitutes 'a small scratch'. In fact, his whole life had been punctuated by their bad tidings:

'I'm afraid those tonsils will have to come out, Henry lad.'

'In cases such as these, amputation is the safest option.'

'I'm sorry, Mr Morris, there was nothing more we could do for your mother.'

'It's a difficult choice, but as her father it falls to you to make it on her behalf.'

'I'm afraid your wife's diagnosis is indisputable.'

He couldn't recall a single time in his history that a white coat and stethoscope signalled anything other than trouble. And today was no exception.

He'd been waiting in the sterile silence of the doctor's office for well over half an hour when Dr Johnson waltzed in, whistling. Because to him, armed with his white coat and youthful privilege, it was just another day at work. Chloe was just another name on a file. Just a date of birth and a condition.

"Mr Morris." The doctor smiled, too widely. Black news comes after flashes of white teeth.

He sat down and opened the lime green tome of a file on the desk.

"I've been reviewing your wife's case. In light of the information you gave my colleague over the phone, I think it's safe to say her current dose of Hepraxin is no longer sufficient. Would you agree?"

"Yes." Henry shivered a little when he remembered coming home the day before to discover the front door wide open, and Chloe nowhere to be found. "Yes, I would."

Dr Johnson nodded. "Well, that in itself is nothing to worry about. As the disease progresses, it's perfectly normal for a patient to require a higher dose. I would suggest we try doubling it. If you still wish to continue treatment, that is?"

Henry's cheeks burned. "Of course I do."

"I understand." The doctor nodded slowly. "I see no medical reason why we can't put her up to 40mg. However, I'm afraid I am only able to authorise three months' supply today."

The bile churned in Henry's guts. Had the time come so soon? Perhaps not. Perhaps there was another reason. Supply problems, maybe? Or the need to review the drug's effects?

"Why is that?" he asked, praying he didn't already know the answer.

Dr Johnson exhaled. That one release of CO_2 confirming Henry's fears. This was it. End of the line. Game Over. You do not have enough credits to proceed.

"I'm afraid three months' supply will take you to the limit of your overdraft, Mr Morris," he said at last. "If you prefer, I could prescribe six at her current dose? You won't see any improvement, of course, but there might not be *too* much of a decline. If you need more time to… make arrangements?"

Make arrangements. The phrase lingered in the air.

Henry eyed the young, virile doctor. Anger twisted in his solar plexus, radiating down to his fingertips which began to shake, and burn. This guy knew nothing about life except its monetary value. He'd never had to watch the light and passion fade slowly from eyes that had once burned with conviction and courage. He'd never built love with someone, learned to recognise the subtle movements in their face that belied their every mood. He'd probably never even held a little miracle of his own creation in his arms. What did he know about life, apart from its mechanics?

He wanted to shout, rage. Scream his despair at the white-coated epitome of youth in front of him. But instead he whispered, "I'll take the three. Everyone gets older, you know."

"Indeed" – Dr Johnson nodded solemnly – "and it is something we must all prepare for. Mr Morris, I understand how hard this must be. But, there comes a time when you must think of yourself as well."

"What do you mean?" Henry thought of nothing *but* himself, if he was honest. All the praise, all the well-meaning 'I don't how you do it, you must be saint' comments from friends and neighbours made him uncomfortable. Chloe was his world. He couldn't let her go. Not without losing himself as well.

"Have you thought about how you would cope, if you continue to care for your wife once her medication runs out?"

"I'd cope."

"We are fortunate these days, Mr Morris. Dementia has been effectively eradicated. The trouble is, because it's no longer a part of everyday society, we've forgotten how hard it is to deal with. What it means for those trying to look after the patient."

"I'm well aware of what it means," Henry snapped. "I stand by my decision. I will not be making any *arrangements*."

Dr Johnson just smiled again, which made Henry want to smack him in the chops, not that he ever would. "Well," he said, far too congenially, "I am just a humble physician. All I have to go by is the current repayment plan you have in place. That's not to say there might not be other options. Why don't I make you an appointment with the financial department?

There's a slot available tomorrow? Maybe they'll come up with something?"

Henry nodded and took the small scrap of paper the doctor handed him, along with the prescription. He stood up and headed to the door.

"Mr Morris?" Dr Johnson called out to him before he grabbed the handle. "I do respect your decision; I'm just concerned about *your* health as well. I sincerely hope we can find some way to continue treating your wife. But if we can't—"

"I'll manage."

Dr Johnson sighed. "Mr Morris... how did you get that cut on your cheek?"

Henry walked out and slammed the door.

"Jumped-up little son of a bitch," he muttered to himself as he clung to the handrail, easing down the staircase one step at a time. Every movement chafed. He was long past due a new prosthetic, but that was the least of his concerns right now. When he reached the bottom, he headed for the gents, hoping to get some relief from the pain that burned in his bladder.

Picturing Dr Johnson's face in the urinal wasn't as satisfying as he'd hoped. But a little of the vitriol built up inside left his body with the dwindling stream of urine. It wasn't the young doctor's fault, any more than it was Chloe's. Or his. The anger he held was all the more bitter because it had no direction.

The mirror was smeared. Hastily cleaned by a harried worker with a low EP and high hourly targets. He grabbed a coarse paper towel and gently rubbed the streaks away. Maybe the supervisor would be coming round with their clipboard soon. Maybe that one small gesture might save someone the sack. Chloe always said a person's character was made up of a series of small gestures. A cup of tea every morning was worth more than a dozen roses once a year. He used to worry she only said that to make him feel better. But then, he never used to understand what was important.

He stared at his own reflection, and half wished he hadn't cleaned the mirror. Sixty years had flown by, leaving only grey hair and deep lines to prove their passage. *Sixty years.* It seemed like nothing. He remembered his grandfather turning sixty. The whole family gathered together, laughing and joking. He could still taste the creamy frosting on the cake his grandma had made for the party. It was the start of a new adventure, the adults had said. The dawn of his Golden Years. Joseph Morris still had twenty years ahead of him on that day. By the time the cancer took him aged eighty he'd spent two decades in retirement, and taken a sunshine holiday every single year of it.

Nowadays nobody celebrated turning sixty. Nowadays people his age held very different types of parties. It wasn't fair.

The jagged cut on his right cheek added a shock of colour to an otherwise pallid canvas. Henry ran his finger along it, making it sting. It ought to sting, he thought. It ought never heal, because the memory of what it means never would.

The door was open. He swore when he saw it. Not at Chloe, but at himself. He knew he shouldn't have gone out and left her, not without someone to keep an eye. But he'd only meant to be gone ten minutes. How was he to know they'd be digging up the sodding roundabout again? Damn temporary lights. He abandoned the car in the drive and limped into the house, his heart racing.

"Chloe?" He hobbled to each room in turn, but she wasn't there. When he reached the kitchen he was confronted by a puddle of water in the middle of the blue linoleum floor. It rippled rhythmically. Looking up, he saw the steady drip coming through the ceiling.

"Chloe, turn the taps off!" He heaved himself up the stairs, grimacing at the pain in his stump from the hard, ill-fitting plastic. The sound of gushing water grew louder as he neared the bathroom. But she wasn't in there either. He turned off the tap and pulled the plug out of the overflowing sink, soaking his left foot in the process. The clean-up would have to wait.

He was halfway back down the stairs when he heard the crunch of footsteps on the gravel path.

"Henry? Henry, are you there?" He recognised the sing-song tone. It was Kimmy, from number 34. When he reached the front door, he saw his neighbour standing there, her arm around Chloe.

"Oh thank God!" He rushed to his wife.

"I was coming home from work," Kimmy said. "I found her down by the post box. What happened, Henry?"

"I'm sorry. I had to pop out. I thought she'd be okay." Chloe shuffled toward him, one stiff leg then the other. She didn't look up from the ground.

"Oh Henry, you could have asked me to watch her. I'm free this afternoon," Kimmy said. "You know I don't mind."

But Henry minded. He didn't want to ask for her help. Or anyone's help. He didn't want people to know how bad things had gotten. He didn't want to admit it, even to himself. He ignored Kimmy and gently placed his hands on his wife's shoulders.

"Chloe," he whispered. "Oh honey, I'm so sorry. Are you alright?"

She blinked and lifted her gaze. Her sapphire eyes met his.

"Henry?" she asked.

"Yes!" Henry tried to hide his relief that she remembered him. The same relief he felt every day when she said good morning. She remembered him. For at least one more day, she remembered him.

Her expression turned dark.

"Where's Heidi?" she demanded, throwing his hands off her.

Kimmy looked confused. "Who's Heidi?" she asked, but the Morrises ignored her.

"Chloe, don't you remember—"

"What have you done with her?" Chloe raised her voice, and Henry stepped back instinctively. "You bastard!" She

lunged forward, clawing at his face. "What have you done with my baby! Where's my baby?"

He couldn't put off the trip to the hospital after that. Kimmy had calmed her down, taken her inside. It was only when he'd turned to follow them through the door, pressing his palm to his smarting cheek, that he noticed Chloe's nightdress was tucked into the back of her knickers.

He'd wept. For the first time in thirty years. Kimmy was more understanding than most people her age, but that only made him feel worse.

Kimmy. He shook himself out of his pity trance. She'd swapped her shift so she could watch Chloe for him. He didn't want to take advantage. He needed to get back, after a quick trip to the pharmacy to pick up the higher dose that might bring his wife back to him. For three months.

Still, he reasoned as he made his way out of the hospital, a lot can happen in three months. He didn't hold out much hope for his meeting with the financial department, but he'd find a way. Somehow. He'd try everything, everyone.

The sour-faced woman at the pharmacy clicked her tongue when she looked at the prescription. He knew what she was thinking. Not much call for Hepraxin these days. Not the done thing.

"It'll be ready to collect in half an hour." She didn't add 'sir'. He didn't expect her to. Old age wasn't something to revere any more. Henry's generation hadn't fought for freedom, or built anything of note. If anything, they'd caused more problems than they'd solved. And now they were just taking up room and resources.

He wandered into the greasy spoon next door and took up the last remaining seat. A young waitress with black curls and a dirty pinafore came to take his order. She rolled her eyes when he asked for a small coffee. It was almost lunchtime and patrons with deeper pockets were beginning to line up outside, looking for an empty table. She dumped his flat white down on the chequered plastic tablecloth with a force that caused a third of it to slosh out into the saucer. And there was no sugar. He didn't complain.

At the next table, two silver-haired women gossiped. Their used napkins lay scrunched up on top of the remains of their lunch. The waitress tapped her pencil on her notepad loudly. The pair seemed to be oblivious to the fact they were taking up much-needed space.

"Excuse me," the waitress said at last. "Are you going to order anything else?"

"Oh no," the skinnier of the two replied. "No, we're just fine. Thank you."

She hadn't got the hint. She turned back to her ruddy-cheeked friend and continued.

"So, anyway I said to her you ought to try those new ginger teas. Cos I swear my rash cleared right up after that. Didn't do much for the arthritis, but then nothing ever—"

"Don't you think it's time to *move on*?" the waitress interrupted her, scowling.

Henry gasped a little, but the ladies either didn't notice the double meaning, or chose to ignore it. They apologised profusely and gathered their things. As they stood up a group of young men in overalls took their seats, without waiting for them to finish buttoning their coats.

"Some people really don't know when it's time to get out of the pool, do they?" one of the scruffy oiks said.

The coffee was bitter and still too hot. Henry burned his tongue trying to consume it quickly. He decided he'd just leave it, put his money on the table and go. He looked for the waitress, to make sure she was far enough away for him to get through the door without having to converse with her. He spotted her clearing plates behind the counter. She threw the old ladies' dirty serviettes into the bin, but didn't scrape their plates. Instead, she took a square of cling film, wrapped an uneaten quarter-sandwich in it, and tucked it in her pocket.

Insulting customers *and* thieving. Typical young madam. No wonder the whole world was going to hell in a handbasket.

If the future belonged to her generation then perhaps having less of it to live through was a blessing after all.

But, as he had taken to doing since he found himself alone most of the time, he tried to imagine what Chloe would say. If she was still Chloe. She'd listen to his griping patiently. But for all her tolerance of his bellyaching, she wouldn't be complicit in his old-gititude. She'd reach across the table, put her hand on his.

"Oh hush now, you old goat," she'd say with a wink of those sapphires. "Thieving from whom exactly? The dustbin? I've a mind to think she's got more troubles than we have if she needs to steal a half-eaten sandwich. No wonder she's a little grumpy."

They'd finish their drinks and Henry would leave the exact money on the table. But, before she followed him out of the door, Chloe would fish around in her purse and leave an extra coin or two. Always more than ten per cent.

Chloe wasn't here. But Henry had long known she was the better half of their whole. He stood up, put the correct money on the table, and then added two shiny coins on behalf of his wife before heading to the door.

"Sir?" the waitress called out to someone as he shuffled to the exit.

"*Sir!*"

She appeared beside him. He panicked a little. Had he done something wrong? But she held the door open and smiled.

"Thank you, sir," she said, holding up the coins.

He was taken aback. He hadn't been called Sir since the pepper in his hair gave up and let the salt take over.

It was a small gesture. But it meant a lot.

2

The lunch shift was a nightmare. Kaitlyn dumped a portion of scrambled eggs onto a slice of toast, strategically covering up the burned corner, and vowed never to agree to a swap again. No matter how much Gina pleaded.

It wasn't so much the work itself; she didn't mind being busy, it kept her mind off things. It was more the fact that she'd have to rush to make visiting hours.

"I don't know why you worry so much," Jared said, counting the morning's takings. "It's not like he knows whether you're there or not."

"*I* know," she said. "And that's all that matters."

"Alright, alright," Jared replied. "But the lunch shift is better for tips, that's all I'm saying. Given your situation, I'd have thought that'd be your priority."

"Tips?" Kaitlyn spooned watery tomatoes from the simmering saucepan. "Here's a tip for you, Jared. How about you worry about your shit, and I'll worry about mine, eh?"

He chuckled. "It's a good job I like you, Kaitlyn." He pulled on his coat. "Not many employers would put up with your lip."

"None of your other girls can keep this place moving like I can." She turned the hob down with one hand, pouring a coffee with the other. "You'd be lost without me."

"Yeah? Well, I reckon Gina could give you a run for your money. Just remember to keep things rolling. No one stays more than twenty minutes. If the queue's too long they'll go elsewhere. Bums on seats is great—"

"But hauling arse is better. I know. Don't stress, I can handle a crowd better than Gina."

Jared raised an eyebrow. "I don't know. She normally takes five hundred on a Tuesday lunch."

Kaitlyn smirked. "Pah, I could do double that without breaking a sweat."

"That's big talk, little lady. How about I make it interesting for you?"

She put down the plates and folded her arms. "I'm listening."

"Take seven hundred, and I'll put fifty of it straight in your wage packet."

She grinned. "Deal." She wiped her hands on her pinafore, leaving greasy marks on the white cotton, and shook his outstretched hand.

Jared left just before the first of the lunch crowd arrived, because that was when the bookies opened. All the staff knew. Most of them gossiped about it, but Kaitlyn never went in for that. Everyone had their demons, and she was too busy dealing with her own to judge anyone else's.

She also knew the wager he'd made was about more than money. Yes, she wanted, *needed*, that fifty. But the challenge was the real win. She'd be too busy to think, and that was just how she liked it. As soon as the boss was gone, she marched out the back to drag Alfonz in from his cigarette break.

"Hey, chimney boy!" she yelled at the plume of smoke rising from behind the wheelie bins. "Get your butt back in the kitchen. I want double of everything on, stat."

"Double?" Alfonz wandered in, frowning at her. "No way you sell double, *chica*. Jared'll have a fit if I waste meat."

"Alfonz, how many people does Gina turn away? Twenty? Thirty?"

"At least. Is very busy, when them trains come in. No more seats. Can't sell food without seats."

"Well, today we're not turning anyone away. No one's

settling for sandwiches from the corner shop when they really wanted a fry-up on my shift. So you need to move your arse, capeesh? You don't wait for the covers to come in, you just cook, cook, cook, got it?"

Alfonz shook his head slowly. "I don't know. I cook to order, that's what Jared say. Then there's no waste."

"And that's why we're turning people away. Trust me. You cook it, I'll move it. If it all goes tits up I'll cover the loss myself, no blame on you."

"Okaaay, *chica*. You have loosey screw, if you ask me. But I play your game."

"That's the spirit. If nothing else, at least it makes things more interesting."

It was 11:45. The first train, full of factory workers returning to the housing district after their early shifts, would roll in across the road at ten past twelve. Followed by another, half an hour later. If she was going to clear seven hundred pounds she'd have to get the first lot served and out of the door in just thirty minutes. The place was already full of brunchers languishing over their food. She got busy clearing finished plates from under their chattering noses. A not-too-subtle hint that it was time to get going.

Using a combination of charm and sarcasm, she somehow manoeuvred the customers out of the door before the clock struck noon. Alfonz made it clear he still thought she was loca, but he had everything ready to go anyway. Two old ladies sauntered in just as she saw the twelve-fifteen arrive at the station. They ordered sandwiches and looked a little taken aback when their lunch arrived within seconds.

"Well, that's very fast service indeed," the gaunt-looking one said. "Mind you, at our age everything seems fast, doesn't it, Bea?"

"I bet," Kaitlyn said, watching the crowd of young men and women heading their way. The old crones had taken a four-seater. What was it with people past their sell by date taking more than their fair share? She only hoped they could chew as fast as they could gabble.

The working crowd were grateful for the quick service. They were hungry, tired and had better things to do than wait around. They wouldn't need coaxing out of the door. Time was precious. Kaitlyn pushed the all-day breakfast, the biggest ticket item, with ease.

"You guys must be starving. No joke those four o'clock starts, eh? Let me get you a proper feed up, won't take a moment, it's all ready to go." The patter worked a treat. The ravenous customers hoovered up their pre-prepared lunches, anxious to get home to bed.

But the old women masticated slowly, stopping to swap rambling anecdotes between every mouthful. Kaitlyn tried to hide her contempt, but it made her sick to watch. It wasn't right. People of their age casually dropping twenty pounds for lunch, when they didn't even work? Where was the justice in that? Why did they deserve to reach an age that she, and most of the hard-working customers, could never even dream of? The selfishness was unbelievable.

As if to taunt her, an old man hobbled in and took the last seat just as the stragglers were beginning to queue at the door.

"What can I get you?" she asked, without a smile.

He glanced around the room and shuffled a little in his seat. He gripped the menu too tightly, and didn't look her in the eye. At least he had the grace to feel embarrassed.

"Oh, just a coffee please, Ma'am. White," he said.

Jesus. A fucking coffee? That seat could have been worth far more. She huffed and rolled her eyes. She quickly poured the coffee and put too much milk in it to make it cooler, before dumping it in front of him. Anything to speed him up.

She cleared plates and dished out food as fast as she could, but there was still a queue starting to form. If she couldn't make room quickly, the impatient workers would abandon their wait. She loomed over the two shrivelled-up elders, tapping her pencil on her notepad. They didn't pay any attention. Too absorbed in their own little world to consider anybody else. Typical self-entitled septuagenarians.

It was a widely known truth that those who had grown up before the Roll-Back were lazy, apathetic and inconsiderate. 'The Snowflake Generation' as the press had dubbed them. Now they had the white hair to match. These two had probably never done a real day's work in their lives.

"Excuse me," she spoke loudly. "Are you going to order anything else?"

"Oh no." The thinner one looked even more unnaturally shrivelled than her friend, without any fat to pad out her wrinkles. When she smiled the edges of her lips reminded Kaitlyn of veiny, overcooked beef. "No, we're just fine. Thank you."

She turned away and carried on talking. Kaitlyn shook her head. How do people with so little awareness manage to function?

"Don't you think it's time to *move on*?"

She regretted it as soon as she'd said it. The shock on the old man's face made her flush. The prejudice she tried so hard to keep inside had come tumbling out of her mouth. The pair apologised, and moved as quickly as they could. Kaitlyn kept her eyes on the dishes as she cleared their table. She didn't watch them leave.

One of them had left a quarter of their sandwich untouched. The throwaway generation often did. Fancy having so much that you can afford to write off food like that. It made her feel a little better about her outburst. None of the workers left any food. Nobody her age did. If they couldn't finish what they'd ordered, they would take it with them, or at the very least offer it to someone else. She wrapped it in cling film and tucked it in her pocket. She'd give it to the guy playing harmonica outside the station. The one the old women walked past without a second thought.

A group of factory workers took over the four-seater. When she went back to take their order she realised the old man had left his seat, and half his coffee. She'd offended him. Shame rippled through her when she saw him lumbering toward the door. One leg seemed shorter than the other; he dragged his right foot rather than lifting it. Perhaps he had troubles of his own after all.

He had left money on the table, next to the unfinished beverage. One pound and sixty pence. The exact price of his order, though she wouldn't have blamed him if he'd left without paying. Perhaps he would have if he wasn't too slow to get away. But, when she picked up the cup, she saw two shiny pound coins sitting on the unused serviette.

He'd *tipped* her? She'd treated him like garbage, and insulted his peers. Snowflakes hardly ever tipped, and never if the slightest thing wasn't perfect. She felt terrible.

"Sir," she called out to the back of his brown duffel coat. All the young men in the café looked up, but he didn't turn round.

"*Sir!*" She rushed over as he neared the door and opened it for him. He flinched a little before looking her in the eye. He was afraid of her? Had she been that intimidating? The guilt twisting in her gut answered her question. She held up the two pound coins and made a conscious effort to smile as sincerely as she could. "Thank you, sir."

He nodded, ever so slightly, and mumbled something she couldn't make out. 'You're welcome,' she guessed. The edges of his lips twitched a little, but the smile they hinted at spluttered out before it formed. Then he was gone.

She dropped the coins into her tip jar, and tried to put the encounter out of her mind. She had to get back in the game.

The rest of the shift went smoothly. By the time Gina arrived she'd taken seven hundred and forty-seven pounds. She scribbled a note to Jared, reminding him of his promise before emptying her tips into her purse. She didn't have time to count, but she guessed there was at least sixty pounds in there. Maybe she should switch to lunch shifts like Jared had suggested. After today's takings he'd be begging her to.

"Hey, thanks again, sweetie." Gina dumped her bag down on the counter, wrenched a scrunchie off her wrist and pulled her long blonde hair up into a ponytail. "I owe you one. It was a *very* successful day."

Gina was fishing. Hoping Kaitlyn would ask what she'd been up to. But she didn't have the time or patience to listen to whatever nonsense Gina had to say.

"That's great." Kaitlyn grabbed her bag. "Glad I could help. Catch you later."

Gina pouted. "Don't you want to know where I've been?"

Where haven't you been? Kaitlyn thought. "Tomorrow, hon, tell me tomorrow. I gotta get to the hospital."

"He won't notice if you're late you know!" Gina called to her as she walked out, slamming the door behind her.

Harmonica guy was sleeping on his tattered blanket, so she left the film-wrapped sandwich on top of the change in his hat, and hurried through the streets. There'd be less than an hour of visiting left by the time she got there, and it was half an hour's walk each way. For a moment she wondered if everyone was right. Perhaps it was a waste of time. Maybe he didn't know, wouldn't *ever* know, that she was there.

But what if it was the only thing keeping him going?

She was out of breath by the time she'd negotiated the labyrinthine hospital corridors. First right, third left, straight on past X-ray, third right. She could have walked it in her sleep. Nurse Richards was at the small reception desk and greeted Kaitlyn with a smile.

"Ah, Miss Thomas. I thought perhaps you weren't coming today."

"Any change?" Kaitlyn wheezed.

"No. Sorry, sweetie."

"Okay." Kaitlyn tried to smile. "Maybe tomorrow, eh?"

"Maybe," Nurse Richards said, unconvincingly. "I'm sorry to have to bring this up, but there's a note on the file today. The financial department need to see you urgently."

"Yeah, yeah." Kaitlyn turned away, heading for the door to the right. "I get paid tomorrow. Tell them I'll come see them then."

Kaitlyn couldn't think about that now. Right now, she just wanted to see Jack.

3

Chloe was asleep when he got home. Tucked up for her midday nap, like a toddler. He thanked Kimmy profusely, as she ran through the morning's events.

"She's been fine. We chatted for a bit, then she had a cup of tea and biscuits. She was tired, so I helped her to bed."

It was just like getting the rundown from the babysitter when David had been young. But back then, he'd have been coming home from a cocktail party, or a show, his first wife Carolyn hanging from his arm, inebriated and dripping with diamonds.

There'd never been any nights like that with Chloe. They'd never had the money for shows, or diamonds. Not after the divorce settlement. Not that Chloe was interested in such things anyway. She was so different to Carolyn. And of course, there'd never been any need for a babysitter. Chloe wouldn't have entertained the idea of going out and leaving David when he came for his weekend visits. "Time with children is too precious," she would say. No, she'd never been anything like Carolyn. It was the cruellest of tricks that she'd never really had a chance to be a mother. David would be a better man if he'd been raised by Chloe, he had no doubt of that. And Heidi... oh God. What could Heidi have been? With her mother's guidance?

"I'll be going then," Kimmy interrupted his train of thought, "if you're okay?"

"Yes, oh yes, thank you." Henry held the pharmacy bag aloft. "All good. I shouldn't need to trouble you again. The doc is confident she'll be right as rain with these."

Kimmy nodded, but her smile looked forced. "That's great, Henry. But it's really no trouble. Just ask if you need anything, anything at all."

She left, hurrying to catch the bus that pulled in at the end of the lane. Off to the medical district, to help package drugs she most likely would never be able to afford for herself. He watched her laughing with the driver as she alighted and wondered how any of them still found anything to smile about. Didn't they know where they were heading? Didn't they know they were just a little further behind him on their journey?

The young ones didn't see it, of course. Because they'd never known any different. Their lives had been mapped out for them from childhood. They didn't have a world of options, of opportunity, to navigate. The endless, sprawling choices laid out for Henry and his generation had been overwhelming at times. So many paths, so many careers, so many routes one could take. But the young ones now seemed content to accept the place where they were told they belonged. They didn't yearn for more, or strive to reach goals beyond their means. They didn't know what hope, or aspiration, felt like. So they didn't feel the sting of its absence.

"Maybe we really are the lost generation," he muttered to his reflection as he passed the mirror in the hall. Stuck between two eras, belonging to neither.

A silver envelope lay on the mantelpiece. Must have come while he was at the hospital; he'd forgotten it was post day. He opened it and pulled out the folded paper, covering the floor with the plastic confetti self-indulgent idiots think will make their invitations seem more fun.

Henry and Chloe,

Moving On Party
12th March
The Starling Club
19:30 – 00:00

You are invited to celebrate the life of Joshua Hughes, as he takes the next step in his journey. Come and join us for an evening of festivities!
RSVP

Josh? Henry screwed the invitation up in disgust, then quickly opened it again to double check. Josh, of all people. He'd always been so against the whole idea. Back in the old days, when they both had young wives and deep pockets, they'd spent many an evening ranting about the credit system, over foamy pints in the company bar.

"*Et tu*, Brutus?" Henry whispered to the paper.

What could have happened? What could have gone so wrong? He wouldn't go. Couldn't go. But Chloe would want to. She'd be better by then, the Hepraxin would have her on an even keel. She'd be back to gently admonishing him, trying to make him a better person.

"You're not going to say goodbye to one of your oldest friends?" That's what she'd say. "Surely your principles aren't more important than your friendship?"

Fine, he thought, trying to smooth out the wrinkles in the paper. *I'll bloody well go. Actually, I bloody well WANT to go. I want to know why he's turned tail, why he's such a bloody hypocrite. I'll fucking well march right over to him, corner him by the punch bowl. I'll look him in the eye and demand to know where the man with convictions went. I'll tell him straight. He's a god damn disgrace. A coward and a sell-out...*

He made his way into the kitchen and poured himself a large brandy, which he knocked back in two gulps. He was rinsing out the glass, feeling calmer, when Chloe's voice echoed from upstairs.

"Heidi? Heidi? Where's Heidi? Henry? Hen-reeee! Where's Heidi?"

She'd woken up in distress. Henry moved as quickly as he could, grabbing a tumbler of water and shoving a strip of Hepraxin into his pocket, to leave one hand free for the bannister. "I'm coming, Chloe, don't worry. Just sit tight," he yelled, hoisting his prosthetic up one step at a time, his right hand wet from the water that sloshed out of the glass with each bump. When he reached the bedroom, she was sitting bolt upright, pulling the pale pink covers up around her, her eyes wide as they searched the room.

"It's alright, my love, it's all alright." Henry put the glass and tablets on the nightstand, and perched beside her on the bed, not so close as to scare her. Sometimes she had forgotten he'd grown older. Sometimes she thought he was a stranger, until her eyes met his. He reached out a tentative hand, brushing her sandy hair behind her ear and drawing her gaze to his face.

"It's me, love, it's me," he whispered.

She paused for a second, studying him. Then she inhaled sharply and threw her arms around his neck. "Oh Henry, Henry. Thank God. You have to tell them, Henry, you have to tell them."

"Who, my darling?"

"The doctors of course, the doctors! They've taken her, Henry. They've taken Heidi. They've taken my baby." She sat back and shook his shoulders, her nails digging in. "Do something, Henry! You have to do something."

"Hush, my love." Henry tried to keep his voice steady, even though Chloe's words were painful to hear. She'd not shown this panic, this desperation, back then. But she must have felt it. "I will, I will."

"You'll go get her? Bring her to me?" The hope in her eyes was more crushing than the fear.

"Yes," he lied. But it was a *good* lie, he told himself. A lie that would calm her, make her happy. A lie she would forget in a minute, in any case. When he'd promised her all those years ago that he would never lie to her, neither of them could have predicted this. There had to be a clause in that oath somewhere, had to be. "I'll go get her. You take these" – he held two little blue pills out in his palm – "and I'll go get her."

She shook her head. "Don't want pills. Don't need pills. All I want is my baby."

"Now, darling" – Henry tapped her bottom lip gently, encouraging her to open her mouth – "you must take these. I can't go get her if you're not well enough, can I?"

It was a dirty trick. A low-down dirty trick. But the end justified the means. She complied, and he sighed with relief when she swallowed her salvation. Or was it his salvation? He questioned himself. Something he had done a lot of lately, and something that made him very uncomfortable. Was he giving her Hepraxin purely for her own sake? Or because he couldn't bear to see the true depth of what he'd done, now that her disease had taken her inhibitions.

Was it karma? There were no mementos of their infant daughter on display, anywhere in the house. He hadn't wanted to be reminded. Chloe kept her picture, her hospital tag, and her bonnet, in an old box in her wardrobe. He wondered now how many times she had looked through it over the years. How many times she had waited for him to be gone, and then wept alone for her only child.

How cruel it was, how unfathomably, horrifically cruel, that the thing he had spent thirty years trying to forget was the one thing Chloe could remember.

4

Kaitlyn grinned when she opened her wage packet. The extra fifty was there, as promised, and Jared had left her a note:

Switch to lunches? Same bet every shift?

"I oughta be steaming mad at you," Gina said, reading it over her shoulder. "You were supposed to be doing me a favour, not showing me up."

"Sorry," Kaitlyn replied. "I needed the money. But I'm not going to switch permanently. Your shifts are safe. I wouldn't screw you over, you know that."

"It doesn't matter anyway." Gina winked, and leaned in. "Between you and me, I'll be leaving in a few months. You should probably think again, maybe take my shifts when I go."

"Leaving?" Kaitlyn was surprised. "How come?"

"I've made a little… investment." Gina grinned. "I'm pregnant!"

"You're… you're pregnant?"

"Uh-huh. Designer sperm baby." She rubbed her concave abdomen. "It's gonna put me through college! That's where I was yesterday, getting the results confirmed."

"I don't believe it!"

Gina had always talked about getting an education, getting out of 'this shithole, hamster wheel life', but Kaitlyn had never taken her seriously. "How did you afford it?"

"Easy," Gina said, "I'm using my credit overdraft. £5,000

for the sperm, £10,000 for pregnancy costs. You've got to speculate to accumulate, that's what Dad says."

"Your dad agrees with this?"

"Haven't told him. But he will. It's solid economics. £100,000. That's the average return. I'm surprised everyone isn't doing it. I can pay for college, and get my own place. All for nine months' work. It's a no-brainer."

"You're talking like it's stocks and bonds," Kaitlyn said.

"Got to be pragmatic," Gina replied. "And anyway, I'm giving TWO kids a better life, at least, when you think about it."

"How's that?"

"Well, this one " – she patted her tummy, like it was a prize-winning puppy – "is gonna have parents rich enough to fork out 100k just for the privilege. That means he or she is bound to get a good education, not have to drop out early like we did. Plus, I'm gonna be rich, so my proper kids will have a great future too. If I'm not too busy running the country to have any, of course."

"Sounds like you've got it all figured out," Kaitlyn said, tucking her wages into her bag. She could see from the self-satisfied look on Gina's face there was no point raising any counter-arguments. Anyway, the bun was already cooking in the oven. No point in doing anything other than hoping it turned out well. "I gotta get to the hospital, I'll be back later for my shift."

"You know, you ought to think about doing it yourself. I mean, realistically, Jack's overdraft's gonna run out sometime, isn't it?"

"Yeah," Kaitlyn replied, walking out the door. "Sometime."

She hadn't told anyone that it already had. Three months ago. Or that she'd been dipping into her own credit, to help cover the costs when her tips were down. She couldn't tell anyone, because there wasn't a single person who would understand. Jeopardising your own future health, to pour money into a machine just so your brother, who most likely won't ever wake up, and would probably be a vegetable if he did, can keep breathing? It was insanity. To anyone who hadn't been through what they had.

She half wished she hadn't bothered stopping by the café to pick up her wages, but the hospital wanted its pound of flesh. It was tough to see Gina so excited about her prospects, when she herself had none. Kaitlyn didn't think about the future, it hurt too much. She didn't know what she was going to do if Jack never woke up. So she just kept paying the piper, trying to keep the tune playing. Pouring good money after bad, some would say. But they didn't have a brother like Jack.

She didn't recognise the nurse who cornered her when she arrived on the ward, but she knew what she was going to say. Yesterday there'd been an asterisk next to Jack's name on the white board; today there was a big red exclamation mark. The symbols had nothing to do with his condition.

"I already know," she barked at the wiry, redheaded nurse before she could open her mouth. "I'll take care of it. After visiting."

"Oh, that's wonderful. I… I just wonder, perhaps would you mind popping down to finance now?" The nurse was blushing. "It's just that every time we have to fill in his obs record, we get beeped at by the damn computer. Idiotic machines. Hate them, don't you?"

"*Now*, I am visiting my brother," Kaitlyn replied. "I will 'pop down' to finance later. Disconnect the damn speaker if it bothers you that much."

She left the shocked nurse standing there and stormed into Jack's room. As soon as she closed the door behind her, she felt a pang of guilt. The poor woman was only doing her job. She had to take a few deep breaths, compose herself, before she lifted her gaze from the shiny white floor to the bed in the centre. She always did. It was a shock, every single day.

Beep. Beep. Hiss.

The endless rhythm of the machines that merged with her brother was both a song of hope, and a chorus of despair.

Beep. Beep. Hiss.

He was alive. Suspended in time. Absent, yes. But alive. Beep. Beep. Hiss.

It taunted and tortured her. The beat would end, one day. That was certain. There would come a time when those sounds were no longer a part of her life. What was uncertain was whether they would be replaced with squeals of joy, or screams of grief. Would that soundtrack fade? The mechanical whoosh of the breathing tube replaced by a cough, a splutter, and then a deep inhalation of air. The chime of the monitors silenced one by one by the hands of a beaming doctor, shaking his head as he declared it to be a miracle.

Or would the refrain one day reach a terrifying crescendo? The beat becoming faster and faster until all the beeping merged into one, horrifying, note?

There was no way of knowing how the tune was going to end. For now, Kaitlyn just had to keep it playing. She forced herself to look at Jack's sleeping face, trying to ignore the machines' tendrils going in, and coming out, of his flesh. Pulling the hard, plastic chair next to the bed, she sat down beside him.

"Hey, shithead," she whispered. "Still haven't moved your lazy arse I see. What am I going to do with you, eh?"

She stared at his face, holding her breath, desperately hoping to see some flicker of recognition. A movement behind those closed lids perhaps, something to suggest her voice was getting through. Something to suggest he was still in there, somewhere. But his long, thick eyelashes were criss-crossed, like a Venus flytrap lying dormant.

She'd tried every scrap of bait she could think of to get them to open. Pleading, swearing, crying. Nothing. But the doctors assured her talking to him was the best thing she could do. She had a strong suspicion they were telling her that for her own sake, rather than his. The feeling of impotence, of waiting and wishing but having no control, was surely more than anyone could bear. She doubted her daily diatribes had any effect, but all the time there was the slightest chance she was helping, she would continue.

She chatted at him. About the café, about the weather, about her neighbours. She was just launching into a tirade about Gina, and her little investment, when the door opened and a gruff-looking doctor waltzed in without knocking.

"Looks like the doc's here to stick pins in you again, Jack," she said, standing up. "Guess that's my cue to get going."

"Actually, Miss Thomas," the doctor was holding bright yellow invoice slips, not lime green medical records. "It's you I've come to see. I'm afraid I have just been asked to sign off on disconnection, due to arrears. I must inform you that, unless the balance is paid immediately, we will have no choice but to turn off your brother's respirator at midnight."

5

The woman behind the desk had more make-up than brain cells, Henry concluded. She held a ball point pen in her right hand, and clicked it relentlessly as she read through Chloe's file. He already knew what the outcome would be, and so did she. The appointment was nothing but an exercise in futility, and a waste of what little time there was left. In fact, he was pretty sure she was too dumb to even read the file properly. He wouldn't be in the least bit surprised if someone had simply stuck the word *NO!* on a Post-it note at the front, and all this was play acting to make him think they were trying everything they could. Well, he wasn't falling for it. If she didn't stop clicking that damn pen he was going reach across, grab it, and throw it out of the window.

"Well, Mr Morris," she interrupted his pen-lobbing fantasy, "I'm afraid we have reached the limit of what we can offer you in terms of credit for treatment."

No shit. Henry hauled himself to his feet, and slung his coat over one arm. What a fucking fiasco. This idiotic pantomime of hoop-jumping was never going to end any other way. He wondered why he hadn't just told the doctor where to shove his appointment.

"Right," he said, turning toward the door, "well, thank you for your time."

"Hold on, Mr Morris," she said, "I do have some good news for you."

"What's that?"

"Well," she said, smiling so wide he could see the lipstick on her teeth, "I am delighted to inform you that, in deference to your wife's regular tax contributions, I have been given direct authorisation from the Moving On Corporation to offer you their gold package for a reduced rate, as a sincere thank you for a lifetime of credit contributions."

She thrust a leaflet toward him. Moving On Corp propaganda. Shiny, smiling grey-haired people standing in front of golden gates, surrounded by white fluffy clouds. Equally ecstatic-looking young models, supposed to be their children, waving them off. They'd stopped short of adding naked cherubim to the design, but there was a white dove or two. *Moving On. For your future, and theirs.*

For. Fuck's. Sake. Henry tasted the bile. Who bought this crap? Enough people to make the Moving On Corp the fastest growing conglomerate in England, that's who. God, he ought to snatch the pamphlet, screw it up and ram it down her throat.

"No," he said, as assertively as he could. "No thank you. I'll find a way. I still have assets."

She withdrew her hand, tucking the leaflet back in Chloe's file, and gave an insincere smile. The type people give when they think you're nuts, but want to seem like they empathise. The type he'd been getting a lot of lately.

"Mr Morris," she said. "You do know Hepraxin isn't a cure, right?"

He wasn't sure what she was getting at.

"I mean" – she dropped her voice to a whisper – "it only masks the disease, for a while. It isn't intended for long-term use. I would hate to see you lose everything, just chasing the end of the rainbow."

"I beg your pardon?"

"Just… don't do anything drastic, okay? At the end of the day, medicine is business now, it's not like it was back in your youth. You could give every penny you have to the drug company, or you could leave it to your loved ones. The end will be the same for Chloe."

Oh, now he understood. She was working for commission. He'd heard the rumours; talk was rife down the darts club. Old Al was always ranting on about it, but Henry had never given him credence, given that he was four sheets to the wind whenever he saw him.

"It's all a big bloody circle, you mark my words," he'd wheeze, shifting his weight from side to side in an effort to remain on his bar stool, almost knocking over his oxygen tank in the process. "Socialism's dying. They're all creaming it off, any way they can take it. S'all new to 'em of course. Personal wealth, enterprise. They actually think they're onto something. That's why they want rid of us. We've seen it all before. They're heading down the same shit creek we already bin down. An' they don't want us pointin' out the rapids. Fuck 'em. Nobody tells THIS old cracker when to get outta the pool."

Maybe Al wasn't a crackpot after all. Henry had fallen into the trap of thinking the generation before him were ignorant, and out-of-touch. Just as this woman in front of him now thought about his own generation. But perhaps Al had the measure of it, after all. She was skimming. She probably got fifteen per cent of any death deals she managed to peddle. Well, she'd not be getting any blood money out of him.

He stormed out. In his mind he slammed the door behind him, but to anyone close by it was nothing more than a slightly irritating thud. The youngsters in the waiting room probably just thought he'd misjudged the weight of the door, what with his being an irrelevant old cripple and all.

In truth, no one would have noticed even if he'd slammed it with enough force to make the walls shake, not with the commotion that was already going on at the reception desk.

A young woman with long, black curls was pushing her way through the queue, much to everyone's disgust. She elbowed the waiting patients out of the way, and threw a bag down onto the desk in front of the startled receptionist.

"Here's your thirty pieces of fucking silver," she yelled.

Despite himself, Henry smiled. Gutsy. So few of them were gutsy. A pang of envy hit him in the stomach. He wasn't gutsy either. He never said what he really thought. He betted this young firebrand would have told that money-grabbing financial 'advisor' exactly where to stick her offer. She reminded him of Carolyn; he'd always admired her brass. Bloody nightmare to live with, of course, and she'd used that killer instinct to take him to the cleaners, but still.

The firebrand turned round, storming away from the desk. This time the queue parted, still shaking their heads at her intrusion. Her lips were tightly pursed, face almost purple with the rage she exuded, but he recognised her still. The waitress from the greasy spoon.

Chloe had been right, even in his imagination. She did have troubles of her own. He was glad he'd left her a tip. In fact, he wanted to burst into applause, or at the very least congratulate her on her outburst. But she was already half way down the corridor, and he didn't have an icicle's chance in a volcano of catching up to her.

6

She felt white hot. The people she passed as she strode down the corridors were just blurred shapes behind the wall of water in her eyes. Thank God she couldn't see their faces. The scorn, the stares. What a way to behave. Shame twisted through her and her pace quickened. The automatic doors opened as she approached and the cold air made her gasp.

The bench at the other end of the mostly deserted car park was as far away as she could manage to get before giving in to the tears. As if it wasn't bad enough to be broke, and alone. Had to go and add public humiliation into the mix too.

Across the road, the school children were emerging from the New Church, after lunchtime prayers. Young girls in yellow cotton dresses, bright faces full of wonder and hope. Loaded up on divinity. She hadn't been to a service for years. But she could remember how it felt to emerge into the sunlight, cloaked in the sweet, thick blanket of belief. That feeling of protection and purpose. A hand on your shoulder, and the world full of omens you need only look for.

The clergy were people you could always rely on to make the world seem better, brighter. People who had time to listen, and an infinite supply of godly advice. Until you disagreed with their counsel, then they cast you adrift. Just when you needed them most.

Jack had never been religious, but he used to take her to

the services anyway. Watching the girls outside the church smiling and twirling in the sunshine, she understood why. They were peaceful, secure in the sure and certain knowledge they were part of a plan far greater than themselves. They were the future. It all belonged to them. What harm could befall you, if you were a channel of God's love? If only she could feel that way again.

"He wanted me to feel safe," she whispered to herself. Her own epiphany sending a shiver through her.

He'd wanted to see that look on her face. That serene, opiated smile. Taking her to the New Church was his way of cloaking her in armour, showing her an alternative to the violent decay of home. And Sister Rochelle had been an alternative role model. Someone to show her not all women had to act like their mother.

When he'd quit school to work in the farming district, he'd instructed her to always go directly to the New Church, as soon as her own lessons were finished.

"Not home, Kat." His hands firmly on her shoulders, the fire in his eyes telling her he was serious. "Never home. Not without me."

So she did. Every day she would walk the two miles from school to the church, and complete her homework on the pews, surrounded by the bright, white statues of angels and saints. But sometimes it got late. Sometimes, she listened for the roar of Jack's motorcycle long past six. On those days, Sister Rochelle would come to her, with a bowl of pea soup, a chunk of bread, and a patient smile.

She was beautiful. The kind of beautiful that made Kaitlyn feel dirty in her own skin. She could have been a star. But instead her long blonde hair was tied in a neat bun, and her lips were pale pink and unadorned. The lemon yellow habit, despite its shapelessness, couldn't hide the swell of her hips and breasts entirely, though Kaitlyn tried not to notice. It was wrong to notice. It was wrong to compare. To envy. To aspire.

To dream.

But she did dream. She dreamed of her own life in God's service. She dreamed that one day she would be radiant, wise and serene. She would have the answers to all the questions, just like Rochelle did. And she'd never have to leave.

She thought that day had come when her test scores came through. It was always a defining moment in a child's life: the EPT results. Two little numbers that determined your Earning Potential, and the path you to ought take. The amount of Social Credit that would be available to you, for use on education and healthcare, was entirely dependent on your EP score. Class sizes always dropped by half the day after the results came out. Spending credit you could never hope to repay on a pointless education was a prideful man's folly... so Rochelle told her.

"We must accept, and rejoice," she said, holding Kaitlyn's lower-than-expected scores in her hand. "God gives each of us the tools for the job we must do. What use is a tractor to a fisherman? Or a trawler to a doctor? We must not covet the tools of another, we must look to those we have been given to find our appointed task."

"So, I should leave school?"

"Unquestionably."

"I want to join the Order."

"And oh, what an asset you would be! But first, you must be older. A life in God's New Order involves commitment. Spiritual and material. Body and soul are yours to give already, but I'm afraid the law does not allow you autonomy over your credit until you are eighteen. A dismal throwback to darker times if you ask me, but there we have it."

"So what should I do?"

"I can organise something, if you'd like? There's a commune just outside Hampshire, where girls such as yourself can live together, under God's protection, while they wait to take their vows. A far better choice for a forward thinking young lady like yourself than high school, or your... current situation. And it doesn't cost a thing."

43

"Doesn't cost? How doesn't it cost?"

"It is funded by the donated credit of those who have already devoted themselves. Kaitlyn, I lived there myself for three years, and they were some of the happiest days I ever knew, all thanks to the generosity of those who came before me. Now I have the privilege of donating my earthly assets so girls like you can have the same opportunity."

It had sounded like a miracle. She'd been bursting with happiness. Surely, it was the right choice? The only choice. But Jack didn't think so.

It had been gone 8 p.m. when he rolled up on his bike, but Kaitlyn was still bouncing with excitement. Sister Rochelle called him inside, to tell him about their decision. But he was having none of it.

"She's staying in school," he said. "And I don't want you filling her head with this nonsense. She's a clever girl."

"That may be your opinion, Jack. But I'm afraid the scores don't agree."

"Fuck the scores!"

"Mind your language in the house of God! Are you really going to allow her to be saddled with a debt she can't repay, just because of your own agenda?"

"As opposed to your agenda? Her debt is none of your damn business. She will have choices, she will have options. I'll make sure of it." He grabbed Kaitlyn by the arm and started storming out.

"She's becoming a woman, Jack," Rochelle called out, and Jack stopped and turned around to face her. "What then? Can you protect her then?"

He stared at Rochelle for a long moment, then yanked Kaitlyn by her arm and led her to his bike without saying a word.

She was young, and stupid. In that moment, she hated him. Rochelle had painted such an idyllic picture that Kaitlyn had already set her heart on life in the commune, full of fun and friendship. She yelled at him, punched out at him. Called him names she was ashamed to remember. She had no idea.

The next day he was waiting for her at the school gates, with suitcases in his hands.

"I've got us a flat, Kat," he said. "Nothing fancy, but you can have the bed and I'll have the sofa. You won't need to go to the church after school any more, you can go home. Our home. Just me and you."

"But, what about Mum? Won't she miss us?"

Jack snorted. "She doesn't need us. And we definitely don't need her. I don't want you ever going to see her, you hear me, Kat? Never. She's no good for you. And I was wrong about that Sister too. You stay away from her, as well. People will use you, Kat. If you let them. Mum and her both. They want something from you, and you're too young to realise what that is. So you're just going to have to trust me, okay?"

She did. To an extent. Leaving their mother wasn't hard, not like she thought it would be. After a couple of days, Kaitlyn realised she didn't miss her. At all. If anything, being away from her gave Kaitlyn a sense of calm she'd never experienced before. So she had no trouble following Jack's command. But Sister Rochelle was a different story.

Now there were things, so many things, she wanted to say to Jack. So many apologies, so many realisations. But she might never get the chance.

7

He was almost at his car when he spotted her. The firebrand. Burned out and sobbing. What had been bold and glorious just minutes before was now crumpled and defeated, like a spent firework lying in the rain. He opened his car door and started to get in. But Chloe's voice spoke in his head.

'You wanted to congratulate her, didn't you? Well, this is your chance. She looks like she could do with a little support.'

The voice of Chloe had been right about her yesterday, so he decided to roll with it. He fished around in his pocket and found a tissue. She didn't seem to notice him approaching, even as slow and lumbering as he was. Her gaze was on the New Church.

"Excuse me, miss?" he said, when he was close enough for her to hear.

She looked up, startled.

"Would you like a tissue?" He offered the crumpled paper. She stared at it, and her nose wrinkled as if he'd tried to hand her a mouldy sock.

"I have a handkerchief, thank you," she replied, waving the fabric that had been scrunched in her palm.

He winced. He should have known. They were all militant about their reusables. He'd just played right into the 'throwaway' snowflake stereotype.

"I just wanted to say, I thought you were brilliant back there." He gestured to the hospital. "Wish I had your guts."

She stared at him. "Do I know you?"

"Ah… well, not really. I was in your café yesterday. You held the door for me."

"You tipped me, after I was rude. I'm sorry. And I'm sorry I caused a scene back there. I always speak before I think. I hate it."

"I always think, but never speak. Even when I should. Trust me, I reckon there's more regret in that. I wanted to applaud you, you know? I should have done, but I didn't. I regret that now."

"Now that you've seen what a mess I am? It wasn't anything to applaud. I didn't accomplish anything, other than making a fool of myself."

"Well, it's probably not much comfort, but you made my dark day a little brighter, if it helps."

She stared at him, salty liquid still spilling slowly from the corners of those dark green eyes, and her lips curled ever so slightly into a smile.

"Actually," she said, "it does a bit. Thanks."

The silence was awkward. Henry jangled the keys in his pocket, trying not to stare at the young woman whose private tears he'd intruded on.

"Well," he said at last, "I suppose I should get going."

"Okay." The firebrand pulled her coat tighter as an icy wind swirled through the car park. "Well, nice to meet you…"

"Henry. Henry Morris."

"Kaitlyn," she said. "If you ever stop by the café again, I promise not to be an arse. I'll even shout you a free coffee."

"That's very kind, Kaitlyn. I hope your day gets better."

She laughed. A gulping gasp of a laugh that teetered on the edge of hysteria.

"It couldn't get worse," she said. "But no, unfortunately it won't get better. Not unless they're right" – she gestured to the New Church – "and miracles do happen."

"I've never known them to," Henry replied. "Tragedies, yes. Miracles, not so much. But I'm an old, selfish cynic, eh? Their God isn't interested in the likes of me."

"That makes two of us then," she said. "Because he certainly isn't listening to me."

It was a surprise to hear a youngster talk that way; most of them were devout these days. Another example of Old Al's wheel, he guessed. It had always been fashionable to rebel against the values of the elder generations. And his lot had been decidedly secular. Whoever would have thought that conformity could become rebellion? But with the slow death of the socialist ideals underway, the new brand of religious dogma peddled by the New Order was taking hold of young hearts and minds. As though it was something new, and progressive. Not the same old shit recycled and repackaged.

Yet for some reason, Kaitlyn, who should be enjoying the self-righteous privilege her youth allowed, seemed to have some big problems of her own. What could have happened to this young firebrand to make her so desolate? The sight of her shivering beneath her long curls, the winter sun making the tear-streaks on her cheeks glisten, kicked in an instinct he hadn't felt in a long time. He wanted to protect her, to shelter her.

"Are you heading back to work?" he asked. "Would you like a lift?"

"You've got a car?" It sounded like an accusation. Henry felt irrationally ashamed. Another stereotype. He looked across the car park; there were less than a dozen vehicles, and he betted most of them belonged to old farts like him.

It was a different story when he was a kid, of course. He remembered sitting in the back of his dad's 4x4, listening to him curse the traffic as they queued to take their ticket and get through the barrier. Then driving round and round the hospital car park, desperately looking for someone winking out of a spot so they could nab it.

Nowadays, the car park was the half the size. Bus lanes had

taken over, and even then it was mostly deserted. He couldn't argue that it made life easier.

"Well, it'll be less wasteful if we share, won't it?"

She laughed. "I guess you're right. I suppose it's my duty as an ecologically aware citizen to accept your offer."

"Are you going to work?"

"Yes. Well, my shift doesn't start for a couple of hours, but I might as well."

She was smiling now, lips still trembling in the cold.

"Perhaps I can buy you a coffee first, warm you up?" he asked. Then he remembered seeing her steal that sandwich the day before, and felt guilty at how he had judged her. "Or maybe something to eat?"

"I'm not hungry," she said, "but a coffee would be nice, thanks."

"Okie dokes," he said, belying his era.

"But… can we go somewhere else for it, not Jared's?"

"Oh God, of course," Henry said as they walked across the car park. "The service there is terrible!"

Kaitlyn feigned an offended gasp before letting out a small chuckle. They smiled at one another as the first fat drops of November rain began to fall around them.

8

She hadn't been in a car for years. Not since Grandpa had visited and taken her and Jack down to the coast for the day. She hadn't seen Grandpa for years either, after he'd had that row with Mum. He must be older than Henry, so she supposed he was dead, and was shocked at how little pain that caused her.

Henry turned a dial on the dashboard, and hot air blasted her.

"Clears the windscreen," he explained when she jumped a little at the unexpected onslaught of noisy warmth.

He was a strange creature, this elderly man beside her. Grey hairs protruded from his oversized nose and ears, and he swore under his breath every time they hit a bump in the road.

"Sodding potholes," he said. "Bloody well be going back to horse and cart soon, I expect."

She just smiled, not really knowing what he meant, but not wishing to be rude. Old people often talked nonsense; their brains were full of holes. That's what happens when you think you know better than God, Sister Rochelle had told her. 'Our bodies are perfectly designed for the correct lifespan,' she'd explained, 'but the greedy man tries to thwart his mortality, rather than embrace it. Scared of the judgement that is to come, no doubt. But you will see, if you ever happen to meet such a wretched being, that they bring Hell upon themselves by trying to outwit their creator. Their very bodies turn against them. Cells multiply and attack them; their brains addle and torment them. Because you cannot turn your back on what is natural, on what is inevitable, without consequence.'

Kaitlyn wasn't at all sure she believed in God any more, but she still thought Sister Rochelle had a point. Why would anyone choose to endure the agony of old age, unless they were scared of what might lie beyond death?

"Here do?" Henry pulled up outside a coffee shop, interrupting her musings on sin and mortality.

"Yes, great." Kaitlyn got out of the car and walked toward the café. She pushed open the door and held it, expecting Henry to be right behind her. But when she looked around he was still several metres behind, limping slowly. The patrons already seated glared at her for letting so much cold air in, and tutted when they saw it was because of the slow, wizened man she was with. She felt dizzy with shame, realising the scorn this old man, who had been nothing but kind to her, had to endure just for going about his daily business.

"What happened to your leg? Is it why you were at the hospital?" she blurted out as they seated themselves at a corner table.

"Well, you're a curious one, aren't you?" Henry replied, but he was smiling, so she hadn't upset him. She hoped. You had to be careful with snowflakes, they took offence at everything. Even using the wrong title by accident could result in them getting aggressive, so she'd heard anyway. Generally, it was best just to avoid asking them anything, in case they found your question to be an affront. But he seemed happy enough to answer. "I lost it years ago, in an accident. Damn lorry jack-knifed in front of me. I was going too fast, of course. Couldn't stop in time. Lucky to get out with my life, so they told me anyway. Don't remember much about it. One second I was slamming my foot on the brakes, the next I was lying in a hospital bed being told said foot was going *adios*. Still hurts sometimes, if you can believe that? Phantom pain, it's called."

"That's weird," Kaitlyn replied. "So, that's why you were at the hospital? This... phantom pain?"

Fancy spending credit on seeing a doctor about pain that doesn't really exist, in a limb that isn't even there.

"No," Henry replied. "It was about Chloe, my wife. She's having some... problems. What about you? I'm guessing the finance department pissed you off about something, from your little display earlier?"

She must have turned red because Henry's face fell.

"Oh God, I'm sorry," he said. "Please, I didn't mean to embarrass you. I already told you, I thought you were brilliant. I can't wait to tell Chloe all about it... when she's better."

The waitress deposited their coffees in front of them, and Kaitlyn stared at the swirling, freshly stirred liquid. "It's my brother. He's in a coma. Used up all his credit. They were going to switch off his respirator at midnight, unless I settled up."

She didn't look him in the eye, but braced for the usual backlash. You shouldn't be putting yourself into debt for a hopeless case, you can't go throwing good money after bad, yadda yadda. Nobody ever understood.

"Bastards." Henry's clenched-teeth whisper took her by surprise. "God damn Dickensian fucking bastards."

She stared at him, shocked at the genuine rage that seemed to dance behind his eyes.

"It's not their fault," she said, surprised to find herself defending the hospital she'd been cursing just an hour before, "everyone has to pay their own way, how else can they function?"

"'From each according to his ability, to each according to his need.' Karl Marx. *That's* how it should function. That's what we tried to do, you know? But there's always some fucker up the top tilting it their way."

She had no idea what he was talking about, so she changed the subject. "Do you have any children?" she asked.

Now it was his turn to stare into the warm, dark liquid in front of him, she noted.

"Just one," he said, after too long. She wondered why such a simple question had caused him to pause. Perhaps he couldn't remember offhand, what with his age. "A son, David. He's married with his own children now, of course."

"That's nice," Kaitlyn replied, wondering what the point of it all was if you couldn't even remember your own children clearly.

"What about you?" he asked. "Married? Kids? A partner?"

"No, none of the above." She smiled, trying to look like she was fine with her situation, in control of it even, but it hurt.

She'd been close, once. Finn had seemed like the one. Not in a fireworks-in-the-sky type of way, but everyone knew such things were fantasies invented in the olden times to distract people from the reality of the inequality they endured. He'd been hard-working, reliable. A solid EP and no inherited defects. A sensible match that would have produced healthy children with decent scores. At least, that's what she'd told herself.

She had always tried to be pragmatic when it came to relationships. Jack had cautioned her against letting her heart rule over her head. So, when Finn had come along she was sure she'd made the decision to marry him purely for practical, sensible reasons. But having him in her life had brought a sense of peace, perhaps even joy, that she hadn't been expecting. She'd enjoyed the feeling of belonging that came with having someone to meet her after work, walk her home through the dark streets safely. Because it meant she was worth protecting. She liked his arms around her, and waking up to his soft, blonde curls tickling her nose as she snuggled in behind him. She loved his laughter, and the way he would stroke her hair as she lay on his chest. If she was honest, she loved him. More than she'd care to admit. But, like everyone else, he hadn't understood about Jack.

Oh, he'd been sympathetic at first, when it had no impact

on his own future. But once Jack's overdraft ran out, and Kaitlyn made it clear she was not ready to submit the Moving On application that Finn had helpfully already filled in for her, everything changed.

He didn't want to tie himself to someone who was in credit debt. He called her selfish, stupid, an unfit spouse.

"What about the children we were planning? I thought we were supposed to be a team! How can you justify spending so much credit on a lost cause? You're spitting on your kids' chances, on their future!" He raged, and stomped, and threw insults. But she wouldn't budge.

So the ring he had been saving for was never bought. The lease on their flat was never renewed. He found a new partner, one with a higher EP than Kaitlyn. And now, her finger remained unadorned, and she walked home alone through the midnight streets, with no one to care if her corpse should be found, frozen and bloody, by some early morning joggers the next day.

But she tried not to think about the pain. Never let herself use the word 'heartbreak', not even in her own mind. Such self-indulgent woes wouldn't help anyone. No one ever changed their situation by dwelling on it.

"So," she said, trying to steer the conversation away from her, "did you get everything sorted? For your wife?"

"Not exactly," Henry replied, "she has dementia."

He looked her straight in the eye as he said it, like he was gauging her reaction. She tried not to show any emotion, or shock. But she knew what it meant. He'd been at the hospital filling in a Moving On application. The twinge of sympathy she felt took her by surprise.

"I'm so sorry," she said. "How long will you have to wait?"

"For what?"

"The application to be approved? I've never had to do one myself, I don't know how long these things take."

"I haven't made an application," he replied. "She's not going anywhere. She's staying on Hepraxin."

She couldn't hide the shock this time, and her mouth did its usual trick of running off without permission.

"What? But... you've got grandchildren? Why would you use all your credit on..."

A lost cause, a walking corpse.

"On the woman I love?" he asked, still smiling. "Anyway, I'm not using credit."

Must be rich, she concluded. Must have savings. He didn't look rich, though. But appearances can be deceptive.

"Oh, I see. I'm sorry, I shouldn't have assumed."

He started to laugh. A deep belly laugh that was half amusement and half despair.

"I'm not using credit, because neither of us have any left!" he said.

Why was he laughing about that? What was funny about leaving nothing behind to help the future generation? 'Those that came before were raised in greed. Selfishness was their milk, and pride their nursemaid,' Sister Rochelle's voice echoed in her memories. Perhaps it was true, after all. Those who were born before the Roll-Back really were self-centred, despicable people from a godless age of hedonism. But, Henry hadn't seemed like that earlier.

Beware the wolf in sheep's clothing.

"I can't believe you're laughing about it!" She raised her voice, not caring that it caused people to look. "Are you actually proud? Proud that you've used up everything, left nothing behind for those who come after?"

"No, Kaitlyn." His expression turned dark now. "No, I'm not proud. I don't have anything to be proud of, except Chloe. And she's an exceptional person in spite of me, not because of me. No, I'm laughing at the hopelessness of it all. The dream turned to dust."

"What do you mean?"

"Do you know the owner of the Moving On Corporation is a hundred and two? A hundred and two!"

He was cuckoo. Veering off on tangents, not to mention

delusional. Hugo Jensen was the owner of Moving On. Everyone knew that. A handsome, suave-looking man, no more than forty. Henry's brain must be like Swiss cheese. He didn't know what he was saying. Maybe it wasn't his wife who had dementia? Maybe it was him.

"Hugo Jensen isn't a day over forty," she said slowly, as if to a child. "I think you might be confused with someone else. Maybe someone from the olden times?"

Henry just chuckled. "Hugo may be the face of Moving On, but it's his grandfather, Stephen, who founded it. And runs it in all but name, of course. A hundred and two. Are we to believe that he reached that staggering age without ailment? Or is it more likely that he himself has chosen to spend his descendants' inheritance on keeping his old body ticking over, rather than practising what he preaches? Some animals will always be more equal than others."

Was he right? A hundred and two? The guy who saved the country from the crisis of aging, who made people see – at last – how selfish it was to use up the Earth's resources chasing an unnaturally long lifespan, and the wrath that had befallen man for flouting God's order?

"That can't be true! That's… that's…"

"Hypocrisy, my dear. Hypocrisy. The very thing my parents' generation revolted against. Yet here we are. Inequality. Of course, we don't see it as much. Back before the Roll-Back it was on display, to anyone who had access to a computer, which was everyone. They had nowhere to hide."

"But, computers dest—"

"Destroyed jobs and created a culture of fantasy and entitlement. Yes, yes. I know the rhetoric. And it's not wholly untrue. But nothing is ever that black and white. Or it didn't used to be. You forget, some of us *remember*. And what we remember isn't quite what the books say. But, soon we'll all be ushered off this mortal coil. Then it won't matter. History will be whatever the New Church, and the Jensens, decide it ought to be."

She doubted he could remember anything at all. And began to wonder if accepting his offer of a coffee wasn't a huge mistake. It wouldn't do to be seen with a raving madman, spouting radical nonsense. He couldn't even easily recall how many children he had, so how could he possibly have any insight into the past? Everyone was looking now. Some with condescending smiles, some with reproach. If she didn't correct him, she'd be considered complicit in his treacherous talk.

"History is history," she said, as calmly and sweetly as she could, "facts are facts. They can't be changed."

"Oh yes they can," he replied. "I could prove it to you, were you so inclined."

"Look." She raised her voice a little. She had to shut this down. "I don't want to be rude, but I really don't think this is appropriate. I'm sorry about your wife, and I'm sorry about your leg. But I'm not interested in your fantasies, or whatever loony conspiracy theories you buy into."

She expected him to be angry, but he just laughed.

"I'm sorry," he said, "I should have known it would be like trying to tell a fish about life on the land. Hopeless and pointless. Even if they did believe you, they could never experience it themselves."

"I should get to work," she said.

"Hold on," he replied, "I'll give you a lift, I just need to visit the gents first."

She watched him hobble across the café. When he was out of sight, she picked up her belongings. She'd just leave, not wait for him. Just walk out and be on her way; she still had plenty of time to get there on foot. She pulled her coat on quickly and headed to the door.

9

The firebrand was gone when he came out of the toilet.

"God damn it," he muttered, feeling conspicuous as hell as he made his way to the door alone, trying to ignore the smirks and whispers from the other patrons. He'd scared her off. She must think him a crazy old crackpot. Just like Old Al. Offer to buy a young lady a coffee, and then assault her with a political monologue. He got into the car and stared at his grey, wrinkled face in the rear-view mirror.

"Smooth," he said to his reflection.

It was so unlike him, too. He rarely spoke so freely, even to people he knew well. But something about Kaitlyn had made the words fall out, and now his mind replayed them from her perspective. In the mental montage he came off as an overbearing loon. No wonder she'd made a run for it.

She was on his mind the whole drive home. To be so young, and have so many problems. If she was using her own credit to keep her brother alive, she probably wouldn't make forty. Not on a waitress's wage. It was foolish. But no more foolish than pumping an ailing brain full of overpriced pills to try to keep your elderly spouse by your side. They were both idiots, in the eyes of everyone else.

Chloe was still asleep when he crept through the door. He knew she would be. Hepraxin had knocked her off her feet for over a week, pretty much, when she had started taking it. Upping the dose had the same effect. Her body needed to adjust.

It seemed like a miracle the first time. It had been so hard to get the first tablet down her. She was raving, screaming. Storming round the house in a nightdress, searching every cupboard.

"Where's it?" she'd demanded. "Where's the oodle?"

"I don't know what you mean, love?" He'd tried to reason, tried to be patient.

"The oodle! For the tea kettles. In the dub dub. What have you done with it, you wicked man!"

She'd refused the pills. "Oh, you'd love it wouldn't you? You and your getty! I haven't got time for tablets. Need to find the oodle!"

And what was worse, his repeated attempts to give them to her made her suspicious of any food and drink he prepared. In the end, he crushed her first pill and hid it in the milk jug, knowing that eventually she'd pour herself a drink from it. He felt like he'd betrayed her when she did. He'd watched her sip the cool liquid, believing she had outfoxed him by refusing any of his refreshments and getting her own.

When it kicked in, her eyes glazed over. The oodle was forgotten, and he just managed to walk her to their room before unconsciousness overtook her. For seven days she'd stayed in bed, waking only briefly to stagger to the toilet in a drugged-up haze, and take the next dose, meekly, when he prompted her. Then, all of a sudden, on the eighth day, she'd come downstairs at 11 a.m., fully dressed and clouded in her favourite perfume.

It was like a caterpillar going into a chrysalis and emerging as a butterfly. The strange, eerie faraway look was gone. The nonsense speak, plucked out of the ether in lieu of the ability to find the correct words, a distant memory. The demon that had possessed her had fled, exorcised by the pills.

Would it be the same this time? The bedroom door creaked as he pushed it open a crack to check on her. She rolled over in response, but did not wake. It certainly looked the same. But doubt would not allow itself to be banished. That jumped-up jobsworth's words crept unwanted through his thoughts.

"Hepraxin isn't a cure, you know."

She was worse this time. Deeper in the abyss. What if, when she came back, some trace of the hell she'd been to still lingered on her?

The doorbell rang, and he quickly pulled the bedroom door shut, worried it would disturb her if it rang again. Which it inevitably did, because it took him so long to descend the stairs.

"Alright, alright," he said, too quietly for the unwanted caller to hear, "hold your bloody horses."

He yanked the front door open, to be greeted by David's slick smile.

"Hey, Dad." His son was suited and booted, as always, and walked in past him without waiting for an invitation. "Thought you'd gone deaf for a minute."

"I was in the loo," Henry lied. It wouldn't surprise him if David kept note of how long he took to answer the door each time, searching for a downward trend. Making a mental forecast of physical decline per annum, and the projected impact on his inheritance. Maybe a bathroom excursion would introduce a new variable and throw his projections off course.

David laughed. "Ah, I see," he said, perching himself on the sofa and tugging his trousers at the knees to make sure the fabric didn't touch his buffed shoes. "How are you keeping?"

"Oh, you know," Henry replied, "can't complain. How are you and Fiona? And the kids?"

"Oh, great. Just great," David said. "Jerome's just enrolled in advanced physics, and Lisbeth's really taken to the clarinet. Like a duck to water, so the tutor says."

"Well," Henry chuckled, "they're not likely to say she's tone deaf and shouldn't waste her time, not when you're paying them Christ knows how much an hour, eh?"

David's smile slipped. He never did have a sense of humour.

"But that's great," Henry backtracked, "really great. All of it. Great kids. Just great."

"Yeah." David reached forward and helped himself to an apple from the fruit bowl on the coffee table. Henry couldn't remember when he last replenished them, and prayed it wasn't rotten underneath. "But anyway, enough about us. We're peachy. I came to see how you're doing? What with the cold spell, and your leg. Are you managing okay? Getting out to the shops alright? You know you only need to ask if you'd like me or Fi to pick groceries up for you, if it's getting too much. I worry about you, Dad."

Oh, here it was. The 'concerned son' act. Did he really think it washed? Did he really think Henry didn't know exactly which boxes his son was hoping to tick on the Parental Incapacity form? It was hard for Henry not to bite right through his tongue.

"I'm fine, son. Thanks for your concern. You'll be the first to know when I'm scrapheap-ready, I promise."

"Don't be like that, Dad. I didn't mean anything by it. It's just… well, you know a lot of my friends are finding they're having to help out a fair bit now, with their parents I mean. It made me realise I've been negligent; I haven't been coming over regularly enough. Haven't been making sure you're coping. I feel terrible about it, to be honest."

What a shedload of steaming hot bullshit. How the hell had the only surviving fruit of his loins turned out to be such a manipulative, selfish arse? Henry wanted to place the blame firmly on Carolyn, but deep down he knew he'd played his part too.

"No need to worry about me, son. Strong as an ox, and anyway, I've got Chloe. If you want to worry about someone, worry about your mother; she's alone after all." *Because she's a vindictive, spiteful cow.*

"Mum's a lot younger than you and Chloe, Dad.

Remember?" David cocked his head to the side like he was instructing a puppy. "Speaking of Chloe, where is she? Gone out and left you home alone, eh?"

"No. No, she's having a nap. Bit of a migraine. Think she had some cheese last night. She knows she shouldn't, but she's a sucker for a bit of Stilton."

Henry had managed to keep Chloe's dementia a secret from David. It hadn't been hard. He didn't visit very often. Once, before she'd started on the Hepraxin, he'd knocked at the door, with the children, when she was in the middle of a bad spell. But Henry had thought fast, and told David he'd better not come in because Chloe had the measles. Fiona was one of those wealthy pseudo-hippy whackos who didn't believe in vaccines, so David wouldn't want to risk the kids getting it. He imagined it gave Fiona great satisfaction to be able to wax lyrical about how vaccines definitely didn't work, because her husband's stepmother got the measles despite having had them. Some people really will believe anything.

"Oh, I'm sorry," David said, getting to his feet. "I didn't realise, I hope I haven't disturbed her? I should be going."

"No worries, son," Henry replied. "Nothing much wakes her when she's got a head on."

As if to prove him a liar, Chloe's voice rang out from upstairs. Except it didn't sound like Chloe's voice. Chloe's voice was usually soft, an unassuming lilting melody full of kindness and cheer. This sounded more like the unholy wail of a tormented beast.

"HEIDIIII! My Heidi! Henreeeeeee!"

David jumped at the sudden noise, and the guttural calling of his sister's name. "Jesus Christ!" he said. "Dad, what the hell is wrong with her?"

"Just a nightmare, son. Just a nightmare. Perfectly common. Cheese, eh? Really does a number on her. I'll have to put my foot down. It can't be worth it, no matter how tasty." He hurried to the bottom of the stairs. David stared at him, with a look that bordered on terror. Henry wondered how many years it had been since he'd heard Heidi's name. Did he ever even think about her?

He put his good foot on the bottom step and stopped. He needed to get to Chloe. Christ knows what she might say, what she might do, if she got out of bed. There'd be no hiding her condition if David saw her face-to-face. But he didn't want his son to see him struggle up the stairs either.

"Do us a favour," he said, when inspiration hit. "Pop the kettle on, would you? I'll just nip up and make sure she's not too freaked out by the nightmare, then I'll be back and make her a nice sweet tea. Always sorts out a bad dream that, eh?"

"Sure, Dad." David turned and headed to the kitchen. Henry exhaled. He wouldn't be 'popping' anywhere, not with steps involved. But at least the noise of the kettle would mask any further outbursts from Chloe.

He'd almost reached the top step when a thought struck him like a lightning bolt, and made his heart speed up in horror.

He'd left the box of Hepraxin on the kitchen side.

10

She felt a little bad when she pictured Henry coming out of the toilets to find her gone. But he was clearly missing a few screws, and she didn't have the time or energy to deal with that. Typical, the one person who seemed to understand her decision to keep Jack alive was senile. What did that say about her own mental capacity? She tried not to dwell on it.

She took a right turn at the deli on the corner, deciding to cut through the pedestrianised zone in case Henry came looking for her in his car. It was market day, the best time of the week to pick up fresh produce. The shopping zone was full of people going about their business, striding purposefully in all directions clutching their canvas bags full of potatoes, apples and meat. Kaitlyn's stomach growled its discontent, as if it were watching through her eyes and protesting that she fed it nothing but cheap pasta and bread.

A woman of around Henry's age came out of the butcher's, clutching a small bag of off-cut scraps. Her socks were visible through the holes in her shoes, and Kaitlyn betted she thought herself terribly hard done by. But she would have meat this evening, and no doubt every evening.

It didn't do to be self-indulgent. Envy wouldn't fill her belly. Besides, she should be grateful that Jared so often allowed her to eat at work. There were plenty of jobs that paid no more than hers, but didn't have that added perk. She lifted her gaze, looking straight ahead and ignoring the stalls full of food.

Once out of the precinct, she bypassed the rows of skyrise flats where she had grown up, choosing instead to take a scenic route through the slightly more affluent districts where the clerks and secretaries typically lived. The wooden cabin-style houses each had their own small square of grass, outside their front doors. Many had dug out most of it, choosing to grow vegetables instead of wasting their coveted outdoor land on pointless, inedible lawns. Their small but precious crops were protected by boxes made of razor wire.

Further down the lane, past the small school she had once attended, the Moving On complex stood, on a plot of gated-off land as large as a hundred cabin-houses put together. She stopped at the tall, gilded gates to admire the well-kept gardens that lined its sweeping driveway. The old manor house, now remodelled so that its entire front was made of gleaming frosted glass, was partially obscured by the rows of cherry trees and firs that made the whole grounds feel like an ancient, peaceful forest grove. Squirrels darted from one tree to another, while the tall stone fountain provided a soundtrack of tranquillity. It was designed to look like paradise, of course. A haven of comfort and rest that one entered, but never emerged from.

At least, not consciously. The black hearse winding its way down the driveway was a stark reminder of how its patrons physically exited the grounds.

"Excuse me, ma'am," a soft, weak voice interrupted her thoughts.

Kaitlyn turned around, and was confronted by two greying faces smiling meekly at her. A couple, old enough that streaks of silver snaked through their hair, but not so old that all pigment was gone, stood arm-in-arm.

The man was dressed in a faded tuxedo, clutching a bottle of champagne in his free hand. The woman wore a lacy white blouse, and matching ivory skirt that looked far too young in its style for her jowled, sagging skin.

"Oh, I'm sorry," Kaitlyn said, stepping aside from the gate. "I was miles away."

The woman smiled, her lips a perfect Cupid's bow slicked with a pale pink gloss. "No problem," she said, pulling a bronze token out of her handbag and inserting it into the slot on the wall.

The gates swung open, and the couple entered the grounds. Kaitlyn watched, unable to take her eyes off the pair. They ambled down the drive, stopping now and then when one of them pointed to a beautiful plant, or some frolicking wildlife. The woman's hand curled round her partner's arm, they both smiled and laughed, but she was clinging on so tightly that her knuckles were white. When they finally disappeared out of view, Kaitlyn turned away, feeling giddy.

They were never coming out.

The thought plagued her as she started down the street. She tried to picture it; walking to her own demise. So calmly, so willingly. So properly. She couldn't imagine it.

She pulled her coat a little tighter, but it did nothing to ease the chill. There was no anger in that old couple. But perhaps there should have been? A group of people walked toward her, perhaps seven or eight, and she kept her eyes on the pavement. She was thinking about Henry. He had rage, plenty of it. So did she, but she hadn't equated the two. Hers was justifiable, righteous. But why? Because she was young. That was the only reason she could find, and it suddenly seemed pathetic. They were both clinging on to someone they loved, against all advice. They were both angry. The only real difference, apart from their age, was that Henry knew what he was angry with. Hers was an exasperated, directionless rage that reared its head at undeserving targets. The nurses, the financial secretaries, Finn. None of them had any hand in her situation.

As the group coming the other way passed her, she caught a snatch of their chatter.

"What a fucking farce." A tall, well-built man, a little older than Kaitlyn, pulled at the sleeves of his suit and adjusted his tie. "How much do you reckon it cost to get their bloody wedding clothes dry-cleaned?"

"Oh come on, Tim," the woman beside him chided. Kaitlyn chanced a glance at her. She had the same Cupid's bow as the old woman who had the bronze token, but hers was pulled into a straight, spiteful line. "There's seven thousand left, at least. Be grateful I talked them out of the gold package!"

The man beside her huffed. "Moët and bloody Chandon though, I ask you!"

Kaitlyn felt her chest tighten. When they were far enough away not to notice, she turned around to see them going through the gates.

She stood still, shaking. Her mind ran through vivid, technicolour fantasies. She wanted to leap the gate, find the old couple, snatch the little paper cups full of pills from their hands, sending them scattering across the marble floors. They were cutting their love short, for those they cherished. But the ones they made their sacrifice for were mocking them, belittling them. Begrudging them even their one last indulgence.

They thought they were doing the right thing. Just like everyone else, they'd been bombarded with it, for years. The need to do one's duty. It was the responsibility of all patriotic citizens to think always of the future generations before themselves. It was good, and noble, to end one's life rather than take up more than your rightful share of the world's resources. To make sure you played your part in a fairer, more sustainable, future. That had been Stephen Jensen's innovation. His solution to the problems of old.

Stephen Jensen.

Her mind raced. What if Henry was right? What if they'd all been sold a lie? What if the Jensens were mocking the whole country, just as those awful people heading to the Moving On complex mocked their own parents? There was something so terrifying, yet so liberating, about the questions that assaulted her. Just like the half-forgotten lines of that old poem, they'd been waiting in the shadows. Waiting for her to find them. Waiting for her to give them permission to be asked.

She checked her watch. She still had thirty minutes before her shift began. Quickening her pace, she turned down an alleyway, heading for the library with a feeling of urgency. Now that curiosity had been awakened, it roared and thrashed within her, demanding to be fed.

She hurried through the swooping doors, shedding her coat as the warmth hit her. At the desk, the smartly dressed librarian looked up from behind thick spectacles, and tutted as she stormed past. Kaitlyn didn't care that she seemed hasty and uncouth. There was no time to feign leisurely browsing.

She ignored the shelves full of new fiction, all uniform in their brightly coloured covers and cheery, playful fonts. She wasn't here for escapism. The encyclopaedias were at the back, past the sections on better living and social responsibility.

It took both hands to wrench the latest edition of the *Encyclopaedia Britannica* from its shelf. She slammed it down on the nearby table, and opened it at about quarter of the way through.

Kayaks.

She flipped back through the pages. Juggling, Journeymen, Jihadists. Finally, she found it.

Jensen, Stephen

His picture was in the top right corner of the page. Handsome, suave, with a knowing smile. Next to it, in italics, his most famous quote:

Our lives are short, but our legacies long. Live responsibly, always with the future in mind.

That mantra had become the root of all social conscience. The perfect antidote to the previous generations and their hedonism. The pay-it-forward ethos that influenced every citizen's life choices; from using public transport, to farming sustainably, to dying before you used up more than your fair share.

But it was the small date printed beneath his picture that Kaitlyn was interested in. His date of birth was there, more than century ago. But no dash followed it. No expiration date. She clawed at the pages, opening them randomly, searching for names, any names. Each time she found a biography of a deceased person of influence, she checked the dates beneath the photos. And there they all were. Date of birth and date of death. There was only one logical reason why Stephen Jensen's wasn't the same.

"A hundred and two," she whispered, "a hundred and fucking two."

Henry was right. And the goosebumps made their second appearance of the hour. How could it be? How could a man preach sacrifice to others, but not follow his own commands? And if Henry was right about that, what else might he be right about? How many lies were out there, masquerading as truths?

The clock on the wall beeped the hour, snapping Kaitlyn out of her thoughts. Shit. She was late. She thrust the encyclopaedia back on the shelf haphazardly and rushed outside, pulling her coat back on as she walked. She was out of breath, wrestling with the contradictory sensations of freezing extremities and a sweating torso, when she burst through the door to Jared's.

"Jeez, Kaitlyn." Gina tugged at her apron strings, and picked up her bag from the counter. "I thought you weren't coming."

"Sorry," Kaitlyn huffed out in between gulping breaths. "Got caught up. I'll come in early tomorrow for you, I swear."

"Oh, doesn't matter," Gina replied. "It's dead time anyway, don't even know why we stay open late afternoon. He's basically paying us to twiddle our thumbs until the evening trains come in. Let's not point it out though." She winked.

Kaitlyn smiled, and took the apron Gina proffered. "Thanks, I appreciate you not getting mad at me."

"I am the very model of calm." Gina formed her thumbs and forefingers into 'O' shape, mimicking a meditating Buddha. "Got to be. Stress isn't good for the baby, you know."

Oh God, the bloody baby. Kaitlyn had a feeling she'd be sick and tired of hearing about it, and Gina's glittering future, long before its arrival.

"So they say," she replied politely, busying herself with wiping down the already-spotless tables.

Gina rushed off, in a flurry of exaggerated air kisses and overly-affectionate goodbyes. Kaitlyn watched her as she sauntered down the street. Soon she'd be waddling, not wiggling. Was it worth it, everything she'd be putting her body through? Just for what, a few extra points on her EP, and a shot at a cabin-house instead of a flat? She couldn't imagine enduring it all, physically and emotionally, for something as transient as money.

When Gina disappeared around the corner, Kaitlyn was alone in the café. The evening chef didn't start for a couple of hours. They only served cold food and coffee in between lunch and dinner, so there was no need for two staff during these quiet times. But she found herself wishing for an unexpected horde of hungry customers. Something to keep her busy. Something to distract her from the sickening unease that today's events caused. What she really wanted was to talk to Henry, to apologise. Maybe dig deeper into this... whatever this was. But she had no idea how to find him. And after she'd ditched him like she did, he'd likely never want to come find her.

She was grateful for the evening rush when it came. By the time they closed the doors at eleven, her aching feet and stiff spine occupied the forefront of her mind. The walk home was painful. Freezing rain had been falling for several hours, contributing to the rush of customers ducking into the café for a hot-drink-respite on their journey. Though it had ceased its downpour, it left puddles in its wake, the smaller of which began to form an icy skin.

By the time she reached the two-storey concrete block where she lived, her fingers had turned blue. She lifted her hands to her mouth, breathing warm air onto them to wake her joints up enough that they could work the key. Pushing open the heavily weighted outer door, she could hear the couple in the nearest flat arguing. She stepped over the array of free papers and unclaimed letters that flooded the hallway and headed for the dark stairwell.

Jack's apartment, where she had fled to after her break-up with Finn, was the last door on the right. Most of the other tenants would be sleeping soundly now; this was primarily a farmers' dwelling, a cut above the skyrises but not as prestigious as a cabin-house. Her neighbours had eye-wateringly early starts, for the most part. She'd had to get earplugs to prevent being woken by the mass exodus of the building at 3am each day. She took off her shoes, padding quietly along the cold corridor. There were more of them than there were of her, and she'd only got the lease because she'd taken it over temporarily from Jack. She was on their turf, not the other way around, so it wouldn't do to cause inconvenience.

Key in hand, she made her way toward home, longing for the warm embrace of bath and bedsheets. But when the yellow poster on the door came into view, she dropped the shoes she was holding and they clattered to the ground.

NOTICE OF EVICTION

Dear Occupant,
You are hereby given one week's notice to evacuate
these premises, due to non-payment of rent arrears.

11

"Why didn't you tell me, Dad?" David held up the box of Hepraxin accusingly.

"Just didn't want to worry you, son," Henry replied. There was no point in trying to downplay it, not now. "You've enough on your plate."

"Don't be stupid, Dad. Chloe's family, after all."

Funny, David had spent most of his youth saying the exact opposite. No matter how hard Chloe tried to be a kind and loving parent to him, he'd never shown her anything but contempt.

"You've got your own family to worry about. I'm on top of things, no need to fret."

David let out a noisy exhale, and smiled. "Oh good. Good. I was worried for a moment there. But, you know, you don't have to go it alone. It's quite an undertaking, so I'm told. You know Fi is great with events and things, she'd be more than happy to help. Her *hors d'oeuvres* are amazing too. You should definitely ask her to do the catering."

Catering? *Hors d'oeuvres*? David's smile suddenly made sense.

"No," Henry said firmly. "We don't need any catering, thank you."

"Oh, come on, Dad." David put an arm on his shoulder. "I know it's overwhelming, but we'd take care of it. It's only right, after all she's done for me. I never really had a chance to thank her, y'know. Let me do this for her, let me give her the party she deserves."

"There's not going to be a party, David. She's not going anywhere. She's staying right here, with me. Where she belongs."

"What? I thought you said you were on top of things? What the bloody hell are you thinking? Have you gone gaga too? You can't keep looking after *that*." He pointed upstairs. "Jesus Christ, Dad. I know you're a stubborn old goat, but I never took you for a fool before!"

"Now watch your mouth, boy" – Henry raised his voice – "you're in *my* house. She is my wife, and incidentally the first time you've ever shown a scrap of respect for her was just now... when you thought she was going to die! And look how fast that faded when you realised she wasn't. When you thought about your fucking inheritance."

David sighed, and ran his fingers through his hair. "Dad, it's not like tha—"

"Oh don't play the innocent with me! That's exactly what it's like. Are you worried you won't be able to buy gold-plated clarinets for your spoiled little brats?"

He'd gone too far. He knew it. He may as well have declared war. But the words had run away with him, propelled by anger with no thought of caution. Not until after they'd been spoken, and the fallout ignited.

"How dare you speak about my kids, your grandkids, like that." David was yelling now, his eyes narrowed. "You sad, selfish old bastard."

"Selfish? Selfish?" Henry had to place a hand on the sideboard, he felt dizzy with rage. "Oh you ungrateful, spiteful son of a bitch! You have no idea what I sacrificed for you, what Chloe sacrificed for you, for your education. For all the things you've got now. But still you want more."

David huffed out a sarcastic laugh. "Oh here we go," he said, nodding slowly. "Here it is. I wondered how long it would be before you went there."

"What do you mean?"

"Heidi," David replied; the sound of her name falling from his lips made Henry flinch. "Yes, I know what you're getting at. You're trying to pin that one on me. Fucking typical of you. Well you know what, Dad? Maybe it's time we took a good hard look at that elephant in the room. I was eleven fucking years old. Don't you dare, don't you even fucking dare, try to claim you did it for me. I was a kid, Chloe was unconscious. YOU made the decision. Just you. And you told yourself it was for me. That's how you live with it. That's how you look at yourself in the mirror. But it wasn't, Dad. It wasn't. It was for you. You were selfish then, and you're selfish now. You think you're doing this for Chloe? Is that what you actually believe? You think this is what she wants? You're not keeping her alive for her sake, you're doing it for yourself. Just like when you let her daughter, *my sister*, die. I actually feel sorry for Chloe. Not because of the dementia, but because she had to spend her life with you!"

Henry shook. The force of David's vitriol sending shockwaves through his body. His blood roared in his ears.

"Get out," he yelled. "Get out of my house, right now. And never, ever come back!"

"Truth hurts, doesn't it?" David said, picking up his jacket from the back of the sofa. "Mum was always right about you. She tried to warn Chloe, you didn't know that did you? She tried to tell her, but you'd already filled the poor woman's head with poison. You didn't deserve Mum, you didn't deserve Chloe, and you don't deserve any sympathy from me!"

"Leave, now. Or I'll call the police." Henry could hardly see. Everything looked blurry. He had to remind himself to breathe.

"Oh, I'm going," David replied, heading to the door, "don't worry about that. But this isn't the end of it, Dad. Someone has to speak up for Chloe, someone has to do the right thing."

When he stepped through the front door, Henry slammed it with all his might, almost losing his footing in the process.

The force made the doorbell chime, and the letterbox clatter. He limped to the lounge window, standing far enough back from the net curtains that his silhouette wouldn't be visible. David was in his car, both hands gripping the steering wheel tightly, though the engine wasn't on.

His son sat there, in his car, for several minutes. Probably calculating his next move, seeing his inheritance getting ever closer.

When he eventually drove away, Henry took a few deep breaths to steady his pulse, and tried to think rationally.

What was he going to do? The anger gave way to fear, and he couldn't control the trembling in his hands as he made his way to the kitchen for a swig of brandy. He'd gone and done it now. There was no way David would back down. Stubborn, self-obsessed bastard. He'd be straight down to the social workers. And Henry had just had a little taste of the reasoning he'd use.

He was a clever one, alright. Brains from that scheming mother of his. Henry had assumed he'd been looking for a way to declare him incapacitated, so he'd made damn sure not to show too much weakness, physical or mental, in front of him. But he was going to try a different tack, he was going to paint him as abusive. Claim he wasn't a fit advocate for Chloe's wishes. Surely that would be harder to prove?

But the burden of proof wouldn't be on David, Henry realised. That's not how it worked any more. It would be up to him to prove he was acting in Chloe's best interests. And seeing as he was swimming against the tide in his interpretation of what her best interests were, he was likely screwed.

He finished his brandy, just as the last light was fading outside. Supper time, but he couldn't face eating. Instead he made his way upstairs, changed into his pyjamas and slid into bed next to Chloe. She groaned when his weight made the mattress shift, but didn't wake. He lay beside her, listening to her rhythmic breathing, and stroked her hair gently. He loved her so much. So much. How could anyone think they could take her from him? How could anyone have that right?

He'd sell the house. They didn't need all this space. It would take months for any legal action to be carried out. He could use the profits to buy up as much Hepraxin as he could. He'd put it up for sale tomorrow, before David had the chance to file a claim against his capacity. All he needed was Chloe; a cabin-house would be more than adequate, if only she was with him.

He lay awake for several hours, watching the shadows on the walls grow indistinct and merge with the darkness. When the initial fury subsided, he was surprised to find his thoughts turn to Kaitlyn. When he realised he was comparing her to David, the sick knot in his stomach tightened.

He'd always attributed David's self-centred attitude, in part at least, to the wider, external influences of the world they lived in. He'd been solid in his comforting, self-righteous view that the younger generations were just out for what they could get. They'd taken the post-revolution ideals of equality, and spat on them. Picking and choosing their morals. Looking out for themselves, whilst claiming to be more socially responsible than those who came before. Buying the rhetoric of the New Church and its biggest supporter, the Moving On Corporation, without question, without analysis. But Kaitlyn didn't fit those stereotypes.

Sacrificing her own future, her own prospects, for her brother. That didn't fit in with the story he'd told himself. Causing a righteous scene, even though she regretted it; that didn't fit with his belief that they were docile, brainwashed sheep. She was younger than David, by at least ten years he guessed, yet there was a spark there that he hadn't expected. Some kind of fire, burning behind those deep green eyes that she couldn't hide.

By the time the clock struck 2 a.m., she was consuming his every thought. He resolved to go find her at the café the next day. The need to apologise for his behaviour was overwhelming, and unexpected. He'd never cared what any of the youngsters thought of him before. He'd take her some flowers. Did young women still like flowers? Or was the giving of them an affront to some new ecological rule? He wasn't sure. Things changed so quickly these days, what was expected courtesy one moment was an unforgivable insult the next.

It was a hard world to grow old in.

12

She knew she'd gone too far when the security guard came marching toward her. That heartless housing clerk must have pressed the button under her desk.

The tall, muscular man in the navy uniform grabbed her arm, and marched her out of the housing office, past the winding queue of desperate citizens patiently waiting their turn. When they reached the door, he let go of her with a shove, and she almost lost her footing on the icy pavement.

Her humiliating removal complete, the guard positioned himself in front of the entrance, arms crossed.

"It is my duty to inform you," he said, looking straight ahead, not at Kaitlyn, "that your verbal assault on a member of Council staff has resulted in an official mark against your social conduct. Should you receive any further marks in the future, your entitlement to housing allocation will be revoked."

Having reeled off his script, he looked down at her and raised a thick, bushy eyebrow. "Two strikes and you're out, get it?"

"You don't understand," she pleaded, "I did all the right things. I filled out their forms in triplicate. I applied for mitigating circumstances, six months ago!"

"I have no part in the decision-making process, miss."

"But they didn't even tell me." Kaitlyn couldn't keep the anger from her voice. "No letter, nothing. Just a bloody bright yellow eviction notice. I didn't even know they'd turned down my application. When I put the form in, the lady behind the desk said she was sure it would be approved."

"Well" – the security guard bent down a little to speak to her – "frankly, if your behaviour today is anything to go by, I expect she just wanted you gone."

That hit Kaitlyn like a punch to the stomach, mostly because she could see the truth in it. She had been just as desperate, just as angry, the day she'd first gone down to explain the situation. With Jack in a coma, his rent hadn't been paid for two months. Something that, in the chaos of his accident and her break-up with Finn, hadn't occurred to her. When she'd applied to take over the lease, to keep his flat for him, she realised that whilst she could just about afford the monthly payments, there was no way she could cover the accrued arrears as well. The lady behind the desk at the time had seemed sincere. But Kaitlyn had been ranting at her, pleading and crying. Maybe she had just wanted rid of the unstable woman sobbing all over her paperwork. So she had just said what Kaitlyn clearly wanted to hear, knowing it would likely be someone else's problem when reality came knocking.

She couldn't trust herself to say anything more to the security guard. She'd already lost Jack's flat; she didn't want to make things worse. So she just turned away clutching the application form the clerk had given her.

With unpaid arrears and now a mark against her conduct, a skyrise would be all she'd qualify for.

Back at the beginning. After Jack had worked so hard, given up so much, to get them out.

To top it all off, she'd spent the whole morning queueing and now she didn't have time to visit him before her shift. She made her way to work, arriving a little early to take advantage of any leftovers from lunch. Alfonz had three sausages and two rashers of bacon going spare, he and Gina having already eaten their fill. So she took up a table by the window while it was quiet and tucked into the cold, greasy meat.

When she had eaten, she took a long swig of the warm coffee Gina had poured for her and stared out of the window. There were no trains at this time of day. No shifts ending or beginning. During the lull, the street outside was occupied only by rats searching in vain through discarded bags of rubbish for food scraps. No one came down the dead-end road where Jared's sat unless they were heading for the station, or the lorry depot next to it.

Yet, as she watched the vermin scuttling and fighting, and the spilt rubbish tumbling in the wind, she noticed a slow, lumbering figure emerge from the alleyway opposite the café.

"No," she said, "it can't be. It can't be him."

But when the old man got nearer she realised it was. Henry, bedecked in the same brown duffel coat, shuffled toward Jared's clutching a bunch of pink and white flowers.

Kaitlyn stood up quickly and wiped the grease from her lips. With all the drama of her impending eviction, she'd forgotten how desperately she'd wanted to see him again after her trip to the library.

"Hey," she called out to the kitchen, "Gina, Alfonz. You guys get going, I can finish up the cleaning in the dead time."

"You sure?" Gina poked her head round the door, scouring pad in hand.

"Totally. Go put your feet up."

"Ah, you're a peach. Cheers, hon."

Gina wrenched off her apron and started getting her things together. Kaitlyn hastened her and Alfonz out of the back door. "So no one sees you leave early," she said. "Wouldn't want Jared docking your pay."

When they were gone, she rushed back to open the café door just as Henry reached it.

"Henry, I—"

"I know what you're going to say," he interrupted her "but I've only come to apologise. See?" He held up the flowers. "I come in peace. These are for you, I hope they don't break any new conservation rules I didn't know about."

Nobody had ever given Kaitlyn flowers before. She couldn't help the smile that bloomed across her face at such a sweet gesture. Especially after the hostility she'd endured at the housing office. She wanted to hug him. But settled for taking the flowers and trying not to cry.

"Oh no," he said, staring in alarm at the lone tear that escaped down her cheek, "I've upset you again."

"No, no," Kaitlyn said, pulling out a chair and gesturing for him to sit. "This is lovely. So lovely. I didn't think I'd ever see you again, after I was so rude. And I wanted to, I wanted to apologise. Something happened after I walked out on you."

"Oh?" Henry sat down, and pulled off his thick woollen gloves. "What was that?"

"I went to the library."

"Okay…" Henry said. "Sorry, I don't get the significance."

"I looked him up. Stephen Jensen. You were right, he's still alive."

"Well, of course," Henry said. "There'd have been a big announcement if he'd carked it. Probably a televised funeral even."

"Now that you say it, I can see how obvious it is," Kaitlyn said, feeling stupid. "I just never thought about it before. I just assumed."

"Lots of things are obvious, yet we don't see them unless they're pointed out," Henry said. "We all fall foul of that sometimes."

He was being so gracious, despite the fact she'd humiliated him by doing a runner. Even though she'd so clearly been embarrassed to be seen talking to him.

"I'm sorry," she said. "That's what I wanted to say. You were right, and I'm sorry. Sorry for running out, and sorry for everything I thought."

"And what did you think?" Henry asked, sitting back in his chair.

"Oh, you know, that you were a whacko. That your brain was turning to mush. That you're being a typical selfish snowflake, spending your grandchildren's inheritance on a lost cause."

Shit. She heard how her honesty sounded only after it had poured out. She clamped her hand to her mouth, but Henry just grinned.

"Well now," he said. "Don't hold back, eh? Say what you really feel."

"No!" she replied hastily. "No, what I'm saying is that's NOT what I think. Not any more. See, it wasn't just the library. I saw this old couple, going into the Moving On estate. Then I heard their children, at least I assume it was their children, gossiping about them. They didn't appreciate them at all. And I wanted to stop it, you know? I wanted them to stop, to not do what they were about to do. To keep loving each other, not throw it away for people who didn't give a shit about them. And then I realised, that's what you're doing. That's exactly what you're doing. And I'm doing it too. The whole world thinks we're mad."

"That they do," Henry agreed. "And maybe we are."

"But maybe we're not," Kaitlyn whispered.

13

He couldn't remember the last time he'd been so entranced watching someone talk. Kaitlyn spoke with such passion, her emphatic words accompanied by equally zealous hand gestures. Her emotions were right there, so close to the surface that they came spilling out. One moment she had fire dancing in her eyes as she recalled her experiences at the library, and the Moving On grounds, the next her face was ashen and her hands shaky as she told him of the eviction notice, and what it meant for her.

He wondered if he'd ever met anyone so unable to conceal themselves before. Certainly not Carolyn; poker face was her default. Not even Chloe. Though she was warm and open, his wife still kept some of her emotions locked away, though he hadn't realised it until recently.

It wasn't the done thing. To be so candid, so without veneer. But he liked it. He liked it very much.

"So, anyway. I'm unloading on you, I'm sorry," she said, as she came to the end of her tale. "You've got your own worries, I know. I'll think of something. Maybe I should just do a Gina!"

She snorted a laugh, but Henry didn't get the joke. Do a Gina? Was that some new phrase he'd not heard of?

"Do a Gina?" he asked. "Is that slang for something?"

"No, no." She grabbed the coffee pot from the counter and

poured them each a cup, "Just an inside joke. One of the other waitresses, she's having a baby to pay for college."

It took a moment for Henry to comprehend. What a strange, topsy-turvy world it was now. When he was young, pregnancy tended to get in the way of a woman's ambitions, not facilitate them. He shuddered a little when he realised just how out of touch he was.

It stood to reason, of course, that there would be a black market in babies. There's a black market for everything that can't be acquired legally. And he could remember the agony his aunt Sarah went through trying to conceive.

He hadn't understood it fully at the time of course. All those mornings she'd spent with his mother, drinking coffee and crying. But he'd been vaguely aware that she wanted a child, and couldn't seem to get one. He'd known nothing of the birds and the bees, or what cycles had to do with infants, but she was very upset.

Until one morning, when she'd arrived on their doorstep crying again. But this time she was also laughing. And jumping up and down, hugging his mother. He was eight years old when his cousin Lydia had been born. And he still hadn't really understood what the mewling little newborn had to do with test tubes, but he loved her anyway.

Just a few years later, when IVF was outlawed, her birth would have been impossible.

How strange to see the world turn, and have no one seem to care that all that was once one way is now another. The zealots back then would protest abortions, some would even condemn contraception. Not to mention euthanasia. But now, sterilisation and termination were considered responsible, and sacred. The converts to the ideology of the New Church upheld that overpopulation was a sin; causing the destruction of God's planet which his children were charged with keeping. IVF was the new enemy, the moral scourge. Now, creating life was considered 'playing God' in the way ending it used to be.

He only had to remember Aunt Sarah's despair, and

eventual joy, to know just how much people would be willing to go through for a child. How much they would pay, for their heart's desire. It was obvious, when you stopped to think about it. He just never had before.

"Wow," he said at last, when the notion had sunk in. "I hadn't ever thought. How common is it, this having babies for profit thing?"

"Not as common as you'd think, given the return."

"Which is?"

"Gina reckons a hundred thousand."

Henry whistled. "Christ. I had no idea."

"Yeah, but it's risky. Too risky, really."

"In what way?" Henry had a feeling she meant more than just the physical strain on a woman's body.

"Well, you can't get a buyer if there's any inherited defects," Kaitlyn explained. Henry shivered a little. Inherited defects. Like Heidi. "And it's not easy getting the... the sperm."

Henry was surprised. Of all the obstacles he could think of, that wasn't one that sprang to mind. "Really? I mean... well, I didn't think acquiring *that* would be a problem..." He couldn't look her in the eye.

Kaitlyn roared with laughter. "Oh, the hedonistic, irresponsible age is gone," she said. "You can't get a guy to do anything these days without using protection, you know? Most of the time they even insist on seeing your injection certificate. They don't want to get lumbered with half the pregnancy costs. And there's a fair few predatory girls around, looking to get some free sperm and offload half the birthing bill."

What an extraordinary world.

"Anyway," Kaitlyn continued, "even if you could get a guy drunk and stupid enough not to use protection, how would you know if there are any genetic problems? So, Gina went to one of those back alley sperm banks. They give you a certificate, guaranteeing the father's EP and health. She's silly enough to think a piece of paper from an illegal source is reliable. For her sake, I hope she's right. She says I ought to do it, to cover Jack's bills, but even if I wasn't dubious about the sperm, I could never afford it."

"How much does it cost?"

"Well, it's five thousand cash for the sperm, which of course I don't have. And then ten thousand for the pregnancy, which Gina's using her credit overdraft for. But I wouldn't have that option. I'm down to a few thou now."

God damn. She *was* using her own overdraft for her brother. Henry felt sick. And selfish, and naïve. How could he not have considered these things could happen to young people too? How had he been so consumed with the unfairness of his own situation that he couldn't see others had it worse?

He stood up. "Kaitlyn, what time do you finish tonight?"

"Eleven," she replied, looking puzzled.

"May I come and give you a lift home?" Henry asked. "I have to go run some errands now, but I have something I'd like to talk to you about later."

"Sure," she replied, "I guess I could put up with your gas-guzzler if it means I don't have to freeze my arse off walking home."

He guessed that was her way of saying 'yes, please' so he excused himself and hurried out of the door.

He'd been wavering over his decision to sell the house. The cold light of day makes you see the stark edges of things that seemed softer and more appealing in the half-light of your night-time musings. But Kaitlyn had unknowingly made up his mind. David didn't deserve to inherit it; it was a hard thing to admit about your only child, but it was true.

Perhaps he himself hadn't deserved it either. Most people of his generation had gone into allocated housing after the revolution, and remained there. Property ownership was uncommon these days. Considered unnecessary, given that the state would house you according to your contribution. But his mother had been one of the few who owned their house outright when the concept of mortgages was revoked.

They couldn't take away someone's rightful property, so it had remained in her possession and eventually passed down to him, just after his divorce with Carolyn, thank God. He had no doubt she'd have ended up with it otherwise, knowing how cunning she was.

His neighbour Kimmy had inherited hers too, there's no other way a factory worker could ever hope for more than a small apartment. Perhaps that was why she was always so chipper; she appreciated what she had in a way Henry never did.

Or never *had*, he thought as he reached the end of the alley and got into his car. Meeting Kaitlyn had opened his eyes. He really did have more than his fair share, compared to others. Chloe had always, always told him so. Why hadn't he listened? Why did it take a young stranger to show him the things his wife had long tried to make him see? Had he taken Chloe for granted? Not listened to her, not given her opinions the respect they deserved?

He slowed down as his vision blurred, water filling his eyes. Yes, that's exactly what he'd done. He'd ignored so much. His life would be nothing without Chloe, he knew that. Well, he'd damn well get her back to her old self, and this time he'd be a better man. He'd be the man she deserved.

And he'd help Kaitlyn too.

Determined, he sped across town to the only remaining estate agent in the area. There wasn't much call for buying and selling houses any more. Only those who had inherited were on the ladder, and that wasn't enough to keep the dozens of agencies in business. Soon enough, the descendants of property owners would finally sell up, once and for all, then such businesses would be a relic of forgotten days.

Hancock's was a run-down office staffed by only one man. Hancock himself. The doorframe was rotting, and Henry struggled to push it open. When he did, the small brass bell above it rang, and a middle-aged man with greying eyebrows hurried in from the back room.

"Good afternoon!" Mr Hancock's suit had seen better days; Henry noted the worn elbows and yellowing collar. But his smile was warm. Probably the first customer in days, weeks even. His eyes lit up in the way people's do when they see money strolling in through their door.

"What a pleasure, sir," he continued. "It's lucky you caught me, actually. I was just about to close up for the day."

"I want to sell my house," Henry said, getting straight to the point.

"Wonderful!" Hancock shook his hand vigorously. "Well, that shouldn't take long. Do you want me to take care of allocation at the same time? I'm authorised to do that, you know. We can bypass the Council office, get it all done in-house, as it were."

There was only one buyer; the state. So deals were done quickly. By the end of the week he would have money in his hand, and a cabin-house to live in.

"Well yes," Henry said, "I'd like to get it all done swiftly. I've plans for the money, you see."

"Of course, of course." Hancock's grin threatened to split his face. "A cruise is it? Or perhaps a retirement party?"

"No," Henry replied, "nothing like that."

Hancock nodded, and the smile faded. Henry's desperation must have been written all over his face. He sat behind the wooden desk, and gestured to Henry to take the seat opposite.

"Okay," the estate agent said, putting on his glasses, "I'll just fire up the old digital demon."

He pressed a button and the ancient PC in front of him whirred into life. Electricity was expensive, so it stood to reason he only switched it on when needed. Henry wondered how many days it had sat dormant for. Computers were still used in business, but only when they did not replace a human worker. That was the Roll-Back rule. And, combined with the Moving On Corporation's drive to reduce the population via dubious means, it had led to full employment. The Internet was still accessible, after a fashion. Registered businesses were given user codes that allowed them to access the records needed to do their job, but no more. Hancock would be able to look up Henry's address, and check he was the rightful owner.

"Right, bear with me a moment. Just do the necessary formalities and then we can organise the sale. Name and address?"

Henry gave him the details, and watched as he tapped away at the dusty keyboard. The poster in the window advertised *Five Per Cent Instant Cash Advance! For all state approved house sales*. He should be able to walk out of here with more than enough to give to Kaitlyn to allow her to pay the arrears, and keep her brother's flat. He smiled to himself, picturing her face. She'd rant a little, no doubt. She'd try to talk him out of it, but he'd insist. Then those deep green eyes would fill with tears. And for once they'd be tears of relief, not despair. Chloe would want this. She'd be right there next to him if she could understand. It felt right.

He knew he'd never talk Kaitlyn out of her hope; any more than she could talk him out of his. Perhaps they were both fools, but at least he could do something to ease her pain. A gift, from one fool to another.

"I'm terribly sorry, Mr Morris." Hancock's sudden sombre tone caused Henry's daydream of Kaitlyn's grateful face to dissolve. "I'm afraid I can't authorise a sale for you."

"Why not?" he asked, but he already knew.

"There's a..." Hancock couldn't look him in the eye, "capacity claim against you. I really am most sorry."

"Bastard!" Henry clenched his fists in his lap. "Not you," he added quickly when Hancock's expression turned to shock.

So David hadn't wasted any time at all. All that nonsense about how he rarely visited because he was busy. 'Working late most nights these days, Dad. Gotta keep my nose to the grindstone, just like you taught me,' he'd said. Funny, he'd found time in his crippling schedule to get onto this straight away. Henry thought he'd get in first, pull the rug out from under his selfish son. Perhaps he would have, if only he hadn't doubted himself this morning.

"Sorry," Henry said, "I didn't mean to swear at you. But, Jesus Christ! The ungratefulness, you know?"

Hancock wasn't his junior by very many years, Henry guessed. He nodded, with a half-smile on his lips.

"Don't feel embarrassed, Mr Morris," he said. "I'd say at least a third of my potential clients are scuppered in the same way. It's become something of a trend, I gather."

"What do you mean?"

"You know how it is, with the young. They talk. And with times getting tougher… well. One young chap finds a way to stop what he considers his birthright being taken from him, he tells his friends about it. Maybe his claim was genuine, who am I to say? But before you know it they're all at it. Sharing tips, discussing the best way to phrase things on the forms… recommending lawyers, even. My daughter tells me it's a hot topic of conversation. Of course, she's only telling me because it directly affects my livelihood, which in turn affects the credit I'll leave behind. I'm not blind. She's no more selfless than any of them. They'd all sell their loved ones down the creek given half a chance."

"No," Henry replied, thinking of Kaitlyn, "not all of them. Maybe our brats, but not all of them. There is some good out there, I know it."

"I hope you're right" – Hancock smiled – "but the closer I get to the scrapheap the more cynical I become, I'm afraid. Fortunately, cynicism and curiosity go hand in hand. I can't sell your house, Mr Morris. But there is a little loophole we could explore."

14

The pavement outside had already taken on a silvery sheen when she turned the sign on the door to Closed. She pressed her face up to the glass, her breath creating a fog she had to wipe away. He wasn't there.

She hadn't realised how much she was looking forward to a warm ride home until the absence of his beat-up old car made the street seem even colder, and emptier, than usual. She waited a few moments, her coat pulled tight around her. The scuttle of rats in the alleyway opposite unsettled her. This wasn't the time of day to hang around.

She started for home, annoyed with herself for being disappointed. You should never let yourself rely on anyone. Jack had always told her that. Of course, she *had* relied on him. But there was an unspoken understanding between them that they were excluded from such generalisations. When Jack talked of the world, he did so as though they themselves were not part of it. As though they were travellers, just passing through a foreign land full of strange customs and unfamiliar dangers.

Now she journeyed alone.

'Don't ever get yourself into a situation that you need someone else's help to get out of, Kat.' She remembered Jack's words as she scanned the dark corners and recesses of the streets. 'Don't ever give anyone leverage. Because one day they'll want a favour in return, and you can bet it will be a favour you won't want to give.'

He'd always been dead serious on the issue. He didn't want her indebted to anyone. Not even their mother. No, *especially* not their mother. But for all the sacrifices he'd made for her, to ensure that nobody in this world could ever demand from her any type of return on their kindness, he'd forgotten what that meant. It meant that without him, she was alone.

She turned the corner into the main shopping lane, where all the stores lay shrouded in darkness, their drawn metal shutters a reminder of the dangers that come at night time. The street lights overhead blinked three times. A warning that they would soon be going off. All law-abiding folk ought now be off the streets, or at least be quickening their journey, before the plunge into darkness. She wouldn't make it all the way home before the 11:30 blackout. She never did. But she would at least be away from the town centre, which was where any trouble was likely to happen.

The roar of an engine was swiftly followed by the violent glare of oncoming headlights. Kaitlyn turned her gaze to the pavement, partly to avoid being dazzled by the sudden light, and partly in a futile attempt to remain unseen. Nothing was hidden from the garish beams; the ground that had been concealed by darkness gave up its secrets when the light fell upon it. A river of dog's pee trickling from a telegraph pole, discarded gum, small tufts of moss defying man's best efforts to concrete over the world.

The car slowed, and she looked up, mentally preparing to run if needed. But she recognised the scratched paintwork, and the grey driver, straight away. He'd come after all.

Her heartbeat slowed to a dull thump, and she didn't know whether she ought to be grateful for him coming or angry that he was late. Opening the passenger door, she decided to go for snarky.

"Hard to tell time at your age, is it?" she said, expecting

him to laugh. He'd seemed to like her humour, even her teasing, earlier. But, his expression didn't change.

"I'm sorry," he said, "I'm so sorry. Chloe wouldn't settle. And honestly, I didn't know whether I should come at all; things didn't go as planned. But then I thought of you, thought maybe you were waiting, and I didn't want to let you down."

"Hey," Kaitlyn said, clipping in her seatbelt, "I'm only messing. You don't owe me anything. I can take care of myself. I never expect people to keep their promises anyway."

Henry turned to face her. "That's a very sad attitude."

"It's a very sad world," she said, shocked at how true she felt it was.

"You must be exhausted," Henry said. "Where do you live?"

Kaitlyn duly gave directions. Right at the end, straight on past the fountain, left by the crematorium, until they finally pulled up outside her, *Jack's*, apartment block.

"Thank you," she said. "You really didn't need to come out just to give me a ride. I wouldn't have held it against you. You must need your rest."

"What with my quite staggering age, you mean?" Henry said, and smiled slightly for the first time that evening. "No. I said I'd take you home tonight, and I try to always keep my word. Besides, when you're my age you realise your days are numbered, and you don't want to waste them asleep."

She didn't really know how to answer that. "Do you want to come in for a coffee?" her mouth stepped in to fill the silence before her brain could stop it. Images of dirty underwear hastily thrown on the floor, and last night's dinner turning rancid on the kitchenette worktop, flashed through her mind, and she instantly regretted the offer.

"Oh." Henry looked as uncomfortable with the idea as she was. "Well yes, that would be lovely."

"Great." She tried to calculate how much of her slobbish detritus she could cover up in the few seconds between her opening the door and him stepping inside. What was it about politeness that made one person offer something they didn't want to, and the other accept equally as unwillingly? But, he had said earlier that he wanted to talk to her about something, and curiosity made her wonder what that could possibly be. His eyes were probably too bad to see all the dust, and the mould round the windows, anyway.

He struggled on the stairs, she noted. But she didn't comment, or offer help. She didn't want to offend him. But she turned and raised a finger to her lips when they reached the corridor that led to Jack's apartment; his generation were known for having little regard for the needs of others. 'Self-absorbed,' Sister Rochelle had told her. 'It's not that they deliberately wish to inconvenience others, but rather that they simply do not consider anything outside their own needs and desires. They are a product of their upbringing, they were taught to value self above all else. To think always of the effect of any action, or any new philosophy, upon their own fleeting existence. We cannot hope to change them. But as they die out, so will their ignorance and greed.'

She'd never questioned the teachings as a child. But Henry's look of bewilderment at being shhed like a toddler made her flinch. Rochelle had been wrong, about lots of things. Maybe she was wrong about the older generation too. Maybe all the stories about their obsession with technology, to the point where they barely spoke to their fellow man, let alone had any consideration for them, had been exaggerated. In every picture book she'd read at church, the people from the old times always held small screens in front of their faces, staring at them and ignoring the world around them. Kaitlyn had always just accepted that snowflakes had no idea *how* to be considerate members of society.

She hurried inside, and kicked some old clothes under the sofa before Henry could follow. He paused, reading the eviction notice still taped to the open front door, so she rushed into the bathroom and hid her knickers.

"I'm sorry about the mess," she said, dashing into the kitchenette and quickly pushing the dirty dishes into the sink to be concealed by the murky water still in the bowl. "Moving, y'know?"

Henry looked horrified at the state of the apartment. For a moment she felt embarrassed, but she soon realised it wasn't the mess he was worried about.

"You sleep on the sofa?" he asked, pointing at the duvet and pillow piled up on the fraying settee. "Isn't there even a bedroom?"

It was the size that was bothering him. She wondered what type of accommodation he had; what job he used to do that meant a perfectly average-sized dwelling seemed so objectionable.

"Yes," she replied, "there is. But it's Jack's." She couldn't bring herself to sleep in his bed. Or even change the sheets. To disturb any of his things would be to acknowledge that he wasn't here. That he might never be here again. A prickle ran down her spine. She'd have to now. She'd have to pack up all his things, move them to a smaller home. Because she'd failed him. She tried to blink away the tears, but it didn't work.

"Oh Christ," Henry said, stepping forward and putting an arm on her shoulder. "I'm such an idiot. I'm sorry, I didn't mean to remind you."

"It's not the bed," Kaitlyn said, liking the warmth of a sympathetic hand but stepping back from it anyway. "I've let him down. I wanted to keep everything just as it was for him. So that he could come home and just get on with his life. But I've lost it. I've lost everything he worked for. Now if he wakes up, he'll be back where he started. In a skyrise."

15

The weight of Kaitlyn's situation hit Henry like a ten tonne truck, and he felt his limbs go numb from the shock. He'd spotted rats in the entrance hall, and cockroaches on the stairs. The apartment comprised of a tiny lounge, no bigger than the box room of his own house, with a kitchenette smaller than the larder where Chloe kept her preserves and pickles. He hadn't seen the bathroom, or the bedroom Kaitlyn was obviously keeping as a shrine to her unconscious brother, but he had a strong suspicion they weren't exactly luxurious.

How bad were the skyrises, that she mourned the loss of her brother's achievement in getting this place? How unbearable was life for this new generation?

"Oh God, Kaitlyn. I'm so sorry." He couldn't stand any longer, his good leg couldn't take the strain. So even though she hadn't offered him a seat, he moved the duvet aside and perched himself on the edge of the sofa. "I wanted to help. But that bastard, he got there first."

Kaitlyn leaned against the windowsill. "What do you mean?"

"I tried to sell my house," he said, staring at the stained carpet. "We don't need all that room. I thought I'd get a cabin-house, and a few years' worth of meds for Chloe. We'd hole up, just live out our lives together. And I was going to give you however much you needed to pay your debt, so you could keep this place. But my son, that selfish, ignorant arse, he's filed a capacity claim against me. So I can't even sell it, at least not until it's resolved. And you know how things are, how people feel about my generation, d'you reckon that's going to go my way?"

"What? Would your son really do that?" Kaitlyn looked confused.

"We had an argument, David and I," he explained. "Chloe isn't his mother, you see. He found out she was on Hepraxin, and he marched straight down to the Council offices. Trying to make out I'm not in my right mind, or not caring for her properly. So when I went to the estate agent, they couldn't sell the house for me, not with an open claim. He's just worried about his fucking inheritance, of course. He doesn't actually care about Chloe. But that's my plan scuppered. The only thing the guy could do, and I swear he only even told me about it because he's not too far behind me on the old biological clock, was an equity release."

Hancock had got up and locked the door, and then dropped his voice to whisper. Needlessly, Henry had thought, there was no one around. But perhaps he had become paranoid. The attitudes of those around you tended to have that affect as you got older. It was an 'emergency measure', in recognition that some claims made were done so purely out of spite, and greed. Henry could borrow, instantly, ten per cent of the value of his property, to be repaid upon his death, or the sale of the house should he win the claim.

For a few almost joyful seconds, Henry had thought that someone in power actually did care about him and his peers. That there were some safeguards in place. Perhaps, even, that they cared about the rights and well-being of his generation after all.

But then he pictured himself walking into the bar, lifting a pint to his lips and telling Old Al he shouldn't be so cynical after all. Al's mocking, rasping laughter soured his fantasy.

Even in his daydream, the old crackpot deconstructed his

optimism in seconds. Who did it really benefit, this equity scheme? Everyone knew the state was after full control of all housing, hence the constant pressure to sell. Now the debt would have to be repaid. David would have no choice but to sell the house, at whatever price he was offered, as soon as he inherited it. Served him bloody right, of course. But the state was the ultimate beneficiary of this little deal. They always were.

He couldn't read Kaitlyn's expression. At best guess, she seemed to be wrestling with several emotions all at once. Probably a mix of pity for his situation, anger at his son, and gratitude that he'd been trying to help her. She was practically a stranger. He'd given her a lot to process. But then of course, he'd disappointed her, too. He regretted having told her about his plan to help.

But... maybe he still could? He'd thought to use all the ten per cent on Hepraxin, but seeing this place made him feel even worse for her. How much could a couple of months' rent arrears on this dump be, really? Maybe it would mean a few weeks less for him and Chloe. But he knew what his wife would want him to do, given the choice.

"I can still help, is what I'm saying," he said, hoping she didn't realise that hadn't been what he was saying at all. He'd been explaining why he couldn't. "How much do you need to cover your debt?" He started pulling a few notes out of his pocket... fifty, a hundred, two hundred... but she just stared at them, her mouth slightly open now. It couldn't be much more than three hundred, could it? "Just say when," he said, wondering if perhaps she hadn't realised that was what he was waiting for.

"You're unbelievable," she whispered. "You are un-fucking-believable! How dare you?" She stepped forward, and knocked his hands causing the bank notes to fall to the floor.

"I... what?" Of all the reactions he'd envisioned, rage wasn't one of them. Now he knew why he couldn't decide which of the mixed emotions he'd thought she must have was reflected in her strange expression. She wasn't any of them. She was apoplectic.

"You think I want your charity? You think I want hand-outs? Have you listened to a word I've actually said? Jack did this. By himself. Nobody gave him anything. You have no idea what we went through, how hard he worked to get me out of it. To make sure we never had to answer to anyone, ever again. How do you think he'd feel if I threw all that away by making us indebted to someone else?"

"You misunderstand, Kaitlyn, it's not a loan. There's no debt. It's a gift."

"It's always a debt," she whispered.

"No." He tried to look her in the eyes, but she turned her head and stared out of the window. "Kaitlyn, I promise, I don't want anything from you. I'm in a position to help you, that's all."

"That's exactly the problem with you lot, isn't it?" she muttered. "You think money is the answer."

"Isn't it?" Henry stood up, with a fair bit of effort, and took a tentative step toward her now that the fire seemed to have died down a little. "I agree it shouldn't be, but it seems to me like it is. Perhaps not to everything, but certainly to both our situations."

She wiped her eyes with the sleeve of her jumper and stared straight at him.

"We must accept our lives as they are, not as we would wish them to be," she said. "That's what the New Church taught me. But Jack disagreed." A faint smile formed on her lips. "He was a bit of a rebel."

"I think I'd like him," Henry said, returning the smile.

"I can't take your money," Kaitlyn said. "But I do see your point. It's not money itself that's the answer, it's what it can do. So I'm pleased you've got enough to keep your wife with you, and let's just leave it at that."

"It's a temporary solution, at best," Henry said. "If I could have sold the house things would be brighter."

"How long?" Kaitlyn asked. "How long will it buy you?"

"In terms of Hepraxin? Maybe a year, if the current dose is enough."

"A lot can happen in a year," she said. "At least that's what I'm hoping. The rate I'm dipping into my credit, if he doesn't wake up by then… well, I'm just going to have to find a way to make some more money."

"Sounds like we both need a miracle, or an investment."

"I haven't got anything to invest," Kaityln said, "financially anyway. I suppose there's always my feminine wiles," she laughed, "like mother, like daughter maybe."

So that was what her brother rescued her from? Their mother was a hooker? She must have seen the shock on his face, because she added quickly, "I'm only kidding. Jack would rather I switched that machine off now than go down that road. I know that much. Christ, I'd do a Gina way before I'd end up like my mother."

Do a Gina. The other waitress who was a having a baby for money. Hadn't Kaitlyn said she couldn't afford the outlay?

"Would you, if you could? Do a Gina, I mean?"

"I've never really thought about it that hard. I mean, it's not an option. I don't have the credit."

"What if you did?"

"Morally, you mean?"

"Yes. Would you create a life to save another?" Or perhaps two others…

"I guess, when you look at it, it doesn't harm anyone. It's not like the baby suffers, they probably have great lives in fact. The mother gets the money they need, the adoptive parents get their hearts' desire, and the kid gets a great upbringing. The whole overpopulation thing makes it a bit dubious I suppose, but otherwise it's win-win all round."

"If you had the means, would you do it to keep Jack alive?"

"I'd do anything to keep Jack alive."

"What if I invested?"

"What the hell are you saying?"

"Okay, so you don't want to take my money. I get that. But what if I invested my money in you. Covered the costs for the sperm and pregnancy, then we split the profit. We could buy more time for both of them. For Jack and Chloe."

Kaitlyn shook her head. "I already said before, I wouldn't touch that back-street sperm. Don't trust it. I could end up with a kid I can't sell, and can't afford to raise."

"Is there someone else? A male friend perhaps? Someone who would... you know. We could cut him in on the deal."

"I don't know anyone that well. I mean, like, on a genetic level. Plus, the type of people I meet round here don't exactly have high EPs."

"I do," Henry confessed. "I mean, I was too old to have to take the test when it was rolled out, I was already employed. But, I took one anyway, even though it's not an official score, just out of curiosity. And David does, too."

"Oh Christ!" Kaitlyn screwed up her face. "Are you suggesting we... Is that what this was all about? You're a dirty old perv?"

"Oh no! No! I wasn't suggesting we do it *naturally*... Just a, erm... deposit? Like what you'd get from the bank, but a guaranteed source."

"Can you, even...? I mean... even—"

"Yes!" he snapped. "I'm fully functional, thank you!" At least he was last time he checked, which admittedly had been a while.

"Okay, sorry. I didn't mean to offend. Sorry."

"Look," he said. "It's just an idea. It only just came to me. But, on the surface at least, it could solve both our problems."

"I'll have to think about it. I mean, I only met you a few days ago. You're a crazy old man, with a beat-up gas guzzler and a sick wife, no offence. You're very confusing. You tipped me when I was rude, came looking for me after I walked out on you, rocked up in the dead of night to take me home.

And now you've come in here, turned your nose up at Jack's apartment, tried to give me money and then offered to get me pregnant. It's all a bit of a head-fuck quite honestly."

Henry didn't take offence. He allowed himself to visualise their encounters from her perspective, and it made him chuckle. A lumbering old man, with a lumbering old car and some wacky ideas, who kept bursting into her life and upsetting the equilibrium. Yes, he quite liked that image. He'd never been a catalyst for anything before, but perhaps he could be for Kaitlyn. She didn't know it, of course, but her entry into his life had turned his world upside down too.

16

"Look." Jack pushed two chairs close to each other, and spread his frayed bedsheet over the top. "It's a fort, Kat. Come in the fort with me."

"Can Emmy come too?" she asked, squeezing her rag doll extra tight.

"Sure."

"Emmy's hungry though," she said, although it was her own belly that was twisting and lolloping.

"Okay." Jack pulled back the sheet. "Well, you and Emmy get in the fort. Women and children first. I'll go get her some biscuits."

She crawled into Jack's fort, cuddling Emmy close when the noises started coming from behind their mother's door.

"Here we are, ladies," Jack's smile stilled her jitters. If Jack was smiling, everything was okay. He was twelve, practically an adult. He knew what was good and what was not. If Jack was grinning and eating biscuits then it must be a smiley kind of day. He slipped his arm around her.

"So this here is a siege," he said. "And these" – he tapped the sheets – "are our castle walls. Ain't nobody getting in here. So we just sit tight, eat our biscuits and relax. Okay, Kat?"

"Okay," she said, resting her head on his shoulder, liking the feel of his breath on her hair. The noises were just the army outside. The grunts and groans just them trying, and *failing, to get over the drawbridge. The knocks and bangs just the battering ram that would never, ever break the door because it was made of enchanted fairy wood. And everyone knows that there's nothing on Earth that can splinter that. Jack told her so.*

But then there was a scream.

Not a low, grunting cry. Not one of the faceless army falling into the river. No, this was a shrill, urgent scream. A lady in trouble, perhaps the queen? Then there were words, deep and shouty. Bad words. Words that hurt God.

"God damn it." Jack squeezed her shoulder, but then withdrew his arm. "Just stay here, Kat. Okay? Stay in the fort."

Then he was gone. And the fort wasn't a fort any more, it was just grubby sheets and old chairs.

She peeked through the crack, and Jack was opening Mum's door. They must NEVER open her door. Then Jack was shouting bad words too, but the man with no trousers on shouted them louder. Mum was shrieking. A loud thump, and Jack was on the floor, clutching his face.

"Keep your fucking kid under control, you stupid bitch!"

The man pulled on his trousers and stormed through the door. Toward the fort, toward her. She shrank back, trying to be still. Hoping he'd go straight past. But the snot was gathering in her nose, bubbly and urgent. She tried to ignore it, but it trickled down her throat. She had to sniff it up, just a tiny sniff.

It wasn't tiny enough.

The sheet was flung back, and a big, hairy face intruded into her fort. Like a fat, ugly ogre.

"Well," the monster said, with a smile that Kaitlyn didn't like. She didn't know what it meant, but it wasn't a friendly nice-to-meet-you type of smile. There was something in the curl of his lips and the raise of his eyebrow that made a panic bloom inside her. An alarm she didn't know she had, and didn't know what type of danger it warned against. "You're a pretty little thing, aren't you?"

He reached an arm through the sheets. A big, hairy arm, with yellowed fingers and a strange metallic smell. "Come here sweetie," he said. "Let me get a proper look at you."

But suddenly he was cursing and thrashing. Jack had leapt onto his back and pulled at his face.

"Get away from her!" Jack yelled, and the big bad man swore and flung him off before marching out of the front door and slamming it behind him.

Jack was a hero, Kaitlyn knew it in that moment. And she's known it ever since. But her mother didn't see it that way. She staggered from the bedroom, her white nightie torn and blood running from her nose, and whacked Jack round the head. There'd be no dinner, she said. Because of Jack. No dinner for any of them, nor any breakfast. And Kaitlyn could thank her stupid brother for the pain in her stomach.

But she didn't think he was stupid. That night he let her sleep in his bed, and she cuddled him tight and thought that she would never let him go.

It had taken a long time for her to realise exactly what Jack had shielded her from. Or at least, what he was worried she might have to deal with if she stayed with their mother. He'd gotten her out of there as soon as he could. At the expense of his own education. Once again, he'd thrown himself between her and danger.

He'd never said it, but she knew it now. He was worried Mum would use her, put her to work, when she was old enough. She wished she could say that was ridiculous. No mother would do that to her own daughter. But Mum had a habit, and she loved it more than her children. She hadn't always been that way; Jack could remember a time when their father was around and she was, if not a doting mother, at least a functional one. Kaitlyn guessed desperation to feed her children drove her to prostitution, and the drink and powder became the tools to help her do that job. Trouble was, somewhere along the way, the priorities shifted.

Or maybe even that was giving her too much credit. Maybe she'd always been a waste of space. She certainly couldn't remember a time she wasn't. Maybe Jack made it up, to soften things for her. Maybe he didn't remember their father being around, maybe they didn't even have the same one.

She stared at his features. Same nose, same mouth, though his lips were a little fleshier than hers. Still, she didn't know. And it didn't matter. He was the little boy who threw himself at the monster to protect her. He was the young man who gave her a safe place to live. He was the person who mattered more to her than anyone, or anything, in this whole fucked up world.

And, in the end, she knew there was nothing he wouldn't do for her, if the roles were reversed.

"I'll do you a deal," she said to him, taking his hand from where the nurses had placed it on his chest. "If you *don't* want me to do this, you gotta wake up before I get up the spout, okay?"

Beep. Beep. Hiss.

"It might not be wrong, you know. Just because the New Church says it is. I know you don't think much of them now anyway. I know why you took me there, and why you told me to stop going. None of it was ever about God, was it? I wish you could chat with Henry, actually. I think you'd like him. He doesn't take things at face value, just like you. At first I thought he was crazy, like one of those old people they show you in those videos at school. I used to think I knew what was right, but now I don't any more. There's things we haven't been told, you know? Things that make you wonder. Things that make me angry. Like, Stephen Jensen. Did you know? Stephen Jensen is a hundred and fucking two!"

Beep. Beep. Hiss.

17

Chloe wasn't beside him when he woke up.

Jesus. Where was she? He cursed himself when his hand reached across to where her warm, sleeping body should have been and found only a cold, desolate sheet. Why didn't he hear her get up? It was his own damn fault for going out late to see Kaitlyn, getting himself too tired.

"Chloe," he yelled. "Chloe, where are you?"

Sitting up was always a mission. You don't realise how much you rely on the weight of your legs to steady your bottom half until one of them is gone. Of course, it used to be a lot easier, when his stomach muscles were stronger. Now he had to have one of those grab handles tucked under the mattress to help him wrench himself up.

He heaved himself into a sitting position on the edge of the bed and gravity conspired to make the pressure on his bladder almost unbearable. He used to wonder why older people got up so early, why they didn't have the lie-ins younger people would kill for. Now he knew. Who needs an alarm clock when your waterworks will conspire to get you out of bed? He pulled the thick, cotton sock over his stump and grabbed his prosthetic. His fingers weren't as nimble as they used to be, and the Velcro fastenings were starting to get fuzzy. But he yanked it on, giving it a good bash on the floor to make sure it was secure.

The first few steps were always a bit wobbly. As if his body had forgotten this is how it moves now. There wasn't time to take it steady, so he grabbed the walking stick he kept by the bed for such moments and tried not to look at himself in the long mirror on the wardrobe door. Hunched over, grey and hobbling. He didn't need to see it to know it.

"Chloe!"

He could hear the TV blaring; it hadn't been on in weeks. And it was light downstairs. Much lighter than usual. It took a few moments to realise why. The curtains had already been opened. He'd been the one to do it for so long, he'd become accustomed to the house being shrouded in shadows when he awoke. The kettle was whistling, and a faint smell of magnolia hung in the air. Chloe's perfume.

As he shuffled through the lounge, past the goggle box on which the morning newsreaders were proclaiming 'record employment and satisfaction levels', Chloe appeared in the kitchen doorway, fully dressed with a tea towel in her hand.

"Morning, sleepy head," she said, smiling wide. The sapphires shining, the hair brushed and secured at the side with her favourite butterfly clip. She was vivid, technicolour. Breathtaking in her shine. As though she'd been a 'before' picture last time he'd seen her, and now here she was, all made over and presented in glorious HD. She walked toward him, and planted a soft kiss on his cheek. "Toast? And I've just made a pot of tea."

"Chloe, I—" What could he say? What do you say when someone's been with you, but not with you? You missed them? Even though they were physically there. Was she back? He wanted to know, but was scared to find out all at the same time.

"It's good to see you," he said at last.

She laughed. A sweet, refreshing aria that seemed to sweep the cobwebs in his mind away. "Silly boy, come, have some breakfast with me."

He took the seat opposite her at the newly laid table, staring at her as though she were a rare and beautiful butterfly that the wrong move could scare off.

"What are you gawping at?" she asked, raising her buttered toast to her mouth. "Have I got jam on my nose or something?"

"No. No, you look… perfect."

"Well, you're very sweet," Chloe said, "and not just for the compliment. I had one of my funny turns again, didn't I?"

He didn't know how to answer. Chloe knew, well, she *had* known, about the diagnosis. But she'd never said it out loud. In truth, he wasn't sure if she really comprehended her situation. She always referred to her erratic behaviour as 'a funny turn' or 'one of my moments'. But then, she had a habit of sugar-coating things, putting a digestible sheen on the unpleasant. He just nodded.

"Well, thank you for taking care of me, love. You always look after me so well."

That wasn't true. But how like Chloe to proclaim it. How typical of his gentle, wonderful wife to see the best in everyone. Even in him. He hadn't always looked after her well, far from it. But it wasn't too late. He'd make up for it, for all of it, with whatever time they had left. He'd be the husband she deserved, the carer she needed. He'd do whatever it took to see those sapphires sparkle, to hear that laughter ring out. She was back with him, and he'd never take that for granted ever again.

"Just so long as you're feeling better, love," he said, "that's all that matters."

"Oh yes. Right as rain now. In fact, I thought I might pop to the butcher's, get some sausages."

"Oh yes? What are you planning?"

She laughed again. "And I thought I was the one with the bad memory!"

"What do you mean?"

"It's Friday, love. Sausage and mash, David's favourite. You know how he hungry he is after school!"

Henry's stomach flipped over, and he tried in vain to stop a solitary tear from rolling down his cheek.

18

"This is so exciting!" Gina clapped her hands together, bouncing in the hard plastic chair. Several of the patrons looked up from their plates of over-cooked bacon and eggs.

"Shhh," Kaitlyn cautioned, "I don't want the whole world knowing."

"We're gonna be like twinsies!" Gina continued, ignoring Kaitlyn's plea for discretion. "Oh, we can go to birthing classes together and everything."

"Hardly," Kaitlyn replied, "I'm not even pregnant yet. I don't even know if I *can* get pregnant."

"Course you can, it's not difficult. Legs in the air, quick squidge of the syringe thingy, and you're off! When do you ovulate?"

Syringe thingy? Ovulating? Crap. Kaitlyn didn't know much about any of it. Perhaps it was just as well she'd confided in Gina after all, even if her over-enthusiasm was painfully embarrassing.

"I… I don't know."

"Didn't you get the kit from the trader? Who did you go to? You've got be careful, there's some right crooks out there. I can hook you up with my guy if you like."

"I haven't been to a trader. I'm not using a trader. I have a donor. Maybe. Possibly. Like I said, I'm only thinking about it right now. You're, like, ten giant leaps ahead of me here."

"A donor? So you're thinking of doing it *au naturel*?" Gina winked, and nudged her in the ribs.

"NO!" Unwanted images of Henry stripping off forced their way into her head. "No. Still just a specimen, but a, err, private transaction."

Gina nodded sagely. "But you're still going to need some equipment, right? I mean, unless your cycle's super reliable."

How long ago had she had her period? A week? Two? She had no idea. Some months it didn't come at all.

"I hadn't thought of that," she confessed.

"No problem," Gina declared. "I was super fertile, this little jellybean came along on my first try! So I've still got a few of those ovulation tests left, you can have them, call it a pregnancy gift. And I'm pretty sure I've still got the syringe too somewhere."

Kaitlyn screwed up her face.

"Oh, don't be such a prude. I'll wash it!" Gina said. "I'm only trying to help."

"I know," Kaitlyn said, cursing herself for not being able to hide her disgust at the suggestion. After all, Gina did know more about it than her. "I appreciate it. It's just all a little overwhelming. I haven't even really decided for sure."

"What about the father? Who is it?"

"I'd rather not say. He wants to keep it private."

"Fair enough. When do you have to decide?"

"We're both taking a couple of days, to think it over. But, honestly, I just can't see any other way. For Jack, or me."

"For Jack?" the smile faded from Gina's lips. "You're doing this for Jack?"

"Of course," Kaitlyn said, "I've done the maths. At the rate I'm dipping into my credit it'll be a year, fifteen months tops, before I can't afford the bills any more."

"Kaitlyn." Gina reached across the table and took her hand. "Sweetie, if he hasn't woken up by then, he's never going to."

"You don't know that." Kaitlyn pulled her hand away. "No one does. There are stories."

"What stories?"

"Stories from before. From back when everyone wasn't in such a fucking rush to die. There were people who woke up after years, sometimes even a decade, and went on to be perfectly healthy."

She'd looked them up. Back when Jack first had his accident. Even then, after just a few days, the doctors had wanted to stop. They'd said it was hopeless, but she couldn't accept that. So she'd spent hours poring over old medical journals in the library, wading through volumes of almost unintelligible medical terminology until she found them. Studies of coma patients who had pulled through, against all the odds, after years on life support.

Of course, back then life was sacred. At any cost. Barbarically so at times, she thought. Every child learned about it in history lessons, every class watched the old news reports. The suffering was too hideous to imagine. Poor wretches living in unending agony, desperately pleading to the courts for the right to die... and being refused.

Between the footage of emaciated, bed-bound patients who moaned in pain as they gasped for every breath, and the documentaries exposing the sickening cruelty at the homes in which the elderly used to be kept like livestock, her education had done a good job of convincing her the old ways were savage and uncivilised. Not to mention the cause of so many of the economic problems the Collective Council now worked to put right.

Preserving life, in any form and at any cost, was an outdated and cruel ideology. She'd always believed that. Until the life in question belonged to Jack.

The old ways were wrong. But, she was starting to realise, that didn't necessarily mean the new ways were right.

"I'm sorry," Gina said. "I didn't mean to upset you. I just worry about you, about your future. I just wish you'd consider yourself in all this."

"I'll be fine, all I need is to keep helping him. That's all that matters to me."

"Nine months is a long time you know," Gina said. "Things change."

Jack might already be dead. That's what she meant. And Kaitlyn knew she was right, but she couldn't dwell on it. Not without falling into despair, and that wouldn't do either of them any good.

"What I really need to know is, how do you find a buyer?"

"Oh, that's easy. Soon as it's confirmed you just go and see Old Martha, down by the river. She sorts everything out. I'll take you, no need to worry."

"Old Martha?"

"Yeah, she's one of those heathen nuns, from the time before. She's big on the sanctity of life and all that. All you gotta do is tell her you got pregnant by accident, but can't bring yourself to terminate. She'll treat you like a queen, tell you you're a beacon of light in an immoral world, or some such crap. She's always happy to help. At the end of the day, she gets ten per cent."

Kaitlyn snorted. "The god of money, eh?"

"Well, what do you expect?" Gina shrugged. "That's just how it was with the old church. You can't teach an old dog new tricks."

19

Henry watched Chloe closely as she busied herself clearing up the breakfast things and hanging out the washing. On the surface, she was her old self again. She hummed as she worked, shooting him a beaming smile every now and then when she realised he was staring at her.

"Haven't you anything you'd rather be doing than watching me?" she asked at last.

"No," Henry replied, "there's nothing in the world I'd rather be doing."

She giggled. A girlish sound that somehow didn't feel out of place despite her wrinkles and greying hair. A sound that had once stolen his heart. He'd given up everything for the chance to keep hearing that melody, to be the one who got to elicit it from her. And he knew, beyond all doubt, he'd do so again if he had to.

"You're a charmer, Henry Morris." She planted a soft kiss on his cheek, right below the scratch she'd inflicted. "But I can't have you cluttering up the kitchen all day. Go find something useful to do, or else I'll come up with a list of chores for you."

He heaved himself up from the table to go and get dressed. She was right. He couldn't, *shouldn't*, study her for cracks. There'd always be imperfections to be found, if you looked for them. Her comment about David had briefly knocked the wind out of his sails. But that was an over-reaction. So what if she was still a little disorientated? She'd only been on the new dose a few days, and just look how well she was already.

And even if she continued to get her years muddled up, what did it matter? Plenty of people had little lapses like that, especially as they got older. It didn't mean the Hepraxin wasn't working.

He made his way upstairs and grabbed the trousers he'd worn yesterday from the dressing table. He'd have to stop doing that. Now Chloe was herself again, she'd not put up with him draping his worn clothes over the furniture. He pulled back the bedroom curtains and smiled as he watched her in the garden, pegging out his shirts.

Normality was bliss. All he really needed was the woman he'd fallen in love with. There was no achievement, no earthly possession that could fill the hole her degeneration had carved out in his heart.

But even as he tried to consciously bask in contentment, his thoughts turned to Kaitlyn.

They'd agreed to meet in two days' time, once they'd both had a chance to really think things through. Would she agree to his proposal? There was no doubt it would be much harder for her than for him. But it made sense. It all made such perfect sense. This was a business offer and one that could benefit them both, plus the people that meant the most to them.

The doorbell rang. A sharp, shrill tone that made him jump.

Chloe was still at the bottom of the garden. He glanced out of the window; she hadn't heard or she'd be making her way inside. So he began his slow descent down the stairs. The bell rang again. And again, this time accompanied by aggressive knocking. Someone was in a hurry.

The sheer rudeness of it had him riled. As he unlatched the door, he made sure his face displayed the irritation and disgust he felt at the unwelcome barrage of impatient noise.

"Henry Morris?" the young man in a blue jumpsuit asked before he'd even opened the door halfway.

"Yes," he replied, trying his best to sound curt and pissed off.

A large brown envelope was thrust at him. "You've been served."

20

She didn't want to go home. The clock ticking above the counter taunted her, a constant reminder that the passing of the time was unstoppable. She didn't want her shift to end, not today. Because it couldn't be put off any longer. Tonight she would have to enter Jack's room and pack his whole existence into the shoddy cardboard boxes Jared had let her rescue from the recycling. There wouldn't be enough room for all his possessions at the new apartment, even as meagre as they were. She'd have to sort through all his private things, choose which to keep and which to discard.

As if he was already dead.

And then, when she reached whichever shitty skyrise hell hole they would allocate her, she'd have to face an even harder decision. Should she unpack his things, or not? Would he ever even enter their new home?

To leave his room untouched was one thing. A hopeful thing, undoubtedly the right thing. But it was a different matter to furnish a new place for him. To stretch his sheets across a bed that he may never lie in, put his mug next to the kettle not knowing if he would ever drink from it again. And what if she went through the pain of it all, only to have pack it all away again if…

No.

Those thoughts could not be allowed to take root. She put down the cloth she was using to clean the tables and squeezed her fists tight, letting her slightly-too-long fingernails create a sharp, burning sensation in her palms. Forcing her brain to concentrate on physical pain, derailing its morbid train of thought.

Jack had never, ever, treated her like a burden. Yet here she was, thinking of the pain it might cause her to unbox his possessions? Such ridiculous, selfish concerns.

He would not die. He would come home. Not to his own home, but it would be home nonetheless because she would make it so. No matter how bad the skyrise was, no matter what its occupants got up to in the stairwells and corridors, there would be a door. A door that would separate them from the rest of the world. And behind that door she would create a haven for the two of them. She would clean, and paint, and make it a home.

And he would come back to her.

No matter what it took, she'd bring him back to her.

The clock struck eleven. She pressed her cold fingers to her cheeks, to soothe the heat that bloomed there. Tightening her ponytail, she marched to the café door and slid the bolt across. Her pocket was full of order tickets; she spread them out across the table until she spotted the handwritten note Henry had given her with his phone number on it.

They weren't supposed to meet to declare their intentions until tomorrow, but now her decision had been made she found she couldn't wait. Her certainty swirled around her mind, looking for something tangible to cling to. She needed to speak it, solidify it.

Jack's apartment didn't have a phone any more. That was one of the first bills she'd stopped paying. But Jared's had one out the back, by the kitchen. She dialled the number, not thinking about the time. It rang for several minutes before a gruff voice answered.

"Hello?"

"Henry?"

"Yes. But who—"

"It's Kaitlyn. I'm in."

PART 2

IT DOESN'T WORK
WITHOUT HEAVEN

"Education is paramount. We cannot be complacent. I think sometimes we, as adults, forget how it is for children. How hard the concept of time can be to really comprehend. When we talk about life before the revolution, there's this sense of 'otherness', as though it was a different world altogether. To a child, we might as well be talking about medieval times. But there's a danger in that, in that feeling of separation from history. It can lead one to believe that such things can never happen again. It can lead to apathy, when there should be vigilance.

"That is why we are so delighted to receive such generous support from The Moving On Corporation. It is my firm belief that our alliance will ensure we are able to provide an ongoing programme of education that nourishes our children, not just intellectually, but spiritually too. That is how we will build a better, safer future. That is the legacy we will leave; one of humility, responsibility and reverence."

Bishop Adley, the New Church

1

The sperm needed to be kept at body temperature, apparently. He'd done a couple of dummy runs, speeding across town to the edge of the skyrise district. He'd even gone all the way up to Kaitlyn's apartment, on the twenty-third floor, just to see how long the journey would take. Best dress rehearsal was completed in thirty-seven minutes, but of course, he hadn't had the actual deposit to contend with then.

Producing the goods and sneaking them out of the house without your wife noticing was no mean feat, he discovered. Not least because three shrill rings on the telephone (the agreed upon 'I'm ovulating' signal), followed by a frantic dash into the toilet was hardly the most seductive of foreplay scenarios. The sound of Chloe banging the hoover against the skirting board on the other side of the door wasn't exactly conducive to sexual fantasy either.

He tried to conjure up the most arousing images he could, but imagination had never been his strong point. It felt too sordid, under the circumstances, to rely on his memories of intimate times with Chloe. Somewhere, in his distant recollections, he could remember huddling around his older cousin's computer. He must have been about eleven or twelve, as the internet was still a free-for-all full of the most outrageous debauchery mankind had ever conceived of.

It felt less treacherous somehow than picturing a real

person, so he decided to concentrate on those half-remembered digital images.

It was quite possibly the least satisfying ejaculation he'd ever had. But it was done.

He screwed the top on to the specimen jar that he'd purchased at the pharmacy, and wrapped it in brown paper before stashing it in the pocket of his trousers, where he hoped it would stay warm for the journey.

Stage one of operation fertilisation complete, it was time for stage two: get the goods out of the house without arousing Chloe's suspicion.

He pulled his shirt down to try to cover the bulge of the specimen jar, flushed the empty toilet and sprayed some air freshener. She was in the kitchen. This was good. His route to the front door was clear.

He entered the lounge, and called out to her across the length of the house.

"Sorry, love, I just remembered I'm supposed to meet Al down at the club. He's got some new flights or something he wants to show me. He was so excited about it, I felt I couldn't say no. You know how he is."

She removed her hands from the washing up bowl and grabbed a tea towel to dry them.

"Okay," she said, smiling, "that's sweet of you, love. It'll make his day I'm sure."

She was walking toward him, still holding the towel. If he didn't move quickly, those hands would be dry, and then those arms would reach out to embrace him, those lips would touch his cheek, and as she pressed against him to bid him a tender goodbye, she'd feel the hard lump in the back of his trousers. What would she do? What would she say?

He backed away from her as quickly as he could.

"Sorry, I'm already late. Can't believe I forgot until now. Better dash, hate to think of him sat there alone."

Snaking through the door and pulling it shut behind him, he was both relieved and ashamed. By the time he'd got behind the wheel, Chloe was at the window, smiling and waving him off. He waved back, though his heart sank at the deceit. He was off to impregnate another woman, and his sweet trusting wife was bidding him farewell.

Sure, he was doing it for her. But it still felt treacherous.

He had thought about telling her, but decided against it. After talking it all through at length with Kaitlyn, it had started to sound like a perfectly normal, rational thing to do. But, objectively, he doubted anyone else would think so, least of all Chloe. Quite apart from the fact that she'd be aghast at the thought of someone going through so much in order to help her, it would be cruel beyond belief for her to have to cope with her husband fathering yet another child when she herself had none, and never would. After a life spent yearning for a child to love, the idea of having a baby and giving it away, even for good reason, would be unthinkable to her.

But, he had resolved that he would definitely tell her about his new friendship with Kaitlyn, once the conception was out of the way. They'd have to stay in touch, because of the pregnancy. It would be too hard, and he'd feel too guilty, to keep spending time with her behind Chloe's back.

The skyrise district was bleak and depressing. Pulling off the circular road, into the shadows cast by the towering apartment blocks, he was at least pleased for Kaitlyn that she was on the top floor. The overcrowded monstrosities were built so close together that each cast shade on the others. He wondered if those on the lower floors ever felt sunlight through their windows.

There was no need to use the intercom system to enter the building. The front door had been long ago torn off its hinges. A violation of every health and safety code that had existed in his youth, no doubt. But nobody paid much attention to the wellbeing of those inhabiting low-EP dwellings these days.

The drawback of Kaitlyn living high enough to see daylight was that it meant he had to endure the elevator. Entering the piss-stained lobby, he was relieved to note that the only other person waiting for the rattling tin-can was a youngish woman carrying shopping bags. She nodded at him politely as he approached, and when the door opened with a terrifying shudder he gestured for her to proceed first.

She hit the button for floor thirteen, and he waited until she had retracted her arm before reaching over and pressing the faded number twenty-three. He tutted and jabbed at it harder when it didn't light up.

"Stops at nineteen today," the woman said cheerfully, as if it were a perfectly normal statement.

"What?" Henry asked.

"Stops at nineteen," she said again, this time reaching across him and pressing the number nineteen to illustrate her point. "I expect it'll break again soon. Wouldn't go down past seven the other day. Yesterday it would only stop on random floors. I had to get out at sixteen and walk down. Easier than walking up from nine, I thought."

Christ. It was like an elevator lottery.

"Hasn't anyone called maintenance?" Henry asked. The woman just laughed.

"We're all just praying someone's in it when it gives up the ghost completely."

"What? Surely that's the worst possible outcome?"

"That's the only way we'll get someone out to fix it. If there's someone trapped they'll have to do something about it. Otherwise they'll just stick that yellow 'Out of Order' tape on it and it'll sit there for nine months or more like last time."

The creaking box spluttered to a halt and the doors opened, causing the floor to shake.

"Well," she said, "that's me. Cheerio. Good luck getting back down."

As the doors closed again, he could hear her chuckle. He swallowed hard, and concentrated on the digital display, watching the numbers slowly ascending. His relief at reaching floor nineteen, and leaving the rickety death box behind him, was short-lived when he was faced with the reality of having to drag his prosthetic up the remaining flights of stairs.

He was dripping with sweat, and struggling for breath, by the time he rang Kaitlyn's doorbell.

She greeted him with a smile, a paintbrush in her left hand and speckles of magnolia peppering her scraped-back hair.

"Henry." She stepped aside to let him in. "Fifty-seven minutes? I guess it took a little longer than we thought to complete the, err, task in hand?" She stifled a laugh, and despite his exhaustion he couldn't help but grin. It was good to see her looking bright and happy.

Looking around the apartment, he marvelled at her resilience. When he'd visited a few days ago, the walls had been stained yellow and covered in mould, and all her, and Jack's, earthly possessions had been piled up in soggy cardboard boxes. Now the place looked bright and clean. She'd thrown open all the windows, despite the winter chill, and swathed the walls in light, airy colours. She was feeling positive. Probably because they had a plan. It's amazing what agreeing on a course of action can do for one's spirits.

"Yes," Henry replied, still looking round, "sorry. One or two setbacks."

"Never mind," she replied, "I'm sure it'll go better tomorrow."

"T-tomorrow?"

She laughed. "Of course. I'll be fertile for four or five days, might as well give it the best chance we can, eh?"

"Four or five days?" Henry felt giddy. "In a *row*?"

2

Things were looking up.

The skyrise wasn't as bad as she'd feared. For a start, it was on the south side of the low-EP district. Mum's apartment, if she was still there, was along the north edge, next to the river. There must be four thousand souls, at least, living between them. As long as she always exited the area close to her own block, and never cut through the estate, there was no reason why they should ever bump into one another. Mum had no cause to go south.

And then there was the place itself. She'd never envisioned being given a top floor apartment. It was incredible luck, something which the housing officer made sure to remind her of.

"You should consider yourself extremely fortunate, Miss Thomas," the scowling woman said as she handed over the keys. "Usually, we'd have put you with the SDs, because of your antisocial behaviour. But, given that you've been in continuous employment for more than two years, we've decided to be generous and place you among the LCWs. I hope you appreciate how lucky you are, and don't do anything to make us regret our kindness?"

Being scolded like a naughty child made hot rage churn inside Kaitlyn, but she managed to keep her composure and smile.

"Oh yes," she said, taking the proffered keys before the

stuck-up bitch could change her mind, "absolutely. I am most grateful. Most humbly grateful for the mercy you have bestowed upon me."

The woman didn't seem to pick up on the sarcasm, probably because she assumed such snivelling gratitude was actually deserved. Kaitlyn resisted the urge to salute her before retreating from the Council office.

If you had to live in a skyrise, being on the top floors among the Low Credit Workers was the best possible outcome. There were hierarchies according to your contribution to society, even within the housing blocks. The highest storeys belonged to those who worked hard, but whose jobs were not considered of enough value to the community to warrant a cabin-house, or even a larger apartment in one of the two-storey blocks like Jack and the other farmers had. Her immediate neighbours would be hard workers, but undervalued ones.

As the floors descended, so did the social status of those inhabiting them. The middle storeys were occupied by those who worked only part time, or had now retired from low-ranking occupations. Women with young children who worked only during school hours, widows who had once been supported by their husbands but were now alone and could only find a few hours' work each week, even army veterans whose injuries meant that they could only physically manage a small amount of work.

At the very bottom were the SDs. The social deviants. Those with marks against their social conduct, or those who somehow had enough money to pay rent but no discernible form of employment. Criminals yet to be caught, in other words. The bottom floors of a skyrise were where you could find pretty much any illegal service you were after.

Kaitlyn had grown up on the ground floor. Their mother had told them this was a good thing, because the elevator never worked. But sometimes she and Jack had gone mountaineering, on bold and ambitious expeditions up the seemingly unconquerable stairwells to the very peak. The corridors smelled cleaner the higher you got, and the people you met looked happier and better dressed. Mrs Finch, on the sixteenth floor, would give them fresh orange juice and sometimes even a chocolate biscuit if she happened to be in when they knocked. She was a smiley, plump white-haired lady who liked children, and Kaitlyn enjoyed visiting her, mostly because her apartment always smelled like cinnamon.

Until one day it didn't.

They hadn't been on one of their expeditions for several weeks, because Jack had twisted his ankle. Kaitlyn had missed having adventures, and the sweet treats Mrs Finch offered. So she'd decided to go it alone. It wasn't as much fun without Jack, though. The endless flights felt like a chore, rather than a magical outing full of laughter and chatter. By the time she reached the fourteenth floor, she resolved to turn back and head home after the 'pit stop' rather than continuing to the peak. But when she reached it, the corridor smelled bad. So bad it made her gag.

When she opened the door that separated the corridor from the stairwell, covering her mouth and nose with her grubby sleeve, there were men in white coats outside Mrs Finch's apartment, filling in paperwork on clipboards. Neighbours stood around, handkerchiefs tied to their faces, shaking their heads and saying things like, 'How dreadful. Makes you think, doesn't it? We must check in on one another more often.'

And just like that, there were no more chocolate biscuits or cool glasses of sweet fruit juice to be had.

Kaitlyn shuddered as the elevator to her new home passed the sixteenth floor and vowed to herself that she would keep an eye out for her new neighbours, particularly any who lived alone.

She smiled when she saw the door to her apartment. It was a good door. A sturdy door with a robust lock and a spy hole that looked out, but not in. A door fit for purpose. The apartment itself was small, but no smaller than expected. She'd give herself the luxury of the bed, for the time being.

When Jack came out of hospital she'd simply sleep on the sofa. Or put a second bed in the bedroom, or even in the lounge. It's not like they'd be entertaining. There were so many options. So much possibility.

Where there's life, there's hope.

It seemed silly now, to have been so distraught about losing his old apartment. Rationally, even when he woke up it would be a long time before he was fit to work the fields again. So he'd have lost his allocation eventually anyway. At least this way she could prepare a comfortable place for him to recuperate in, rather than him having to go through the upheaval of moving himself.

Having a task, and a plan, made everything seem more hopeful. She took a few days' annual leave from Jared's, and set about making the apartment as comfortable and inviting as she could.

When Henry had visited, the day after she moved in, they had chatted all about their scheme and she felt herself growing excited. It would work. It had to.

He'd insisted she needed a phone. They'd have to be able to contact one another easily. She hadn't planned on having one, she'd been managing perfectly well without, but she could see his point, so she'd transferred the existing landline to her name.

When two little lines had appeared on the ovulation stick that morning, she'd given him the three-ring call to arms and tried to focus on painting the window frame while she waited for him to arrive. But the butterflies in her stomach were too active to ignore.

Would this work? Surely, it had to. But then what? She'd be pregnant. A whole new life growing in her belly; a whole little being entirely dependent on her to bring it into the world. But not her world... a better one. The child would have a life she had never known. It would grow up with parents who loved it, parents who actively went out and chose it. It would wonder, perhaps, if its conception had been an accident. It would never know how precious it was, never know that it had saved lives just by being born.

She'd make sure, when she went to see this Martha, that the family who'd adopt it would be the very best. An archetypal happy family. Mother all smiles and patience, father hard-working and big on education, but with a penchant for tickle fights and family outings. The child would be a saviour; the very least she could do was to make sure it had the most charmed life possible. The type of life she could never hope to give it.

She was daydreaming about a blissful childhood in the suburbs, a garden full of vegetables and a mother whose soap-scented arms could fix any ills with their loving embrace, when the doorbell rang.

Henry looked a state. Wheezing and sweating, his cheeks bright red yet his overall complexion somehow pale and sickly. She was just relieved to see him. Glad he hadn't changed his mind about the whole idea, now that she was so certain it was the right thing to do.

When he handed her the package, sheathed in brown paper, he couldn't look her in the eye. Opening it in front of him would have been excruciating, for both of them. So she just nodded, and headed to the bedroom.

"I'll just be a few minutes then," she said, trying to sound as casual as she could, as if she was referring to something as run of the mill as popping to her room to get changed. "Stick the kettle on would you? There's coffee and sugar in the cupboard by the sink."

"Oh, right," Henry replied, "right you are, yes. Coffee. Good idea."

3

It wasn't nearly as awkward as he'd expected it to be. Mostly due to Kaitlyn's easy manner. He set about making coffee, and after a few minutes she came out of her bedroom. She lay on the sofa, positioning pillows under her bottom and putting her legs up so they rested on the back.

"Gravity," she said matter-of-factly as she reached for the mug he offered. "White with two?"

He nodded.

"Perfect." She took a long slow sip, before putting the mug down on the upturned box that served as a coffee table.

"How are you feeling?" he asked, not knowing what else to say.

"Well, no morning sickness yet." She grinned. "No need to be so awkward, Henry. It's all just biology, right?"

"I suppose," he said, "it's just a little… strange. Don't you think?"

"I guess," she conceded, "but it seems right. I've got a really good feeling about this, the more I think about it the more I'm sure we're doing the right thing. For everyone."

Her conviction was contagious, and he relaxed a little knowing she was steadfast in her resolve.

"I'm a bit worried about you, though," she continued.

"Me?" Surely, effort-wise, he had the cushy end of the stick by far?

"You look done in," she said, "how are you going to manage doing this again tomorrow?"

Having to repeat the whole nightmare of sneaking out and racing across town wasn't something he was looking forward to. Especially if that horror show of an elevator was still playing up. But compared to what Kaitlyn would be dealing with if their transaction was successful, it didn't seem right to complain.

"Oh, I'll be fine," he said, "don't you worry about me. The journey's a bit stressful, I'll admit. But only because I'm trying to get here as quickly as possible, and of course without letting on to Chloe."

"You should do it here," she said.

"What?" The whole idea was hideously embarrassing.

"I'm serious, Henry. The journey's stressful because you're trying to get here quickly, you said so yourself. So, take your time getting here and then use my bathroom."

"I—" The thought was mortifying. Doing the deed in a young woman's apartment? With her just a few feet away, and fully aware of what he was up to?

Kaitlyn burst into laughter. "Oh come on," she said, "don't tell me you're embarrassed? I'm currently lying here legs akimbo hoping gravity will help out. If anyone should be blushing it's me."

She had a point. The situation was equally as uncomfortable for her as it was for him.

Feeling a little ashamed that he'd not thought of it from her perspective before, he agreed. It did make sense, logistically.

So he arrived the next day, with an empty specimen pot and a crippling feeling of embarrassment. He felt unbelievably self-conscious, especially when Kaitlyn asked if he'd like her to dig out one of her brother's old magazines. It seemed to take him an age to relax enough to get the job done, which in itself caused a vicious cycle of anxiety. The more he worried about how long it was taking, and what Kaitlyn must think, the more his body conspired against him.

But if she did have any thoughts on the length of time he took, she kept them to herself. When he emerged from the bathroom, she simply took the wrapped pot from him, without saying a word, and disappeared into the bedroom, leaving him to make drinks for them both.

He filled the old, scaly kettle and spooned coffee into the two mugs Kaitlyn had left out on the side for him. While he waited for it to boil, he picked up the newspaper that lay folded up on the small wooden kitchen counter. The *National Herald* was delivered daily, free of charge, to every household. The Collective Council made a big deal about the notion that information should be freely available to every citizen, for the sake of education and transparency.

Indeed, the paper's by-line read: *Empowering the nation*.

Most people thought it was a wonderful idea, and a prime example of the Council upholding the promises made to the people after the revolution. Never again would those in power hide behind the shields of billionaire tycoons and their gutter-presses. Never again would private business control public information. Every man, woman and child, regardless of their situation, now had full access to the most up-to-date news. No one need live in ignorance; every citizen was entitled to know what was happening in the world around them. Knowledge is power, after all, and the whole idea of the Collective Council was to return power to the people.

Henry didn't view the publication that way, though. In fact, he tended to throw his copy straight in the recycling bin. Yes, on the surface it was it a public service to ensure even the poorest in society were armed with information about current affairs, but he didn't need Old Al to point out the double-edge on this particular sword.

The *National Herald* was the only national paper, just like the BBC were the only news broadcasters. Back when there'd been a myriad of sources to choose from, online as well as in print, there'd been a huge amount of misinformation. In a competitive market, journalists and commentators stretched the truth as thin as gossamer to win views and readers from one another. The bias and slander peddled by the tabloids had been so obvious it was farcical. But therein lay its only saving grace… it was obvious.

With only one purveyor of news, and no experience of conflicting sources, the younger generations assumed the facts they were given were unspun, and indisputable. Growing up in a world dominated by the Internet had had its problems, but it meant that Henry and his peers had, from a very young age, learned not to believe everything they read.

Today's front page featured a photograph of a smiling young man with neat cornrows and deep brown eyes wearing a white coat, and holding up a gold plaque.

Skyrise Success!

From slums to stethoscopes, Menye Habdila scoops the Jensen Medical Award.

As the youngest ever recipient of the prestigious JMA, Menye attributes his success to the selfless actions of his parents. Speaking to our reporter, he told us:

"We didn't have much growing up. My parents were hard workers, though. They taught me the value of making a contribution to society. When I said I wanted to be a doctor, I didn't think it could really happen. My EPT scores weren't high enough, I just didn't have the credit available for college. But they believed in me, they knew I could do it."

Menye's parents saw his potential, and knew he was destined to have a positive impact on society.

"My mum always said, it's all about making the world a better place, about helping others.

She knew I could do that, and she knew that by supporting me she herself would be doing it too."

When he was eighteen, Menye's parents chose to Move On, bequeathing all their remaining Social Credit to him, so that he could train to be a doctor.

"Whenever I heal a sick patient, or save someone's life, I know they're looking down on me. Those lives I save, they're saving them too, because without their sacrifice I wouldn't be able to do it."

Henry folded the paper and turned it over as he put it down so that he couldn't see the young doctor's face. And so it began. The next level. How many parents would be reading that, right now? How many teenagers living in small homes, harbouring big ambitions? Everyone wants their children to do better in life than they did. Here was a seed, a seed that would grow. It wouldn't be enough any more, Moving On to avoid the cost of long-term treatment and instead pass your credit down to your kids. Even that huge sacrifice wouldn't be enough. Now they'd be a spate of perfectly healthy people ending their lives to give their offspring an education. Poor ones, of course. The rich would be just fine.

Was this the next level of natural selection? Peer pressured into removing oneself from the land of the living? How long before no one from the lower ranks lived past forty any more? It was the exact polar opposite of what the revolutionaries had intended, yet no one seemed to see it.

Feeling disgusted, he put the coffees down on the upturned box and made his way to the bathroom. When he came back out, Kaitlyn was on the sofa in her after-insemination position.

"Hey," she said, smiling, "are you okay? You look a bit pale."

There was something different, more sedate, about her behind closed doors. As if the fire that seemed to burn close to her surface retreated once she was away from the outside world. Her whole demeanour changed, and not just because she was lying on the sofa. Her face seemed softer, her voice quieter.

It was this time, after the deed was done, that he enjoyed. She insisted on keeping still, legs up, for half an hour because she believed it would help. Henry wasn't at all sure it made the blindest bit of difference, but it gave them a chance to chat and it was conversation that he missed the most.

"Yes," he said, taking a seat on the armchair opposite, "yes, I'm fine. Just got myself riled up, that's all. I should know better than to read the news."

"What's got you in a rage this time?" she asked, picking up her mug.

"I'm not sure I could explain myself properly," he said, "it's just... it's not how it was supposed to be. It's not what the revolution was about, or at least, not what I thought it was about."

"What was it like?" she asked, leaning forward a little, "living through the revolution?"

"Pretty boring, to be fair," he said, smiling at the look of shock on her face. "I was just a kid, remember? My parents were obsessed with it all, but it didn't really affect me at the time."

"But... the uprisings? The crowds tearing down the bastions of power? The tanks on the streets? How could that be boring?"

"That stuff was only in the big cities. For most of us life just carried on as normal, until the Council came to power."

The chaos of the unelected interim government had been all over the news, but he'd been too young to really care. The only thing that really irked him had been the disappearance of American products from the shelves after transatlantic relations broke down. The instatement of the Collective Council had been supposed to bring stability, but nothing had seemed particularly unstable in his life until after they were elected.

That had been the first time he'd been old enough to vote, and he put his cross next to the 'working class hero' standing for the newly formed Council. It made perfect sense. A new government, run by the very people who had been disenfranchised and underrepresented by the old establishment. That had to be the best way to achieve equality.

The whole country had thought so. They voted in their droves, not realising it would be the last vote they'd ever have.

Kaitlyn was fascinated by his tales from his childhood, and Henry found himself looking forward to this time each day, when they would chat and relax together.

He took to giving her a lift to the hospital to visit Jack afterwards. She seemed to have forgotten her former disgust with cars entirely, and was more than happy to accept his offer. When he watched her step through the front door of her apartment, the change in her was instantaneous.

She stiffened up, standing taller. Her shoulders raised, her arms crossed. Her eyes never stilled, constantly surveying everything around her. Even in the elevator, she didn't stand still. Small, subtle movements. Her fingers tapped on her folded arms, she shifted her weight from one foot to the other. Like an animal gearing up to pounce, or run.

Fight or flight, that's what it was. The very act of being outside her own home was flooding her with adrenaline. A constant state of high alert. He'd seen it before, with Carolyn. A nervous anxiety that his ex-wife used to take pills, and see endless expensive shrinks, for. Kaitlyn wasn't a firebrand because she was angry, or feisty. It was self-defence. She was afraid.

He wondered if she even knew. The younger generations didn't go in for things like self-help, or seeking diagnoses for their non-physical ailments. If he dared mention to her that he thought she might have some kind of anxiety disorder, possibly even PTSD, she'd probably laugh, or fly off the handle. Such things were now considered the self-indulgent weaknesses of times gone by. Invented illness that the snowflakes hid behind to justify their laziness. The modern way was to just soldier on, stiff-upper-lip. Another full-circle.

On the fourth day, he pulled up outside the hospital to let her out.

"Well," he said as she unfastened her seatbelt, "see you tomorrow."

"Oh," she replied, "well, I don't think there's any need. I won't be ovulating."

His stomach flipped a little. Why was that? It took a moment to realise – it was disappointment.

"Oh, right. Right you are, yes," he said.

"So... I guess I'll call you in a couple of weeks, let you know if it worked, or if we'll need to try again?"

"Yes. Yes, that'll be fine."

"Okay then." She started to open the door, but then stopped and turned to face him. "Bye, Henry," she said, before getting out of the car.

He couldn't help but smile as he watched her walk away.

4

There was an asterisk next to Jack's name on the patient board again. The weeks rolled by so quickly, she'd forgotten payment was due once more.

Remembering what happened last time filled her with shame. She'd not put it off again. She couldn't trust herself not to get snappy if she was confronted about it, so she turned around and walked back out of the ward, hoping none of the staff had spotted her.

The problem with taking days off from work was the lack of tips. Her wages for this week wouldn't be enough to cover the bill, not once rent and utilities were deducted, so she made her way to the lobby. The credit transfer machines stood amongst the racks of magazines, toiletries and other gifts one might buy for an ailing relative.

There was a queue, of course. There was always a queue. When she reached the machine, housed inside a semi-private booth, she placed her index finger on the scanner to bring up her account. She knew Jack's SC code by heart, having done this so many times. She entered the required amount, and pressed Transfer. *Are you sure you want to transfer credit from Thomas, Kaitlyn to Thomas, Jack?* the machine quizzed her. She hated that; it felt like judgement. As though even this non-sentient bundle of wires and electrodes thought she was crazy. She stabbed at the Yes button, as if it would somehow register her annoyance.

Watching the numbers go down in her account, she tried to think of them as nothing more than that. Just numbers. She tried not to wonder what they represented, what she was actually giving up. A year's worth of pills for some chronic illness she was yet to endure, perhaps? A course of antibiotics for a nasty infection she was yet to contract? If she kept doing this, she'd be overdrawn herself soon. Perhaps one day she would be old and out of credit, and a cut finger would lead to sepsis. She'd die from carelessly chopping vegetables for her supper, and all because the credit that would have saved her had been spent today to keep her brother breathing.

Or perhaps she was giving up the chance to have a child she'd get to keep.

The thought came out of nowhere, and took her by surprise. The person behind her tapped her on her shoulder, tutting their impatience. She'd been lost in her own musings, taking too much time, holding people up. She felt embarrassed, but scowled at the woman rather than apologising. Didn't anyone have any patience?

"Excuse me for existing," she snapped, stepping out of the booth.

Annoyed with herself, she headed for the East Wing, without looking back at the people she'd inconvenienced. But instead of taking a left by the elevators, she found herself turning right, following the signs to Maternity.

Peering through the criss-crossed glass in the door to the post-natal ward was like looking through a portal to another dimension. A world she'd heard of, but never experienced. Every bed was occupied, and every woman in them wore the same stiff and shapeless gown emblazoned with the hospital's name, written diagonally, and unendingly, across the fabric.

Not one of them noticed her staring from behind the glass. Not one of them would have noticed if the sky outside turned green. For in their arms they each cradled their own treasure, and from the looks on their faces Kaitlyn could tell it shone brighter to them than any jewel on earth.

She wiped at her eyes with the back of her fists, digging her fingernails into her palms.

Had her own mother ever looked at her, or Jack, the way those mothers gazed at their new sons and daughters? Like they were the only thing in the whole world worth looking at? Had she ever spilt tears of sheer wonder and joy at the slightest movement of their fingers or toes, or gasped in awe when they yawned?

She didn't know. She didn't know if her mother had ever held her that tightly, or loved her that much. She moved her hands down to her abdomen, splaying her palms and pressing, ever so slightly. Feeling for something, though nothing could possibly be felt. Was there life beginning in there? A spark so small she couldn't feel it ignite? And if there was, she would never get to cherish it. She wouldn't be able to allow herself to fall in love the way those women had. It wouldn't be her that got to swoon at its perfection, to count every hair on its head and lose hours to the study of its toes.

But at least someone would, she told herself. That would be the criteria, the very bare minimum. The arms that took her child from her would be ones that could never tire of holding it. The eyes that looked upon her infant's face would be misty with love. Her child, if it existed, would be the object of unconditional adoration.

But would she ever get to look that way, at anyone? Would there ever be another chance, a child she got to keep? If she spent much more of her credit on Jack, then probably not.

"Are you visiting somebody?" A robust-looking nurse in a navy uniform opened the door to the ward, eyeing her with disdain.

"No," Kaitlyn replied, "I mean yes, but not here… I think I took a wrong turn."

The nurse just nodded briskly, and pulled the door shut again. But she remained on the other side of the glass, watching until Kaitlyn walked away and headed back along the corridor toward her brother's ward.

Jack was just the same. Same position, same serene but vacant expression. Someone had shaved him, she noted. But other than that, today could have been yesterday, or a week last Wednesday. Did he even have any concept of time, locked away behind those closed lids?

"So," she said, scraping the chair across the floor to sit by his side. "I might be pregnant."

Breath held, she watched for something... anything. Some kind of reaction. But there was nothing.

"And the father's a married man, sixty years old."

Not even a flicker.

"Come on, Jack. Yell at me, tell me I'm a screw-up. Tell me you're disappointed in me. Anything. Anything at all." She stared at his eyelids, willing them to twitch. "I need something here, Jack. I need to know you're there."

I need to know I'm not giving up everything for nothing.

But it was futile. Like shouting at a rock, or pleading with a fence post. Not only did it get you nowhere, but it made everyone around think you were crazy.

She must have raised her voice more than she realised because a worried nurse came scampering in.

"Is everything okay in here, Miss Thomas?" she asked, cocking her head to one side like a spaniel.

"No," Kaitlyn snapped. "Everything is not okay, everything's just the same as it was yesterday, and the day before that. Everything's shit."

The nurse sucked her bottom lip in over her teeth. "Would you like some water?"

Kaitlyn laughed, and then sobbed. And then took the small glass of water the nurse hastily poured for her from the jug on Jack's bedside table. Why did they even do that? Fill a jug with fresh water every day and plonk it beside him, just to remove it later?

"Sorry," she said, after the tepid drink had calmed her slightly, "it's hard."

The nurse smiled. "It must be. Maybe you should give yourself a break? It's so admirable that you come and visit every day, but it must be very tough on you. I'm here tomorrow, I'll sit with him on my break if you like? Read him the headlines, maybe?"

"That's so kind of you," Kaitlyn said, smiling at the thoughtfulness, "but I sort of have to come, if you know what I mean. Even though it hurts, even though it doesn't change anything. I feel like if I don't keep coming, keep reminding him I'm here and I won't give up, he might let go of whatever it is that's keeping him here… I know it must seem crazy."

"It doesn't seem crazy at all," the nurse replied, putting her hand on Kaitlyn's shoulder. "If only we were all so lucky as to have someone who loves us that much."

She did. She did love him that much. She loved him so much that she lost hours, every day, to studying his face. She loved him so much that the slightest movement of his fingers, or toes, would make her gasp with joy, just like those mothers holding their newborns.

Oh God, how stupid she'd been. How selfish. To worry that she was giving up the chance to love someone that may never even exist, when someone she loved so deeply was already here, and needed her every bit as much as those infants needed their mothers. Maybe Mum never did look at Jack with such pure, unending love. But someone did, and that someone was her.

"Thank you," she said. But it wasn't for the kind words, or even the understanding. It was for the epiphany.

I am doing the right thing, she told herself with renewed certainty. Now she just had to hope the scheme would work.

The next two weeks were painfully slow. At first she missed Henry's daily visits, finding the apartment very quiet and lonely without them. She found herself smiling when she recalled his anecdotes and rants, or the embarrassed look on his face when he emerged from her bathroom with the brown paper bag in hand. But she soon fell back into her usual routine of walking to the hospital each morning, which was closer now she'd moved apartments, and then wandering to Jared's to eat any leftover lunch before beginning her shift.

It was hard to tell if her period was late or not, seeing as it didn't always come. Henry had told her that was likely a lack of nutrition, but he had some strange ideas so she wasn't sure whether to believe him. Snowflakes were obsessed with every tiny physical problem. They used to call in sick for splinters, so her teachers had said. Always looking for any excuse to be lazy, any reason that wasn't their own fault to get out of pulling their weight. That was why the Collective Council had had to revoke sick pay, even though it went against their ethos. They'd been forced to go back on their own promises because the snowflakes took advantage of it too much, spoiling it for everyone else.

Fourteen days after Gina's test kit had told her she was ovulating, she had no cramps or spots. She checked ten times a day for any signs of her impending cycle, relieved each time when there were none.

So she stopped by the pharmacy, and spent money she could ill afford on a different type of test.

The instructions said that the result would be most accurate first thing in the morning. Trying to sleep with that little box, the one that held the answer to the most urgent of questions, on her bedside table was near impossible. She tossed and turned, and almost gave in to the temptation to just do it there and then. But eventually exhaustion overtook her, and she slipped into dreams of positive tests, pregnancy clothes and birthing classes.

When she awoke she dashed to the toilet, tearing open the box and unwrapping the test on the way. The relief of expelling the built-up urine was short-lived, replaced by nerves at what the test might say.

Two minutes, the package said. *Two minutes?* She left it on the edge of the sink and paced around the living room. Opening the curtains only killed ten seconds. Filling the kettle and putting it on only twenty. One minute thirty to go. She picked up the *National Herald* and tried to read the front page, which today was all about a new initiative to improve wheat harvests, but she couldn't concentrate on the words.

One minute ten.

She sat down. She stood up.

Forty-five seconds.

She walked as slowly as she could to the bathroom, and wrapped her hand around the door handle.

Thirty.

Big breaths. Deep breaths. Breaths that took five seconds to inhale and another five to expel.

Ten.

She pushed the door open, moved toward the sink but kept her eyes away from the stick.

Five.

This was it. Time for one more deep breath and then...

Inhale, and look.

Two little pink lines...

Exhale.

5

The women's health clinic had changed a fair bit since he'd last had cause to visit. Back when he'd accompanied Carolyn, and then Chloe, to their pre-natal appointments the walls had been covered in bright, cheerful posters featuring wide-eyed and chubby-cheeked infants. They had proclaimed things like 'Breast is Best' or 'Immunisation for Life'. Every noticeboard in the waiting room had been packed full of tips on maintaining health and vitality during pregnancy, or warnings against indulging in alcohol, smoking, or unpasteurised cheese.

But as he sat beside Kaitlyn, waiting for her name to be called, there wasn't a chuckling little bundle of joy, or a ridiculously smiley gestating woman, on any of the display boards. Instead there were slim, sensible-looking young women adorning the advertisements for various contraceptives.

'Your fertility. Your responsibility.'

'Bipanon, available without credit cost. Stay radiant, be responsible.'

'Gynaecol. Helping you make the world a sustainable place.'

Well, they certainly weren't mincing words. With the young generation being bombarded with anti-procreation propaganda at every turn, it was a wonder there were still children coming into the world at all. But, despite the youngsters being so impressionable, that all-consuming longing for a child must still be stronger than any message the Collective Council could peddle. He shouldn't be surprised; he'd seen that maternal drive first hand. No amount of posters could ever have dissuaded Aunt Sarah, or Chloe, from their burning desire.

Of course, it wasn't just the notice boards that made this a very different experience, it was Kaitlyn. Of the three women he had sat in this clinic with, she was by far the most bewildering, and amusing.

Carolyn had treated the whole pregnancy, and ensuing infant, as a huge inconvenience. Until the time came that she could use David as a bargaining chip in the divorce proceedings, of course. If she could have made Henry go to the appointments in her place, she would have. Sitting beside her in the waiting room had been awful; all she did was huff and tut and moan about how she'd had to miss a meeting for this. Chloe, on the other hand, had been overwhelmed with excitement and emotion. Every check-up was marked, and circled, on the calendar, and she looked forward to each milestone as though it were Christmas morning.

He felt painfully conspicuous sitting beside Kaitlyn, and not just because of the age difference. Her assertiveness in public embarrassed and impressed him in equal measures. He'd felt himself turn crimson when she interrupted the two middle-aged receptionists, who had been chatting about their weekends despite the mounting queue. She wasn't even first in line, but she'd leaned around the women ahead of her and said loudly, "Do you think you could check us all in before you have your catch-up?"

She'd laughed when she saw the look of shock on his face. "Oh, you are funny," she'd said, "we're here because you got me pregnant, but you're more embarrassed at me saying what everyone else is thinking to those two than the fact I'm carrying your baby?"

All eyes in the room had turned on him, and he sank into the chair next to Kaitlyn, resolving never to show any hint of embarrassment in front of her again, lest she pour gasoline on the fire.

But he had already seen the other, more vulnerable, side to Kaitlyn, and now he knew her better the tell-tale signs of her own nervousness were obvious. She tapped her foot, fiddled with her sleeve. She was just as uncomfortable and jittery as he was, maybe more so. She was the one who would have to go in to the consulting room, after all.

"Kaitlyn Thomas?" A plump nurse with horn-rimmed glasses and overly-thick eyebrows appeared in the doorway, holding a clipboard. Kaitlyn stood up. "Follow me, then." The nurse turned and headed down the corridor, but Kaitlyn just stared at Henry.

"Well?" she said. "What's the matter? Do you need a hand up?"

"I—" She wanted him to go with her? Why? He'd thought he was just here to give her a ride, and pay the bill at the end. "I thought I should wait here."

"Oh no, you don't!" She grabbed his hand and yanked him up. "This is a two-way transaction, mister. I'm not doing this all by myself."

He trailed behind her, head spinning. He'd never gone in to the consulting room before, not for the confirmation tests or even the routine check-ups. He'd only accompanied his wives for the cool stuff, like scans and heartbeats. The world of female tests and examinations remained a terrifying mystery. He had no idea what went on behind those closed doors, but he was pretty sure it was undignified and hideously embarrassing.

"So," the nurse said as they took their seats on the opposite side of her desk. Two seats, Henry noted. Perhaps the men were expected to attend these days after all. "What can I do for you today, Kaitlyn?"

He was relieved that she addressed Kaitlyn, and ignored him.

"I've had a positive pregnancy test," Kaitlyn replied. "I conceived two weeks ago."

"I see." The nurse nodded. "Well, you've done the right thing coming in so quickly. Did you bring a sample?"

"Oh yes." Kaitlyn reached into her handbag and produced a pot of bright yellow urine, plonking it on the desk as though it were nothing unusual.

Perhaps it isn't, he thought. *Perhaps women are so used to such things that walking around with pots of urine in their bags is as passé as carrying lipstick.* How would he know?

"Excellent." The nurse unscrewed the top. Right there. On the desk. Neither woman batting an eyelid at it. She opened the drawer and unwrapped a test strip, dipped it in the urine and then left it on a piece of tissue whilst she poured the sample down the sink and threw the used pot into a yellow bin.

"It'll just take a minute to get the result," she continued, "no need to scan you or fill in any paperwork or anything, there's no credit charge for the pills." She opened another drawer and pulled out a small box of tablets. "There" – she glanced at the pee stick – "I can see the second line forming already. So, here you are. One now, there's a water cooler in the waiting room, then one in six hours' time. Stock up on sanitary towels, if you haven't already. You might need to rest today, but you'll be fine to work tomorrow."

"Oh, no," Kaitlyn said, "I don't want pills, thank you. I just want the confirmation certificate, and to book a midwife. I'm having the baby."

"I see." The nurse made no effort to hide her disapproval, sighing audibly as she retracted her hand and put the pills back in the drawer. "Well, in that case we'll have to go through all the paperwork." She walked across the room, and pulled a large folder from the filing cabinet. As she sat back down, he noticed the small silver crucifix, embedded with three tiny diamonds, pinned to her lapel. A convert to the New Church. Their views were finding their way into everything these days. Apparently even into private medical consultations. Surely it was unprofessional to be so obviously judgemental of a young woman's choices?

"Of course, no problem," Kaitlyn replied, wearing a saccharine smile, "thank you so much." She either hadn't picked up on the nurse's disdain, or was being overly cheerful in order to annoy her more. He suspected the latter.

"I'll need you to fill these in." She thrust a pile of papers toward Kaitlyn.

"Perfect."

"Black ink. Print in capitals."

"Super." Kaitlyn produced her own pen from her handbag, still smiling.

"And I'll have to scan you for credit deductions."

"Oh, no need for that," Kaitlyn said. "I'm not using credit." She elbowed Henry in the ribs. "He's paying."

He'd been quite enjoying watching the dance between the two women, and admiring Kaitlyn's tactics, until she brought him into it.

"Is that so?" The nurse raised an eyebrow at him.

"Yes," he replied, when Kaitlyn nudged him again. "Yes, that's correct."

"And who might you be?"

"Oh, he's the baby's father." Kaitlyn grinned, and put her hand on his arm.

Right about now would be a good time for a heart attack, Henry thought. Or perhaps a random sinkhole, or fluke lightning strike. Anything to end this excruciating moment. He opened his mouth to speak, but didn't have the slightest clue what to say. Kaitlyn coughed to stop herself from chuckling.

"So... you're *together*?" the nurse asked, flicking her eyes up and down Henry's body, nose scrunched as if he smelled of rotten fish.

"Is that one of the questions on the form?" Kaitlyn's pitch was still high, almost lyrical.

"No. But—"

"Well then" – her tone dropped – "I don't suppose it's any of your business, is it?"

The dance was over. Kaitlyn wasn't smiling any more. She stared directly at the nurse.

"Miss Thomas, have you thought this through?"

Kaitlyn turned the pages of the document in front of her, scanning the text. "Nope," she said, "can't see that question on here either. Are these new forms? You don't seem very familiar with them."

The nurse let out a small huff of a laugh. "Have it your way then, dear," she said. "It's your mistake to make."

"I'm glad we could agree." Kaitlyn turned her attention to completing the forms, leaving Henry to suffer the awkward silence. He couldn't meet the nurse's eye, instead staring at the floor, listening to the ticking of the clock on the wall and the scratching of pen on paper, desperately wishing each second away.

"There," Kaitlyn said at last. "All done. So, if you would be so kind, I'd like my confirmation certificate, and for you to book me a midwife."

The nurse pulled a pink form from her drawer, scribbled her signature on it and shoved it at Kaitlyn. "There's your confirmation," she said, "but I can't book you a midwife, not until you've completed the course."

"Course?" Henry asked. "What course?"

"She will be required to watch an educational film, and answer questions. By herself, you won't be permitted to accompany her. It's so she can be sure she's making the right decision."

"What film?"

"The Reality of Reproducing," the nurse said, with a wry self-satisfied smile. "We find it's very instructional. Helps women make a more informed choice."

"Scares them into making the choice you want them to, more like —" he heard the words as they came spilling out from his mouth, and was shocked he'd said them. Maybe Kaitlyn was starting to rub off on him? He glanced at her, and she gave him an approving nod.

"It's vital we ensure women have the correct information, and are making their own decisions. They are the ones who have to go through it, after all."

"Well, I think it sounds empowering," Kaitlyn said, "sign me up."

"There's a session running next Wednesday morning."

"I'll be there with bells on."

Kaitlyn stood up, and Henry followed her lead. They walked out, leaving the nurse staring after them, shaking her head.

"Oh, that was hilarious," Kaitlyn said as they walked to the car, "her *face*!"

"I had no idea it was going to be such an ordeal," Henry said.

"You've got a funny idea of what an ordeal is," she replied. "I don't think getting sarky with a stuck-up nurse really qualifies."

"What about this 'educational film' stuff? Sounds like persuasion tactics to me."

"Oh, it is," Kaitlyn said, "but it's perfectly standard. They just show you scenes of childbirth. Women screaming and all that. Try to put you off. I'm not stupid though, I know it's scaremongering. They show you worst-case scenarios. I mean, people give birth every day, right? If it was really that bad, nobody would do it!"

6

The daylight was fading fast. The low sun elongated her shadow on the gravel, and created swirling patterns of orange and purple on the tinted windows of the New Church. It had been years since she'd last been here. Her fingers curled around the opaque door handle; it felt smaller in her grip than it used to.

She wasn't sure what she was hoping to find inside. Sympathy? Forgiveness? Compassion? Or perhaps answers, though the right questions still eluded her.

The door was unlocked. She stepped through into the nave, her worn plimsolls making no sound on the shiny marble floor. At the end of the aisle, a woman in a yellow habit knelt before the huge silver cross that dominated the space above the pulpit. The light Kaitlyn let in reflected off the three jewels in its centre. "Humility, responsibility and reverence." She whispered the tenents, at once feeling their gravity.

Alerted by the sudden shift in light, the sister stood up from her hassock and turned around. Rochelle, framed in twilight's hues and even more beautiful than Kaitlyn had remembered.

"My goodness." Rochelle hurried up the aisle toward her, hands outstretched, and Kaitlyn wished in that moment that she was still a little girl. Just a child, without sin or remorse. A child deserving of this woman's embrace, and patience. "Kaitlyn" – fingers as smooth and white as porcelain prised

her calloused hands from her sides and held them gently – "it's been such a long time."

"Yes," she replied, not knowing how else to respond. Hoping Rochelle would know the words to say to coax out her own, just like she always had before.

"I heard about your brother's accident. I'm so sorry." Rochelle reached up and tucked a strand of Kaitlyn's hair behind her ear.

"Thank you. I'm sorry, I'm sorry I stopped coming to church. I'm sorry I've turned up like this, I just didn't know what else to do."

"Hush now. There is nothing so large as to be an obstacle to God's love. You're here now; all else is past."

Rochelle drew Kaitlyn's head to her shoulder, and she found she couldn't hold back the tears any longer. Was it God's presence that had opened the floodgate, or Rochelle's words? She didn't know, but the sweet and sharp relief of letting them flow was at once exhilarating and exhausting. What else is there left, when all is so bleak, but to succumb to the embrace of sympathetic arms?

Jack in a coma. Finn gone. Not one spark of hope, or love, left, anywhere in her life. Nothing to do but to beg for divine intervention, or at least understanding.

"What made you come to see me today, Kaitlyn?" Rochelle asked at last, when the shuddering sobs had subsided.

"I just needed to talk things through. Get some guidance."

"I see." Rochelle gestured to the pew, and they sat beside each other, still holding hands. "Well, I'm very glad you did. I was worried for a moment you might be looking for someone to conduct the service. I'd hate to have had to disappoint you."

"The service?"

"Jack's funeral. I had a lot of respect for your brother, Kaitlyn. You know that. But, he wasn't a member of the church, so my hands are tied. Whatever my personal feelings, we can only perform those rites for our parishioners."

"He's not dead."

"Oh, I'm sorry. I just assumed. I heard he was in a coma?"

"Yes. He is."

"Still?"

Kaitlyn took a deep breath and withdrew her hand from Rochelle's. Without looking up from the floor, she explained it all. How Jack was still asleep, and no one knew if he would ever wake up, or what condition he would be in if he did. How everyone was pressuring her to turn off his life support. How Finn had called her selfish, and packed his bags.

When she was done, Rochelle let out a deep sigh.

"Well," she said, "you've been through a terrible time, Kaitlyn. You have my deepest sympathy. But you came to me for counsel, and I cannot in good conscience tell you what I know you want to hear."

"What?"

"I know, I know" – she took her hand again, but Kaitlyn instantly withdrew it – "it's not an easy thing for you to hear. Believe me, it's not an easy thing for me to say, but I think Finn's right."

"You think I'm selfish? You think helping my brother is the wrong thing to do?"

"Your brother was not a godly man, Kaitlyn. He loved you, very much. There's no doubt about that. Concern for your well-being was perhaps the only thing he and I had in common. But he was misguided. Prone to flights of hedonism and fantasy. You need look no further than that awful bike of his to see that. A reckless and irresponsible indulgence that flies against the very ethos of a sustainable ecology that God's children are working for. And it was his undoing in the end, wasn't it?"

How dare she? How dare she speak about Jack like that? The rage churning inside Kaitlyn made her dizzy, and blurred her vision. Rochelle no longer looked serene and beautiful. Her face was contorted, her small blemishes amplified, as *if the ugliness of the words she spoke was manifesting itself on her flesh.*

She stood up. "If you're telling me God wants me to kill my brother, then he and I are done with each other." She headed for the door, not looking back. Not wanting to see the hideous creature that the woman she had once so admired had morphed into.

"You're doing him a disservice, Kaitlyn," Rochelle called after her. "His love for you was the best of him. He wouldn't want this for you. Don't make everything he did for you be in vain."

She slammed the door behind her, vowing never to pass through it again.

"C'mon." Gina pulled her by the hand, snapping her out of her memories. "It's just up here. She's totally whackadoodle but she's harmless. So just humour her, okay?"

"Sure." Kaitlyn covered her nose with her mouth to try to block out the pungent smell of the river. "Whatever you say." The rats were even more prevalent here than in the alley by Jared's. They scuttled along the bank, squealing at the paradise of fly-tipped waste man had created for them. She wished she'd worn sturdier shoes, or brought a torch. The dirt track was uneven and in the half-light of dusk she couldn't tell whether the occasional squelch underfoot was a patch of mud or something foul and rotten.

When they reached the cottage, Gina fiddled with the rusty latch on the old wooden gate until it squeaked open. The whole fence would probably come down with a hard shove, broken and leaning as it was. Stepping into the overgrown garden, the small, ramshackle house at first appeared to be in darkness.

"It doesn't look like she's home," Kaitlyn whispered, keeping very close to Gina's side.

"No electric," Gina replied, "she does everything by candlelight. And it's not because she can't afford it, I reckon she must be rolling in it with all the deals she makes. Look." she pointed to the first floor window, and Kaitlyn could just make out a dim orb of flickering light dancing behind the curtain. "It's a wonder she hasn't burned the place down yet. Told you she was cuckoo."

Gina lifted the large ornamental door knocker that was more tarnish than brass and banged it loudly three times against the heavy oak door. Kaitlyn was still staring at the upstairs window, and watched the flickering light fade from view. "Takes her a while," Gina said, "she's like a tortoise."

Both girls jumped a little when the small shutter in the door was pulled back. "Who is it?" two eyes, one light blue and the other covered in a milky film, peered through the hole.

"Hi, Martha, it's Gina."

The door rattled as bolts were pulled back. "Gina, my dear." Martha's voice was soft and warm. "How are you? Have you brought the scan pictures for me?"

"No, not yet. I've brought a friend. She needs your help."

"I see." Martha was smiling as she opened the door. Kaitlyn couldn't help but think that Gina's description of her as a tortoise was incredibly apt, and not just because of her speed. A tiny woman, no more than five foot, her neck seemed too long and her head too big. She wore a torn and faded black habit, but no head covering. The garment was far too big for her shrivelled frame; it trailed around her feet and had been rolled up at the sleeves. Her wrinkles were far deeper than Henry's. The lines in her face looked unnatural, sickening. Kaitlyn shivered a little at the sight of her.

"And who might you be, my dear?" Martha asked Kaitlyn.

"Kaitlyn," she replied. "Kaitlyn Thomas."

"Well, Kaitlyn Thomas, it's a pleasure to make your acquaintance." Martha reached out her spindly, withered hand and Kaitlyn realised with horror she was expected to shake it. The old nun let out a laugh that was as close to a witch's cackle as she had ever heard in real life. "No need to fear, child." She winked her blind eye. "Old age may be considered disgusting these days, but it still isn't contagious!"

Oh God. Her repulsion had been obvious. Gina scowled

at her, and Kaitlyn could feel the heat rising in her face. She tried to smile and took Martha's hand. Cold, it was so cold. The skin was gnarled and loose. Just like the oversized habit, it seemed to hang from her as though she were wearing flesh that didn't fit. And, oh good heaven, she could feel the bones. It was like shaking hands with the reaper himself.

The desire to wipe her hand on her skirt was almost overwhelming, but she settled for putting it in her pocket, resolving not to touch anything until she'd scrubbed it.

"I take it you are... in the family way?" Martha asked, looking her up and down.

"I... what?"

"She means are you up the spout," Gina interjected, "and yes, she is."

"Very well, follow me." Martha picked up the candle from where she had left it on the windowsill and slowly shuffled inside. Gina gestured to Kaitlyn to go first, so she stepped through the door into the dark, cramped cottage. They followed Martha, at snail's pace, to the back room past dusty bookshelves and cobweb-covered antiques. She set the candle down on a small table and pulled a box of matches from her pocket. She moved around the small drawing room, lighting candles as she went.

A wooden crucifix took centre stage above the unlit fireplace. Upon it, a horrific plastic depiction of Christ stared down at the room, blood dripping from the thorny crown on his head. It looked like something out of a horror movie. Was this really how the old nuns chose to honour God? By putting up figurines of half-naked Christs with their faces contorted in pain?

'The old ways were dark and sadistic' – Rochelle had told her that many times. Certainly, the image of torture and blood sacrifice in front of her seemed more suited to the altar of a devil worshipper than a follower of enlightenment and love. But Martha bowed to it, and crossed herself before bringing the crucifix she wore around her neck to her lips and kissing it.

"Now, my dear," she said, pulling a large leather-bound

ledger from the shelf next to the fireplace, "how far along are you?"

"About three weeks," Kaitlyn replied.

Martha began scribbling in the book. "That's lovely," she said, "an autumn baby. Well, don't you worry, Kaitlyn, I'll find your son or daughter a wonderful family, no doubt about that."

Son or daughter. She hadn't thought in those terms before. She'd always just referred to the child as 'the baby', even in her mind.

"I'll need you to bring me scan pictures, when you have them of course, then we will be able to really get the ball rolling."

Kaitlyn gazed around the room while Martha carried on writing in her book. The left hand wall was covered in photographs. Children with their parents. Happy, smiling families in various poses. First days at school, birthday parties, even graduations.

"My families," Martha said when she saw Kaitlyn looking, "they like to send me updates and mementoes from time to time. Just look at them, dear. All those happy children, all those happy parents. So many lives changed for the better, because of courageous young women like you."

"Courageous?"

"These are dark times, my dear. End times. Times when even the churches themselves are overrun by the devil's prophets. The Antichrist walks among us, and the sinners are deluded by his pretty temples and clever words. To do what's right, in times such as these, is courageous indeed."

"You think I'm doing what's right?"

Martha nodded. "Unquestionably, dear. Unquestionably."

"But I'm unmarried, don't you believe getting pregnant is a sin?"

"We're all sinners, my dear, we're all sinners. That's why he paid such a price for our souls" – she gestured to the crucifix – "but the way to absolve one sin is not to commit another. Life is sacred, my dear. And motherhood is the purest act of love and selflessness on this earth. You would not have been given this child if this child was not meant to be. Your body has a higher calling now, a purpose. And you have chosen to honour that, just like Mary did."

Martha pointed to the painted portrait hanging in the centre of her wall of photographs. The Virgin Mary, looking serene and wise. Just like a mother should. Just like Rochelle had always seemed.

"She was unmarried too, was she not? Suppose she had subscribed to all this modern nonsense, suppose she had let those idolaters tell her to kill her child! Where might humanity be then, without its saviour? No one but God can choose the hours of our births and deaths. To think otherwise is an aberration, an affront to the Lord."

What a load of nonsense. Gina was right, the old nun was stark raving nuts. Mary, if the story was to be believed, had conceived immaculately. Her baby the child of God himself, no less. Hardly to be compared to a young, not-exactly-virginal woman who was carrying the offspring of a sixty-year-old atheist who swore like it was going out of fashion.

Martha laughed again, filling the musty room with her eerie, throaty chuckles.

"Oh, I know you're not a virgin, dear," she said. Kaitlyn's skin prickled. "And I know this" – she poked her finger toward Kaitlyn's abdomen – "is not the second coming! But the principle remains. Bringing life to this world is a sacred, divine task. Maybe you are not a saintly Madonna, and maybe your child is not a prophet of the Lord. But it will answer someone's prayers, will it not? Somewhere, my dear, there is a barren woman who pleads with heaven every day to bring her a child. For her, this child is the answer to the yearnings of her heart. And you, by your selfless actions, are indeed a saint."

The baby she carried was the answer to someone's prayers. Martha didn't know how right she was.

Kaitlyn looked again at the photographs on the wall. The rows of happy faces, the contentment in the women's eyes. Families. Real families. Blissful just in the act of being.

"Do you know what a mother is, Kaitlyn?" Martha's hand on her shoulder somehow felt warm, despite the coldness of her skin. She thought about her own mother, about how far removed her memories of childhood were from any of these picture-perfect images.

"No," she answered honestly, "no I don't."

"A mother is someone who puts their child first, above all else. Just like you're doing by coming to me instead of one their death-clinics. You're giving your child the chance of life, and a wonderful family. Kaitlyn, you are a mother, in the truest sense of the word. Don't ever doubt that."

A mother? Her stomach lurched. The onset of morning sickness, or something else? She hadn't thought of herself as a mother, just as she hadn't thought of the embryo inside her as her son or daughter. Would her baby be on this wall someday? Grinning as they held hands with the loving couple they called Mum and Dad? And if she were to return to Martha's house and gaze at the photos then, would she even know which one was her child?

"Well, thanks, Martha" – Gina grabbed her by the arm – "but we ought to get going, if that's everything?"

"Oh yes," Martha replied, "that's all I need for now. But just be sure to bring me your scans as soon as you have them, both of you, it's very important."

"Will do. C'mon, Kaitlyn." She pulled Kaitlyn away from the wall of pictures and toward the front door. "We need to shift it, the lights will be going out soon."

Martha chuckled again. "I'm afraid you're too late, girls. The darkness is already upon us." Her laughter grew louder and louder as she cackled at her own, somewhat macabre, joke. Kaitlyn could still hear her when they were halfway down the garden path.

"See?" Gina said. "Totally batshit."

"Yeah…" Kaitlyn replied, but she couldn't stop thinking about the photographs, or Martha's definition of motherhood. "Totally."

7

Henry groaned when he saw the tinsel. Christmas had always been something he'd endured through gritted teeth, rather than enjoyed. But Chloe loved it, and never let his grumpiness distract her from her festive spirit. One year she'd even bought him a grey woolly jumper with *Bah Humbug* written on the front. David was about six or seven then, and he'd laughed so much he'd had to rush to the bathroom.

David. His heart sank as he watched Chloe hanging up the stockings, dancing to the godawful tinny version of 'Rocking Around The Christmas Tree' that was blaring from the radio as she did so. She didn't know yet. He'd barely been able to confess it to himself; the court summons had been hastily stuffed into the bottom drawer of the bureau as soon as it arrived. He'd had more pressing matters to worry about, what with Kaitlyn ovulating. Well, that's what he'd told himself at the time. But, that was weeks ago and, apart from making a mental note of the date – six months from now – he'd not looked at it again.

He wasn't sure what to do. He couldn't spare any of the money from the equity release for lawyers, not if he was going to cover pregnancy costs and keep Chloe in Hepraxin until the investment paid off. He supposed he'd have to represent himself. It wouldn't make any difference, he'd lose no matter what he did. No point throwing money away on a brief. The house would be transferred into David's name, and he'd be prevented from selling it. It didn't even matter any more, not with the baby on the way. The money to keep Chloe with him would come. The only real concern now was whether David's lawyers would argue for more than just the material assets.

Would he try to take control of Chloe's future? Get himself declared her legal next of kin, with power of attorney, if his claim against Henry's capacity was successful? Would he force her to Move On?

He didn't think so. David was selfish; he only cared about protecting his inheritance. Once the house was legally his, he'd have no reason to go through the rigmarole of taking over control of Chloe's care. There was nothing to be gained, no reason to do it, except maybe pure spite. But, for all David's faults, he didn't think him capable of cruelty for cruelty's sake. But he couldn't be sure.

The only thing he could be sure of was that David and the kids wouldn't be coming for Christmas, and he'd have to tell Chloe why.

"Oh, there you are." She turned around to face him, eyes shining. "I wondered where you'd got to. Grab the other end of these, would you?" She handed him a string of fairy lights, and he dutifully began untangling the knotted-up end while she weaved around the tree, zigzagging them through its branches.

"We're a bit late this year, aren't we?" she said. "Sorry about that. Bad timing for me to have to one of my turns, eh?"

"Oh don't be silly. I'm just glad you're okay. You always loved Christmas, didn't you?"

"I really do." She moved round and round the tree, almost skipping, as if it were a maypole. "I don't suppose you've reserved a turkey, have you?"

"No, love. Not yet."

"Ah, never mind. I expect there's still some left, we'll need a big one though. Or two smaller ones, if not. They've got quite an appetite these days, those kids."

"Listen, darling, David's not coming. Or the kids."

"Oh? Is Carolyn having them over?" Chloe asked, looking puzzled. Carolyn never cooked. Most Christmases she went away, somewhere up north with whoever her latest fancy man happened to be. She hated all the forced merriment and tackiness even more than Henry did.

"No. I mean, I don't know but I doubt it. David and I..." Chloe was rummaging through the box of baubles, but Henry's tone made her stop and look at him. "We had an argument."

Chloe exhaled and waved her hand dismissively. "Oh, is that all?" she said, returning to the task of separating the white and gold baubles from the red and green ones. "You boys are always arguing about something, you'll both have forgotten what you're even angry about by then."

"Not this time," Henry said, taking one of the red and green ornaments and hanging it in the centre of the tree.

Chloe shook her head, and moved the decoration a few centimetres to the right, "Why? What's going on?"

"I should have told you before, but I didn't want to worry you."

"Well, you're worrying me *now,* Henry Morris, so spit it out before *next* Christmas comes."

"Okay." He took her hand, and squeezed it. "He's taking me to court."

"He's what?"

"I know. It's unbelievable isn't it? Ungrateful little sod, everything we've done for him and this is how he—"

"Never mind all that," Chloe interrupted him, "save your ranting for after you've told me what's going on. What is he taking you to court for?"

"He's claiming I lack capacity, trying to get the house put into his name."

"Why ever should he do that?"

"To stop us from selling it."

"Selling it? Where did he get a fool notion like that from?

Why on earth would we sell it? Whatever have you been saying to him?"

"Why do you assume this is my fault?" Henry asked, feeling a little irked that Chloe didn't automatically take his side.

"Because I know you," she replied, "you must have given him some cause to be worried. Probably one of your jokes, or else you said something in the heat of the moment that you didn't mean."

"I did no such thing. In fact, it's because of you."

He shouldn't have said that. Why did he say that? Her face fell, and the pained look in her eyes hit him like a sucker punch to the heart. The very last thing he wanted to do was dull the shine in those sapphires. Hadn't he been pleading with the fates just a few weeks ago? Promising to himself, and to the unknown ether, that if only she came back to him he would do everything he could to be the husband she deserved? How quickly the heartfelt oaths made in times of woe fade to dust when normality returns.

"Me?" she said. "What did I do?"

He'd have to sugarcoat it. Play it down. She may walk and talk like the Chloe of old, but she was ill. Underneath the clean, dry clothes and the plans she was making there was still an ailing brain that was fighting its assailant. Hepraxin may be helping, but the disease would continue battling, looking for any way to conquer her, to claim her for its own. She shouldn't have to deal with his problems too.

"Nothing, my love." He stepped forward, put his hands on her shoulders and kissed the top of her head. "You didn't do a goddamn thing. It's me. He thinks I'm not capable of looking after you. He loves you, see? Wants you to have someone better than me taking care of you."

"But that's silly," she said, "I know I wasn't quite myself last week, but I'm fine now, aren't I?"

"Better than fine. The weather is fine, a nice bottle of Merlot is fine. *You* are perfect."

She laughed, and batted him away. "Well then, just call him. Or I'll call him. Thank him for his concern, but explain that everything's okay now."

"I don't think it's a good idea, Chloe. He's dead set on getting the house transferred. Even if he sees you're alright now, he's worried we'll sell it out from under him. I wouldn't be surprised if that wife of his, or his scheming mother, had a hand in it."

"But Christmas will be very odd without them." She put the baubles she was holding down, all joy in the preparations gone. He couldn't bear it. As much as he disliked Christmas, seeing her lose her festive cheer was a thousand times worse than putting up with crappy songs and ridiculous paper hats. "Isn't there anything we can do?"

"I don't think so," he replied with a heavy heart. "I know you like to think the best of him, Chloe, but he's a selfish man when all's said and done."

"He's just young," she replied, "he's building a life, he hasn't seen as much as we have. They all think of themselves first at that stage. Give him time, he'll come around."

"I used to think it was just his generation, just a sign of the times. But they're not all like that."

"All who?"

"All young people, they're not all the same." He took a deep breath; he'd never get a better in than this. It was time to bring up the subject of Kaitlyn. "In fact, I met this young girl at the hospital, when I was there getting your pills. She really made me see things differently."

"Oh yes? Who was she?"

Henry told her all about Kaitlyn. How feisty she was on the outside, but how vulnerable underneath. He explained about Jack, her eviction, the skyrise apartment with the elevator from hell. He even told her that Kaitlyn was pregnant, though he left out the part about her having a baby for money, as well as the fact he was its father.

"Goodness," Chloe said when he was finished. "What an

awful lot for a young woman to be dealing with. Doesn't she have a mother nearby, or a father?"

Henry remembered Kaitlyn's comments about her mother's lifestyle. "No," he said. "I don't think she has anyone. I don't think she had much of an upbringing, her brother mostly took care of her from what I can gather."

"Well," Chloe said, picking up the baubles again, "that settles it then."

"Settles what?"

"We can't sit around stuffing our faces and drinking eggnog while that poor girl spends Christmas alone, or at her brother's bedside, with no presents or dinner! She'll have to come here, we'll have far too much food for just the two of us. It's the least we can do."

Now that she brought it up, the thought of Kaitlyn all by herself on Christmas, pregnant, alone and penniless, was hideous. But then, the thought of her sitting across the table from Chloe, eating dinner and pulling crackers with her, all the while incubating his foetus in her abdomen, was a bit unnerving.

But, seeing Kaitlyn smile as she tucked into a decent meal, giving her a shiny present topped with one of Chloe's metallic bows... well, that was a very pleasant thought indeed.

"I'll ask her," Henry said, "you're right, of course. It's the decent thing to do."

Chloe beamed and kissed him on the cheek before hanging the last of the baubles on the tree.

"Wonderful," she said, "we'll have to get her something nice. A scarf perhaps? Or one of those sets. You know, with the gloves and hat and everything. They do some lovely ones this time of year. Now, I just need the star." She fished around in the box and pulled out the tatty, yellowed star that always sat atop their tree. "There it is!"

"It's seen better days, hasn't it?" Henry said. "Perhaps we ought to pick up a new one when we go into town. They're pretty cheap, you know."

"No," Chloe said, and he was shocked at the emphatic tone, "*this* is our star. I don't want another, ever."

"Alright, love. Alright." He took a step back, worried the dementia might be peeking out from behind its curtain. "Whatever you'd like."

She nodded, and tried to reach the top of the tree. But even on tiptoes she couldn't quite place the star on the highest branch. "Let me," Henry said, and she handed the ragged, fading ornament to him. He turned it over in his hand, and gasped. There, on the back, a name was engraved: *Heidi*.

Beside his infant daughter's name was a date. Just one date. The date of her birth, and the date of her death.

Every year. Every year that star had been placed on their tree. Every year Heidi's memento had been there, through the dinners and the gift-giving. Always looking down on them, always a part of Christmas at the Morrises'. How could he have forgotten that it was the star Chloe's own mother had given her when she was pregnant, to be hung on the tree. He'd never realised she had carved Heidi's name into the back of it, but he should have realised it was special to her nonetheless.

"I'm sorry," he said, pulling Chloe close, fighting back his tears. "Oh, Chloe. I'm so sorry."

8

She'd never been to such a big house. It had a front garden. Not a patch of uniformly square lawn like the cabin-houses, but an *actual* garden with bushes and flowers. His gas-guzzler sat on the gravelled driveway that led to a large red door, upon which someone, probably his wife, had hung a holly wreath. Four windows were visible. *Four*. On one side of the house. How many did they have altogether?

No wonder Henry was upset that he couldn't sell it; you could pump all manner of drugs into someone for twenty years or more with the money this place could fetch.

She felt extremely self-conscious walking up the driveway, clutching a small blue present in her hands. Why did she agree to this? Surely, it was going to be excruciating. But then, spending the day alone, or chatting to a comatose Jack, wouldn't exactly fill her with festive cheer. There was something about Christmas that made loneliness unbearable. Even if you were generally the type of person who was quite content in their own company. Somehow, being alone on Christmas was the epitome of failure, and misery.

The chance to have a decent dinner had been quite high on her list of reasons for saying yes to Henry's invite. She was supposed to be eating for two, but lately she'd barely eaten enough for one, and certainly nothing as enticing as the roast turkey and sweet potatoes Henry had promised.

She rang the bell, adjusting her position on the doorstep several times while she waited for it to be answered. Not too close, she didn't want to seem overbearing. Were her shoes okay? She checked the bottom of them for mud, or would this be the kind of place where you had to take your shoes off? Shit. A wriggle of her toes confirmed her sock had a hole in the end.

The door opened and there stood Henry, smiling. "I'm glad you came," he said, "I was worried you wouldn't."

His sincerity made her relax a little. "I almost didn't," she confessed.

"Well come in, come in. Don't stand on ceremony. Chloe's in the kitchen. She won't let me anywhere near the dinner, apparently I'm a hindrance."

"I brought her a present," Kaitlyn said, feeling embarrassed at the shoddy wrapping, and the cheap contents within, as she held it out.

"That's very sweet of you," Henry replied. "You didn't have to do that."

"It's not very good," she blurted out. "I'm sorry."

"Chloe will love it," he said, taking Kaitlyn's coat and hanging it on the bannister.

"How do you know that? You don't know what it is."

"I know Chloe." Henry grinned. "You'll see what I mean. Come through, make yourself at home."

The house was light and airy. In the lounge, winter sun streamed through the bay windows, leaving square patches of light on the emerald green sofas. The enormous tree was next to the fireplace, where stockings were hung amidst a string of tiny silver bells. Beyond a wide, textured archway was the dining table – covered in a cloth of gold and white. The silverware sparkled as it reflected the changing colours of the fairy lights hung around the imposing oak bookcase that nestled in the corner. Each place had been carefully set with its own tinted-glass goblet, filled with a silver napkin that had been folded so the top protruded in a point. She had never seen such a beautifully arranged table before, let alone sat at one.

"Chloe," Henry bellowed, "Kaitlyn's here."

The clattering and clinking noises that had been coming from behind the kitchen door stopped abruptly. The first sound Kaitlyn ever heard Chloe make was a squeal of excitement.

"Oh, how lovely." Her voice was high, but not screechy. There was something very girlish, and yet self-assured, about its tone. "Hold on, I'll be right there."

The kitchen door opened, and Chloe emerged. She was older than Henry, that was the first surprise. By a fair few years, judging by the wrinkles. Her hair was mostly white, but with a dash of sandy blonde here and there. Either she hadn't gone completely grey yet, or she'd been dying it until recently. She was a little shorter than Kaitlyn, and much fuller-figured. Her skin hung loose around her neck, and the crevices that snaked outwards from her eyes as she smiled seemed to add emphasis to her ruddy cheeks.

But the thing that surprised Kaitlyn the most was how beautiful she was.

Taken on their own, each of the aspects of her would be considered undesirable. She was old, short, a little overweight, her skin too loose and her blouse too tight. But, when the whole package came together – topped off with those sparkling eyes and that enormous smile – she was radiant.

Kaitlyn had often read about smiles that could light up a room; they were a fairly common fixture in the fiction pages of the trashy mags Gina left behind at work. But she'd never thought them real, until now.

Chloe hurried across the room. "Kaitlyn." She threw her arms around her before planting a kiss on each cheek. Her embrace was warm, and she smelled of bread and magnolia. "I'm so thrilled you could make it, Henry's told me so much about you."

"I... I..." The sincerity in the old woman's words left Kaitlyn struggling to know how to respond. Had anyone, ever, been so genuinely pleased to meet her? "I brought you a present." She held out the parcel, which looked even tattier now that she had been nervously fiddling with its edges.

Chloe put her hand to her heart. "Oh my. How incredibly sweet of you, there really was no need." She took the gift, turning it over in her hands, studying it. "Oh, I wonder what it is? May I open it now? I never was very good at waiting."

"Of course," Kaitlyn replied, though she wasn't looking forward to the disappointment once Chloe saw what was inside.

Chloe's fingers shook a little, she noticed. But when she peeled back the wrapping paper, she squeaked in delight at the cheap, unimaginative box of humbugs inside. "Oh, my absolute favourites, how did you know?" She poked Henry on his arm. "Did you tell her, you rascal?"

"No, love," Henry replied, "I didn't say a word."

"Well, how bizarre then. We must be on the same wavelength, Kaitlyn. Oh, I shall enjoy these. I think I'll tuck into them later, when that film's on I want to watch."

It was an extreme reaction to a box of humbugs. From anyone else it would have felt forced, cringey even. But she'd never met anyone else like Chloe. The sheer love of life radiated from her, as though she were surrounded by an aura of happiness. No wonder Henry loved her so much. It was impossible not to smile when you were around someone so infectiously cheerful.

"Dinner's almost ready," Chloe said, "you two take a seat. Henry, pour Kaitlyn a drink, would you? I'll just finish dishing up."

She dashed off into the kitchen, and Kaitlyn turned to Henry. "She's lovely," she said.

"I know," Henry replied, pulling out a chair for Kaitlyn.

"What the hell is she doing with you?"

He roared with laughter. "I've been asking myself the same question for thirty years. Drink? Not wine, I take it?"

"Just water, thanks."

174

Henry poured her a glass of water from the ornate jug that sat in the middle of the table. It had ice cubes and slices of lemon floating in it, and she couldn't remember ever tasting something so refreshing. He busied himself opening a bottle of wine, and as she sat sipping her own drink she could hear Chloe humming to herself in the kitchen.

No wonder Henry couldn't let her go. This life he had was as close to paradise as she had ever seen. How could anyone have this bliss, and stand to lose it? It would be worse than never having it at all.

9

It was one of the most enjoyable Christmas dinners he could remember. Certainly, it beat having to make polite conversation with the ever-critical Fiona like he'd had to for the past decade, ever since David had decided to marry a hippy version of his mother. Watching Chloe try to accommodate her every whim with a smile, while his daughter-in-law rolled her eyes at every perceived misstep and never once showed any gratitude, always boiled his blood. But he knew how important Christmas, and family, were to Chloe so he always kept his trap shut.

It was a relief to savour the epic meal in company he actually enjoyed for once.

Kaitlyn was obviously nervous at first, which was hardly a surprise given that she was being served food by the wife of the man whose baby she was carrying. But, as she always did, Chloe put their guest at ease with her warmth and sincerity. By the time the sprouts were spooned from their buttery tureen onto Kaitlyn's plate, she was visibly more relaxed.

"I think this is the nicest meal I've ever had, Mrs Morris," she said, tucking in to Chloe's exquisite sweet potatoes.

"Oh please, call me Chloe." His wife smiled. "I never was one for formality, especially between friends."

By the time he came back from a bathroom break in between courses, the two of them were giggling like schoolgirls.

"What's so funny?" he asked.

"Chloe was just telling me about your first date," Kaitlyn said, wiping at her eyes with the serviette, not in the slightest bit concerned that it was disposable.

"You remember, Henry," Chloe said, reaching across and putting her hand on his arm. "That waiter, with the droopy baguettes! Poor Henry, he wasn't used to being a toy boy. He was so on edge."

"I was not!"

"Oh yes you were. You were twitchy, always looking around at everyone, worried what they must think about you being on a date with an older woman!"

Over figgy pudding the conversation moved on to Kaitlyn's job and she regaled a delighted Chloe with anecdotes of awkward customers. The two of them gabbled so fast Henry couldn't get a word in edgeways, but he didn't mind. It was lovely to see them both so animated. Chloe congratulated Kaitlyn on her pregnancy, but steered clear of any topics or questions that might upset her. He knew she would. She wanted to give the poor girl a break from her troubles.

If anything, the afternoon passed too swiftly. Most years he couldn't wait for guests to be gone. As soon as they were out the door, after the traditional fanfare of insincere thanks and forced kisses, he'd change into his new pyjamas – a gift that Chloe bought him each year – and finally relax. But this time he felt a pang of disappointment when the day drew to a close.

After their third game of Scrabble, Kaitlyn put on the brand new hat, scarf and gloves Chloe had selected for her, and made her way to the door.

"You're not walking," Henry said, "I'll drive you home."

"I couldn't ask you to do that," Kaitlyn said, "I've taken up too much of your Christmas already."

"Don't be silly," Chloe said, adjusting Kaitlyn's blue scarf so it sat correctly, "you *were* Christmas! It made our day you coming to spend time with us, didn't it, Henry?" Henry nodded. "And anyway, you're not asking, he's offering. And I'm insisting. I couldn't possibly stand the thought of you walking all that way in the cold by yourself. Scarf or no scarf."

Kaitlyn looked as though she might cry as she accepted the ride home. Chloe hugged her tight. "Now, don't be a stranger. Please? Come by any time, any time at all."

"She means it, you know," Henry said as he started the car. "She really liked you."

"I really liked her too," Kaitlyn replied, "maybe too much."

"What do you mean?"

"I feel guilty. You know, about our secret. I felt as though we were deceiving her."

He sighed. "Yeah. You and me both. But we have to remember we're doing it for her, and Jack. The end justifies the means, as they say."

"You never told me she was older than you."

"Ten years," he said, "but damn, it could have been twenty, I'd not have cared. You don't meet many people like her in a lifetime."

"I don't think I've met a single one," she replied. "But then, I've never met anyone like Jack, either. I mean, he's nothing like Chloe. He's not sweet and gentle, at least not to anyone else. But he always is to me."

He heard the crack in her voice, and took his eyes off the road briefly to glance at her. The tip of her nose was bright red, something that always happened when she was trying not to cry. A little tell he had picked up on.

"We're right, aren't we?" she asked him. "When you love someone so much, when they love you, you'd do anything. Anything at all."

"What else is there?" he replied, letting go of the gear stick to squeeze her hand. She didn't pull away.

***

When they drove into the skyrise district the noise was deafening. Music, if you could call the cacophony of bone-jarring drumbeats overlaid with shrill electric jazz 'music', blared from an old stereo hanging precariously out of a third-floor window. Upturned waste bins had been set alight, and dozens of young people were milling about. Some dancing, some fighting, all drinking.

"What the hell?" Henry couldn't see a way through the revellers to get to Kaitlyn's block.

"It's just a Christmas party," Kaitlyn said, "just drop me here, it's fine."

"Looks a bit rowdy. Let me walk you to your block."

"Don't be stupid, they're just letting off steam."

"What if they hassle you?"

"Why should they do that? They're just minding their own business, having fun. Anyway, what are you planning on doing? Brandishing your false leg as a weapon?" she asked, and he realised his age once more. "Seriously, it's a tradition round here. Even when I was kid, there were always block parties at Christmas. They've not even got going yet, by ten o'clock tonight the place will be kicking."

"Well, just get in quick then before it gets worse," he said, disturbed by the thought. "I don't like it."

"You worry too much. I grew up round here, remember?"

"Okay," he said, though he didn't think it was. It didn't sit right, letting a young woman walk through a drunken crowd alone. But he was a dinosaur as far as she was concerned. This wasn't his world, not even his era.

"Thanks again," she said, planting a kiss on his cheek. "I'll call you when I get the scan appointment, yeah?"

"Yes. Yes, of course. Or before that, you know, if you want to. If you need anything."

She grinned at him. "You're very sweet, for an old snowflake. Now go home, enjoy your evening with Chloe.

She'll be wondering where you got to if you hang around any longer."

"Right you are."

She got out of the car and started toward her block. He watched as a group of five or six youngsters leaning against the wall raised their beer cans at her and yelled, "Merry Christmas." She waved back at them before turning around and raising her eyebrow at him as if to say, 'See? I know what I'm doing.'

"Alright," he mumbled, "point made."

She raised her hand and made a shooing gesture at him. He smiled back, and put the car in reverse. But he still wasn't comfortable with it. Turning out of the skyrise district, he went right instead of left and pulled into a lay-by. From there, he could see the top storeys of her block, as well as her lounge window. She'd be mortally offended, no doubt, if she knew he was keeping tabs on her, but he'd never rest easy unless he knew she was safely behind that locked door. She might have the street smarts, but he couldn't shake the feeling that human beings couldn't have changed *that* much since he was young. There were always bad apples.

He checked his watch. It would take five minutes at most, give or take the dodgy lift, for her to reach her apartment. Once the light went on in that window, and he knew for certain she was safe, he'd head home and relax.

10

She couldn't help but smile as she weaved her way between the tower blocks toward home. It was nice to have someone care about you. Even if he was over the top in his concern, it was better than having nobody in this world give the slightest crap. Well, nobody who was conscious anyway.

Plus it had been a lovely afternoon, and one hell of a meal. Her stomach ached from being so full; she felt as though she'd never need to eat again. Her new gloves were smooth and warm against her skin and she couldn't recall ever having worn such luxurious fabrics. Come to think of it, she couldn't remember ever receiving such a special gift, apart from Emmy.

Jack had done odd jobs for the neighbours for weeks to buy her the smiling rag doll. It was the only present she'd gotten that Christmas. Mum had slept through the day entirely. Jack didn't get a gift at all. But he hadn't seemed to mind; they'd spent the whole day introducing Emmy to their apartment, making up a little bed for her out of cereal boxes and old clothes. In the evening he'd read them stories and kissed both her and Emmy goodnight, telling them he'd had the best Christmas ever.

God. How could it be? How could it be that she was here, with a belly full of turkey and pudding, and he was alone in a hospital bed with nothing but tubes and beeping machines?

"Merry Christmas!" Two inebriated teenage girls wearing

deely-boppers made out of tin foil and pipe cleaners staggered past her, their arms around each other.

"Merry Christmas," she replied, trying to smile.

"You coming to party?" the taller one asked.

"Nah," she said, "I'll pass. Have a good one."

"We will," they replied in unison, staggering across the concrete toward the source of the music.

Although she had nothing against the traditional Christmas party, she was glad to put the bulk of the revellers, and the noise, behind her when she turned left at the small patch of grass in the centre of the district and headed for her own block.

The celebrations were more sedate away from the central area. Several young guys wearing thick hooded jumpers sat around the blazing bin outside H block, sipping from cans of strong, cheap cider. They glanced up at her and nodded as she walked past. She returned the gesture. Almost there. With such a full stomach, and such heavy eyes, it would be a relief to collapse into bed early.

She turned the last corner and the broken front door was straight ahead. It was much quieter here, though the drumbeat from the street party still pounded in her ears. A small cough made her turn her head and she spotted the scruffy guy pissing against an unlit bin.

"Sorry," she said instinctively when her eyes met his by accident. "Didn't realise you were there."

"S'alright, darlin'. You can look if you want." He grunted a laugh, and stepped out of the shadows, zipping up his flies. He was swaying slightly, and the flick of his eyes up and down her body made her feel uneasy. When he smiled slowly, first sucking his bottom lip in and then letting it slide back through his teeth with a squelch and a click, she turned away and quickened her pace.

"Ain't ya coming to the party, darlin'?" He was following, getting closer.

Don't speed up any more. Don't make it obvious you're

scared. It's all civil right now, keep it that way. If he knows you think he might be dangerous, it might piss him off.

"No," she said, deliberately using a higher pitch, trying to sound happy, friendly even. "I'm shattered. Off to bed."

"This 'ere's your block ain't it?" He was too close now. His shoulder brushed against hers; she could smell the alcohol on his breath. "Up the top, right?"

She didn't want to answer. But, oh God, she didn't want to anger him either. He moved in front of her, blocking her route to the door.

"Wassa matter? Don't you know where you fuckin' live?"

She stepped backward. He stepped forward.

There was no one around. The guys sitting by the burning bin were out of sight now. She glanced at the downstairs windows of her block, and the one to the left, hoping someone might be looking out. He moved closer, she moved back. He stepped right, she stepped left. He threw his cigarette on the ground, she pulled her arms tighter across her body. One step forward, one step back.

The feints and weaves of this menacing dance were driving her backwards toward the side entrance of L block.

Run or scream?

If she bolted, he'd catch her. He was already close enough to reach out and grab her if he wanted to. He was playing. Toying. Waiting for the right moment.

If she screamed, it would go unheeded amidst the thump of the music and the excited shrieks of the partygoers.

Back. Back. Back. Like a cornered rabbit trying to outwit a fox. Her heels hit the concrete step and she was forced to retreat up onto it. She felt the door against her back. He grinned and stretched out his arms, putting one hand on each side of the wide doorway. She slid her left hand behind her back, feeling for the handle. Maybe if she could get into the hallway someone would be there, by the elevators.

"How's about we have a little party of own?" the fluorescent light above the door gave his pocked skin a lurid yellow sheen.

The small scar beneath his eyebrow disappeared among the lines created by his sordid smile.

Her hand closed around the thick, oblong handle and she pushed. It clicked, but the door didn't budge.

It would be the one fucking door in the district that hadn't been vandalised.

"Nowhere to go, little buttercup." His gnarled, hairy fingers stroked her cheek. She flinched. He laughed. "Nowhere to go."

11

Six minutes. He shuffled in the seat, counting the windows again. It was definitely the right one. No movement, no light. She should be there by now.

Perhaps the elevator wasn't working? That would explain it. He slipped the car into first and rolled forward a little so he could see the stairwell windows. Damn. His eyes were too bad. No matter how much he squinted, he'd never be able to make out a figure on the stairs.

Seven minutes. She was probably making her way up the endless flights right now, cursing the building. Probably. Seven minutes wasn't a long time. She could have stopped to chat to a neighbour, or even paused for a breather halfway up. No, it wasn't long at all.

Unless she was in trouble. Then seven minutes would be an eternity.

He tapped his fingers on the steering wheel. "Come on, Kaitlyn. Come on. Switch on the light."

Eight minutes. He couldn't stand it any longer. He made a U-turn and headed back along the dual carriageway. He'd just park up where he dropped her off and have a look, she'd never know.

12

"No need to be so uptight, darlin'." He moved in closer, running his hand across Kaitlyn's breasts. "Just a bit of Christmas cheer, eh?"

He was all around her. There was nothing in her world but him. Her heart beat faster, her mind whirled. The state of panic simultaneously flooding her with adrenaline and paralysis. His hot, wet breath in her face made her eyes sting.

"I'm pregnant," she blurted out in desperation.

"Great." He pulled at her precious new scarf, winding the end of it around his hand to draw her face closer to his. "Won't need a rubber."

His hand moved to his belt. Hers was still gripping the door handle behind her. She let go slowly, inconspicuously, and slid it into her back pocket. While he fiddled with his buckle, she pushed the sharp edges of her keys through her knuckles. When he looked up from his own trousers and reached out for the fastening on hers she pulled her hand from her pocket and swung.

Her fist made contact with the side of his head. It wasn't a good hit; there wasn't enough space behind her to get a decent swing. But it took him by surprise. When he stepped back slightly, she kicked out as hard as she could. She aimed for the knee, but missed by several inches, catching him on the calf instead.

It made him stumble.

Now, Kaitlyn. Now.

She ran. Not toward home, but back round the other side of the block. Toward the party. Toward people.

"Fucking bitch!"

He was only a couple of seconds behind her. She could hear his feet pounding on the concrete. Taking a sharp right turn, she headed for the throng of people dancing and drinking.

He was gaining. She yelled out to the crowd ahead, but no one heard.

Not fast enough. Not close enough. Her feet kept moving, her lungs kept panting, but it wasn't going to be enough.

She reached the patch of grass, looking desperately around for the guys who had been drinking by the fire. But the bin had been doused, and they were gone, leaving only discarded cans and cigarette butts behind.

Too far. The crowd was too far and too loud. He was right behind her now. She scrambled up the grass verge, trying to get higher, trying to be visible.

She tried to scream, but his hand cupped around her mouth and they both toppled to the ground.

13

There were even more people gathered around than before. A mass of bodies jumping and gyrating in time to the godawful incessant pounding of the drumbeat. There was no way through; they jiggled and loitered across every path.

He pulled over a few yards away from them. He couldn't see Kaitlyn's block, let alone her window, from this angle. Walking through this drunken rabble of miscreants wasn't an appealing prospect, but there was no other choice.

Switching off the engine, he leaned forward in his seat, scanning the closest of the crowd. Perhaps she had simply joined in. If he could spot her among them he could avoid having to venture into the chaos.

Young men with three days' stubble and homemade tattoos, girls in miniskirts despite the chill, even some older people mingled in. He spotted a head of dark curls bobbing up and down to the music and thought for a moment it might be her. But when the head's owner turned around they looked nothing like Kaitlyn.

"Nothing for it then," he muttered to himself, unclipping his seatbelt. But before he opened the door, he glanced right and something caught his eye.

A figure on the grass verge beyond the crowd, hands in the air waving. Trying to attract attention, though none of the revellers took any note. Even in the shadowy firelight he could see the long black curls protruding from under her new hat. Kaitlyn. And she was running.

A second figure topped the slight hill behind her. Taller, bigger. The assailant launched himself at Kaitlyn, and Henry saw her fall to the ground.

"Shit!" He turned the key and the engine roared back into life. Flicking the headlights to full beam, he punched at the horn and accelerated toward the gyrating mob.

They all stopped dancing at the sudden noise and blinding headlights, shouting obscenities as they leapt out of the way of the car.

"MOVE," Henry yelled, his foot on the gas. The shocked and inebriated partygoers jeered and screamed.

"Fucking maniac."

"Watch it, Grandad."

Beer can missiles sounded like gunfire as they hit the roof and windows at high speed. But he pressed on, eyes fixed on Kaitlyn. As he neared the verge, the large figure on top of her looked up, shielding his eyes from the piercing beam. Henry slammed the brakes. The bastard got to his feet and turned tail. But in that moment, the angry mob clued in to what was happening. They stopped shouting at Henry, and turned their attention to the fleeing attacker.

"Come back here, you fucking wanker." A well-built lad of no more than twenty led the charge, followed swiftly by at least a dozen roaring young men who hurtled up the verge in pursuit. Two or three of them paused to pick up empty glass bottles. Justice was coming for the bastard, swift and bloody.

The car door was opened by a tall, scrawny teenager and Henry flinched, expecting another foul-mouthed tirade. But the young man held out his hand, and he realised with surprise he meant to help him get out.

"It's okay," Henry said, heaving his prosthetic out of the door, "I can manage."

"I'm really sorry, dude," the teen said, "I think I made a

dent with my can. I didn't know, I thought you were like nutso or something. Trying to kill us, like."

"It's okay." He didn't give a crap about the bodywork, he just wanted to get to Kaitlyn. "Doesn't matter."

Several young women had already helped her to her feet, and stood with their arms around her offering comfort. There was blood on her cheek and mud in her hair. She shook her head as the well-meaning girls held out their drinks for her.

"Kaitlyn," he said softly as he approached. She looked up, her eyes wide and wet.

"Henry?" She pulled away from the cooing women and threw herself into his arms. He pulled her head to his chest and covered her with his arms as she sobbed and shook.

"It's alright," he said, clenching his jaw and swallowing hard against the lump in his throat. "It'll be alright."

"Did anyone see who it was?" one of the women asked.

"It was Nero, from my block," a voice piped up. "Dodgy fucker. Never did like him."

"Has anyone called the police?" Henry asked. A rumble of laughter rippled through the crowd.

"No point," a guy with a bald head and spiky beard replied. "They never come out to us for stuff like this. They don't care. They'd be happiest if we all just killed each other."

"Eh, well. Danny's gone after him," another lad chipped in. "He'll not be walking any time soon."

"Good," Henry replied, surprised at himself. He'd never approved of vigilante justice before. But, with Kaitlyn trembling in his arms and bleeding on his coat, he couldn't think of a single torture he wouldn't inflict on the one who had hurt her if he could. "Come on," he said, walking her toward the car. "Let's go."

"Where?" she asked, hesitating slightly but clinging to him nonetheless.

"Home."

14

The smell of bacon made its way into her semi-conscious brain, and for a moment she thought she was at Jared's, somehow asleep when she ought to be serving customers. But when she opened her eyes, the pale pastel walls and fluffy lilac duvet threw her into confusion. She sat upright, and the sharp pain in her side brought the memory of the previous night crashing down before she was ready for it.

The fear. The stomach-churning, blood-pumping feeling of helplessness. Running, running, but not fast enough. Crashing to the cold, hard ground with a hot, heavy body on top of hers. Then the deafening horn and the blinding light. Chaos, noise. People all around her, helping her up. Asking her questions, giving her counsel but her head too foggy to hear their words. And Henry, appearing out of nowhere. Driving her home. Chloe, concerned and full of kindness. The fresh sheets, the spare room.

She threw back the duvet. Hot, it was so hot. There was a glass of water on the bedside table, perched on a pretty coaster. She drank quickly, and regretted it when the liquid sloshed in her belly. Sweat beaded on her forehead; she pulled her hair into a ponytail to cool the back of her neck and took a deep breath to try to calm the nausea.

The smell of a fried breakfast was usually a pleasant one, not to mention one she was well used to at work. But when she gulped in air, the stench of half-cooked meat seemed to curdle in her guts, turning the fresh water to bile. Hot, urgent saliva filled her mouth. She rushed out of the bedroom door, pushing past Henry, who was coming out of his room wearing a checked dressing gown.

She barely made it to the bathroom, and hadn't had time to shut the door behind her, when her stomach contracted and the ensuing vomit pebble-dashed the Morrises' pristine white bathtub.

"Oh God," she said, sinking to her knees on the bath mat. "Oh God, I'm so sorry."

It was only three more steps to the toilet. Why couldn't she have made it three more steps?

"Hey, don't worry," Henry said. He walked toward her, but took a step back when he saw the mess. "Happens to the best of us."

"Is everything alright?" Chloe appeared at the top of the stairs, and shooed Henry out of the way. "Oh goodness, you poor thing."

"I'm so sorry." She struggled not to cry at how pathetic she must look. "I'll clean it up."

"You'll do no such thing." Chloe didn't flinch at the sight, or smell, of Kaitlyn's shame. "Come on now, let's get you some camomile tea. Just the thing for morning sickness."

"Morning sickness?"

"Well, possibly. Or it could be shock. But it'll do the job either way, trust me. You get along now, Henry. Go make tea, we girls will freshen up." Chloe shut the bathroom door, and ran a bowl of warm water. "Just you wash your face, now. And don't think about it for one second."

She handed Kaitlyn a soft, thick washcloth soaked in lukewarm water. It felt soothing against her skin. Then there were fluffy towels that smelt like meadows, and a brand new toothbrush plucked from the cupboard over the sink just for her.

"Now," Chloe said, "you go have that tea, and something

to eat if you feel up to it. I won't be offended if you don't, you have to listen to your body. When you're ready, Henry will take you to collect your things."

"My things?"

"Well, I expect you'll be wanting a change of clothes and whatnot. Anything you need. If that pillow's no good do feel free to bring your own, I don't mind at all. Just make yourself at home."

"That's very kind, but… I really should go home. I've intruded too much already."

"Nonsense." Chloe took the towel and hung it on the rail over the bath. "It's our pleasure. Besides, I would worry myself sick if you went back there all by yourself right now. Henry too, he was very shaken up. He thinks an awful lot of you, you know. Says you've restored his faith in the next generation. Trust me, that's high praise indeed from an old curmudgeon like him."

Kaitlyn laughed. Curmudgeon. Yes, that was a perfect description. "It's so nice of you, both of you, but I really can't stay. There's my brother to think of, and my job."

"Henry will take you to visit him, any time you like. No question about that. And anyway, the café's closed until after New Year, you said so yourself. Boss on holiday, right?"

"Well, yes."

"So that settles it. You're staying with us, at least until New Year. A house guest for the holidays! Please, Kaitlyn. I'd feel so much better knowing you're here, where I can see you're alright. Just until you get over the shock, and the sickness. Plus I'd love to have female company for a change. Between you and me, much as I love him that old grouch does my head in sometimes."

It was an enticing prospect. A week of soft sheets, good meals and hot baths. But Jack had always told her never to accept charity, or favours. Not to mention the guilty secret she and Henry shared would be hanging over her if she stayed. The sensible thing to do would be to decline the invitation, politely but firmly. But Chloe's eyes were shining, pleading. How could she say no to her? And oh, her body ached. Every muscle screamed, longing for a little respite, a little luxury after years of hardship.

"Can I think about it?" she said at last.

"Of course," Chloe said. "Why don't you go and have that tea, and think things over. Chat about it with Henry, if you like. I'll clear up in here."

"Oh no." Kaitlyn was horrified. "Please, I can't let you clean up my mess. I'll do it myself."

"That's the very last thing you ought to do if you're feeling queasy. Go on, away with you." She opened the bathroom door and ushered Kaitlyn out. "I've got a cast-iron gut. Don't worry about me."

In the kitchen, Henry sat munching on a piece of toast. He looked up when he saw her coming. "Feeling better?" he asked, pouring strange-smelling tea from the pot on the table and handing it to her.

"Yes," she said, "much."

"Well, best drink that anyway," he said, "Chloe swears by it. Not to my taste, but then I'm more of a two sugars and cream type of guy."

She sat opposite him, and sipped at the scented liquid. It didn't taste of much, but the beast thrashing in her guts seemed to be sedated by it. "She wants me to stay," she said. "I said I'd think about it."

"What's there to think about? She wants you to stay, so do I."

"Really? Don't you think it would be a bit awkward? I mean, given the situation."

"Kaitlyn, I was scared last night. I mean, really scared. You must be in shock. And if you're not, I sure as hell am." He put down his toast and leaned closer to her. "I want to make sure you're safe. You, and the baby. Plus, it would do Chloe the world of good. She loves having guests, gets sick of my moaning and griping I expect."

Kaitlyn let out a small chuckle. "She called you a curmudgeon."

"Well, if the shoe fits." Henry shrugged, and grinned. "It's not just that, anyway. It's good for her to have something to focus on. Some stimulation. It's important to keep her mind active, it helps with the dementia."

"She doesn't seem…" Kaitlyn struggled to find words that wouldn't offend. "… *ill*."

"That's the Hepraxin. It really is a miracle. A few weeks ago she couldn't have held a coherent conversation with you."

"No wonder you're desperate to buy more." The waves of nausea had subsided, leaving hunger in their wake. She still couldn't face the bacon piled up on a plate in the middle of the table, but she grabbed the Tupperware box full of muesli and poured a small helping into one of the empty breakfast bowls. "But, what if she asks questions? I don't want to lie to her, it doesn't feel right."

"What kind of questions?"

"About the baby. About its father."

Henry shook his head. "She won't," he said, "it's not her way. She doesn't pry. Come on, Kaitlyn. What do you think Jack would do, if he was around?"

"What do you mean?"

"Do you think he'd let you be alone right now? After what you've been through? From what you've told me about him, I'm pretty sure he'd be looking after you morning and night, at least until he was sure you were okay. And, if he can't be there for you, I'm sure he'd want to know someone else was."

What would Jack do? Probably hunt the scumbag down and remove his testicles with a blunt knife. But she took Henry's point; he wouldn't want her to be alone. Not now. Not when she was hurting, and scared, and shaken up. Not to mention sick.

"Besides," Henry continued as he tipped several brightly

coloured pills out of a small plastic pot and into his hand, "what if, God forbid, something did happen to you? Delayed shock, or something like that. What if you collapsed? Or got too sick? Who'd be there for Jack?" The thought made her blood run cold. If she wasn't around, those machines would be switched off. She was barely keeping them on as it was. "You know what they tell you when you're on a plane?"

She shook her head. She'd never flown before. International travel wasn't something many people could afford these days.

"Put your own oxygen mask on before helping others with theirs. You've got to take care of yourself first, otherwise how can you help anyone else?"

"Okay," she said, grateful that Henry had found a reason for accepting their offer that she could justify to herself. "I'll stay. But just a week."

15

"Here we are," Chloe said, lifting the lid from the serving dish with a flourish, "our traditional New Year's meal!"

"Lasagne?" Kaitlyn asked, and Henry smiled at her confusion. "Don't get me wrong, Chloe, it looks, and smells, amazing. But I didn't know it was traditional?"

"It is in this house, isn't it, Henry?"

"Tell her the story," Henry said, looking forward to watching her tell her favourite anecdote. He loved the way she came alive when she regaled Kaitlyn with her tales. Come to think of it, he loved the way she came alive around Kaitlyn.

"Well," Chloe said, getting comfortable in her chair as Henry took over the task of serving the meal. "One year, when David was six, his mother decided he could spend New Year with us for the first time. Oh, he was so excited. We promised him he could wait up to see Big Ben chime, and the fireworks and everything. He'd never been allowed to stay up for it before, she always held parties but she sent him to bed, out of the way. He talked of nothing else for weeks beforehand. I swear, he was more excited about it than he was for Christmas!

"So, he'd even gone and got himself books about New Year celebrations out of the library. He was a good reader, young David, and he liked to know everything he could about whatever his latest obsession was. When the day came, he was bouncing off the walls. I can still picture him, sitting right where you are now, Kaitlyn, in his little pyjamas covered in rocket ships and stars. But when I put his dinner in front of him, gammon and roast potatoes it was, wasn't it, Henry? Well, his face fell and he burst into tears.

"We couldn't understand it. He always loved my roast dinners, that's why I'd made it specially. He was sobbing so hard it took twenty minutes, at least, for him to speak. And do you know what he said?" Kaitlyn shook her head. "He said 'We're supposed to have old lasagne!'" Chloe slapped the table and started laughing so hard that she could barely speak. "You see, all that reading. He'd read all about Auld Lang Syne, only no one had told him how to pronounce it!"

Her laughter was infectious. Kaitlyn reached for a napkin to dry her eyes, and Henry couldn't help chuckling even though he'd heard the tale hundreds of times before. The sheer joy on Chloe's face made it impossible to resist.

"So what did you do?" Kaitlyn asked.

"I couldn't bear to see him so upset, so I made a lasagne," Chloe replied in between gulping laughs, "and we've had it every year ever since, in homage to little David. Oh, there really is nothing funnier than children. Just you wait, Kaitlyn. You'll have dozens of stories of your own about the funny things your little one will come out with!"

Henry and Kaitlyn stopped laughing and shot each other dark looks.

"Excuse me," Kaitlyn said, getting up from the table. She looked pale. "I just need to use the bathroom a minute. I'll be right back."

It was always painfully awkward when the baby came up. No wonder she wanted a minute. Probably hoping he'd steer the conversation away before she returned. Damn it. He'd been hoping to talk to her later, after Chloe went to bed. He desperately wanted her to stay longer; the way she brought out the sparkle in Chloe… he didn't want that to end. He had a whole speech prepared, so many reasons why she ought to keep living with them. But it would mean more moments like this one, and with it fresh in her mind she'd be harder to persuade.

"Poor girl," Chloe said, picking up her knife and fork. "Early pregnancy is tough. Sickness, fatigue. I do worry about her going back to work, all those hours on her feet. I hope she'll be alright."

"Yes, it is a worry. But let's not dwell on it now, eh? Let's enjoy the evening."

"Absolutely," Chloe replied, holding up her wine glass. "Top me up will you, love?" She pointed to Kaitlyn's half-empty glass of water. "And pour some more water for Heidi, too."

The chill formed in the small of his back and dispersed across his whole body, making him shiver. She didn't notice. Didn't correct herself. Just carried on eating the steaming lasagne, totally unaware of her mistake.

It was just a slip of the tongue, he told himself. Easily done. Doesn't mean anything. But he couldn't quite make himself believe it. He stared at her. She'd been taking the pills, religiously. She'd been her old self. Better even. Having Kaitlyn around had been like a tonic to her. Like a miracle. But now he worried why that might be. She'd been treating her like family, like a daughter. Had the lines become blurred?

"Eat up, Henry," she said, "it'll get cold."

He tucked into his food, even though he had no appetite now. But when Kaitlyn appeared in the doorway, eyes wide and even whiter in pallor than before, he dropped his fork.

"What's wrong?" He'd never seen her look so scared, not even on Christmas night.

"I'm bleeding," she said, her voice little more than a squeak. "A lot."

He tried to focus on the road as they sped across town to the hospital, but his heart was pounding. Kaitlyn didn't speak, just stared out of the window and nibbled at her fingernails.

Even when he helped her out of the car, and walked with his arm around her to the accident and emergency department, she didn't say a word.

The triage nurse didn't look impressed when he told her the problem. The waiting room was full of drunk youngsters with various bleeding body parts. Several lads held their heads back, covering their noses or jaws with handkerchiefs. A woman in a silver minidress had fallen asleep across three chairs, a bucket next to her. They waited in silence for over an hour before Kaitlyn's name was called and they were ushered into a cubicle by a tall, thin nurse who wore a fraying piece of tinsel in her tight ponytail.

"How far along is she?" the nurse asked.

"About six weeks, I think," he replied. "Is that right, Kaitlyn? Six weeks?"

She just nodded, her fingers still in her mouth.

The nurse scoffed. "Well, it's very common to miscarry at that stage. Most women don't even notice."

"Miscarry?" Kaitlyn looked up at them, the panic obvious. "No. No, I can't. Surely you can stop it?"

"Not all pregnancies are viable," the nurse said sharply, "it's just one of those things. Nothing to be done about it, I'm afraid."

"But you don't know for sure that's what it is?" Henry asked.

"Well, no. It could be nothing at all, or it could be the start of a miscarriage. There's no way to tell, not without a scan. But frankly, it's an unnecessary expense; you'd be better to just go home, take some painkillers and wait and see if the bleeding continues. At this stage you wouldn't see much, but keep an eye out for any mass in the discharge. If that happens, come back next week and we'll make sure the pregnancy has cleared itself completely."

"No." Kaitlyn's voice was shaky, but determined. "I can't. I have to know. I have to know if my baby's okay."

"You want to use credit on a scan?" the nurse asked. "If you are miscarrying, there's nothing we can do, you know."

"I'll pay for it," Henry said, squeezing Kaitlyn's shoulder. "Please, she needs to know."

"Alright, but it'll be a few hours yet."

"We'll wait."

"As you wish." The nurse scribbled something down on her clipboard before leaving them alone in the stark, cold cubicle.

The minutes ticked by slowly. Outside the hospital walls the world was preparing to welcome the start of a new year. Parties in full swing, drinks flowing. Marking the inevitable passage of time surrounded by friends and family. But for Henry and Kaitlyn, time seemed to stand still. Trapped in an anxious limbo while they waited, wondering if the life they had created had spluttered out before it had even had chance to properly begin.

"I'd kinda gotten used it." Kaitlyn broke the silence between them at last. "The idea of it, anyway."

"Being pregnant?" Henry perched beside her on the bed, and slipped his hand into hers.

"Not just that. The child, you know? I mean, I know it wouldn't have been part of my life, but…" She wiped tears from her eyes with her free hand. "When I went to see that old nun, Martha, she had all these pictures on her wall. All the children she's helped find families. They looked so happy. And I started thinking, imagining. I got used to the idea that my child, *our* child, would have a life like that. A really, really awesome life with awesome parents. And even though I'd never know them, I'd feel happy knowing they were out there somewhere, living that way. Living a way I never did."

Henry hadn't thought about the child, not in those terms. He'd not thought beyond the notion of a screaming newborn that would be quickly handed over to its waiting family. The idea of it being a real child, not just a generic bundle of chubby cheeks and cradle cap, was unsettling. A child, with a unique personality. One that he would never know. Christ, how had been so short-sighted?

He started to say it was okay, they could just try again, but stopped himself when he realised how foolish that was. He might be short-sighted, but Kaitlyn wasn't. She'd already built a mental image of the child in her mind. Thought about its family, its childhood. She'd probably imagined its first day at school. She didn't want 'any' baby, she wanted the one she was carrying. However briefly it had been a part of her life, it had made an indelible impact. It wasn't replaceable.

Shit. Memories hit him in quick succession, like missiles from a pellet gun. All Chloe's reasons for not trying again after Heidi, even though a child had always been her heart's desire. Every logical, medical, rational reason she gave him meant nothing. The real truth was that Heidi was irreplaceable. The real truth was that Heidi was her baby, even if she wasn't here. There was no way that wound would ever heal, nothing that could help her move on from the choice he had made. But she couldn't tell him that, because the weight of it would have destroyed him.

He squeezed Kaitlyn's hand tight as his own tears fell.

16

The blue jelly was cold and slimy. She winced a little as the technician pressed the probe hard against her abdomen. He lifted it, moved it, pressed again even harder and wiggled it whilst he stared at the screen that had been turned so that she and Henry couldn't see what was on it.

Still jamming the device into her lower belly so hard that she thought she couldn't bear the pressure, he clicked the mouse with his other hand, squinting at the monitor. She raised her left hand, and Henry took it. Gritting her teeth, she prepared herself to hear the news she was dreading. There was nothing there. No life. The baby was gone.

"Well," the technician said, spinning the monitor around to face them. "There we are. Here's junior, safe and sound."

"What?"

"Just here." He clicked the mouse again and zoomed in on what looked like a throbbing kidney bean. "Happy as Larry."

"That's my baby? My baby's okay?"

"Yes and yes." The technician grinned; he was a lot nicer than the nurses, she thought. "Good strong heartbeat."

No kidding. The poor little thing looked racked by the constant pulsating.

"Should it be that fast?" she asked.

"Oh yes, absolutely spot on that is. Just the ticket."

"So she's not going to miscarry?" Henry asked.

"Well, it's always a risk. Especially in the first trimester. But I'd say your odds are very good. In fact, nine times out of ten if there's a heartbeat at this stage then all will be well."

Relief was sharp and sweet, almost dizzying in its swift arrival. She sat up a little, and hugged Henry tight, partly so the technician wouldn't see her snotty tears.

"Here." The technician handed her a printed out picture of the little jumping bean. "Not much to see yet, of course. You wait for the twelve week scan!"

She stared at the blurry, pixelated image. "My baby," she whispered. "That's my baby." A strange, warm sensation ran through her, coupled with a sense of indefinable dread. This little blob, this tiny little dancing blob, was suddenly the most precious thing in the universe. Was that just because it could save Jack, and Chloe? She tried to reason that it was, but she knew, deep down, it was more than that. It was something primal, unconquerable. The desperate desire to keep this little cluster of cells from harm was hard-coded into her very DNA.

You can't get attached, Kaitlyn. Not now, and not when it's born. You have to be strong, for Jack.

"I don't think I should take this," she said, handing the picture back to the puzzled technician. She looked up at Henry.

"Come on," he said, a chill in his tone. "I think we should get you home."

It was just gone 2 a.m. when they walked through the front door, but Chloe came rushing downstairs as soon as they arrived.

"Why aren't you asleep?" Henry asked her, and Kaitlyn thought there was something accusatory, angry even, in his voice.

"As if I could sleep," she snapped at him, hurrying to put her arms around Kaitlyn. "Honestly, Henry. Stop treating me like a child. Oh, Kaitlyn. I've been frantic. Is everything alright?"

"Yes," she replied, "it's fine. The baby's fine."

"Oh thank heavens." Chloe's eyes were wet with relief; she

hugged Kaitlyn tight. "You must rest now, off to bed. Quite a start to the year, eh?"

Kaitlyn was relieved to slide in between the soft, comfortable sheets and close her eyes. But sleep did not come as readily as she thought it would. She lay awake for a long time, thinking about the little jumping bean growing inside her, and when she did drop off her dreams were full of bleeding and screaming. More than once she woke abruptly, convinced she was lying in a puddle of blood.

It was gone eleven when she finally awoke the next morning, and Henry had gone out shopping. Chloe hummed to herself as she peeled potatoes in the kitchen, and Kaitlyn cleared her throat loudly so as not to make her jump and cut herself when she entered the room.

"Good morning, sleepy head." Chloe put down the peeler. "Can I get you something to drink?"

"No," Kaitlyn replied, "no, please. I'll make tea. I'm sorry, I didn't mean to sleep so late."

"Nonsense, rest is the best thing for you."

Kaitlyn filled the kettle, and grabbed two brightly coloured mugs. "I'll just get dressed, and then I'll pack my things."

"Pack?" Chloe sounded shocked. "Why ever should you pack?"

"It's New Year," Kaitlyn said, "time for me to go home and leave you in peace."

"Peace? Well, that sounds boring," Chloe said, covering the saucepan of peeled potatoes and washing her hands. "Admit it, it's Henry isn't it? You're sick of his cantankerous moaning," she sighed. "Don't leave me alone with *el groucho*, take pity on an old woman."

Kaitlyn put the freshly made tea on the table, and they both took a seat. "No," she said, "it's been lovely staying with you both. But we agreed a week, that was the plan."

"That's the good thing about plans," Chloe said, taking a sip from her mug, "they can be changed. I'm serious. I want you to stay. *We* want you to stay. Henry told me about your block, and the dodgy elevator. Climbing all those stairs is a terrible idea in your condition, and it'll only get harder as the months go on. Why not stay here for now? Take it a bit easier while you're pregnant. The flat will still be there for you to return to once you've had the baby. Wouldn't it be easier?"

It would. Of course it would. Easier, safer, and so much nicer than being alone. But the easiest route wasn't always the right one. "Don't get me wrong," she said, "I love being here. It's been amazing. You're amazing. But I couldn't possibly take advantage of your kindness any more."

"Ah." Chloe put down her mug. "I see the problem. Kaitlyn, I've not been honest with you, I'm sorry. Forgive a foolish old woman her pride."

"What do you mean?"

"I'm trying to sell it to you, trying to make it appealing for you, but the truth is I'm being selfish in asking you to stay."

Selfish? She'd never met anyone less selfish in her life. "How so?" she asked, feeling dubious.

Chloe sighed. She reached across the table and took Kaitlyn's hands. "I have a habit of looking on the bright side, of pretending everything is just fine," she said. "I mean, when you live with someone as grumpy and cynical as Henry, one of you has to be positive, right?" Kaitlyn laughed, and Chloe winked at her. "But I do know, Kaitlyn."

"Know what?"

"I've got dementia. I know what it is, and I know what it means. I play it down, but that's mostly for Henry's sake. He has enough to contend with. So I call it a 'funny turn' or 'one of my moments', so at least he doesn't think I'm scared. But I am, Kaitlyn. I am scared. I don't know what happens, when it gets bad. I don't remember. I've lost days, weeks sometimes, when the meds haven't been right. I don't know what I do, what I say. And I don't know how Henry copes.

"But I'm not blind. I see the way the neighbours look at me, if they see me in the garden. Kimmy, from across the road, she talks to me like a toddler. Do you know what that's like? To know they must have seen me, when I was out of my mind, but not know what it was they saw? I could have been dancing naked in the mud for all I know. It's why I don't go out much now, even when I'm well. I just don't know what I may have done, what people may have seen. That's why I need you, Kaitlyn. I need someone other than Henry to talk with, to laugh with. To help me stay sharp. And I need you to do what he won't."

"What's that?"

"I need you to be honest with me. If I have another turn, if the meds need to be altered again, I need you to tell me, when I'm back, how it was. How I was. I want to know the truth, warts and all. He tells me I was fine, just a bit confused, a bit sleepy. But the way people look at me, Kaitlyn. They're *scared*. I pretend I don't notice, but I do."

Kaitlyn inhaled sharply. Henry didn't know this, he didn't know any of this. He thought he was protecting her by not being honest about how bad her dementia could be, but really she was protecting him by not letting on how scared she was. That level of love, of self-sacrifice, neither wanting to hurt the other, even though it meant they carried a heavier burden by themselves.

"And not just for me, Kaitlyn," Chloe continued. "You being here would help Henry, too. It's too much for him, when I get ill. You'd be helping him, even just being here. And if it got too bad, maybe you could make him see sense."

Goosebumps rose on her flesh. "What do you mean 'see sense'?"

"Oh come now. You know what I mean."

"You… you want to Move On?"

"No. God, no. Leave Henry? It's the very last thing I *want*. But if there comes a time when it's what I need—"

"He'd never be able to let you go."

"I know," she sighed, and stirred her tea absent-mindedly. "It probably seems crazy to you, right? It's all so logical these days, so cut and dried. People don't value life like they used to. They treat it like a product, like something to be discarded when it malfunctions. But that's because they have something to replace it with. It's different without that. It's different when you don't believe."

"In what?"

"Heaven, my dear," Chloe said. "It doesn't work without heaven. None of it. Moving On, accepting your allocated place, putting up with inequality. To say goodbye to someone, to really say goodbye, without any hope that you will see them again, in some form or another, is a pain I can't describe. Without the concept of heaven, of a reward for mortal struggles, it's just too hard. They figured that out quick enough, hence the New Church and its revival."

"Who's they?"

"The Collective Council, of course. It didn't take them long to work it out. People claimed they wanted equality, but when it came to it they didn't really. That instinct, that need to be superior, it was just too strong. Why should a road sweeper earn the same as a doctor? That's what they said. Why should I not pass my hard-earned money to my children? Reasonable, of course. As are most points of view, if you take the time to listen. But then, there comes the problem. Now some children have more than others, yet again. Just like before. Some people have advantages that they neither earned nor deserve. But it couldn't be eliminated. And then came the population crisis. Too many people living too long, the youngsters couldn't get a break because the cost of caring for the elderly was crippling the country.

"No wonder they couldn't wait to endorse the ideas of the New Church, and bring religion back into the classrooms and laws. It solved everything, see? Accepting your station, knowing there would be more for you in heaven. Letting loved ones go, or choosing to go yourself, knowing you would be reunited in paradise. It was the supreme cure-all. The perfect way to take the sting out of the failed utopia."

Kaitlyn stared at her, mouth open. She'd never looked at it like that before. Snowflakes were considered godless, for the most part. They'd grown up without religion. She knew that, yet she'd never realised the implication. They didn't believe in heaven. No wonder. No wonder they fought so hard, no wonder they so often had to be cajoled or legally forced into Moving On. They believed it was the end.

No wonder they raged. No wonder Henry ranted, and raved. She would too, if she thought it was all there was. But she'd been raised to know there was something more, something better. Something wonderful that awaited those who took care of God's planet and lived responsibly. It was a comfort the snowflakes didn't have.

So why are you fighting so hard for Jack, if you truly believe in heaven?

The question filled her mind, and made her queasy. *Because I'm not sure.* She was forced to admit it. *I'm not sure I believe any more.*

"If you don't believe in heaven, why would you even contemplate Moving On?" she asked Chloe, hoping she would be able to offer some insight. Some reason that wasn't tied up with the tenents of the New Church.

"Because something isn't always better than nothing," Chloe replied. "I want to live, of course I do. But only if the living is worthwhile. And only if it doesn't hurt those I love. Oblivion is better than suffering, or causing suffering to others. I don't want to lose who I am, Kaitlyn. So much of who I was has already disappeared over the years, I couldn't bear to lose any more of myself."

"What do you mean?" Kaitlyn asked, feeling confused. "What have you lost?"

"I wasn't born an old woman," Chloe replied, with a wistful smile. "When I was young, I had dreams. Big dreams, ferocious dreams. I wanted to change the world, set it on fire. I used to be a bit of a wild-child in my day, you know."

"You?" Kaitlyn blushed at the unmasked shock in her voice; she hadn't meant to sound rude. But Chloe just laughed.

"I know," she said. "Hard to believe, isn't it? Here, let me show you something." Chloe opened the sideboard drawer and rummaged through a pile of old papers and forms. "Here it is, look. Bet you hardly recognise me there."

Kaitlyn stared at the picture on the newspaper clipping Chloe handed her. A young woman with scruffy blonde curls and a stained T-shirt, her mouth open in a silent shout, pure rage on her face. She was flanked by two policemen who each had hold of her arms. Behind her, a crowd holding placards, their fists in the air.

"Is that *you*?"

"It is indeed." Chloe beamed, and chuckled. "Me, and a whole crowd of students. We were protesting the collaboration between the New Church and the Collective Council. Trying to stop them from outlawing IVF, and from peddling their nonsense in schools. I was right at the front, I hit Bishop Adley with a rotten tomato!"

"Oh my God." Kaitlyn looked from the picture, to Chloe, and back at the picture again. She'd never have thought it in a million years. "You got arrested?"

"Yes." Chloe nodded. "Suspended sentence for assault! Assault, my arse. I got more tomato on my own shirt than on the bishop. But that was the end of my dreams nevertheless. I got chucked out of law school, and nowhere else would touch me after that picture was in all the papers. So I ended up just a humble secretary. I can't really complain though, I'd never have met Henry if I'd gone on to have the glittering career I thought I wanted. But, you see, it just makes all this so much harder."

"How so?"

"I've already been humbled, Kaitlyn. I'm already not the person I dreamed I would be. I was intelligent, passionate, full of potential. I've accepted who I am now, but I can't lose more of myself. I can't go from being that bright, courageous young woman in the picture to losing my sanity, losing my dignity. So promise me, Kaitlyn. Promise me you'll stay. Promise me, if it comes to it, you'll try to make him see it's for the best."

"Okay," Kaitlyn said, squeezing Chloe's hand. "I promise."

17

"Have you remembered the present?" Chloe asked as they pulled up outside the old working men's club, the beat of the disco inside already making Henry's head ache.

"Yes, yes," he said, pointing to the boot. "It's in there."

Stupid idea, bringing presents. What was the point of giving gifts to someone who was about to off themselves? But Chloe had insisted. He'd joked that perhaps they ought to just give him a bag of nails for the coffin; she hadn't been amused. She'd gone for cufflinks. *Cufflinks.* What the hell for? So his shirts could look good hanging in his wardrobe until his widow got round to giving them away? But he'd kept his mouth shut.

Walking in to the party, with Chloe on his arm, was surreal. If he didn't know better, he'd have thought it was a wedding reception, or an extravagant birthday celebration. Adults and children alike wore their best frocks and suits, cheesy music blared from old floor-standing speakers and toddlers jiggled around on the dance floor under garish lights and a spinning disco ball. A long table, covered in an ivory cloth, was bursting with the traditional buffet foods that people would politely pick at, but that ultimately would go warm and crisp at the edges in an hour or two.

Josh's wife, Eloise, came bustling toward them, all lacy blouse and thick make-up.

"Oh," she exclaimed, throwing her arms around Chloe and then planting an unwanted lipstick kiss on Henry's cheek. "You came! Josh will be so thrilled."

"Lovely party," Chloe replied, handing Eloise the shiny present. "You've done a great job."

Eloise responded with the usual insincere modesty before snaking her arm around Chloe's waist and whisking her away. "Chloe, you simply must meet the girls from the bridge club. You'll adore them. And then you'll have no reason not to come along next time. Honestly, it's more about the gin than the bridge. An excuse for a giggle more than anything."

Henry watched as Chloe was shepherded across the room to a corner table occupied by a group of middle-aged women who wore too many bangles and held drinks with umbrellas and straws poking out of them. Straws. Kaitlyn would have something to say about that, he betted. Not very ecologically responsible.

He smiled, picturing her rolling her eyes and tutting about the typical snowflakes. God, he'd much rather be at home chatting with her and Chloe than here at this farce. Kaitlyn had settled in so easily, once Chloe had used her charms to get her to agree to stay longer. Just a few weeks into her extended stay, and it felt as though she'd always been with them. It was good for Chloe to have the company of a young, sharp mind. It was good for both of them.

In fact, he thought, life was pretty much perfect just the way it was right now. If only it could stay exactly as it was. But the baby growing inside Kaitlyn's womb was both a source of hope, and a ticking time bomb. As her abdomen began to swell, so the day of reckoning grew nearer. How would they explain to Chloe why Kaitlyn would not bring the baby home? It was a subject neither of them wanted to broach, but they wouldn't be able to avoid forever.

Worse, what if Kaitlyn couldn't go through with it? He'd seen the look in her eyes during that first scan. It was a look he recognised only too well. If she pulled out, decided to choose keeping her baby over her brother's medical bills, he'd have no way of stopping her. And then, how long before the Hepraxin ran out, and he lost Chloe forever?

She was adamant the plan still stood. "We've got a deal, Henry. I don't go back on my word," she'd said when he asked her, tentatively, if she was having second thoughts. But, since she'd moved in, her visits to Jack had become less frequent. She used to go every day, without fail, but now she was beginning to skip the odd day, here and there. Arguably it was because she simply didn't feel up to it. The morning sickness was hitting her quite hard, and she was back to doing long shifts at the café. But still, it made him uneasy.

Once he lost the court case, he'd have no financial means left. If Kaitlyn welched on their agreement, it would all be over.

"Henry." A familiar voice, and a hearty clap on the back, interrupted his musings. "You came after all, I didn't think you would."

Josh had put on a few pounds, and a lost a few inches from his hairline since Henry had last seen him. But the bushy beard and blue suit were just the same as always. He gripped Henry's hand and shook it firmly.

"Of course," Henry said. "Wouldn't miss it. Lovely do."

Josh frowned briefly, then roared with laughter. "Oh, don't give me that, Henners," he said, punching him playfully on the shoulder. "Don't you start getting all faux polite on me, old chap. I know what you're really thinking. You think this is some kind of macabre farce. You're seething with anger at me for selling out my principles, or else you think I've got a screw loose. You hate the music, the false niceties are making you itch round the collar and frankly you'd rather be going for a root canal than standing here surrounded by pseudo cheer and fake hypocrites. What? Do you think I've forgotten who you are?"

"No," Henry replied. "But I think you might have forgotten who *you* are."

Josh clapped his large hands and grinned. "That's the spirit,

Henners," he said. "I knew you were still in there somewhere, underneath the old-man anorak and the snowy hair. Life's too short for mincing words. C'mon, give it to me straight. Tell me what you really think of my decision, you'll never get another chance, after all."

That made Henry's flesh prickle slightly against the starchy fabric of the new shirt Chloe had insisted he wear. There were a million things he wanted to say. So much rage. How had a man so full of passion and principles, so outspoken about his hatred for the new credit system, and the corrupted morals of the New Church and the Moving On Corporation, come to this? How do you go from being on the front line of every public protest, throwing eggs at the Collective Council, to putting on your best suit and lying down to die at their behest?

He looked Josh straight in his hazel eyes, remembering all the years they spent by each other's side. The times they hid together behind the bike sheds to avoid Kieron Knox and his gang of bullies, the days they snuck out after PE and drank Lucozade in the park, the room they shared at university. And the day those hazel eyes stared back at him, full of compassion, when Chloe lay unconscious in her hospital bed, and Heidi lay lifeless in his arms. His rage subsided, grief rushing in to fill its place.

He'd never see those eyes again.

"Why, Josh? Just... why?"

Josh sighed. He grabbed a drink from the nearby table and handed it to Henry. "Do you remember when my grandad died?"

"Of course," Henry replied. They'd been in high school, about thirteen years old he reckoned. Josh had barely spoken for days; he'd never seen his bouncy, raucous friend so subdued.

"He was a great man, you know," Josh said, "I loved him very much. When I was really young he used to take me fishing, this lovely little river in the middle of nowhere. We never caught anything, mind. But it didn't matter. He'd bring cans of Coke, and those old jelly sweets covered in sugar. All the things Mum and Dad wouldn't let me have because they thought they'd make me more hyper. We just used to chat, sing songs, that kind of thing. He was really the only one in the family who seemed to enjoy my company. I was too much for the rest of them. Too loud, too crazy. But not for him. He used to say the rest of 'em were just uptight.

"It broke my heart when he got ill. I couldn't understand why he had to go into a home, or why they wouldn't let me go and visit him. I hated Mum for doing that, I used to think she was selfish. I thought he should have come and lived with us, we had the room. But I didn't have a clue. Not a goddamn clue.

"A couple of weeks before he died, I overheard my parents talking. They were saying he didn't have long left, he was declining, stuff like that. I couldn't bear the thought of not saying goodbye, so when they were out I went through Mum's drawers and found the name of the nursing home he was in. I never told you this, but that day when I snuck out of school without you, you were really mad because I didn't tell you I was leaving, do you remember?"

Henry nodded, and Josh continued, "Well, it wasn't anything like that. I went to see him, at the home. Really nice one it was, too. Willow trees in the garden, lovely and clean and airy; best money could buy, and the staff were very friendly. I'll never forget the one who greeted me at the door, Wendy her name was. She was all smiley, and perky. Not too bad in the looks department either, as I recall. Far too old for me of course, otherwise I'd have asked for her number."

Henry grinned despite himself, remembering teenage Josh and his constant pursuit of anything in a skirt.

"So," Josh continued, "she greets me at the door with this big smile, enthusiastic patter and all that, and asks me who I've come to visit. But when I told her, her face fell. She asked me was I sure? Had I been prepared? I gave it the old gung-ho, told her yes, I knew exactly what to expect. Even told her my mum had sent me herself. She still looked concerned, but told me to follow her anyway.

"So I trailed behind her, down these wide, bright corridors. There were old people milling about, some of them reading, some of them painting. When we went through the dining room, I could even see some of them in the garden playing boules. And I remember thinking, it wasn't so bad after all. It was a nice place, and all these people seemed pretty fit and healthy considering their age. But then we got to the end of a long, darker corridor and Wendy had to punch a number into a keypad to make the door open, and she locked it quickly behind us.

"You could hear the wailing as soon as you stepped through. We'd gone into the loony section, you see. There was a nurse trying to cajole some old woman into taking her pills, but she was thrashing and cursing, hitting out. We kept walking, quickly, until we reached a grey door with my grandfather's name on it.

"Wendy turned to me and said she thought she ought to come in too. She asked again if I was sure. If I could go back in time, Henners, I'd turn around right then and never open that door. I'd keep my memories of him sacred and intact. But I was young and foolish, I didn't realise what they'd been protecting me from.

"When I opened the door I saw him, dozing in an armchair. The chair looked huge, but I think that was just because he was so thin. He was half-naked, covered in scratch marks. I thought they'd been abusing him. Wendy must have seen the horror in my eyes, because she explained the reality, and it was even worse. He'd been doing it to himself. Couldn't bear the feel of fabric on his skin, apparently. They kept trying to clothe him, to keep him warm, but he tore at anything they tried to cover him with. He'd forgotten, you see, how to take clothes off. So he just clawed at them, and himself in the process.

"He opened his eyes, and for a moment he was Grandad. My favourite guy in the whole world, the one who taught me to tie knots and winked at me behind Mum's back while she was yelling about the state of my clothes, or the cuts on my knees. We locked eyes, and it was him and me against the world, like always.

"I started to walk toward him, holding out my arms to give him a hug. But then he frowned. Not a little frown, not a puzzled frown. It was stern and angry. I'd never seen either expression on his face before.

"Wendy grabbed my arm, and pulled me backward. He picked up the plastic beaker on the table next to him and threw it at us. It just missed me, and only because Wendy had realised what he was going to do. He started yelling, raving. 'Get away from me, demon! Go back to your whores! Fuck off, you bastard, you're not having my silver.'

"He tried to stand up, but he couldn't. So he just kept shouting, and looking around for things to throw, though of course they'd made sure nothing but his drink was in his reach. I could still hear the swearing, and screaming, once Wendy had ushered me out of the room and shut the door."

Josh downed the rest of the whiskey in his glass, and sighed. "He didn't know who I was, Henners," he said. "Where's the justice in that? I wish I'd never gone, I wish it every day. Because now, I can't see him the way I used to. Whenever I try to remember our fishing trips, or the times we would laugh together through Christmas dinner, I can't see his face the way it was. All I can see is that frown. I can't remember how his voice sounded when he told me I was his little champ, all I hear is him telling me to fuck off."

"Jesus, Josh," Henry said, reaching out and putting his hand on his old friend's shoulder. "Why didn't you tell me?"

"I was ashamed," Josh said. "Imagine that. Ashamed of my own grandad, my own hero. Ashamed of myself, for thinking I knew better than my parents. I never told them either. But I'd give anything to have those memories back, untainted."

Henry didn't know what to say. He cursed himself for getting so angry with Josh the day he'd snuck out of school without him. Maybe that was the reason he hadn't confided in him back then? Damn his stupid ego, blinding him to his best friend's suffering.

Josh picked up another drink, and took a long swig. "Anyway," he said, "turns out it can run in the family. Fucking Alzheimer's, eh? The diagnosis was still a bit of a shock though, you don't really expect the inevitable to catch up with you, but it does."

"Shit." Henry's throat felt dry. "Oh, Josh, I had no idea."

"You see those two?" Josh was swaying a little now; he put his arm around Henry and directed his gaze to the two children in the centre of the dance floor. A smart young boy of about ten wearing a blue suit just like Josh's, holding hands with a smaller girl who wore a frilly pink dress with a huge bow at the back. The pair were squealing with delight as they spun round and round together until they fell over, then got up and did it again.

"They're the light of my life," Josh said, "They're the reason I get up each morning. We have them every Sunday, you know? Eloise cooks a roast and then we go to the park, or the river. I'm teaching them to fish. Not that there's any fish in that damn sewer of a river of course, but it's not the point. They think I'm the bee's knees. I'm 'funny Grandad', and I want to keep it that way. I never want them to see me the way I saw my grandad."

Henry was confused. He understood the sentiment but Josh wasn't short of a bob or two. "I still don't get it, Josh," he said. "Why this? Why now? Why don't you just go on Hepraxin?" He stopped short of adding 'like Chloe' at the end. Even after Josh's revelation, he couldn't quite bring himself to confess his own predicament.

Josh just laughed. "I'm already on it, Henners," he said. "How do you think I'm having this, sparkling and coherent, conversation with you, eh? But it's a fool's game, you know that as well as I do."

"What?" Henry felt himself begin to shake. What was

that? Anger? Frustration? Or was it fear? "It's a miracle drug, Josh. Stops dementia in its tracks, reverses it even… so I've heard, anyway."

Josh snorted. "Only temporarily, and only for those who can afford it. Come on, Henners. Don't tell me you've bought in to the hype? You're cleverer than that. We said it ourselves, back when they started this whole credit shit. It amounts to privatised health-care. They'll overprice the drugs, and make sure you keep needing more and more. You predicted it yourself. Perhaps you're the one who's forgotten who you really are."

Henry just scowled at him, feeling foolish.

"I'm not knocking it, as a temporary solution," Josh continued, "I mean, it's given me the chance to put everything in order, to make sure I crossed off my bucket list, as it were. But, it's a bottomless well. They're already saying I need a higher dose, at double the cost. How long before it's triple? Quadruple? How long before I haven't a penny left in the world to give to those I live for, and I'm still facing death or the loony bin just the same? This way, I get to make my own decision. I hate the credit system as much as you do, but we're stuck with it. And I'll be damned if I'm giving everything I ever worked for to some big drug corporation just for the sake of an extra year or two."

Henry felt sick. There was truth in Josh's words, he couldn't deny it, much as he'd like to. Eventually, no amount Hepraxin would be enough to keep Chloe with him. But he didn't care about eventually, he just wanted more time. Just a bit more time. It wasn't the same; Josh was close with his kids and grandkids, he had a reason to want to leave a legacy behind. Henry just wanted Chloe, just his Chloe. Once she was gone, well there'd be no need to worry about what was left. Without her, nothing mattered anyway.

"I just want them to remember me as I am," Josh said, gesturing to his grandchildren again. "Happy, healthy, maybe even slightly tipsy," he chuckled. "I get to choose the last words I ever say to them. To me, that's a gift. I know you might not agree with me, but I hope at least you can understand."

"Of course I do," Henry said, surprised to find he truly did. Josh's reasoning was flawless, for his own situation. But it didn't apply to him and Chloe. There was no reason to think Josh's decision was a comment on his own choices. The two scenarios were totally different. Apples and oranges.

He threw his arms around his oldest friend, hugging him tight, trying to drink in the smell of his cologne, knowing it would be the last embrace. Over Josh's shoulder, he saw Chloe and Eloise rise from the table they'd been sitting at and walk toward them, smiling.

For a second, as they made their way across the dance floor, he couldn't see Chloe's sparkly dress and coiffured hair. For a second, when he looked at her all he could see was an old woman in her nightie shuffling up the driveway, Kimmy from number 34 guiding her home.

18

What kind of sadistic bastard decided to put a water dispenser in the middle of a waiting room full of pregnant women with uncomfortably full bladders? Kaitlyn scowled at the young man pushing his paper cup up against the lever, making the tortuous trickle of liquid fill her ears. She crossed her legs even tighter.

Another woman's name was called over the intercom, and Kaitlyn tutted. "I'm sure we were here before her," she said as the large blonde girl heaved herself out of her plastic seat and waddled off down the corridor. Henry just shrugged. He'd been very quiet lately, ever since he and Chloe had gone to that party. Must be difficult, she supposed. Saying goodbye to an old friend, especially when you don't agree with their decision. Still, the moping was getting a bit much. She could see why Chloe had wanted her to stay with them; Henry didn't talk much when he was in one of his moods.

Henry stood up unexpectedly. "What are you doing?" she asked.

"I need the loo," he whispered.

"Oh no you don't." She yanked his arm, pulling him back into his seat. "If I can't go to the toilet then neither can you."

"Oh, come on. Don't be unreasonable."

"I'm pregnant," she said, "it's my prerogative. Anyway, they could call us any second. I'm not waiting any longer than I have to just because you've got no self-control."

He huffed and rolled his eyes, but sat back down.

When her name was eventually called, they headed to the small, private room and Kaitlyn took up position on the bed, wincing once again at the cold blue jelly. The prodding was even worse this time because of the pain in her bladder, and she worried she might wet herself when the technician wiggled the scanner on her lower abdomen.

It was a female technician this time, and she was much less smiley and enthusiastic then her male colleague. After much clicking of her mouse, and vigorous repositioning of the scanner, she finally turned the screen around. Kaitlyn couldn't help but gasp when she saw how much her little jellybean had changed in six weeks.

"Wow," she said, transfixed by the moving images on the monitor. "It's got arms and legs and everything."

"Well yes," the technician said, with a wry smirk. "Babies do tend to."

"So it's healthy?" she asked, not taking her eyes off the screen.

"As far as we can tell, yes," the technician replied, "everything is growing as expected."

"Should its head be that big?" It looked a little like one of those aliens from the old movies. Head too big, dark shadows for eyes.

"Perfectly normal. It evens out in time."

"Is it a boy or a girl?" Kaitlyn asked.

"We can't tell you that yet," the technician replied. "When you come back at twenty weeks we might be able to, if baby plays along and lets us see. For now, I'll print you off a couple of pictures to take with you."

Pictures. She needed the pictures to take to Martha. She was still staring at the monitor when the technician switched it off and the screen turned black. She sat up, and took the strip of photographs offered to her, smiling at the one where the baby looked as though it were waving for the camera.

Don't look at them. Her rational brain chided her, and

she hastily folded them and stuck them in her pocket. Yes. Don't look at them. Certainly don't smile at them. They're for Martha, that's all. If she looked at them too much, she might not want to give them away. And if she couldn't give Martha a strip of pixelated, black and white pictures, how could she give her a living, breathing baby?

Stay focused, Kaitlyn.

"I think I'd like to pop up to see Jack," she said to Henry.

"But you went to see him an hour ago."

"Still," she said, "I think I need to."

"Alright," he sighed. "I'll wait in the car."

They headed to the toilets to relieve their respective bladders. When she emerged from the ladies, Kaitlyn was surprised that Henry was nowhere to be seen. He must have headed straight for the car, though she couldn't see him making his way down the long corridor. She turned right, and headed up the stairs to see Jack.

She knew Henry was grumpy with her for wanting to see her brother again so soon. But it was easier for him. Chloe was right there, all the time. A constant reminder of why they were doing this. It was so much harder to keep the end goal in mind when it was out of sight.

But even when she sat beside Jack, even when she held his hand and watched the rise and fall of his chest, he still felt far away. It was getting harder and harder to remember him, even though he was right in front of her. She kept trying to chase the memories of his eyes, his voice, but they seemed to have gathered speed and were always just out of reach.

In the montage of memories she ran through her mind, his role was no longer played by a tangible, three-dimensional person. His face was always slightly blurred now, and his speech delivered in her own inner voice, not the crisp, deep tone she knew he spoke with.

It was as though he was already being erased from her life.

She stayed as long as she dared, desperately trying to bring detail and clarity back to her recollections. Henry didn't say much when she got into the car, and she felt a bit guilty about making him wait. She didn't want to inconvenience him any further, but the scan pictures in her pocket were making her feel uneasy, as though they were an illicit, forbidden possession. They didn't really belong to her, yet every fibre of her being wanted to fish them out, open them up, and stare at the images again. They felt dangerous, even through the fabric of her pocket.

"Do you think we ought to stop by Martha's before we go home?" she asked. "I think I ought to get these pictures to her as soon as possible."

"What?" Henry hadn't been listening, too focused on the road.

"The pictures," she repeated, "shall we take them to Martha now?"

"Don't be silly, what do you think the first thing Chloe will ask when we get through the door will be?"

"She'll want to see the pictures," Kaitlyn replied, realising the predicament.

"Exactly. You can't very well not show them to her. Martha will have to wait a day or two, that way if Chloe wants to see them again you can say you left them at work by mistake or something."

"Okay," Kaitlyn said, "you're right."

She wanted to insist. Wanted to plead with him to come up with a reason for coming home empty-handed that Chloe would believe. Perhaps the printer hadn't been working, perhaps the technician had been called away before she could print the pictures. But his gaze was fixed on the road, and his expression stern. How could she tell him that the images in her pocket felt as though they were burning her skin? How could she tell him that she was scared? Scared to look at them again, scared of the primal instinct that they induced.

So she just stared out of the window, and kept her worries to herself.

19

He tried to concentrate on the road, tried to focus on the immediate surroundings, tried to keep his mind from wandering back to that hospital urinal.

He'd been desperate for the toilet by the time they'd got out of the scan appointment. So desperate he hadn't really been able to take in anything the technician had said, but Kaitlyn seemed pleased so all must have been well. The pain of it was almost blinding. Sweat formed on his brow and the world seemed to go fuzzy at the edges. But he hadn't wanted to complain; Kaitlyn had reminded him that she was in the same agony. Surely it couldn't be this bad for her though? Maybe it was worse, and he really was just a weak, griping old snowflake.

He'd never been so happy to see the white porcelain of a latrine before. Like a man who had finally reached a desert oasis after days of walking the arid sands, he could have wept at the promise of imminent relief.

But as he'd stood there, the anticipated release did not come. Try as he might, the waterworks just would not turn on. Yet the pain, the urgent need, was ceaseless. After a good ten minutes, during which he had at least been glad that nobody else had come in with a fully functioning fire hydrant and put him to shame, the tiniest of trickles escaped. It was like putting all your might into opening a bottle of champagne, bracing for the big pop and the ensuing eruption of bubbles, only to find the cork twists out with a pfft, and falls limply into your hand.

Still, he'd thought, at least the stream was flowing now, even if it was more of a stagnant brook than a mighty river. But when he glanced down at the urine trickling into the bowl, panic made his mouth turn dry.

It was tinged red.

Could be any number of things, he'd told himself, most of them entirely trivial. A little infection, perhaps? Or a small nick; even a tiny amount of blood would look so much worse than it really was when mixed with liquid. Yes, that must be it. Though surely he'd have noticed getting a cut or scrape? Maybe not; he still had all kinds of weird nerve damage in random places from the accident. There was a patch on his left thigh that was completely numb, after all.

He'd held his palm to his forehead, to see if he felt hot. He didn't. He'd stared at himself in the mirror, pulling his lower eyelid down to see if there was any discolouration. Not that he'd have any idea what it meant if there was, but it was something he'd seen people do.

"Don't overreact, Henry," he'd instructed his pale reflection, "chances are it's nothing."

But still, he was struggling to put it out of his mind. Kaitlyn was saying things, but he couldn't take them in. Something about the nun, and the pictures. There was an urgency in her tone that worried him, and pulled him out of his thoughts of nightmare-scenarios and back into the present.

She wanted to take them there now?

He knew why. Of course he knew why. She was worried about getting attached. She was absolutely right, taking the pictures straight to the nun right now would be the most sensible thing to do. Get rid of them, don't look at them. But, Chloe was hanging out to see them, she'd been excited about it all week. She was probably pacing around, watching for them to arrive home out of the window.

Sure enough, as soon as they pulled into the close, the

front door opened and there she stood, bouncing slightly on the spot. "Well?" she asked, as soon as the car door opened.

"All fine," Kaitlyn replied. "Perfectly healthy."

Chloe squealed, and threw her arms around Kaitlyn. "And? Did you get them?"

"Yes." Kaitlyn pulled the scan pictures out of her pocket and handed them to Chloe.

"Oh my." Chloe welled up. "Oh Kaitlyn, you clever thing! Just look at that, so perfect. It's got your nose, I think. Look at it waving hello! It knows you're Mummy, see. Oh what a clever little munchkin you've got."

He couldn't stand it. Chloe's excitement, Kaitlyn's awkwardness at all the fuss. Not with his mind still swirling around the urinal bowl.

"I'm going to the club," he said, turning away from Kaitlyn's wide-eyed scowl.

"Alright, love," Chloe called out, wilfully ignoring his rudeness. God, it was irritating when she did that.

He knew he was being a selfish, grumpy old sod leaving Kaitlyn to deal with Chloe's enthusiasm all by herself, but he had to get away. Clear his head. Or maybe cloud it with beer, whatever it took to rid himself of the chaotic thoughts that hounded him.

When he arrived at the darts club, Old Al was in his usual position. Perched on the central bar stool, his oxygen tank on the floor by his feet, the tubes snaking up his body to his nose. At least some things never change.

"Usual please, Mike," Henry said to the bartender as he took the seat next to Al.

"You look like shit," Al said in greeting.

"Look who's talking," Henry replied, and Al burst into a drunken laugh that descended into a coughing fit so severe he had to pull his handkerchief from his sleeve and spit the dislodged phlegm into it.

"Get me another, would you, Mike," Al wheezed when the coughing finally stopped. "Got a thirst on."

"You've always got a thirst on." Mike grinned, pouring another pint.

"What's eating you, anyway?" Al asked Henry. "You've got a cheek coming in here with a face like that. This is supposed to be where I come to forget that the world's shit."

"Nothing," Henry said, feeling too embarrassed to admit he was driving himself crazy over a little bit of blood, when Al struggled for every breath even with the oxygen tank. "Women troubles."

Al scoffed. "Half your luck, boyo. I ain't had a woman to worry about for near on thirty years. That's one trouble I'd be very glad to have. Only it's the one trouble that seems to want nothing to do with me. Despite my devilish good looks and" – Al coughed uncontrollably again – "innate charm."

Henry laughed, and downed half his pint in one go. Much better.

He and Al put the world to rights over several more pints, and Henry gradually forgot why he had been so concerned. When he limped into the gents, after his third pint, his waterworks seemed to have been lubricated by all the barley and hops. This time, all was as it should be.

"Beautiful sight, that," he chuckled at his own stream of urine, "magnificent."

What a twit he'd been. Fancy getting so worked up. It'd probably just been something to do with Kaitlyn having forced him to hold it in so long. Stupid old snowflake. Nothing to worry about. The baby was fine, his stream was clear again. All was right with the world.

20

"Well," Kaitlyn said as Henry departed for the club. "That was rude."

Chloe waved her hand dismissively. "Best he goes out and leaves us in peace, if he's just going to be a misery. I always just pretend I don't notice when he's being churlish, it winds him up more." She winked, and carried on cooing over the pictures. Her enthusiasm wasn't helping with Kaitlyn's resolve not to look at them too much.

"Shall I put them up on the fridge? Or maybe the noticeboard?" Chloe asked, beaming.

"No," Kaitlyn replied, a little too hastily. "No. I'd rather just keep them in my bedside drawer, if you don't mind."

"Of course not," Chloe said, pouring them both a cup of tea. "I'm fussing, I know. I'm just so pleased for you. That's the first trimester ticked off. Oh, that reminds me, I have something for you."

"For me?"

"Yes, now you go sit down with your cuppa and I'll just go and get it, won't be a jiffy."

Kaitlyn sat in the armchair nearest the lounge window. Chloe bustled out of the room, and up the stairs. She'd been watching the news and Kaitlyn found herself staring at the television screen. A young female reporter, holding a huge microphone, stood in front of what looked like an office block.

Its windows had been smashed, and scrawls of red graffiti across the front of its magnolia wall proclaimed *Up the rebels!*

Kaitlyn leaned a little closer to the screen, and turned up the volume.

"The Collective Council have yet to make an official statement about this attack on one of their municipal buildings, but we have received assurances from senior representatives that this is very much an isolated incident."

Chloe snorted a laugh as she came back into the lounge, carrying a large box. "That'll be the third isolated incident this week then," she said, turning off the TV and placing the box in front of Kaitlyn. "Go on, open it!"

The shiny silver box had been topped with a gold bow. Kaitlyn lifted the lid gently, and peeked inside. Bottles of toiletries, a strange triangular-looking pillow, jars of pills, a hot water bottle. She wasn't really sure what it was all in aid of.

"Second and third trimester survival kit!" Chloe pronounced with a grin. "Everything you need to make you as comfortable as possible while you get on with the important job of cooking that little bub of yours to perfection. From vitamins to comfy socks, to scented bath oils to help you relax."

"I don't know what to say, this is incredible. It's the nicest thing anyone's ever done for me." Kaitlyn began pulling the items out of the box, marvelling at the thoughtfulness behind each one. She reached a bottle of bright pink liquid that looked to be a medicine of some sort.

"That's antacid in that bottle you're holding," Chloe said. "Trust me, you'll be swigging it like water, especially if it's a hairy baby."

"I… what?"

"Well, they say it's just an old wives' tale. And I suppose I am just an old wife. But I swear it's true. Got so bad for me toward the end I couldn't so much as bend down to retie my shoelace without feeling like a fountain of lava was springing up in my throat. Hairy, the wives who seemed old to me at the time said, you'll have a hairy one. And lo and behold, they were right."

Kaitlyn stopped looking at the antacid bottle, and stared at Chloe. Was this dementia? Had she forgotten she wasn't David's biological mother? How very strange, to be so on the ball one moment and talking nonsense the next. It didn't even sound like nonsense, and that was the scary part. If she didn't know better, she'd assume Chloe was relating a real experience. She suddenly became conscious that her mouth had fallen open slightly, and hoped Chloe hadn't realised she was scrutinising her for any outward signs of madness.

"Oh, don't worry," Chloe said. "I'm sure you won't have it as bad as I did. I'm sorry. I was trying to help, not scare you off with my horror stories."

"It's not that," Kaitlyn replied, hastily searching for the right questions to ask to check Chloe's state of mind, without offending her. "It's just, I'm surprised. David looks bald in the baby pictures on the mantelpiece."

"David?" Now it was Chloe's turn to look confused. "My dear, I'm not his mother, you know that."

"Oh. Yes." Kaitlyn felt herself turning red. "Yes. Sorry, Chloe. I—"

"Ah." Chloe chuckled, and smiled. "You were worried it was the dementia?"

"No! I mean… well, yes. A bit."

"No need to look so embarrassed, Kaitlyn. I asked you to keep an eye on it, didn't I? Just, please, just say it outright, okay? Let's not have my condition be an elephant in the room for us, like it is with Henry."

"Okay," Kaitlyn agreed. "But, if you weren't talking about David, then who…"

"Well, Heidi, of course."

21

Henry whistled as he walked up the driveway. Amazing what a few pints could do, he chuckled to himself. When he'd left home three hours before in search of alcoholic solace, he'd been carrying the weight of fear and self-pity on his shoulders. Now, the edges of the world seemed softer.

But as he approached the door, Kaitlyn flung it open, scowling. Oh shit. He had been rather rude, rushing off to the bar and leaving her to deal with Chloe in full-on clucky mode, especially because he knew how uncomfortable Kaitlyn found it. Nothing for it, have to just apologise.

"Kaitlyn, I'm sorry I went off like that."

"You bastard," Kaitlyn yelled, and he realised it wasn't a scowl that had crinkled up her features after all. She was crying. Her eyes were puffy, her nose streaming, her cheeks blotchy. "You lying, manipulative, bastard."

She pushed past him, almost knocking him off balance, and stormed down the drive.

"Kaitlyn," he called after her. "Kaitlyn wait, please,"

"Leave me alone!" She carried on walking, almost sprinting, away from the house without looking back.

Okay, so it hadn't exactly been a chivalrous thing to do, leaving her alone with Chloe and the scan pictures, but this was a bit of an overreaction, surely?

"Chloe," he called out as he entered the house. "Chloe, where are you?"

She emerged from the kitchen. There was no misreading the expression this time; she was definitely scowling.

"Oh, Henry Morris," she said, "how could you?"

Oh God. What had happened between them? What had Kaitlyn said?

"What's the matter, love?" he asked gently. "And what's wrong with Kaitlyn?"

"I know you don't like to talk about it. Christ, I know that well enough. But I can't believe you never told Kaitlyn. Never mentioned her, not once?"

"What? Who?"

"Heidi," Chloe snapped, her own tears forming in her eyes. "Don't tell me it's not all an act? Don't tell me you *have* forgotten? Well, would that I could be like you then, Henry Morris!"

"H-Heidi?" Henry felt his leg begin to shake. "You told her about Heidi?"

"Not intentionally! Jesus, Henry. You think I'd bring that up to a pregnant woman? I thought she knew. Thought there was no way she could not know. All the time you two spend together, all the talk of babies in this house, how have you never told her?"

"What did you say to her?"

"The truth. Well, part of it. The part we tell ourselves to make it better than it really is. I told her I had a daughter, but that she died at birth. Is that acceptable? Or is even that too much? Am I not supposed to even speak her name? Am I supposed to pretend I never was a mother?"

Realisation hit all at once. Now he knew. Now he knew why Kaitlyn was so upset, what she must be thinking. She must be terrified for her own baby.

"I'm sorry, Chloe," he said. "I really am. I can never begin to tell you how much. Maybe that's why I don't even try. But right now I have to go after Kaitlyn."

22

The bus was just pulling into its stop at the end of the road so she got on and plonked herself down on a seat near the back, staring out of the window so the other passengers wouldn't see her wet, puffy face. She ran her hands across her belly, trying not to sob again.

Chloe's words echoed through her mind. Inherited defect. Nothing could be done. Died shortly after birth. That's why we didn't try again.

Inherited defect. Inherited defect. Inherited defect.

"Please God, please God no," she whispered, watching a new mother pushing a pram along the street. "Not my baby. Please not mine."

If God was up there somewhere, he probably thought she had a hell of a cheek, what with all the doubt and blasphemy of late. But where else was there to turn, when such heavy gambles hang in the air, but to the fates or the heavens?

When the bus pulled into the hospital car park she got off. The other passengers hurried away in different directions, heading to their appointments or to visit loved ones. But when the bus pulled away again, Kaitlyn was still standing in the middle of the barren parking lot.

She stared at the bench straight ahead, the one she had been crying on when Henry had first approached her and tried to offer her a tissue. So much had happened since then, and so much had been changed by his presence in her life. He'd opened her eyes to things, given her a shoulder to cry on, let her into his home. She'd begun to feel like he was family. It was a messed-up kind of topsy turvy family dynamic, sure. But weren't most families unconventional in one way or another? He was grouchy, cynical, downright moody at times. But he was reliable, kind-hearted and trustworthy. Or so she'd thought.

Jack had always cautioned her against trusting people, and she'd always heeded him, until Henry wormed his way into her affections.

How could he? How could he keep this from her? She thought back to the café they'd gone to, when she asked him how many children he had and he'd taken too long to answer. She'd assumed it was his memory; Christ, she'd assumed so many things. She'd thought old people were all half-crazy, all forgetful. But that wasn't it at all. He'd made a conscious decision to hide the truth from her, even back then. And even when they'd come up with this plan to have a child, he'd still kept it from her. Because it was her risk to own. He had nothing to lose. She was the one who had to carry the baby. She was the one who couldn't walk away if it all went wrong.

What if her baby was sick? She wouldn't be able to sell it, and she'd be unable to afford to look after it. Or Jack. What if her baby died, like Heidi? Jack's life was tied to this little bundle growing inside her, their fates linked. She could lose a child and her brother, in one fell swoop. And she realised she could no longer tell which loss would be the keenest.

Behind her the hospital doors swished open. Doctors and nurses swarmed out, having finished their shifts, and headed for the bus stop. There was still an hour or so of visiting time left. She could go see Jack again, pour her heart out to him, cry by his bedside. But what would be the point?

Guilt pricked at her as she realised it just wasn't enough any more. Talking to someone who couldn't talk back, seeking comfort from someone who could give none. At first she'd been able to imagine his responses to her outpourings and conundrums. She'd been able to hear his voice so clearly in her mind when she'd told him about Finn. 'Fuck him,' comatose Jack had said through the ether. 'He obviously doesn't care enough about your feelings. You're better off without him, Kat.'

Even when she lost his apartment, his voice still formed in her imagination. Telling her it would be okay, he wasn't cross, he was proud. All they needed was each other, after all.

But this? This fucked-up mess? She had no idea what he would say. And because she had no idea what he'd say, she couldn't hear his voice. Which just went to prove it had never really been his voice to start with. He wasn't really with her. He wasn't really listening.

She'd been alone all this time.

So she turned her back on the hospital. Straight ahead, past the bench, was the New Church. Sister Rochelle had a voice. Sister Rochelle would have plenty to say. But Kaitlyn didn't want to hear any of it, not any more.

The two biggest influences in her life were both mere feet away, yet neither of them could give her what she needed right now. With Henry and Chloe in her life, she hadn't noticed just how far away the things she once cherished had really gotten from her.

She reached into her pocket for a handkerchief. When her fingers touched the folded paper she remembered she still had the scan pictures. Turning them over in her hands, she almost unfolded them. The yearning to look at her baby again, to whisper her plea for its health to the images, was almost overwhelming.

"You have no one, Kaitlyn," she told herself sternly. "No one to rely on but yourself. Can't go falling apart. Can't go wishing and dreaming. Just stick to the plan, it's all you can do."

She shoved the pictures back in her pocket, took a deep breath and headed toward to the river.

23

Henry raced across town, his old car spluttering as he put his foot down. He had to find her, had to tell her the truth. The truth he could barely dare to let himself remember. The truth he had tried so hard to forget, the memories he had always forced down, down into the depths of his mind. The memories that now seared through his brain, broadcasting themselves in high definition, making it even harder for him to concentrate on the road.

Chloe's hand around his felt like a vice. He bore the pain stoically, knowing it was the only small thing he could do. The midwife grabbed one of her legs, and pushed it roughly outwards, holding it at the knee at a right-angle.

"Grab the other one," she commanded. "Quickly!"

With his free hand he grabbed Chloe's right leg, pulling it outward from her body as the midwife had done with her left.

"Push, Chloe, push," the midwife commanded. "Baby needs to come out."

"I-I-I-can't do it," Chloe gasped in between cries of pain.

"Yes you can. You don't have a choice. Baby needs you to do this, right now."

Chloe scrunched up her eyes, sweat pouring down her face, and squeezed his hand even tighter still as she let out a deep, guttural groan and bore down.

"That's it," the midwife said, "that's it, Chloe, keep going. Baby's head is coming now."

Henry leaned around Chloe's outstretched leg to look, just as a head of dark, downy hair began to emerge.

Chloe's long moan came to an end and she sucked in air, panting frantically,

"That's it, that's it. Pant. Relax now, relax. The head is coming, then the baby will be born with the next contraction, okay?"

Chloe just nodded in between gasps.

"Oh my God, Chloe," Henry said, stroking her hand. "She's got hair, so much hair. Nearly there, sweetheart. Nearly there."

But when he glanced at the midwife, she was staring at the half-born child between Chloe's legs and he saw her eyes widen as her face fell. She reached across Chloe, slamming her palm onto a large red button on the wall.

"It's just a precaution," she said quickly, though she didn't sound convinced. "But I need you to push again, Chloe. Now. Right now." She pushed Chloe's legs even further back as the door burst open and a gaggle of doctors and nurses rushed in.

"What's going on?" Henry asked, but no one answered.

Chloe groaned again, and the long, slippery body of his newborn daughter slid out from his wife's body and into the midwife's arms. She didn't hold her up. Or say anything at all. Henry watched, confused and anxious, as she handed the blue, blood-soaked creature to a doctor, who in turn placed her in a plastic box on wheels and whisked her out of the door, the whole entourage of white-coated staff disappearing with her.

He hadn't heard her cry.

"What's the matter?" he asked the midwife urgently. "What's wrong?"

He turned to speak to Chloe, wondering why she wasn't filling the air with frantic questions too. She was still, her eyes shut.

"Chloe?" He shook her arm, but she didn't respond.

The midwife tried to rouse her. "Chloe," she said, shaking her more vigorously, "Chloe, can you hear me, hon?" When Chloe didn't stir, she rushed to the door of the small birthing room and yelled out into the hospital corridor. "I need some help in room seven please."

Again the room filled with medical staff that seemed to converge from nowhere. But this time they swarmed round Chloe's bed, and a tall scrawny nurse took him by the arm and pulled him away.

"Come on, Mr Morris. We need you to come out of the room now, let us do our job."

"But, my wife. What's happening to my wife, and where's our baby?"

"We're doing everything we can, Mr Morris."

He pulled into the hospital car park, dumping the car diagonally across two spaces. He made his way through the endless corridors as quickly as he could, finally reaching Jack's ward. The nurse on the reception desk glared at him.

"Yes?" she said. "What can I do for you?"

"Is Kaitlyn here? Kaitlyn Thomas, visiting Jack?"

"And who might you be?" the nurse asked.

"A friend," he said. "Please, is she here?"

"I'm afraid I can't give out that information," the nurse replied, "and it's family and approved visitors only in here. And I know you're not on Jack's list, he only has Kaitlyn."

"Oh for Pete's sake!" He raised his voice, and the nurse looked shocked. But this was no time for being weak and apologetic. It was time to get assertive, to take a leaf out of Kaitlyn's book.

"Kaitlyn," he yelled out to the ward behind the reception desk, "Kaitlyn, are you here?"

"Well now." The nurse stood up, and started walking around the desk toward him. Two other nurses emerged from side-rooms and strode his way too. But before they could reach him, he spotted the name on the board outside the room next to the desk: *Jack Thomas*.

The nurse's hand touched his shoulder, and he threw it off. Moving with more speed, and purpose, than usual, he strode to the door and flung it open. There was no Kaitlyn. Just an unconscious young man on a hospital bed, surrounded by machines. That was him. That was Jack. The person Kaitlyn loved most in all the world. The person she was doing all this for, and the person she was worried she might lose.

The gravity of seeing him in the flesh, not just in his own imaginings, made him stop, and exhale. Several hands grabbed his arms.

"I'm afraid we are going to have to ask you to leave," one of the faceless nurses said.

"Okay," Henry said, letting them manhandle him off the ward without resistance. "Okay."

24

She was going to play it cool, she decided. This was a business transaction, nothing more. You don't tell the person you're selling to that the product might not be up to spec; she may not be an entrepreneur, but she knew that much. If she was going to be a strong, independent woman who could handle any curveball life threw at her, she couldn't go to pieces in front of a stark raving old nun. She straightened herself up, smoothed down her skirt and banged the heavy brass knocker against the door.

The shutter was pulled back and Martha's blind eye, and her good one, appeared in the slot. "Oh, hello, my dear," she said cheerfully, opening the door. "Kaitlyn, isn't it? How lovely to see you."

"I brought the scan pictures you asked for," Kaitlyn replied, as matter-of-factly as she could.

"Oh, how wonderful. Do come in."

"No." Kaitlyn handed her the photos, without unfolding them. "No thank you, I can't stay."

Martha raised an eyebrow, and looked her up and down. "Is there something wrong?"

Kaitlyn avoided making eye contact. "No, everything's fine. The baby's fine."

"The baby might be," Martha said, unfolding the pictures and smiling at the images on them, "but you're not, are you, dear? Something's troubling you. Oh, don't look shocked. You don't get to my age without knowing that puffy eyes and tear streaks on a young woman's face mean pain. Emotional pain, that is. We tend to be much better at hiding our physical complaints than our emotional ones, us empathic types. You don't want to tell me, even though you're desperate for someone to talk to, because you're worried it might affect our little arrangement, is that right?"

How? How did this old woman know so much about her? Was it really just age? Did wisdom come with age after all? She'd always thought brains got mushier as they grew older, not sharper. But then, she used to think a lot of things she now knew were false. She just nodded, scared to speak in case she broke down in front of Martha.

"Well," Martha said, "let me assure you, I won't think any less of you if you're having second thoughts. Nor will I go back on my end of the deal. You have a right to change your mind, you know."

"It's not that," Kaitlyn said. "I'm worried –" Her voice cracked as she spoke in whispers. "I'm worried there might be something wrong with baby."

Martha roared with laughter, not at all the reaction Kaitlyn was expecting. "Why my dear, of course you are!"

"What?"

"You're a mother, Kaitlyn. Worrying is what they do. I'd be shocked if you weren't imagining every possible complication, every little thing that could go wrong. Do you know that lovely Mrs Diggory who runs the bakery on Hinde Street?" Kaitlyn shook her head. "Well," Martha continued, "her son is a judge. A judge. And do you know what? She telephones him every night, to make sure he got home alright and check he's eating properly. Thirty-five he is! My point is, it's all normal. The worry. The scan was fine, yes?"

"Yes," Kaitlyn replied, "everything growing as it should, they said."

"Well, there you are. I'd tell you that means you've nothing to worry about, but you'd continue to do so anyway because that's what being a mother is. So instead I'll just tell you that I'm not worried. In fact, I've already got the perfect family in mind for your little one. So you worry if you must, and I'll just keep on keeping on, alright?"

"Alright," Kaitlyn said, feeling a little less anxious.

"Good." Martha put her arm around Kaitlyn's shoulders. "Your child will be alright, Kaitlyn. I know it."

She didn't know it. Couldn't possibly know it. But Kaitlyn did feel a little better. About the baby, at least. Henry's deceit still burned inside her as she began the long trek to the skyrise district.

A mother. Martha had called her that again. The old nun seemed to have some very clear and idyllic ideas about motherhood. Kaitlyn had never experienced the kind of maternal love and self-sacrifice she talked of, apart from vicariously when she visited her friends' houses as a child, or read about the sweet, patient mothers all the characters in the books she read at school seemed to have. She couldn't help but think that, despite her age, Martha was a little naïve.

Kaitlyn's mum was a mother, after all. The only one she'd ever have. And she was nothing like the ones in books and movies.

Mum.

Kaitlyn tried to think about something else. About anyone else. But as she approached the vast rows of tower blocks where she had grown up, and now lived at once again, she couldn't shake the images of her childhood from her mind. Every time she got away from here, circumstance pulled her back. Maybe you can't outrun your genes, no matter how fast you move. Maybe the whole system of sorting and allocating people was right after all. Maybe you would always be what you were born into, and fate would drag you back if you ever got your head too far above the water.

Maybe, if she ever had a child to keep, she'd be a car crash of a mother, just like Mum.

The grass verge where she had been attacked came into view, and it made her stop in her tracks. Going back to her flat was the last thing she wanted right now. She'd have to walk right past the doorway where he'd cornered her. And what if she bumped into someone who had been there that night? They'd ask her how she was, ask her where she'd been. She couldn't face the questions, even though they'd be well-meaning.

So she kept walking. Instead of turning into the southern part of the district where her block was, she carried on North. Past block after block, small square of grass after small square of grass. Children played hopscotch, clothes torn and faces covered in dirt. Drunk old men sat babbling to each other beside the wheelie bins. Every estate in the district was the same. The same formation of blocks surrounding token greenery, the same smell of festering waste and stale beer, the same people living the same dead-end lives.

When she reached the northernmost edge, she stopped and stared at the block she had once called home. There were different coloured curtains at the window of the corner flat on the fourth floor. They'd always been bright blue when she was a kid. She'd always looked for them if she got disorientated. Sometimes the rows and rows of identical blocks were overwhelming for a small child. The distinctive curtains had been like a beacon, showing her which block she belonged in. She never did know whose curtains they were. Perhaps whoever had hung them had grown tired of the colour and replaced them with the beige blinds that now adorned the window. Or perhaps they had moved out. Or died.

Perhaps Mum had too.

The thought struck her suddenly. Was her mother even there? With Jack unconscious, and Rochelle full of nothing but condemnation and criticism, Mum was the only person left from her childhood that might still be the same as she remembered. Or she might be gone, or changed. Maybe her children walking out on her had been a wake-up call. Maybe she'd sorted herself out. Got clean, got a better job. Maybe she'd even got a better place to live. Adrenaline spiked inside her; she had to know. If her mother could turn her life around, then there was hope that she could too.

Walking through the broken front door of the block wasn't as strange as she'd thought it would be. It was pretty much identical to the block she lived in now, though in her memory the foyer of her childhood block seemed much bigger. There was yellow Out Of Order tape across the elevator, just like there'd always been. The door to their old flat was still the same. Heavy wood, with the number plaque missing and *Flat 4* written on in marker pen. She ran her finger down the doorframe, and found the small initials – *J T* – that Jack had carved into it with a pen knife.

She rested her palm on the door for a few moments before swallowing hard and knocking.

"Who's it?" The yell was shrill, and slurred. The yell was her mother's.

She almost turned around. Almost walked away. Knocking on the door to your past was a stupid, impulsive idea. She'd wanted to find a happy ending to the story of Mum, but that one drunken shout told her there was none.

"It's me," she said, against her better judgement.

"Who's me? Whatta ya playin' at?"

She heard the scrape of the chain being put on. She'd recognise that sound anywhere. She'd put it on herself every time she got through the door, scared of the monsters outside. The door opened a crack, and the stench of smoke and booze spilled out into the hall, briefly covering the scent of ammonia.

Her mother's eyes were wizened, and more wrinkled than she remembered. But they were still the same eyes that stared back at Kaitlyn whenever she looked in the mirror. The same eyes that Jack was hiding behind his closed lids.

"Kaitlyn?"

"Yes, Mum. It's me. It's Kaitlyn."

"Whadda you want? What you doin' here? You ungrateful

little brat. Walkin' out on me like that, you and your good for nuthin' brother."

She was swaying, her head bobbing from side to side. Even though the door was only open a crack, Kaitlyn could see the bottle she clutched in her right hand. And the bruise on her cheek.

"I'm pregnant, Mum." She didn't know why she said it. It just fell out in the absence of anything else to say.

Her mum snorted. Then chuckled. Then erupted into a raucous, hysterical belly-laugh. The door closed. Kaitlyn heard the scrape of the chain being taken off. Mum threw it wide open, still laughing like a demented demon.

"Ta da!" she shrieked.

Kaitlyn stared in horror at her mother's ripe, engorged abdomen.

"Like mother, like daughter, eh?"

She turned and ran from the building, Mum's grotesque inebriated laughter ringing in her ears.

25

She must have gone back to the skyrise. At least, he hoped she had. He was all out of ideas if not. He'd already checked Jared's, but a quick look through the window told him she wasn't there. Just a few customers having afternoon tea, and that blonde waitress whose pregnancy had inspired this whole arrangement. What had Kaitlyn said her name was? Jemma? Jemima?

"Oh, damn. As if it matters," he muttered to himself as he struggled up the last flights of stairs. "Need to concentrate on making it there in one piece, not worrying about some waitress' name."

But when he reached her door, it was obvious she hadn't been there. Mail was still sticking haphazardly out of the letter box, and when he peeked through he could see all the curtains were drawn. He called out her name and banged on the door anyway.

Where now? Where else could she possibly have gone? Perhaps to that old nun, but he had no idea where she lived. Damn it, why didn't he just take her there when she asked him to? All of this could have been avoided.

He couldn't face the trek back down to the elevator just yet, so he leant up against the low windowsill in the corridor, trying to rest his aching leg a little. But he straightened up when he heard footsteps.

The heavy door to the stairwell flew open and Kaitlyn burst through.

"Kaitlyn," he said, "Kaitlyn, I've been looking for you."

She stormed past him, pulling her keys from her pocket. "What are you doing here? Leave me alone!"

She tried to put the key in the lock, but her hands were shaking. "God damn it. God damn it all." She thumped her front door with her fist. "Just fucking open, why won't anything go right?"

"Please." Henry took a tentative step forward. "Let me help you."

"Help me? Help me?" She turned to him, face red and breath coming in gasps. "Look what happened last time you helped me. You lied. You let me get pregnant knowing the child could be sick. You manipulated me. You let me take a risk without telling me all the facts. I could have found another way, found another donor. But you let me gamble my brother's life on this."

"No," he said gently. "No, Kaitlyn. I didn't lie."

"Well you sure as hell didn't tell the truth."

"Because I didn't think it was relevant."

"You didn't think the fact you had a child who died at birth because of an inherited defect was relevant?"

Henry sighed, and looked her straight in the eyes. "It was from Chloe's side, not mine," he said. "So, no, it wasn't relevant. Medically, at least. But I should have told you. I know that. This is more than just a business arrangement now. You're like… like family to us. I did owe it to you to be honest, and I wasn't. I'm sorry."

"Chloe's side?" The relief was obvious on her face.

"Yes." He nodded. "Her sister lost a child in much the same way, though hers lived longer. But then, there were other issues with Heidi."

"So why didn't you tell me?"

"Because I was ashamed."

"Ashamed? Of Heidi?"

"Oh God, no." Henry blinked fast, trying to stop the tears from coming. "Ashamed of what I did."

26

She was still reeling from the shock of her mother's pregnancy. But Henry looked so broken, so vulnerable. Just a few moments ago she'd been livid with him, anger coursing through her veins like a drug. But now she felt guilty. She hadn't waited to hear his explanation, even after all he'd done for her. She'd stormed out without giving him a chance to explain. Impulsive, that was always her problem. Even going to see her mother had been impulsive, and she regretted that now too.

The relief she felt at hearing the defect wasn't on Henry's side was short-lived, replaced by shame. Shame that she'd been glad to hear the news. Chloe was the kindest person she'd ever met; she didn't deserve such terrible misfortune. No one did.

She finally got the door open and ushered Henry inside. He was shaking. She vowed she would let him tell her whatever it was that was burdening him, and wouldn't rush to judge.

"So, tell me what really happened," she said as they both took seats in the lounge area.

"It's not something I ever talk about. Not even with Chloe," Henry said, staring at the carpet and wringing his hands. "I've always just tried to forget. But it doesn't work. I know that now. And when Chloe was ill, it was like torture. Like karma, come to get its revenge. She would scream for Heidi, all the time. Can you imagine what that's like? To hear someone you love wail in pain, listen to their heart break over and over again, all because of what you did?"

"I don't understand," Kaitlyn said. "I thought Heidi was sick? What did you do?" She wasn't sure she wanted the answer, especially when Henry began sobbing so hard he buried his head in his hands. But she had to know. And more importantly, she had a strong suspicion he needed to tell her.

"It was a difficult birth," Henry said, when he'd managed to compose himself a little. "Hours and hours she was in labour for. All through the night, and most of the next day too. Christ, she was in so much pain. But she wouldn't have drugs, they'd convinced her at one of those birthing classes that it was bad for the baby. And she'd have endured anything for her baby. But when Heidi finally came, they whisked her away, we didn't even get to see her. She wasn't breathing, they told me after, they had to resuscitate her. But Chloe was in a bad way too. She fell unconscious, and before I knew it they'd whisked her off too. Loads of them, doctors and nurses, rushing her down the corridor in her hospital bed, shouting medical jargon to each other.

"One minute I was holding my wife's hand as our daughter was born, the next I was alone in a hospital corridor, both of them gone God knows where and me with no idea what was going on. I was terrified."

Kaitlyn shuffled forward to the edge of her chair, and reached out to take Henry's hand in hers. "Henry," she said softly. "It must have been awful."

"It was," he continued. "It felt like an eternity, just waiting. Not knowing. I thought nothing could be worse than that. But then a doctor came to see me, took me into a small office, said he needed to talk to me about my daughter. He told me she had a hole in her heart, that if she had any chance of survival she'd have to be operated on, as soon as she was strong enough, and he needed to know if that was what I wanted."

"So what did you say?"

"I said of course, but it turned out it was more complicated than that. She'd been starved of oxygen for a while during the birth. For too long. He said she would have permanent brain damage. They couldn't tell the extent of it yet, but it was likely she wouldn't be able to walk, or talk. Maybe not even communicate at all. Even if she survived the heart surgery, she'd need care for her whole life. And her EP would automatically be zero. We'd have to use our own credit, or find the money. He asked if I had other children, so I told him about David. He said I ought to consider the impact on him, on his future."

"That's terrible," Kaitlyn said, trying to comprehend the choice Henry had been faced with.

"Yeah," Henry replied. "But that's not the worst of it. I told him I'd have to talk it through with Chloe, but he told me there wasn't time. Chloe had haemorrhaged, she was in surgery. He said she'd be sedated for hours yet, and they needed a decision immediately."

"Why?" Kaitlyn leapt up, feeling indignant on Henry's behalf. "Why couldn't they wait? How could they possibly expect you to make a decision in that state, and without Chloe?"

"I was in such shock," Henry said. "I was so confused. I didn't know up from down, or right from wrong. He went on and on about how much intervention Heidi would need if we were going to keep her alive long enough to undergo surgery. They'd stabilised her, for the time being, but she wouldn't live more than a few hours without assistance. He talked about how cruel it would be to put her through it if we weren't going to go ahead with the operation, how painful it would be for her, all the tubes and needles she'd need. Told me there was no guarantee she'd survive surgery anyway, and went on about how little quality of life she'd have even if she did. 'Better to let her slip away in her sleep than put her through it all if you've any doubt,' he said. I can hear it now. Clear as day."

Kaitlyn shook her head, squeezing his hand.

"I tried to think about what was best, for everyone. Especially David. He was my child too, you know. Carolyn had insisted he went to a private school, which of course I had to pay for. If we had to fund Heidi's surgery, and all her future care, he'd have to drop out. I wouldn't be able to give him the best start in life, or any help down the line if he needed it. There would be nothing left for him if he had problems of his own later on. And what would happen to Heidi anyway, when we became too old to look after her? We'd not survive any major illnesses ourselves, with no credit left."

"So what did you decide?" Kaitlyn asked, although of course she already knew the answer.

"I decided to let her go." His voice broke, his whole body shook. Kaitlyn threw her arms around him, her shoulders soaked by his tears. "I let her die in my arms. Chloe never even got to see her alive; by the time she woke up Heidi was already gone. I chose my existing family over my new daughter. I chose David over Heidi."

"Is that what you think?" Kaitlyn's mind whirred. It all made so much more sense now. No wonder he was so angry at David. He'd sacrificed so much for him, and now he was throwing it back in his face. Trying to take even more from him. "Henry, you said it yourself. They said she might not have even survived the surgery."

He just shook his head. "It doesn't matter. I thought I was being practical, logical. Thought it was the rational thing to do, her odds were so slim anyway, why prolong things? But I know now what I didn't back then. We all lose each other eventually, Kaitlyn. It's the time we have together that matters. And Chloe didn't get any. Not a single hour to treasure. I don't know how she forgave me; sometimes I worry that she didn't."

"She did," Kaitlyn said, certain it was the truth. "I've seen the way she looks at you. She loves you. More than I ever knew it was possible for one person to love another."

"And David," Henry said, "I can't believe how selfish he is. I gave up my daughter, Chloe's chance to be a mother, for him. And he still wants more. Taking me to court, trying to prove I'm incapable. He wants to take Chloe away from me too, just so he can get his hands on what's left of my money."

"We won't let him," Kaitlyn said, feeling her resolve set in. "*I* won't let him. Come on, let's go home. We need to figure out how you're going to win that court case."

PART 3

THE GHOSTS OF OUR CHOICES

When we look at back at the time in between the revolution and the instatement of the Collective Council, it's clear that we are looking at a time of acute chaos. The revolution was born out of anger; a shared, primal outrage at the corruption and lies of the previous government. But the revolutionaries had no plan beyond bringing down the establishment. There was no clear idea as to what should happen next. So the interim government failed because it had too many factions to try to appease.

When the Collective Council were elected, it was clear they would need to consolidate power quickly if they were to bring about stability and govern effectively. One cannot achieve much in power with the constant threat of being overthrown by any of the multitude of groups who sprung up in opposition. The revolutionaries, of course, had used the power of technology – specifically the internet, which was at that time accessed daily by almost every man, woman and child to organise their activities and spread their message. The Roll-Back then was not only an attempt to return to better, more productive times, but also a means of preventing such uprisings whilst the Council put its plans into action.

But of course, History shows us that revolutions occurred in many places across the world long before the advent of the information superhighway. And in all likelihood, they will again.

Thomas Sandrid, *The Revolution in History*

1

It was a stifling afternoon in mid-June when he sat in the court room with his wife on one side of him and the young woman who was carrying his child on the other.

Chloe squeezed his hand as they all sat wiping sweat from their brows and fanning themselves with the business cards a young lawyer had thrust at them on their way in. Henry hadn't wanted to put her through it, but Kaitlyn had insisted. True to her word, she'd spent the last few months learning everything she could about similar cases, including what counts in the defendant's favour and what doesn't.

"How can we argue that Chloe is well, and of sound enough mind to make her own decisions, if we don't bring her with us?" she'd said. "They'll just think we're hiding something. She has to be there, it's the best hope we've got."

He had to concede she was probably right. He could only hope David wouldn't say anything too cruel or upsetting; he couldn't bear for Chloe to be hurt any more.

On his right side, Kaitlyn wiggled in her chair. Her belly was huge now, and her fuse even shorter than ever.

"You alright?" he asked her.

"I'm fine," she huffed, "just this bloody chair. You try getting comfortable in this tiny little plastic seat when you're the size of an obese mountain goat."

"Must be tough," he said, treading carefully. He'd learned not to downplay her suffering, and never, ever to give unsolicited advice as to how she could improve her levels of comfort. Ever since his suggestion of lavender oil on her pillow to help with the insomnia had been met with her own suggestions regarding where he could shove his 'witchcraft flower-oil', he'd kept his advice to himself.

"Yeah," Kaitlyn continued. "Well let's hope this son of yours doesn't keep us waiting much longer."

Before she'd even finished her sentence, Henry spotted him. Swaggering into the room in his best suit, Fiona on his arm wearing a frosty smile. Damn disgraceful little ingrate.

His son and his wife took up their seats on the opposite side of the room, and the judge called for hush, even though no one was speaking. David hadn't hired a lawyer, Henry noted. He meant to present his case himself, probably thinking it was a foregone conclusion. He smirked a little when he noticed the look of shock on David's face at seeing Chloe present. Not just present, but radiant. Kaitlyn had done her hair and make-up for her, and taken her shopping for a new outfit too. A far cry from how she'd been last time David had visited.

The judge called the court to order with a ceremonious bang of his little wooden gavel, and then invited David to explain why he had brought the case before him. Henry eyed his son as he flounced before the judge.

"Well, your honour," David began, "I have some serious concerns about my father's ability to care for my beloved stepmother, Chloe, and have cause to question whether his actions have been in her best interests."

Henry couldn't stop the low growl from rumbling in his throat. Kaitlyn widened her eyes at him, and he felt like a scolded schoolchild. 'Play nice,' she mouthed, and he knew she was right. He had to be the epitome of calm, otherwise he'd just go and prove David's point. But damn it, it was hard to listen to such bile.

"I hadn't seen her in quite some time," he said. "There was

always some excuse, some reason, why it wasn't a good time to visit. I took it all at face value, of course. But now I believe he was keeping me away from her deliberately."

"And why do you think that might be?" the judge asked.

"I believe he knew he wasn't taking care of her properly, and he knew I would intervene. Your honour, my stepmother is a kind, wonderful and dignified lady, and I love her very much." Henry couldn't stop the snort of disbelief. Kaitlyn glared at him, but David continued. "She took great care of me as a child, more so than my own biological mother at times. I know she would not want to continue in the state she was in when I was finally able to visit."

"And what state would that be?" the judge asked.

Henry gripped Chloe's hand even tighter, but he couldn't look her in the eye when David began to recall hearing her frantic wailing. "I wasn't even able to see her," David said. "My father was keeping her hidden upstairs, I have no idea what physical state she was in, but the anguish in her cries... No human should have to endure that, least of all someone as sweet and gentle as Chloe."

"So you didn't see her," the judge asked, "on this one occasion you were present? So really, you can't be sure this wasn't an isolated incident?"

Hot damn. Henry couldn't believe it. The judge was pressing for more evidence, not just taking David's word for it? He grinned; this might go better than expected after all.

"No, as I told you before my father was deliberately keeping me away from her. However," David continued, "I do have some witnesses to other events who can help to prove my case."

Witnesses?

"Very well," the judge said, "let's hear from your witnesses."

Henry felt the blood drain from his face as Kimmy entered the room and took up the stand. Of all the back-stabbing witches. Pretending to be so concerned and helpful, and then testifying against him? She caught his eye as she sat down, her eyes wide, and mouthed, 'I'm sorry.' But he didn't want to know. He crossed his arms and stared straight ahead.

She told them everything. How he'd gone out and left her unsupervised and she'd wandered the streets. The times when she'd been 'minding' Chloe for him and witnessed her erratic behaviour. The time Chloe scratched his face and she'd had to calm her down for him.

And it didn't stop there. More neighbours were paraded in front of the judge, telling tales of the times they'd seen Chloe searching through the bushes in her nightclothes, raving about nonsense, or the screams they'd heard late at night when she'd woken looking for her baby. The rage inside him threatened to boil over. But when he looked at Chloe, it was the slow tear that trickled down her cheek as she listened to their accounts that really hit the hardest.

2

"Alright." The judge took his glasses off and rubbed the sides of his head. "Well, we've heard all the evidence from Mr Morris Junior. I think we will take a short recess now, and then the court will hear from Mr Morris Senior before I pass judgement."

"All rise," the court clerk bellowed, and Kaitlyn wrenched herself to her feet, grateful to stretch a little. She followed behind Henry and Chloe as they headed outside for some fresh air.

"God damn sneaky, selfish bastard." Henry started ranting as soon as they were out of earshot from the court room. "Bringing our neighbours in like that? Who the hell does he think he is?"

"He's got nothing," Kaitlyn said. "All of those accounts were from at least six months ago. Before the new dose, before I moved in. It's all irrelevant. Anyone can see for themselves that Chloe is fine now."

Except she wasn't. In truth, Kaitlyn was worried about her speaking in court; she hadn't been quite herself recently. Just little things, nothing like the stories David's witnesses had recounted, but the warning signs were there. Keys in the fridge, clothes on inside out, answering questions that hadn't been asked, forgetting briefly who Kaitlyn was. Nothing drastic, but enough to make her worry that Chloe's medication might not be as effective any more. Henry hadn't seemed to notice, and she hadn't brought it up with him. With this case looming, she didn't want to add to his stress.

But, true to her word, she had told Chloe. Even though it broke her heart to see pain in the eyes of the old woman she had come to love so much. A promise was a promise. So she'd let Chloe know, gently. Pointing out when she'd put something in the wrong place, rather than just discreetly moving it like Henry always did, telling her straight when she wasn't making sense, instead of humouring her. Sometimes, Chloe didn't seem to believe her. But other times, Kaitlyn could see the look of realisation flash across her face. On those occasions, Chloe would thank her for her honesty. But, that didn't stop Kaitlyn feeling guilty.

But compared to the tales they'd just heard in court, Kaitlyn's concerns really were minor. It had been shocking to hear the testimonies. She couldn't imagine how horrific they must have been for Chloe to listen to. It pained her to imagine how hurt she must be feeling; she slipped her arm around her and kissed her cheek.

"Are you alright?" she asked.

"Me?" Chloe replied. "Oh yes. But the important question is, how are you doing? Very hot in there isn't it? Not much fun when you've got a little furnace inside." She patted Kaitlyn's tummy gently, and the baby kicked.

"And again," Kaitlyn exclaimed. "Seriously, every time. Baby must like your voice, Chloe."

Chloe beamed, the pain completely gone from her eyes. But Henry didn't react. "We best get back in there," he said. "Show them what we've got."

Henry's testimony went better than she'd expected it to. When they'd practised, he couldn't help going off on sweary tangents and she'd been worried he'd do the same here. But either the solemnity of the court room, or the proximity of his son calmed his impulses, and he made his points sensibly and rationally. He explained that there had been teething problems with Hepraxin at first, but now the dose was sorted she hadn't had an incident in over six months.

Then it was Kaitlyn's turn. She'd come up with the plan to tell the judge that Henry had hired her as a home-help, and a carer for Chloe. Genius, even if she did say so herself. Not only did it explain their unusual living situation, it painted Henry in a much better light. David was trying to prove he wasn't responsible enough to make decisions for Chloe, but what could be more responsible than hiring someone to share the load?

It worked like a charm. The judge smiled and nodded as she told him how Chloe and Henry were very much in love, and both very capable. "I'm only really there to help a bit with the housework, and to be some company for Chloe when Henry's playing darts," she said. "I'm more like a professional friend really. And I certainly haven't seen anything like what the neighbours described."

"And you've been living with them for how long?"

"Almost six months, your honour."

"So, you've been with them, day and night, for all that time, and haven't encountered any of the..." He picked up his notes and squinted at the page. "...'wailing' or 'raving' the other witnesses described?"

"No, your honour. And I might add that all of those incidents were before Henry took charge and sorted out her medication."

"Thank you, Miss Thomas," the judge said. "Well, it seems to me that the only thing left to do is to hear from the lady herself. Mrs Morris, are you able to answer some questions for us?"

"Of course," Chloe replied, getting up from her seat next to Henry. Kaitlyn winked at her as they swapped places.

The judge asked all kinds of condescending questions. What year it was, where she lived, who was the current Council spokesperson. Kaitlyn felt pained, imagining how awful it must be, to be treated like a child. Though from the stories about her bad times she'd heard today, she knew there had been days when she couldn't have answered them correctly. And that there might be again.

"That's lovely, Mrs Morris," the judge said at last, "I just have one last question. The most important question, in fact. What do you want?"

"Well that's the easiest one," Chloe said, "couldn't you have started with that, instead of the year?" The whole room chuckled, except David and his wife. "What I want, your honour, is exactly what I have. No more, no less. Henry takes great care of me, and having Kaitlyn around too is the icing on the cake. The only thing I would love more would be if you" – she turned and addressed David directly – "and the kids would join us this Christmas?"

"I... I don't..." David stared at the floor, shuffling in his seat.

"Well, I've heard more than enough." The judge saved him from having to answer. "Mr Morris Junior, I thank you for bringing this matter to the court's attention. From the testimony of the witnesses you provided, I can see you were justified in your concerns, and acting as a loving son, and responsible citizen ought to."

"What?" Henry leapt up, but the judge shot him a dark look.

"However," he said, "I am also satisfied that, whilst there was once cause to worry about Mr Morris Senior's ability to act in his wife's best interests, that is no longer the case. He has taken all reasonable steps to ensure Mrs Morris' health and well-being, and therefore this court rules in favour of the defendant. Mr Morris Senior will retain his legal position as his wife's next of kin, and also retain control of all his material assets."

The relief was indescribable. Henry cheered, and hugged his wife tight. But although Chloe smiled, Kaitlyn thought there was something missing from it. Her lips made the right shape, but that was all.

David tried to approach them as they got up to leave.

"Chloe, I…" His face was ashen.

"It's alright, David," Chloe said, "I know you meant well."

"Like hell he did," Henry snapped. "Damn ungrateful little brat."

"I'm sorry you feel that way, Dad."

"Don't call me that." Henry's face had turned a shade of red Kaitlyn had never seen him wear before. "Don't you dare call me that, after what you've put us through."

"I think it might be best if you left them alone now." Kaitlyn stepped forward, putting herself in between them. "It's all very raw."

David nodded, and took a few steps backward. But as Chloe and Henry walked through the door ahead of her, he grabbed Kaitlyn by the arm.

"Miss Thomas?"

"What is it?"

"I really was worried about her. I know he thinks it was all about money, but that's his own mind, his own guilt. He's just projecting his own standards onto me."

"What do you mean?"

"Can you imagine what it's like?" David said. "Owing such a debt? What could I ever do, ever have done, to make him proud? To help him justify his choice to himself?"

Kaitlyn glanced out the door; Henry and Chloe were heading to the car. "You're talking about Heidi?"

"Yes," David said. "I know he blames me. But I never asked him to do what he did. He feels as though he bet on me, and I let him down. But really, what hope was there for me to ever be enough? How could I ever be worth it?"

"You couldn't," Kaitlyn whispered. "No one could."

She knew it to be true. She'd realised it the minute Henry told her about that day. He hated David for his actions, sure. But more than that, he was disappointed in him as a son. And that wasn't fair. How could anyone ever prove themselves worthy of the loss of another child's life? They couldn't. Because nobody was. There was nothing she could do for

267

him; she'd never convince Henry his son was anything other than the selfish money-grabbing bastard he'd built him up to be. But she knew a woman who might.

"Chloe will talk him round, you'll see," she said.

"I hope so," David said. "I meant what I said in there, she was more of a parent to me than either of my own. I couldn't bear it if she thought the same as Dad."

"You've met Chloe, right?" Kaitlyn said, and David laughed. "She sees the good in everyone. Even me. And I know she loves you, she's always telling me stories."

"Oh dear," David said, smiling now. "Not too embarrassing I hope?"

Kaitlyn shrugged. "Depends if you think trying to give yourself a crew cut with her best scissors when you were ten is embarrassing, I guess."

They both laughed, but David's wife approached, looking stern, and cleared her throat. "It's time we were going, David," she said, without acknowledging Kaitlyn's presence.

"Okay, Fi, I'm coming." He shook Kaitlyn's hand. "Thank you, you've made me feel a bit better. I'm sorry we had to meet like this, I hope things will be more congenial next time."

She just nodded, and rushed off after Henry and Chloe. When she got in the car, Henry was still bouncing with exhilaration.

As they drove home, Henry waxed lyrical about their victory. Kaitlyn joined in, making all the right noises and agreeing how well it had all gone. Chloe was quiet while the two of them chattered. But when they eventually stopped talking, she spoke. Calmly, and gently.

"I think I should like to hold the baby," she said. "I think I should like that very much. And that will be quite enough for me then."

3

Over the coming weeks, he told himself Chloe hadn't meant it. Or at least hadn't meant it the way it sounded. He was good at that; he'd spent most of his life coming up with alternative explanations for things he didn't like. Or ignoring them.

He didn't mention what she'd said. And she didn't bring it up again. With Kaitlyn getting bigger by the day, he focused his attention on practical things, like making sure she had a hospital bag packed, and some nappies for the first few hours before the transaction. Of course, with the case won, he wouldn't need the money from the sale of the baby. He'd already resolved to tell Kaitlyn to keep it all for Jack's bills, and to help her get back on her feet. But he wouldn't say anything until after the birth; she was too proud to accept without putting up a fight.

No, he'd sell the house, just like he planned. Tell Chloe he wanted somewhere smaller, somewhere without stairs, because he was struggling now, with his leg. He didn't want her to know it would really be for her pills.

Not just her pills, in fact. He'd be able to get a new prosthetic, and a proper check-up. The red tinge had reared its ugly head a few times, but it came and went. Even though his natural predilection was toward burying his head in the sand, he thought it might not be wise to leave it unchecked for too long. He had Chloe to look after, after all. And once Kaitlyn was gone, he'd not be able to afford to get sick.

Kaitlyn leaving. That was something else he didn't want to think about. The way Chloe laughed with her, the in-jokes they shared and the meals they cooked together, his wife teaching her all the things her own mother never had. And the evenings spent chatting on the sofas, Chloe rushing to rub her belly every time she told them baby was kicking. Those were magic times. Family times, almost.

They even nagged him in stereo, just like a real family. Especially about David. Both of them had tried to make him see his son in a better light. Too damn full of heart for their own good. It must be nice to be so innocent, to believe the good intentions people profess to have. He could never be so naïve. He'd seen too much of human nature not to know its goals were usually selfish.

He said as much to Al, down at the club, on one of the nights he left the ladies home alone watching the soaps Chloe had got Kaitlyn hooked on.

"Blood is thicker than water, my arse," he ranted, launching his dart at the board and hitting a disappointing single twenty. "Blood doesn't mean anything to the likes of him, and you know why?"

"Why?" Al asked, in between coughs.

"Because it's red. They're only interested in the green." Henry rubbed his fingers together. "After all I did for him."

"Gave him everything, did ya?"

"Everything. And then some." Henry had had at least five pints, and his tongue felt looser than usual. "Chose his future over his sister's life!"

Al whistled. Henry had told him about Heidi once or twice, but never made that confession before. Usually, if he spoke of it at all, he just gave the line he'd tried to tell himself. No chance of survival, no point in operating.

"Thassa biggun," Al agreed. "But you know you can't expect any more from their generation. All greed and self-righteousness they are."

"I wish I could believe that," Henry said. "But I know

270

they're not all that way. Which means my son is just a bastard, and it's probably my fault somehow."

"Or it's his," Al said, downing the dregs of his pint, "for not being his sister."

"What do you mean by that?" Henry put his darts down and stared at Al.

"Ach, nothing offensive. Just, it's natural isn't it? To romanticise the road not taken. Imagine how much easier it would have been to walk, imagine the views would have been more spectacular. That's what decisions are, Henry. They're choosing to take one path over another. But you always wonder how the journey would have gone if you'd chosen different."

"I guess you're right."

"Course I'm right! Take me, eh? Forty years ago, I had two lasses vying for my attention. Hard to believe now, isn't it?" Al wheezed a laugh. "I went for Georgia, hair like the blazing sun and a voice like music. Turned down Hannah, though she were just as pretty and good-natured. But I wonder all the time, where I'd be now if I'd taken the other road. Not sitting here on a shitty bar stool yammering to you, that's for damn sure. So, even though I thought I decided not to make Hannah a part of my life, I did."

"How'd you mean?"

"The other choice. You can't escape it. It never stops coming to mind. Like the other version of your life is unfolding somewhere, and you want to just reach out and touch it, see if it's better. They haunt you, the things you could have chosen."

"I never thought of it like that before." Henry waved at Mike to fetch him another, his mind racing. Was Heidi still with him? Was the thought of how things would be if he'd opted to try to save her infecting his life? Was it colouring his view of the world, of his son?

"Hard to live with them, eh?" Al said.

"Live with who?"

"The ghosts, Henry. The ghosts of our choices."

4

Gina had left Jared's a week before her due date, and Kaitlyn had been sad to see her go. They'd had fun going to the birthing classes together; squeezing ice cubes and trying to 'breathe through the pain', laughing at the almost demonic-looking doll the midwives passed around for them to practise changing. Gina made everything seem light, and upbeat.

She'd promised to come see Kaitlyn at work, after she'd handed the baby over to Martha. But she hadn't visited yet, so Kaitlyn figured she must have gone overdue and prayed that wouldn't be the case for her. With just five weeks left until her own due date, she was really feeling the strain. Heartburn, mysterious cramps, not to mention the fact the baby had turned and now insisted on kicking her ribs morning, noon and especially at night.

The last time she'd seen Martha, just after her twenty-week scan, she'd given her the full low-down on how it would go. As soon as the baby was declared healthy, and discharged from hospital, she was to take it straight to the old nun. The new family would be on standby, but not present. She wouldn't have to meet them, she could return the next day for her money.

Kaitlyn had opted not to find out the baby's sex because she knew if she did she'd not be able to stop herself from thinking of names. 'You should never name something that can't be kept'; Jack taught her that when he worked on the farm. 'Imagine if we named all the calves?' he'd said when she'd asked him if he had a favourite and what they were called. 'How could I send little Toby, or Buddy, off to become hamburgers? No. Numbers only. 15346, can't get attached to him.'

She'd worried Martha might be cross, that it might be harder to place the baby without knowing, but she hadn't minded at all.

"Oh, don't you fret, dear," she'd said, taking the latest scan pictures (which Kaitlyn had forced herself not to look at) and filing them away. "The family this baby belongs with will love them no matter who, or what, they are."

It was all very reassuring. But still, she wished Gina would hurry up and pop so she could find out how it went, and if the adoption process really was as simple as Martha made out. "Henry's turned me into an old cynic," she said, staring at herself in the mirror. Just a few months ago she'd have taken it all at face value, no questions asked.

She settled herself sideways on the sofa, the triangular pillow Chloe had bought her between her knees, just in time for the evening soaps. Henry couldn't stand them; he'd gone off to drink at the club. But Kaitlyn loved these evenings with Chloe. She'd never realised how riveting watching other people's scripted version of daily troubles could be.

"So," she said. "What do we think? Is Dimitri cheating on Anne? Or is there a reasonable explanation?"

"I don't know," Chloe sighed.

"What's wrong?" Normally she was full of smiles and anticipation when *Skyrisers* began.

"There's toothpaste in my handbag," Chloe replied.

"Okay, well that's random."

"I don't remember putting it there," Chloe said, "and it's not exactly the kind of thing I could mix up because I was busy, is it? Anyway, it's not just that. Earlier I was thinking about my niece's birthday, and I couldn't remember when it was. Kaitlyn, when you moved in, you promised you would be honest with me, and you kept your word. But I'm starting to worry. It's getting more frequent, isn't it? I'm doing funny things more and more."

Oh God. She didn't want to upset her, but she didn't want to lie either. It was true. The odd behaviours had been happening more often recently. She'd been pointing it out, gently, as Chloe had made her swear she would do. But half the time Chloe didn't remember what Kaitlyn had said. "Yes. But you know it's nothing major, only silly little things. The odd wrong word, putting things away in the wrong places. Nothing like what those people said at the trial. I promise."

Chloe nodded slowly. "It's coming though, isn't it? I mean, that's how it started last time. It's coming again, and for good."

"You probably just need a higher dose. Nothing to worry about."

"Yes," Chloe said. "Yes, I expect you're right. I'm sorry, I'm feeling dreadfully tired. I think I'll just go to bed, tell me what happens, okay?"

"Sure," Kaitlyn said, feeling sick to her stomach as Chloe made her way upstairs. She tried to concentrate on the latest gossip from the L7 tower block, but it just wasn't any fun without Chloe. So when the show ended she switched off the TV, deciding to forego the other nightly dramas, and went to bed herself.

But sleep eluded her, as it had a habit of doing of late. And not just because of the physical discomforts of late pregnancy. She hadn't told anyone about going to see Mum. Somehow, she just couldn't find the words. There was no way to relay the encounter that didn't fill her with shame, even though she couldn't quite work out why she should feel that burden. Emotions don't always have rational explanations and she couldn't quash them with logic, no matter how hard she tried.

Rochelle had once told her that confession was important, because keeping bad things inside makes you sick. Although she now firmly believed most of the New Order's teachings were nonsense, there was still the odd lesson that seemed to ring true. Holding this memory inside her was making it worse. Or at least, making it impossible to put out of her mind.

Her mother had to have been much further along than she was, judging by the size of her. Which meant she must have had the baby by now. Probably several months ago. Did she have another sibling in this world? And if she did, was her mother capable of taking care of it?

Perhaps she'd sold it. Perhaps she too had walked along that riverbank and knocked on Martha's heavy door. Perhaps the old nun looked at their names in her book, put two and two together from the surname, and cackled to herself late at night, saying, "Well there's a thing."

Stop it, she commanded herself, sitting bolt upright and checking the time. It was 3 a.m. She'd lain awake for near on six hours tortured by questions she couldn't answer. It couldn't go on. She had to tell someone. Enough was enough; she'd recount the whole sorry tale to Jack tomorrow. At least he wouldn't be able to react.

The sunlight streaming through the slight crack in the curtains woke her up. But it was the sharp pain that stopped her dozing off again.

"Jesus," she cursed, sitting up in case the stabbing, gripping throb had been caused by an awkward angle. Instinctively, she leaned forward, resting her arms on the footboard and arching her back to take the pressure off her abdomen. The pain eased a little, then stopped abruptly.

She didn't feel like having breakfast; a lumbering kind of nausea hung low in her stomach, probably a hangover from having hardly slept.

"Fresh air," she declared, throwing open the curtains to be greeted by the bright, hazy July sun. "That's what I need."

Henry had been driving her everywhere. To work, to visit Jack, to her flat to pick up her post, to midwife appointments. She'd barely used her legs in weeks. That could well be half the reason she couldn't sleep, she realised. Lack of exercise. It's not natural.

"I'm going to take a walk to visit Jack today," she declared as she entered the lounge where Henry and Chloe were sitting drinking coffee.

275

"What?" Henry said. "Kaitlyn, it's nearly two miles."

She laughed. "Oh, you lazy old snowflake! You've turned me soft too. I used to walk more than that every day without a second thought. I need to stretch my legs."

"In your condition?"

"I'm pregnant, not struck down with typhoid," she said. "Please, don't worry. I just need some summer air. Anyway, I'm sure you've got better things to do than cart me around."

"Alright," Henry replied. "If you're sure."

"I'm sure." She kissed Chloe on the cheek and walked out of the front door.

The sun on her bare skin and the breeze in her hair were exhilarating. But not long after turning the corner into Fulcett Street the vice-like pain struck again. Visions of gnarled, clawed hands squeezing her insides flashed through her head as she reached out an arm to lean on a nearby fence post, bending over with the agony.

It flew away as quickly as it had descended. Sharp, hot pain replaced by sweet relief so swiftly that it seemed almost imagined.

Perhaps she should go back? No, that was silly. Just have to take it steady, not too fast.

It was actually a pleasant walk, through the more affluent streets of Henry's neighbourhood and past the shopping district. The spell of the season was in full force, making it seem as though days full of warmth and vivid greenery would be eternal. Summer always did that; made the sting and misery of cold, driving rain and bitter frosts hard to remember. They always came back though. Summer always deserted in the end.

She was halfway down the long hospital corridor when the pain struck again. This time it made her cry out, more from the shock of its sudden appearance than its severity. Leaning against a wall, half-bent, it struck her that all the people staring must think she was in labour. She couldn't be though. She still had a few weeks to go. When it subsided she carried on walking, deliberately avoiding eye contact.

Jack was just Jack. Motionless flesh. Expressionless face. Eyes that wouldn't open and ears that, she strongly suspected, didn't hear. But still, he was her brother. Who else could she talk to about the wrecking ball that was their mother?

"I went to see her, Jack," she said, getting straight to the point without so much as a hello. "I know you told me never to go back, but I just had to see if she was still there. I was hoping she'd changed, pulled herself together. I guess I thought that—"

The vice-like grip of pain took hold again, causing her to gasp. She breathed steadily, waiting for it to pass, listening to the machines to distract herself.

Beep. Beep. Hiss.

Just breathe. Just breathe. Just breathe.

"Anyway," she continued when the pain ceased. "I think I thought that if only she could change, it meant anything could happen. Anything could turn out alright in the end. But she hadn't changed, Jack. Not a bit. She was drunk. A mess. And the worst thing was…"

It was back. Swifter and stronger. Crushing her middle, causing a stab in her spine that forced her up onto her feet. Longer this time too.

Beep. Beep. Hiss.

But she couldn't make herself breathe in time to the mechanisms any more. She leant over the chair, involuntarily letting out a long moan.

"Is everything alright?" Nurse Richards rushed in, and put her hand on Kaitlyn's shoulder.

"I don't know." Panic had arrived. *It wasn't a pulled muscle, how could I have been so stupid?* "The pains, they keep coming."

"Well," Nurse Richards said. "I'd say we better get you down to delivery."

"But I can't be in labour," she protested. "I'm not due for another five weeks."

"Tell that to baby. They don't much care for our plans and schedules, I find."

5

He was in the downstairs toilet when the phone rang.

"Chloe," he yelled. "Chloe, can you get that?"

The bad colour. It was back. It had started happening too often to ignore. There'd been no getting around it, he'd had to bite the bullet and make an appointment. He'd probably just need a pill, and then he'd curse himself for having put up with it for so long out of fear. The moment of truth was scheduled for tomorrow. Kaitlyn had a midwife appointment, so he'd figured he'd kill two birds with one stone and booked in to see the men's health specialist at the same time, though he hadn't told anyone.

The ringing stopped, and Chloe's cheery voice greeted the mystery caller.

"I see," she was saying. "Of course, of course. We'll be right there, tell her we're coming straight away."

What was going on?

"Henry," Chloe shouted, her hasty footsteps getting louder until she hammered on the door and made him jump. "Henry, it's Kaitlyn."

"What is it?"

"She's in labour, Henry! We have to go, we have to go right now!"

No. No, it was too early. It couldn't be. "Are you sure?"

"Yes, I'm sure! That was the delivery suite on the phone, I'm pretty certain they'd know. Now, where's her bag?"

She was flapping around, gathering things whilst simultaneously pulling on her shoes when he emerged from the toilet.

"Come on," she said, "Kaitlyn needs us. Don't just stand there like a stunned goldfish! Get your keys, get your shoes. Come on, get yourself in gear already."

She held the open hospital bag in one hand, dashing round the downstairs throwing things into it. A packet of tissues, a bottle of water, a packet of biscuits. He watched, confused, as she raced into the kitchen and opened the cutlery drawer, scooping a handful of teaspoons into the rucksack.

"Chloe?" He stepped forward and touched her arm. "Chloe, what are you doing?"

"Packing, what does it look like?"

"But... teaspoons?"

She stopped bustling and stared into the bag at the cluster of small silver spoons strewn haphazardly over the nappies and baby clothes. "Oh," she said, the colour fading from her cheeks. "I... I thought. I don't know. I don't know what I thought. But, they seemed so important."

"It's alright, love." He reached into the bag and removed them. "You're just in a fluster. It's all a bit unexpected."

"Just a fluster," she said slowly. "And I thought I was the one who always put a positive slant on everything."

6

"Four centimetres," the stocky, cheerful midwife between her legs declared. "Established labour. Baby's on the way, sweetie."

"Where are my…" Kaitlyn struggled to find the right word to describe Henry and Chloe. "My friends?"

"Don't worry." She removed her gloves and deposited them in the yellow bin in the corner of the small blue room. "They've been called, they're on their way. The receptionist will send them straight through when they get here. In the meantime, just relax. I'll check in on you again in a couple of hours."

"A couple of *hours*?" Surely, with the pains this strong, and this frequent, it must be nearly time?

The midwife chuckled, which irritated Kaitlyn. "Yes. Still a long way to go, I'm afraid. But don't you worry, it'll be over before you know it and you'll have that beautiful bubba of yours in your arms. You took the birthing classes, right?" Kaitlyn nodded. "Okay, so just breathe through the pains when they come. I'll stick the radio on, shall I?" She flipped the switch on the small box on the cupboard without waiting for an answer, and cheery, cheesy music filled the room. "Right then, well you just rest in between contractions and I'll be back to check you at" – she glanced at the upside-down watch pinned to her uniform – "one-thirty. I'm Jan, by the way. So if you need anything in the meantime just ask for me."

"Ask who?" Kaitlyn enquired, but the door was already closing behind the whistling midwife.

"Well that's just great." She stared at the stark, white ceiling. She tried to relax as instructed, but the godawful racket coming from the radio was hardly conducive to finding her zen.

The pain bloomed again, sharper and more urgent than before. And it had moved. This time, the evil grip tightened across her lower back, and it felt as though she were lying on jagged rocks. She gripped the rails on the side of the bed and wrenched herself up to a sitting position. *Breathe through it, Kaitlyn. Breathe through it.*

In.

Out.

In

Out.

The door flew open and Chloe rushed in, swiftly followed by Henry. She didn't think she'd ever been so relieved to see anyone before.

"Kaitlyn!" Chloe hurried forward and Kaitlyn found herself reaching out to hug her, tears suddenly unstoppable. "Oh, Kaitlyn. Are you alright?"

"It hurts, Chloe," she squeaked. "It hurts so bad."

"I know." Chloe nodded. "I know, sweetheart." She stroked her hair and Kaitlyn gulped back sobs. "How far along, did they say?"

"Only four centimetres."

"Alright, well don't fret. We're here now. We're with you."

Henry looked awkward, standing in the corner like a spare part, clutching the hospital bag.

"For goodness' sake, Henry," Chloe scolded. "Take off your coat and sit down, you're cluttering up the place."

Kaitlyn felt the tide begin to rise again. "It's coming again. Not again!"

"It's alright." Chloe held her hand. "It's alright. Tell me what you need."

"It's… my… back," Kaitlyn gasped. "It feels like it's in my back."

"You need to get up," Chloe said. "Trust me."

She did trust her. More than she trusted the midwives, or Henry, or anyone she'd ever met. So she nodded, even as the pain made her cry out, and let Chloe help her to her feet.

"Lean forward, over the bed," Chloe commanded. She obeyed and instantly discovered Chloe was right. The pain was still horrendous, but it had definitely eased a little.

The radio host stopped talking, and another obnoxiously upbeat pop song blared out, just as the agony reached its peak. "Henry," Kaitlyn said. "Turn off that fucking radio."

"With pleasure," he replied.

7

He flicked the switch, just as Kaitlyn turned around and sat on the edge of the bed, breathless from the effort of the contraction.

"Thanks," she panted. "It was driving me nuts."

The next couple of hours passed slowly. Kaitlyn and Chloe got into a rhythm. In between contractions, Kaitlyn would perch on the end of the bed, and Chloe would try to take her mind off things by chatting about their insipid soap operas. As soon as Kaitlyn felt the first rumble of the next pain, she would spring up, turn round and lean over the bed, Chloe furiously rubbing her back. When it was over, they would carry on the conversation, from mid-sentence sometimes, as if nothing had happened.

By the time the midwife appeared to check Kaitlyn's progress, the contractions were only a minute apart, and Henry had learned far more than he ever wanted to know about the love-lives and dark secrets of the miscreants of block L7.

"How are we doing in here?"

"I think she could do with some gas and air now," Chloe piped up. "They're a minute apart, and very strong."

"Alright, well if you hop up on the bed after this contraction, Kaitlyn, I'll have a quick check and see how we're doing."

Kaitlyn obeyed, and the midwife seemed surprised to discover she'd progressed faster than expected. "Eight centimetres," she declared, grinning. "Well, that's terrific work. I was expecting about six by now. Baby is in a hurry!"

"Great," Kaitlyn replied, heaving herself up in preparation for another contraction. "Now how about that gas?"

She seemed to find it a little easier to cope once she had the Entonox to suck on, though her talk of 'devilish Dimitri' and 'homewrecking Ali' was slightly slurred. He'd begun to feel claustrophobic and it seemed like a good time to slink off down the corridor and get some fresh air.

As the moment of birth drew nearer, his worry grew. Five weeks early. Surely that meant more chance of complications? Made it more likely that the baby would have health problems? He wasn't sure he was strong enough to handle it, not again. Christ, he didn't really handle it the first time. But he couldn't show his fear to the two women in that birthing room. He had to try to be positive, stoic. He'd have to be there for them if things went wrong.

"Come on, you old fool," he whispered to himself. "Keep it together. Whatever gets thrown at you this time, just keep it together."

Back in the birthing room, Kaitlyn had got up onto the bed and Chloe was arranging pillows behind her.

"Everything alright?" he asked.

"I think the baby's shifted," Chloe said as Kaitlyn clutched the gas and air tightly to her mouth, and inhaled frantically. "The pain's all out front now, and there's no gap between contractions."

Kaitlyn pulled the mouthpiece out. "I need to push!" she cried in a squeaky voice before shoving it straight back in and sucking even harder.

"Henry!" Chloe ordered. "Get the midwife. Now."

"Right, yes." He hurried back through the door and called out along the corridor. "Hello? We need a midwife here. Hello?"

8

"Are you feeling like you need to push?" Jan asked.

"Yes, damn it," she growled, biting down on the mouthpiece so hard her teeth hurt.

"Alright, let me just have a look…" Jan's head disappeared between Kaitlyn's legs. When it popped back up, she was beaming. "Ten centimetres, Kaitlyn. When you next feel the urge, give it all you've got. I can already see the head, you're nearly there."

'The urge' was overwhelming. She roared her exhale into the mouthpiece as she gritted her teeth even harder around it and pushed with muscles she never knew existed. Her long moan sounded like the low rumble of a mooing cow, and she was briefly amused at herself despite the pain.

The urge flew away, just as the contractions had been doing. She panted frantically, trying to take as much oxygen, and Entonox, on board as she could before the next round.

Sure enough it came again, and again, and again. She was just beginning to think she couldn't go on, didn't have the strength to keep doing this, when Jan said, "Alright, Kaitlyn, big push next time, biggest one yet. The head will be born with the next contraction so push, and then breathe through the sting."

Sting? *Sting?* A sting was what happened when you brushed against a nettle, or had a run-in with a disgruntled wasp. It bore no similarity to the searing, molten fire that overtook her as she pushed, and groaned and strained with all her might.

"That's it, Kaitlyn," Jan enthused. "Baby's coming, baby's coming right now."

She let out one final roar as first the head, and then quickly the whole baby, exited her body in a rush of fluids. Jan grabbed the tiny infant, wiping it gently with a towel, and holding it up. When Kaitlyn heard its first, urgent cry she thought her heart would stop from the shock.

"It's a baby," she whispered. "It's my baby."

"It's a girl," Jan said, passing the naked bundle to her. "Congratulations, Mummy."

Mummy. It sounded so strange, and yet so right. The soft, warm little body was placed on her chest, and she stared down at its smooth, delicate face. Tiny little nose, half-closed eyes, gorgeous puckered lips with the smallest, pinkest tongue she'd ever seen wiggling behind them. All topped off by a shock of dark, downy hair.

A daughter. A beautiful, precious and perfect daughter. Kaitlyn looked for Henry, expecting him to be right beside her, marvelling at the little miracle they'd made. But he was still standing on the other side of the room, just staring at the little bundle in her arms. She gestured at him to come closer, but he shook his head.

"I'll have to check her stats in a minute, after you've had a cuddle," Jan said. "She's a bit early after all, so don't be alarmed if they're not quite tip top. I've got to say, she looks pretty damn strong and healthy for five weeks early though. I think you might be a bit of a superstar, Kaitlyn."

She couldn't take it in. Couldn't fully comprehend the words Jan said to her. Couldn't take her eyes off the baby girl in her arms. She didn't know how many minutes passed before Jan's arms intruded to take her baby from her, but they weren't enough.

"You did so well, Kaitlyn," Chloe said, stroking her back. "So well."

"Five pounds and one ounce!" Jan declared from across the room where she had Kaitlyn's new daughter curled up in a large metal bowl to be weighed. "And great reflexes too. Not quite as pink as we'd like, but that's no worry. We'll have to take her down to special care, but that's only a precaution."

"S-special care?" Kaitlyn was horrified. What was wrong? Something must be wrong.

"Strictly just procedural," Jan assured her. "It's what we do with all babies born before thirty-six weeks. It's just to be absolutely sure she's thriving. Between you and me, I don't think she'll need to be there more than a day or two."

"A day or two?"

"Oh, don't look so worried, Mum," Jan said. "You can go down and see her whenever you'd like, and of course we'll be bringing her to you every few hours for feeds. You'll barely notice she's gone! I expect she'll be on the ward with you permanently soon enough."

"On the ward, how long?" She'd been expecting to be discharged a few hours after giving birth. That was the plan. Then straight to Martha's. Rip off the plaster, quick and clean.

"It's policy to keep you both in until the thirty-six week mark," Jan explained. "I know that isn't what you want to hear, but think of it as a chance to get some rest, and get to know baby before you get home and the hard work begins."

A *week*? They'd have to stay in for a week?

"Now," Jan carried on, "speaking of feeding, shall we give it a go now? Be good to get a feed in her before I take her down, then you can have a little sleep and start to recover."

"Oh." Kaitlyn widened her eyes at Henry. "Oh, I was planning on bottle feeding."

"Yes, that's right," Henry replied, picking up on his cue and pulling the new bottles and cartons of formula from the bag.

"Oh." Jan sounded disappointed. "Well, that's your choice of course. But with preemies we really do feel that breastfeeding, at least for the first few feeds, is vital. She's not as strong as she would be if she'd gone full-term, not as developed. So the antibodies in the colostrum really are an important part of helping her catch up."

"Okay," Kaitlyn said meekly. How could she object? Her baby needed all the advantages it could get. "I'll try."

"That's a girl," Jan said. "You just get comfortable and I'll help you get the latch right. It's easy as pie, you'll see. But I think it might be best if your visitors left now, you need peace and quiet, and plenty of rest."

"Oh." Kaitlyn looked desperately at Henry and Chloe. Suddenly scared to be left alone in this strange new reality.

"It's alright, Kaitlyn," Chloe said. "The midwife's right. You've been through quite an ordeal. You really must try to sleep once they take baby, promise?"

She nodded, trying to be brave. She'd have to face this alone sooner or later. She just wished it could be later.

"We'll be back first thing in the morning," Henry said.

"Yes," Chloe enthused. "With presents! Oh I'm so proud of you, my darling. So, so proud."

Chloe bent down and kissed first baby, and then Kaitlyn on their heads. Henry just stared at the baby, and Kaitlyn couldn't read his expression. When they disappeared through the door, Jan showed her how to hold baby's head and guide her mouth to the breast. Within seconds, her clever little girl had clued in to the process and happily suckled away.

"Feels strange, eh?" Jan asked.

"Feels amazing," Kaitlyn replied, staring down at her daughter, utterly transfixed.

9

'Urgent scan', and 'same day appointment', aren't phrases you want to hear when you'd been hoping for just a magic pill or two to sort the problem out. Henry mentally added the young, lanky specialist to his long list of doctors who had thrown a spanner into the workings of his life.

Fortunately, it hadn't been hard to sneak off to his appointment, or the ensuing scan. They'd come back to the hospital to visit Kaitlyn and the baby first thing that morning, armed with grapes, chocolates and an enormous helium balloon proclaiming *It's A Girl!* that Chloe had insisted on getting. Both the women in his life wore faraway smiles as they cooed over the little girl, barely noticing the world around them.

He had to admit, she was a cutie. Damn perfect, in fact. He didn't dare hold her. The can of worms that might erupt if he let himself kiss her head, or stroke her cheek, didn't bear thinking about.

Kaitlyn's can was well and truly ripped open already. Any fool could see that. This was going to be so much tougher for her than she had ever imagined, and he hated himself for that. She hadn't known, couldn't possibly have known, how it feels to gaze at your own child. No one ever knows, until it happens. But he had. He'd known exactly. And more than that, he'd known how a mother feels when her child is no longer with her. He'd known that decades don't heal that wound. Nothing does.

There hadn't been a day that had gone by in the last eight months when he hadn't worried about their little scheme. But, until now he'd been worried it wouldn't work. For the first time, he was starting to worry it would.

10

At first, Kaitlyn was steadfast in her resolve not to see her daughter any more than was necessary. The midwives brought the hungry little creature to her whenever she needed feeding, and then took her away again. That was fine, she told herself. That was just doing what was necessary. Of course she had to cuddle her while she fed, how else could it be done? It didn't mean anything. And of course she had to watch her breathe, study every little movement in her features. She had to make sure she was healthy after all.

But once Chloe and Henry had left on her second night in hospital, she just lay awake worrying. They hadn't brought her for three hours. Surely she must be hungry? What if they were too busy to take care of her? Images of her crying out, and being ignored, flashed through her mind and she couldn't banish them. She was so tiny, so helpless. It couldn't be good for her to be by herself.

So she pulled on her dressing gown and headed down to special care. Her daughter was fine, of course. Fast asleep, making sweet little squeaks as she exhaled. But Kaitlyn sat beside her anyway, falling asleep in the chair next to the crib, with her hand on her baby's soft, warm belly.

11

When a solemn-faced doctor says the word 'cancer', you don't hear much of what comes after it.

There were lots of phrases. Lots of jargon. The odd word managed to cut through the white noise that roared in his head. Advanced. Inoperable. Terminal. The words themselves didn't matter. Phrasing didn't matter. It all boiled down to one thing – he was going to die.

"I see," he said, without emotion.

"Mr Morris." The doctor leaned forward. "I know this is a shock, but I need to be sure you fully comprehend this diagnosis. Is there someone with you? Someone you could call in here to talk this through."

"No," he lied. "No, I'm here by myself. And I fully comprehend, thank you."

"You must have lots of questions."

"Just one. How long?"

"Well, if you let it run its course naturally, perhaps three months. But I wouldn't advise that. It can be very unpleasant in its final stages." He opened his drawer and pulled out a Moving On application, and a shiny glossy brochure, from the large stack. "Here, let me give you this literature, it might be of use."

"No thank you," Henry replied, standing up. "I don't need any propaganda. I just want to get some air."

"Mr Morris, please come back any time if you have any more questions, or if you need any advi—"

Henry shut the door behind him so he couldn't hear the doctor's witterings any more.

"Well," he muttered out loud, not caring that those waiting in the corridor could hear. "Isn't that just the cherry on the fucking cake."

He wandered the hospital grounds for more than an hour, going nowhere in particular. Completely numb and yet full of adrenaline, his mind wouldn't stop whirring. It was only after he'd been walking, and thinking, for all that time that he realised none of the worries he'd been contemplating were about himself.

Surely this was the most personal, terrifying scenario anyone could ever face? If ever someone had a right to be selfish, to wallow in their own misery and mourn the loss of their own future, it was in a situation such as this? But none of it had even crossed his mind; not the pain, not the fear of death itself, not the things he would miss out on.

Instead, he'd been thinking about the futures of those he loved the most. Worrying for them and wondering how he could make their prospects brighter in his absence. He'd always been selfish, he knew that. Oh, he'd gotten good at hiding it. Saying the right things, asking the right questions. He'd tried to show concern for others, even if he didn't really feel it. But inside, his concealed gut-reactions had always been self-absorbed. Even if someone else had a problem, or a tragedy, his first thought had always been how it would impact on him, and his tiny little world. Had he finally learned to put that aside?

"Well, I'll be," he chuckled to himself. "Fucking typical that, eh? It's taken me until my damn deathbed."

It was liberating, and sobering, to look at things without the filter of ego, or the drive for self-preservation colouring your view. Like switching on a floodlight and illuminating that which had once been in darkness. It was all so clear now: the way forward, the choice he ought to take. Perhaps there was still a chance to find absolution after all.

But, as with all true acts of redemption, it would have to begin with a confession.

12

Jan had been right. On the third day, the doctor checked Baby Girl Thomas – as she was known to the staff, in the absence of a real name – over and declared she could join Kaitlyn on the post-natal ward for the remainder of her stay.

"Oh how wonderful!" Chloe, who was sitting by her bedside, said when they came to tell Kaitlyn the news. "See, told you she was a strong one."

Kaitlyn smiled, though she felt exhausted. She'd been in the chair in the special care unit most of the night, and not long made it back to her own bed before Chloe and Henry had arrived. The midwife placed Baby Girl in the little plastic crib on wheels at the end of the bed, but Chloe scooped her straight back out and covered her with kisses.

"Well damn if she isn't the sweetest, most perfect thing," she said, bouncing her ever so gently in her arms.

"She is," Kaitlyn agreed.

"Oh, she's rooting around," Chloe said as the infant snuffled at her. "Is she due a feed?"

"Probably," Kaitlyn said, "she's a thirsty one, that's for sure."

Baby Girl started to exercise her very impressive lungs and Chloe moved toward Kaitlyn. "Hush now, it's alright," she whispered to the child. "Here's your mummy, don't worry. Don't worry, Heidi."

"Oh," the midwife said, "have you named her now?" She

grabbed her pen from her pocket and the clipboard from the end of the bed.

"No," Kaitlyn said hastily. "No, I haven't."

"No." Chloe's face turned red. "Sorry, my mistake. I got a little confused for a moment."

The midwife said nothing, but raised one eyebrow and stared at Chloe for a second too long before walking away.

"Oh no." Chloe handed Kaitlyn her baby and sat back down. "Oh, I'm sorry. She just looks so much like her, uncanny really. Please, please don't tell Henry."

"Of course not," Kaitlyn replied, reaching out to Chloe with her free arm and squeezing her hand. "Where is Henry anyway? I thought he just went to get a coffee? He's been gone ages."

As if summoned by the sound of his name, Henry appeared at the end of the ward, limping toward them. Something was wrong. She could tell from his expression, and the lack of colour in his face.

"Chloe," he said, sounding out of breath. "Chloe, I'm sorry but can we go home?"

"What's the matter, Henry?" Chloe asked. "Are you alright?"

"No. I mean, yes. But I really need to talk to you."

Chloe looked surprised, but gathered up her coat and bag and followed after Henry, in a flurry of apologies and kisses. Kaitlyn watched them leave, a strange knot of worry in her stomach as Baby Girl snuggled into her, feeding and snuffling.

13

"I've waited a long time for you to be honest with me, Henry Morris," Chloe said, slow tears escaping from her sapphire eyes. "And now I'm going to be honest with you, too."

"What do you mean, love?"

She'd sat and listened to it all. Every last confession. From the cost of her drugs to the fact they had reached the limit of their credit overdraft, how bad it had truly been when the disease had hit her hard. Kaitlyn. The arrangement. The baby. The cancer. The guilt he still carried about Heidi. His plan to put things right.

She'd listened with tears, shock, anger. But never once interrupted him.

"You've always underestimated me," she said. "You always think I'm blind, or stupid, or can't handle the truth. Even now. Keeping the state of the credit from me, thinking you're protecting me. You never listened, did you? You never asked me what I wanted, and even when I told you, you just pretended I hadn't. I never wanted to carry on taking more and more pills. I never wanted to lose myself. But I knew you couldn't bear to hear it, so I didn't keep on about it. But now I wish I had. If I'd have known for one second that you'd go and do something so hare-brained and reckless as you have, I'd have set you straight."

"You mean, the baby?"

"Of course I mean the baby! How could you? You must have known how I would feel about it. You, more than anyone, know what I've been through! All I ever wanted was to be a mother, all I ever wanted was my baby! I'd have laid down my life in a second in exchange for Heidi's. You know that. And yet you... you treat creating life like some sort of get-rich-quick scheme? Were you trying to break my heart even more than you already have? And Kaitlyn! How could you drag Kaitlyn into such a ridiculous scheme? You took advantage of her, of her situation! She couldn't possibly have known what it truly means to create a child, but you did. You knew all about the risks, about the heartbreak, about the bond between mother and child, and you let her go through with it? And what if it had gone badly? What if she, or the baby, had got ill, or died? There are risks a woman takes to bring life into this world, you know that. How could you be so selfish?"

Chloe rose from the table and rushed upstairs, barely able to even look at him.

"Chloe," Henry called after her as she disappeared into the bedroom and slammed the door.

"Leave me alone!" she yelled through choking sobs.

Henry paced the downstairs for well over an hour, cursing himself. He'd done the very thing he vowed he'd never do again and hurt Chloe. He could hear her cries coming from the bedroom they shared, and imagined her getting the little box from the wardrobe and looking through Heidi's things. What had he done? He tried to distract himself while he waited for her to come out, but the tea he made tasted bitter, and he couldn't focus on the television.

Eventually, he heard the familiar creak of the bedroom door, and Chloe made her way downstairs. Her eyes were puffy, and her skin blotchy, but there was a determination in her eyes.

He took a step toward her. "I'm so sorry, Chloe," he said, his voice starting to crack. "I just couldn't bear it. I couldn't bear the thought of letting you go. I'd have done anything, sacrificed anything, I couldn't see clearly, couldn't see past how much I love you."

"I know," Chloe sighed, and took his hand. "You've been stupid, selfish and thoughtless and I can't pretend I'm not seething at you. But for all your faults, of which I might add there are *many*, Henry Morris, I've never once doubted how much you love me. You've put me through hell at times, and I you, no doubt. But we journey together, that's the agreement. That's the vow. And that's my condition."

"What are you saying, Chloe?"

"I'm saying I agree. Your plan. I think it's right. Right for *both* of us."

"Chloe, you don't have to—"

"I listened to you, Henry. Now you listen to me. We have to put things right for that poor girl. Christ, we owe her that and then some. I told you before that I just wanted to hold the baby, and I'm grateful for the chance. I also told you once that I would follow you anywhere because, even as stubborn and grumpy as you are, I love you and I always have. I mean the things I say, Henry. I never speak a word that I don't believe in. You know that."

"I-I—" He couldn't find words.

"But there's one more thing I need you to do. One more thing you *have* to do, if you really want to set things right."

14

Henry and Chloe didn't come back again that day, or the next morning. Kaitlyn found herself taking care of Baby Girl all by herself for the first time, albeit on a ward where midwives were around if she ran into problems. But still, she felt entirely unprepared. She hadn't paid much attention to the nappy changing portion of the birthing classes, other than to laugh with Gina about the strange anatomy of the plastic doll. She hadn't thought she'd need to know.

Baby Girl was cute as a button, that was true. But the stench of the tar-like substance that was spilling out of the edges of the nappy she wore was something straight out of the bowels of hell.

"Jeez, girl," she said to the wide, blue eyes that stared up at her from the changing table in adoration. "How does someone so sweet-looking produce something that foul?"

It took about twenty minutes, and almost a whole pack of cotton wool balls soaked in tepid water, and then several attempts to work out the logistics of folding and securing the fresh cloth nappy. But she felt pretty proud of herself, until she picked Baby Girl up and the nappy promptly fell down.

One of the midwives happened to be passing by the changing station, and she smiled at Kaitlyn's failed attempt.

"Never mind, sweetie," she said. "You'll get the hang of

it soon enough. Here." She deftly unfolded and refolded the nappy, securing it properly this time. "See? Easy when you know how."

Kaitlyn got a shock when she walked back to her bed. A young woman with long blonde hair and sparkly fake nails was perched on the end of it, waving frantically as she approached.

"Gina?"

"Hey!" Gina leapt up, and threw her arms around her. "I went to see you at Jared's when I got out of here, just like I said I would, and Alfonz told me what happened. Tried to beat me to it, did you?"

"No! I... Well, she came early, it was a bit of a shock," Kaitlyn replied, gesturing to Baby Girl, who was happily cooing at them from her plastic crib.

"I'm only joking! Oh just look at her. Aww," Gina leaned over and stared at her. "She is so tiny! You lucked out there, nine pounds my one was. Christ, I don't think things will ever be the same. Y'know" – she leaned closer to Kaitlyn and dropped her voice to a whisper – "*down there*."

Kaitlyn screwed up her nose, and winced a little at the thought of a nine-pound baby. So Gina had had the baby. She looked remarkably spritely.

"So it all went well?"

"Oh yes," Gina said, "all according to plan."

"So you gave the baby to Martha, and you got your money? It really was that easy?"

Gina plonked herself back down on the edge of the bed. "Well, I pushed out a nine-pound baby and needed several stitches. Then I handed my son over to a bonkers old nun with no idea where he'll end up. So yeah, if you wanna call that easy, then I guess it was."

My son. She'd had a boy. A son. She hadn't had 'a baby', she'd had a son. And Baby Girl wasn't just 'a baby' either. She was Kaitlyn's daughter.

"Do you think... no, don't worry." Kaitlyn had so many questions, but they all seemed too insensitive to ask.

"No." Gina looked up at her, and suddenly Kaitlyn could see the veneer had gone. Beneath the perfectly straightened hair and the bright nail varnish, something had changed. "Go on, Kaitlyn. What?"

"Do you think we were naïve? Do you think, maybe, we didn't realise how hard it might be?"

"The birth?" Gina asked. "Or giving them up?"

"Both."

"The birth was the most painful, horrific thing I'd ever experienced," Gina said, reaching a hand into Baby Girl's crib and touching her cheek gently. "Until I gave my son to Martha."

Kaitlyn sat beside her, put her arm around her.

"I can still hear him crying, you know," Gina said, her right hand flicking swiftly under her eyes. "Late at night, or when no one is around. I hear him. In my mind I mean. It makes my boobs leak, even though he's not really there. How can that be?"

"I don't know, Gina. I don't know."

"I'm sorry, Kaitlyn. It was a stupid idea, I should never have got you into it. I didn't know how it would be."

"I made my own decision, Gina. You have nothing to apologise for."

"Yeah, but I put the idea into your head in the first place, didn't I? Still, it's different for you."

"How do you mean?"

"Well, look at me. Okay, so I've got this money now, I can get my own place, go to college, get a better job. But, there'll always be this nagging doubt in my mind. I'll always be wondering if I'd have been happier if I'd kept him, if *he'd* be happier if I'd kept him. All those things I want to get, they're all just for myself. And are they worth it? I'm just not sure any more. But you, you're not being selfish. You're doing this to save a life; your brother's life. It's completely different to being a foolish little ditz who thought she could make a quick buck without any consequences."

"Oh, Gina." Kaitlyn hugged her tight. "You know you're not that."

"Aren't I?" Gina stood up. "Look, I better go. Seeing all these babies is just making me feel worse. You understand, right?"

Kaitlyn nodded.

"Thanks. Well, good luck. I'll be seeing you." She started striding out of the ward, but then turned around again abruptly. "Oh, and Kaitlyn?"

"Yes?"

"She's really beautiful."

Gina walked out the door. Kaitlyn stared deeply at Baby Girl. She really, really was.

15

David's house was the largest on the street. His company had taken over the whole neighbourhood, and allocated homes according to the seniority of the employee. As Regional Manager, David had been given the imposing detached property.

Henry made his way up the long shingle path, past the flowers and the small homemade swing that hung from a large oak. The car was in the drive; he must be home. Henry swallowed hard before he rang the doorbell.

It was his granddaughter, Lisbeth, that answered. When she pulled open the door and Henry saw that long auburn hair, and that pale freckled face, he felt his heart swell.

"Grandad!" She leapt over the small step and threw herself at him, almost knocking him over in her enthusiasm.

Kids. They know what it's all about. They don't care about silly things like court cases and feuds. They love their family furiously, and without prejudice.

"Hello, sweetheart," He croaked a little, his voice distorted by the lump in his throat. "It's good to see you!"

"Grandad, I been painting. I been painting a horse with silver wings and a great big purple bow on her head," Lisbeth said. "You want to see it?"

"Yes," Henry said. "Yes, I want to see it very much. But I think I'd better speak to your daddy first, if that's okay?"

Lisbeth nodded, just as David appeared in the doorway behind her, looking puzzled. "Dad? What are you doing here?"

"David, I wondered if I could talk to you?"

"Go on in, Lisbeth." David stroked his daughter's hair. "Go and finish your drawings." She nodded, and skipped off inside. David stepped out and pulled the door almost closed behind him. "Well that depends, Dad," he said. "If you've just come to have a go at me, tell me what a disappointment I am, well frankly I just don't want to hear it. And I won't have you upsetting the children. They don't know anything about our little disagreement, and I mean to keep it that way."

"No. No, son. It's nothing like that." Henry shuffled his feet, watching the pattern his toes made in the shingle. "Would you believe me if I told you I'd had an epiphany of sorts?"

David snorted. "Don't tell me you've found religion, Dad. Bit late in the day for all that isn't it?"

"No. Not that kind of epiphany. But, I've had cause to rethink a lot of things lately. And I've come to say I'm sorry."

"Well, there's two words I never thought I'd hear you say. What is it you're sorry for?"

"You think I blamed you, don't you? For Heidi? Or at least, you think I was always judging you, because of the choice I made. You think that nothing you could have ever done could make me proud, because I was comparing you to someone who never really was. You've been living with the shadow of your sister's ghost as long as I have."

David turned his head, staring intently at the flower beds. "Yes," he whispered. "Yes, that's exactly what I think. No, more than that. It's what I know. So if you're going to try to tell me I'm wrong, that I imagined it, you can just save your breath."

"No, I've come to tell you you're right," Henry said.

"Ha! Well, there we are. That's your grand gesture is it? I'm right that you blame me for my sister's death. Well thanks, Dad. Thanks for interrupting my time with my kids to let me know that little gem. What is it you're hoping for? What am I supposed to feel? Vindicated? Happy?"

"I'm not trying to make you feel bad, David, I'm trying to be honest. I owe you that. I have judged you. I have been disappointed in you. I have hated you, sometimes, for being the reason Chloe never got to have a child. But you weren't. You weren't the reason. *I* was. Everything I put on you, it was really directed at myself. But I was just too blind to see it. And that's why I'm sorry, son. I'm sorry for thirty years of holding you to a standard that could never be reached. Of blaming you because I was too much of a coward to look inside myself."

"You have no idea," David replied, shaking his head. "You have no idea how it felt. No idea how much it hurt. You had no right to make me feel that way. You were a shitty father, and still I wanted so badly to make you proud, but I never, ever could."

"I know. I've ruined so many things. I've hurt so many people. I can't go back and make it all right, no matter how much I want to. I don't want anything from you, David. I don't expect your forgiveness. But I just have to tell you that I regret it, all of it. I wish I'd been a better father, and a better man. I was wrong, and I need you know that I know that now."

David sniffed, blinking fast. "You know, I've seen a lot of things in my life, but I never thought I'd live to see the day you'd admit—" He stopped abruptly. "Thank you."

"It's too little, too late," Henry said. "I know that. But, although I know I can never earn your forgiveness, I beg you to at least accept my apology." He extended his hand.

David stared at it for a long moment. "Okay," he said at last, and Henry shook his son's hand firmly.

"Thank you, David. You're a better man than I ever gave you credit for. And a better man than me."

"Well, it is a pretty low bar," David said with a half-smile.

Henry roared with laughter, partly fuelled by the relief of having said his piece. "Yep, you got me there, son."

David smiled, and Henry felt the distance between them begin to close. If only he had more time. Time to really heal the wounds, time to show his son he meant what he said. But that's the trouble with deathbed revelations, he realised. You don't get the luxury of acting on them at your leisure. It's now or never.

"I'm afraid there's more I have to tell you, and some of it may come as a shock. I've messed up, big time. But I've a way to put things right. You see, I once made a choice between two people I loved, and it tore me, and you, apart. I can't put someone else through the agony of making that decision. So I've come up with a plan, but I'd like to know you're on board with it. If you can spare the time to listen."

David frowned, but pushed open the door to his home. "Come in, I'll put the kettle on."

16

After Gina left, the ward felt noisy and oppressive. The cries of the other babies, the coos of the other mothers, the bustle of visitors coming in and out. New dads bringing flowers to their wives and girlfriends, grandparents clucking over the little bundles they'd be sharing Sunday dinners with for the rest of their lives. Mums packing their bags, getting ready to take their new children home with them to start the next phase of their lives.

Life. New life. Family life.

A life she wasn't going to have.

She watched for Henry and Chloe, hopeful each time a shadow appeared in the doorway, but they didn't come. She couldn't stand it any longer. She scooped Baby Girl into her arms and marched up to the reception desk.

"I'd like to go and visit my brother, in High Dependency," she said.

"Of course, sweetie," the cheerful midwife replied. "Just make sure you're back for the drug round, you're a little bit anaemic, doctor said. So we're giving you some iron, okay?"

"Okay, no problem."

When she reached Jack's ward, Nurse Richard squealed and got up from behind the desk, rushing over to her with a big goofy grin on her face.

"Oh my goodness!" She didn't even look at Kaitlyn's face, just stared wide-eyed at Baby Girl. "Oh, she is just *precious*! I've been wondering how you were. I did pop down to maternity to check, they said you'd had the baby, but wouldn't tell me anything else. Oh, Kaitlyn. She's just perfect."

"Thank you," Kaitlyn said, feeling a little uncomfortable at all the clucking. "How's Jack doing?"

"Just the same, sweetie. Just the same. Though maybe having his new niece come visit might perk him up."

"Yeah," Kaitlyn said as she moved toward Jack's room, though she didn't believe it, "maybe."

Beep. Beep. Hiss.

"Hey," Kaitlyn called out to her unconscious brother. "Sorry I haven't been in to see you for a few days. I've been kinda busy."

Beep. Beep. Hiss.

"There's someone I'd like you to meet, Jack. This is your niece."

Beep. Beep. Hiss.

Baby Girl gurgled and wriggled in her arms, but Jack's lids didn't flutter. Not even when the wriggling got more urgent, and she started to cry.

"Where are you, Jack?" Kaitlyn whispered. "Where are you that's so far that even she can't reach you?"

She gazed down at Baby Girl's wide, bright eyes. The same wide, bright eyes Jack hid behind those closed lids. She'd been wanting to see them for so long, never knowing if she ever would again. And now here they were, staring up at her from the baby in her arms. If she gave her to Martha, she may never see them again.

Beep. Beep. Hiss.

She left Jack's room and rushed to the desk where nurse Richards was wrestling with a stack of forms.

"He's never going to wake up, is he?" she asked the startled nurse.

"Never say never, sweetie."

"He's not though, is he?" she demanded. "Tell me honestly."

Nurse Richards put down her pen and sighed. "In my professional opinion? I would be surprised if he did, hon... but that's not to say it's impossible. Just... highly unlikely."

Kaitlyn could feel the tears coming.

"Oh, sweetie." Nurse Richards left her desk again, this time ignoring Baby Girl and throwing her arms around Kaitlyn. "I'm sorry. I don't mean to upset you."

"No." Kaitlyn shook her head. "It's alright. It's nothing I haven't been told, ever since the day it happened. Everyone told me, time and again. But... I just wasn't ready to hear it."

17

"I meant what I said before, Dad," David said when Henry had finished recounting his tale and laying out his plans. "I never cared about your money. I don't need it. Look around, I'm doing pretty well for myself and my kids. I never wanted to take anything from you. You're not the only one who felt like you'd given me way more than I deserved, you know. I've always been trying to prove something to you, and it's never been about money."

"So you're on board?" Henry asked.

"Yes, Dad. If it's what you and Chloe want, then I'm all for it."

Henry hugged his son again before going to find Lisbeth in her bedroom to admire her drawings. He passed a very pleasant couple of hours listening first to her list of facts about sparkle ponies, and then to her rendition of 'Three Blind Mice' on the clarinet. Jerome wandered in, back from football practice, and Henry chatted to his grandson all about quantum theory and penalty shoot-outs. He got so absorbed in the chatter, he only realised how late it had gotten when there was less than an hour of visiting time left.

He said a hasty goodbye to his family, and raced across town hoping to make it in time to see Kaitlyn.

When he arrived on the ward, she wasn't there. The midwife told him she'd gone to see Jack, but shouldn't be long. So he sat by her bed and waited, but the minutes ticked by with no sign of her. All the other visitors began to gather their things and say their goodbyes as the visiting hours drew to a close. He waited as long as he could, but when the midwives started to give him stern looks he thought he'd better get going.

Scribbling a note and leaving it on Kaitlyn's pillow, he left the hospital and headed home to Chloe. She'd promised to make a steak pie tonight, with garlic potatoes and a nice bottle of wine to wash it down. Then they'd snuggle up on the sofa, chinking their glasses together and chatting over whatever film came on the television. He couldn't think of anything more perfect.

18

Kaitlyn,
Sorry to have missed you, meant to get here earlier
but got held up.
We'll be in tomorrow morning, with chocolate!
Love, Henry.

Kaitlyn smiled at the note on her pillow. It was nice to
know she hadn't been forgotten. But still, when she settled
down to feed Baby Girl, her mind was racing.

"What should I do, my love," she whispered. "I don't want
to let them down, either of them. Jack, or Henry. But I don't
think I can let you go. Not now, not ever."

Baby Girl just suckled, one big eye open and the other
closed. It wasn't long before she fell into a milk-induced
sleep, but Kaitlyn didn't put her down in her crib. Instead
she sat awake, staring at the heart-melting complication
she'd created.

As promised, Henry and Chloe arrived the next morning with
a big box of chocolates, and a huge bag full of baby things.

"Mostly clothes," Chloe said, pulling out a little pink
top with *Lil' Superstar* emblazoned on the front. "I just
couldn't resist."

"Guess what," Kaitlyn said, handing Baby Girl to Chloe for a cuddle. "We're being discharged tomorrow."

"Wonderful," Chloe replied. "Clean bill of health?"

"Yeah, she's doing great. Gaining weight, scores are up. I'm a little anaemic, they said. But they've given me some pills for it. So we'll be able to get out of here first thing tomorrow morning."

Henry and Chloe shot each other a look that Kaitlyn couldn't read.

"Ah, yes." Henry coughed a little. "About that. I'm afraid I won't be able to pick you up then. We've got... an appointment."

"Oh," Kaitlyn said, feeling a little anxious. How would she get anywhere? She didn't have a pram, or a carry cot.

"But not to worry," Henry continued, "that's why we bought you this." He produced a baby sling from the large bag.

"Oh, okay." It was thoughtful. And she *was* grateful. But still she felt a little pang. She would be leaving all by herself. It made sense, when she thought about it. Henry was expecting her to go straight to Martha's after all, and then back to her flat, she supposed. The end of the arrangement. And the end of their friendship?

Well, it certainly would be once he found out she was going back on the deal. How would she ever pay him back for the pregnancy costs? She'd have to find a way. Work extra shifts or something. Maybe Jared would let her bring Baby Girl in; she'd still have two hands free to serve food if she wore the sling.

And she'd lose Chloe. Either way. If she gave up the baby, she'd never be able to face her again, and if she didn't Henry would be too livid with her to ever want to see her again. It wasn't just Jack she would have to let go in order to keep her daughter, it was them too.

They stayed for hours. Chloe rocking Baby Girl, singing to her and planting soft kisses on her head, both of them chatting. Even Henry. But Kaitlyn felt numb. This was the last time it would ever be like this. Like family. She was going to miss them both so very much.

When it was time for them to leave, Chloe hugged Kaitlyn's daughter even tighter, staring at her as though she were the most precious jewel on earth. "It's hard to say goodbye to her," she said, smiling. "But I know she's in the best possible hands with you, Kaitlyn."

"Come on, love," Henry said. "We can't stay forever."

"That we can't, Henry Morris, that we can't." She handed Baby Girl to Kaitlyn, but bent down for one last kiss and whispered, "Goodbye, Heidi."

Kaitlyn felt a shiver snake down her spine. But then Chloe kissed her on her cheek and said, "You're family to me, Kaitlyn Thomas. Don't you ever forget that, you promise?"

"I promise," Kaitlyn said, a strange unease creeping over her.

Chloe began to walk out of the ward, but Henry lingered behind by Kaitlyn's bed. "Do you still have your key, to our house?" he asked.

"Oh, yes." Kaitlyn felt flustered. Looking around for her handbag, hoping she'd remembered the key.

"Good," he replied. "I want you to promise you'll stop by there, before you go to Martha's, alright? There's something there for you, something I want you to have. So make sure you go to the house first. Swear it."

"Okay," she said, confused, "I swear it."

"Good. Thank you. Kaitlyn I... I just want to say, I'm so very glad I met you." He bent down, and kissed Baby Girl. Kaitlyn gasped a little; he'd never touched her at all before. "Goodbye, sweet one," he said.

She watched him lumber through the ward and out of the door, pulling her dressing gown tighter against the chill in the air.

19

"Is everything ready?" Chloe asked.

"Yes, love," Henry said, sealing the envelope and placing it on the table.

"Then come and have your breakfast. Bacon and eggs, just how you like them."

He raised an eyebrow when he spotted the small plastic cup full of vitamins next to his orange juice. "Really?"

Chloe laughed. "Old habits die hard, I guess," she said. "I tell you what, I'll let you skip them, just this once!"

When they'd finished eating, Chloe cleared the plates and Henry wandered into the garden. He sat down at the small table where they had spent so many summer evenings, sipping on wine and watching the sun go down. Sometimes, they'd even stayed there long into the night, just talking.

"It wasn't a bad life," he said to himself, "when all's said and done."

"Henry," Chloe called from the back door. "It's time to go, love."

"Yes," Henry said, stepping inside and closing the back door before taking her hand. "Yes, I suppose it is."

20

She handed the signed papers to the doctor standing by Jack's bedside.

"Are you ready now, Miss Thomas?" he asked.

"Could I... could I just have a minute alone with him, please?" Kaitlyn squeaked.

"Of course." Nurse Richards touched her arm. "Would you like me to take baby for you for a moment?"

She nodded, and passed Baby Girl to the waiting nurse. When all the medical staff had stepped outside, she approached Jack's bed.

Beep. Beep. Hiss.

"I'm sorry, Jack," she whispered. "I'm so sorry. I've kept you here too long, I know that now. I just hope it's like they say, that you just don't know. I couldn't bear it if you were in there, suffering, for all this time. I was being selfish. Clinging on. I couldn't let you go, because I didn't think I'd cope. But after everything you did for me, I know you would do it all, and so much more, for your niece. God, I just wish you could see her. But I'm going to tell her all about you. I promise. I love you so much, but I can't throw everything I have at keeping this twisted fantasy that you'll somehow pull through. You wouldn't want that, and I'm sorry it's taken me so long to realise."

She stroked his cheek, and kissed his forehead. "Thank

you. Thank you for giving me a chance at life. I promise, I won't waste it any more."

Beep. Beep. Hiss.

Unable to speak, she opened the door and nodded at the waiting staff. They entered the room silently. Nurse Richards handed Baby Girl to her, and stood beside her with her arm around her shoulder as they watched the doctors take up their positions.

The tallest doctor began flipping switches on the machines as the other two observed, their hands cupped in front of them in reverence.

Beep. Beep. Hiss.

Beep. Beep.

Beep beep.

Beep beep beep.

Beep.

Kaitlyn's tears rolled down her face, dripping onto her baby daughter's clothes.

21

The Moving On grounds were truly magnificent. He'd never really been one for horticulture, but he had to admit they'd done an excellent job. Gorgeous blooms lined the long driveway, and the landscaped lawns were interspersed with ponds, fountains and rose bushes. Arm in arm with Chloe, he thought it might be the most serene place he'd ever been to.

There was a surprise waiting for them as they walked through the glass doors and into the impressive marbled entrance hall.

"David?" Chloe spotted him, and the kids, first. "Oh, and Jerome, and Lisbeth! Oh goodness, how you've grown!"

"What are you doing here?" Henry asked his smiling son.

"I know you said you didn't want a party, or any fuss," David said. "But we just wanted to come and say goodbye, and to show you how much we care."

"These are for you, Nana Chloe!" Lisbeth proclaimed, pulling a bunch of red roses from behind her back.

Chloe hugged her tight, and when Henry saw the sheer joy in her expression as she stared at the beautiful flowers, he felt ashamed.

Just a few months – hell, even a few weeks – ago he'd had scoffed at the idea of giving flowers to someone at a time like this. What a waste, he'd have said. Why give them something they'll only have for a few minutes?

But now he knew the truth. Now he knew that joy isn't measured by its duration, but by its intensity.

22

The bus ride seemed to take forever, with Baby Girl tired and grouchy. The hospital bag was cumbersome, and she had to move it out of the way every time someone needed to walk down the aisle.

She was still fighting back tears, the pain in her heart almost too much bear, when they pulled in at the end of Henry's road. She knew she'd done the right thing. The truth had finally revealed itself to her, heavy as it was. She could have given her daughter up, and poured all the money into keeping him breathing for longer, but he wasn't really there. He'd never come back to her, and eventually it would all run out and the machines would be turned off just the same.

But even though she knew that now, she couldn't regret a single penny she'd already paid. If she hadn't believed, so strongly, in a forthcoming miracle she wouldn't have the one now resting in her arms.

She just hoped Henry would see it that way.

"I'll wait here, until he gets back from that appointment of his," she told Baby Girl as she put her key in the door to Chloe and Henry's house. "I'll explain myself, then we'll just have to take it as it comes. If he hates me, he hates me. All we really need is each other, right?"

The house was quiet. Eerily so. No enticing smells coming from the kitchen, no news blaring from the television. She noticed the items on the dining room table straight away: a pile of cash, an envelope addressed to her, and the title deeds to the house... in her name.

Her heart sped up as she ripped open the envelope and unfolded the letter inside. "Oh, Henry. What have you done?"

> *Kaitlyn,*
>
> *I hope you've done as I asked, and come here before the old nun's.*
>
> *I once had to make a choice between people I loved, and it almost destroyed me. I can't ask you to do the same. So here is the rest of the money from the equity release, and the house has been bequeathed to you. You'll have to sell it, of course, to pay back the release. But I hope you can use the profits to keep both your brother, and your daughter, in your life.*
>
> *Now, don't go thinking me a selfless saint just yet, because there's something else you don't know. I've got cancer. Started in the prostate, but they say it's spread. I only found out recently and I've not got long left anyway, and Chloe doesn't want to keep upping her pills. So we thought we'd bow out a few months early, for such a good cause.*
>
> *You really have been like a daughter to us, Kaitlyn. And we know you'll be an excellent mother, if you decide that's what you want. Thank you, most sincerely, for bringing so much happiness to us both.*
>
> *All our love,*
> *Henry and Chloe.*

"No. No, no." She slammed the note down on the table, shoved the money in her pocket, and rushed back out of the door. "Come on, Baby Girl," she said. "We have to get there, we have to get there quick. Maybe there's still time."

23

They said their long goodbyes, full of hugs and well wishes, before making their way to the door at the end of the hall. Henry was more grateful than he could express that David had disobeyed him and come to say farewell.

Beyond the beautiful, ornately engraved wooden door lay a bright, airy room painted in subtle shades of shimmering gold and white. A king-size double bed, topped with silver pillows and sheets, was in its centre. A smiling nurse, bedecked in a yellow uniform, waited for them at the small, oak table.

They signed their respective papers, and the nurse handed them each a small gold pot containing four brightly coloured pills.

"How long does it take to work?" Chloe asked.

"About fifteen minutes," the nurse replied, still smiling exaggeratedly like an enthusiastic air stewardess.

"Well," Henry said. "Bottoms up?"

They tipped the pills into their mouths and chinked their tall, frosted glasses of water together before swallowing them.

"Now," the nurse said. "Would you like me to stay, or would you prefer to be alone?"

"Alone, thank you," Henry replied. She nodded, and left the room.

They wandered over to the window and stood hand in hand

watching the birds and squirrels in the magnificent garden. About ten minutes passed before Chloe broke the silence.

"Henry," she said. "I'm starting to feel a little sleepy."

"Shall we lie down?"

Chloe nodded, and they climbed onto the huge, soft bed. Henry suddenly felt afraid. "Chloe," he said. "What if it's not exactly the same time? I couldn't bear it, if yours worked faster. I couldn't stand to be in this world without you, not even for a minute."

"Well, let's make a pact," Chloe said, smiling. "Let's agree to both close our eyes one last time, and never open them again, and we'll not say another word. That way, we'll never have to know."

"Okay," Henry said.

"I love you, Henry Morris."

"I love you, Chloe Morris."

"On three?"

"Yes."

"One." They took each other's hand again.

"Two." Chloe squeezed Henry's, and he squeezed back.

"Three."

Henry closed his eyes for the last time, concentrating on the feel of Chloe's hand in his and marvelling at how lucky he had been to have her hand to hold for so much of his life.

24

Breathless, she rushed up to the looming gates of the Moving On complex, jabbing at the intercom button.

"Come on, come on, let me in damn it!"

Baby Girl must have found the constant bouncing of the hurried dash through the shopping district soothing, for she breathed deeply against Kaitlyn's chest, unperturbed by her mother's frantic pleas.

"Why does nobody answer?" Kaitlyn shouted, mashing the button with her palm in frustration.

"Miss Thomas?" A voice from behind her made her stop and turn around. A smart, middle-aged man in a sharp black suit stood staring at her, a young boy and girl in tow.

"David? You knew about this? Was this your idea? What have you done to them?"

"It wasn't my idea, Miss Thomas. But yes, I knew. Dad and I... we... well, we made our peace."

"Well good for you," Kaitlyn replied. "But I'm not going to stand around in my Sunday best and let this happen." She stabbed at the intercom again. "I need to stop them."

"Miss Thomas." David reached out a hand slowly, gently. He touched her lightly on her shoulder. "Kaitlyn, it's already done."

"What?"

"They're already gone, Kaitlyn. I'm sorry."

"No!" She threw his hand off. "No. No. No."

The world blurred. Gasping, gulping breaths still didn't provide enough oxygen. She leaned forward, holding the gate to steady herself as her stomach contracted.

Gone. They were all gone. Henry, Chloe, Jack.

"I really am sorry, Kaitlyn," David said again. "They didn't do it to upset you, they wanted to help you. You meant the world to them."

"He left me a note," Kaitlyn said in between gasping sobs. "He didn't want me to have to choose between my brother and my daughter. But… I did. I already had. I switched his life support off this morning. They did this for nothing!"

This time, when David's arms reached out to her she did not resist. She buried her head in his chest and screamed her grief.

When the initial shock and pain finally subsided, she was briefly embarrassed at having sobbed all over a near-stranger, his wide-eyed children looking on in bewilderment.

"I'm sorry," she said, pulling back and nuzzling into Baby Girl.

"Don't be," David replied, "we're family, of a sort, after all."

"What do you…" What had Henry told him? "I mean, why do you think that?"

"Dad told me everything," he said, tentatively reaching out to touch Baby Girl's head. "Kind of a last confession, I guess. He wanted to make sure we were all square before he went ahead with it. So, this is my sister, right?"

"Yes, yes I suppose she is."

"Wow." His smile grew wider, and she thought she saw a misty sheen take over his dark eyes. "I've waited a long time, to cuddle with a sister. May I?"

"Oh." Kaitlyn was surprised, but she fiddled with fastenings and gently removed her from the sling. "Sure."

David took her into his arms, staring at her intently. "She's perfect," he said. "Kids, kids, come here. This is your... well, auntie, I guess."

The girl and boy moved closer, looking at the baby in wonder.

"What's her name?" the girl asked. "She can't just be auntie. It's always auntie something. Like Auntie Rachel, although I don't like her. She makes me drink kale shakes."

Kaitlyn laughed. What a gorgeous little girl.

"I don't know," David said. "That's down to her mummy. Have you named her yet, Kaitlyn?"

"I-I'm not sure." There was one name that seemed to fit. One she'd already been called. "I was thinking I'd like... But only if it's alright with you, only if you don't think it's weird, or disrespectful or anything..."

"Spit it out," David said, grinning.

"I think I'd like to call her Heidi," Kaitlyn said. "Chloe kept calling her that, and I know it was probably because of her condition. But, it just seems right."

"I think it's perfect." David planted a soft kiss on Heidi's head.

"Auntie Heidi!" The little girl clapped her hands.

"Heidi Chloe," Kaitlyn decided as she said it out loud. "Heidi Chloe Thomas."

"Even better." David handed her newly named daughter back to her. "Is there anywhere I can take you, Kaitlyn? I've got my car."

He was being so kind. So gracious. Guilt sent another wave of nausea crashing through her. Would he be this nice once he found out about the inheritance? "No," she said hastily. "No, you've been very kind but I better not impose."

"Kaitlyn, if you're worrying about the house, I already know."

Jesus. Why was she always so transparent? Like a piece of wet paper. Easy to see through, and easy to tear. "You do?"

"Yes. He told me his plan. And I agreed."

"You *agreed*?"

"I really wasn't after his money. I told you, Kaitlyn. We're family now."

Family. She'd lost three people today, all of them family as far as she was concerned. She'd thought Heidi was the only family she had left, but now Henry's son was extending the title to her as well.

No, it's not true. The thought struck her suddenly. *You do have more family. You have Mum, and her baby.*

"In that case," she said. "Would you be kind enough to take me to the skyrise district?"

David stopped the car by the river. Mum's block was straight ahead, its shadow looming over the water, and over Kaitlyn's whole life.

They'd chatted the entire way. His kids were awesome. Bright, witty and full of character, just like Henry. She hoped Heidi would turn out just the same.

"You sure you don't want us to wait?" David asked.

"No, no, thank you. I'll be fine from here."

"Well." He fished around in his pocket and handed her a small business card with his address and phone number on it. "Don't be a stranger, I mean it. I really want to be part of Heidi's life, and I know these two do too, right, kids?"

"Yeah! Yeah!" Jerome and Lisbeth cried from the back seat.

"So call us, pop by. Anytime." David said. "And Christmas… You're coming to us for Christmas. It'll be our new tradition."

"Like having lasagne on New Year's Eve?" Kaitlyn asked with a smirk, and David looked embarrassed, but chuckled nonetheless. "I will, I promise. And thank you."

Once out of the car, she reattached the sling and headed to the broken door of her mother's block, cuddling Heidi through the fabric. "Just stay close to Mummy, Heidi," she whispered, as if her tiny daughter had any choice. "It'll all be alright."

The door to the flat was slightly ajar, just enough that the stench of booze wafted through it into the foyer. She didn't knock, but called out as she entered the squalid, cluttered apartment.

"Mum?"

No reply.

"Mum?" she called again, stepping into the dark lounge. The curtains hadn't been opened, and the air was thick with the cloying scent of tobacco. She nearly tripped when she trod on a pile of assorted rubbish, and discarded bottles, in the middle of the floor.

Reaching across the small, wonky table, she grabbed at a fraying curtain and pulled it back enough to allow sunlight to illuminate the room.

When she turned around she gasped. In one corner there was an old, mould-covered travel cot. Its blue fabric worn and marred by small cigarette burns. Inside it, a baby much larger than Heidi lay wriggling, but silent. Just staring at the yellowed ceiling above its head.

In the other corner, Mum was snoring in the armchair, an empty bottle at her feet and vomit on her nightgown.

Kaitlyn shuffled forward quietly, to look at the poor child in the bio-hazard of a crib. She gasped again when she saw its face.

Its lip wasn't properly formed, or wasn't in the right position. It seemed to peak too high in the top right corner, leaving its gums and tongue exposed even when its mouth was shut. But that wasn't what shocked her. What shocked her was its eyes. They were the same as Jack's. And Heidi's. They were family eyes.

Even through the baby-gro, Kaitlyn could see that its nappy was bulging.

"Whatta tha'!" Mum woke with a start, and stared straight at her. "You! What are you doing here!" She got up, swaying and belching as she moved toward Kaitlyn and Heidi. "Come to show off your perfect baby, eh?" she spat as she slurred. "Well, I hope it fucks up your life, just like you and your brothers did to mine!"

Brothers. The baby in the crib was a boy? She had another brother?

"I think you did a fine job fucking up your life all by yourself, Mum," Kaitlyn snapped at her inebriated wreck of a mother.

"Don' you fuckin' dare talk to me like that, you ungrateful bitch!" her mother shouted. But then she flopped herself back down in the armchair, picked up another bottle from the floor and took a swig. "He was supposed to make up for it," she said, pointing at the crib. "He was supposed to get me out of here. I was gonna sell him, get myself some nice clothes, and a nice job and all that. But look at 'im! Nobody wants to buy that face! Cleft fucking lip, they said. Needs surgery, they said. Why do I get all the shit kids, eh?"

Kaitlyn could barely contain the rage that boiled inside her at the words her mother spoke. Her hands shook as she stroked Heidi, and walked over to her baby brother. Bending down to pick him up, she whispered to him.

"Hey there, sweetheart, I'm your sister, Kaitlyn. Our big brother got me out of here once. Now I'm going to do the same for you."

She lifted him to her, and felt goosebumps on her arms. Maybe this was why. Maybe this was why Jack had saved her, maybe this was why he *had* to save her, and to leave her. So that she would be here, right now, to save their brother. To be a real mother. To make sure at least one of them had a shot to make something of themselves.

With Heidi dozing in her sling, and her baby brother in one arm, she reached into her pocket with her free hand and pulled out the wad of cash Henry had left on the table.

"How much is he worth to you?" she shouted at her mother, throwing the money at her. "This do? Go on, Mum. You take that, drink yourself to death. I'm taking my brother."

She stormed out with the children, leaving her mum on her hands and knees picking up every last note, counting each one.

"Come on," she said to the two babies as they walked along the river. "We'll go back to Henry's, just for a bit. We'll be just fine, the three of us. You'll see."

Holding her head high, she walked through the streets with her little family. She'd fill Henry and Chloe's house with love. Even if it was just for a little while, until the house was sold. They'd have liked that. They'd have liked that very much. And then, who knows? They'd be allocated somewhere, it wouldn't matter where. All they needed was each other. With the profits from the sale she could give both her children the best start in life, and with all Henry and Chloe had taught her, she could give them the best home.

All this time. All these years, she'd been looking for someone to guide her. She'd been looking for a mother. First Mum, then Rochelle, and they'd both let her down. But Martha had been right, all along. She didn't need a mother, she *was* a mother. She just never realised it before.

By the time she reached the Morrises' house, both babies were sleeping soundly. Heidi in her sling, and her brother in her arms. She laid the snoring boy gently down on the rug in the living room.

"I guess at least you can't fall and hurt yourself, if you're on the floor already," she whispered, grabbing a throw from the sofa to cover him with. She caught a glimpse of the photograph of Henry and Chloe that was sitting on the mantelpiece. "Am I crazy? Can I really do this? I wish you were here, I have no idea what I'm doing."

Feeling overwhelmed with the weight of reality, she carefully undid the sling and placed her tiny daughter on the rug next to her uncle.

She didn't have any equipment. Or any experience. Or

anyone to guide her. Except maybe David. She pulled out his business card and ran her fingers over the embossed telephone number. Call him? Ask him for help? No. Not yet. She needed to try, to prove to herself that she could do it. She couldn't be completely dependent on someone else, especially someone she hardly knew. Jack had always taught her that.

Jack.

The weight of his absence from the world was heavy on her heart. She sank onto the sofa, staring at her new brother. "You look just like him," she cooed to the child. "I wish you could have known him, both of you. He'd have known exactly how to take care of you, to keep you safe. And Henry, oh I wish you could both have him in your life! Okay, he'd teach you to be cynical, but that's not always a bad thing, especially when it comes with such fierce love, like he had for Chloe. And for me, I think. And Chloe? God, she'd love you both so much. She'd spoil you, though. No doubt about that. You'd be the most cuddled children in all of the world!"

As the babies slept, Kaitlyn ran through all the precious memories she held of those she'd lost. Some made her smile, like Jack and the wild games he invented when they were kids, or Henry and his grumps about silly things, Chloe being overly cheerful to wind him up more, winking at Kaitlyn as she did so. Others, like the memories of the last time she saw them, made her ache with loss.

"I'm going to tell them all about you," she whispered to the empty air. "Everything you ever taught me, all the love you ever gave me. I promise. I won't let you down, I'll take care of them both."

She wasn't at all sure any more if there was an afterlife, or if it was anything like Rochelle had claimed it to be. But she hoped that, somehow, her loved ones could hear her fervent vow.

The letterbox rattled, making her jump. Today's *National Herald*. She rose and picked it up, meaning to throw it straight in the recycling like Henry always did. But the pictures on the front page caught her eye. More protests. More unrest. More Council buildings defaced or burned down. It was happening so frequently now, even the national paper couldn't avoid reporting it.

"Change is coming," she said out loud, and the notion made her shiver in anticipation. She wasn't scared of it any more. In fact, she realised, she welcomed it.

She smiled at the sleeping infants, so tiny and content. She had a feeling that the world they would help create would be very different to the one she lived in now. And she couldn't wait to see it.

"I'm ready," she said, moving swiftly toward Heidi as she started to stir. "Let's do this."

The old nun bent down to pick up the envelope that had landed on her doormat. Her fingers were stiff and sore today, but she managed to pull out the note inside.

Dear Martha,
You were right. I am a mother. And now I have my baby. Two babies, in fact (long story!). I'm sorry to let down the family you had waiting, but I can't let my daughter go. Though I've got a feeling you always knew that, didn't you?

She squinted with her good eye at the accompanying Polaroid. A young woman with dark messy curls grinned back at her from the picture. Martha recognised her instantly. In her arms she held two chubby-cheeked infants, one larger than the other but both had those same deep, wide eyes. Along the bottom of the picture, their names were written:

Heidi Chloe Thomas and Henry Jack Thomas.

Martha smiled as she placed Kaitlyn's photograph in the centre of her wall of mementoes. Of all the families in her montage, she was the most proud of this one.

ACKNOWLEDGEMENTS

I have been completely overwhelmed by the support and encouragement offered by so many people. *Overdrawn* has been a joy to write, in no small part because of those who have helped it on its way.

I'm forever grateful to Lauren, Lucy, Tom, Ditte and everyone at Legend Press for their hard work and dedication. It's a pleasure to work with such a committed and dynamic team.

Heartfelt thanks go out to my agent, Emily Sweet. She never fails to offer support and encouragement and is always there for me. I feel very blessed indeed to have her on my side. Thank you for all your hard work, enthusiasm and general loveliness!

I'm indebted to my friends and family who have read and given feedback on *Overdrawn* in its early stages. Barbara Evans, Roberta Crosskey, Sharron Swan, Mike Grant, Melanie Sedlmayr and Aisling Mills – thank you for your continued support.

Massive thanks to Helen Robins for sharing her neo natal expertise with me.

Thanks also to the very talented Wendy Burke and EL Rowe for their comprehensive critiques of the first draft. Their input helped shaped the novel, and I treasure their friendship.

I am so grateful to fellow Legend Press author Joanne Burn for her support and camaraderie, and count myself very lucky to call her a friend.

As always, I could not have written this novel without the constant encouragement and critique of GJ Rutherford. The words 'above and beyond' don't even begin to describe his value to me as a critique partner and friend. Thank you, from the bottom of my heart.

My husband Kev has been my rock. His belief in me and his unfailing enthusiasm for my writing has made all this possible – and, of course, the endless cups of coffee he deposits beside me as I'm writing have fuelled each word! My daughter Mya and my son Riley have given me so much support and shown such pride in what I do – they are my reason, and my rhyme. Thank you, my wonderful little family. I'd be nothing without you.

If you enjoyed what you read, don't keep it a secret.

Review the book online and tell anyone who will listen.

Thanks for your support spreading the word about Legend Press!

Follow us on Twitter
@legend_press

Follow us on Instagram
@legendpress